T0190683

Berkley titles by Katie Shepard

NO ONE DOES IT LIKE YOU

SWEETEN THE DEAL

BEAR WITH ME NOW

NO ONE DOES IT LIKE YOU

Katie Shepard

BERKLEY ROMANCE

NEW YORK

BERKLEY ROMANCE
Published by Berkley
An imprint of Penguin Random House LLC
penguinrandomhouse.com

Copyright © 2024 by Katie Shepard
Penguin Random House supports copyright. Copyright fuels creativity,
encourages diverse voices, promotes free speech, and creates a vibrant
culture. Thank you for buying an authorized edition of this book and for
complying with copyright laws by not reproducing, scanning, or
distributing any part of it in any form without permission. You
are supporting writers and allowing Penguin Random House
to continue to publish books for every reader.

BERKLEY and the BERKLEY & B colophon are
registered trademarks of Penguin Random House LLC.

Library of Congress Cataloging-in-Publication Data

Names: Shepard, Katie, author.
Title: No one does it like you / Katie Shepard.
Description: New York: Berkley Romance, 2024.
Identifiers: LCCN 2023059759 (print) | LCCN 2023059760 (ebook) |
ISBN 9780593549339 (trade paperback) | ISBN 9780593549346 (ebook)
Subjects: LCGFT: Romance fiction. | Novels.
Classification: LCC PS3619.H45425 N6 2024 (print) |
LCC PS3619.H45425 (ebook) | DDC 813/.6—dc23/eng/20240116
LC record available at https://lccn.loc.gov/2023059759
LC ebook record available at https://lccn.loc.gov/2023059760

First Edition: September 2024

Printed in the United States of America
1st Printing

For Jeeno, Rebecca, and Celia, my beloved fellow travelers

You were the perfection of my life
And I couldn't have you. That is, I didn't.
　　　　　　　—KENNETH KOCH,
　"To Marina," *On the Great Atlantic Rainway:*
　　　　　　　Selected Poems 1950–1988

We are never, ever, ever getting back together.

　　　　　　　　　—TAYLOR SWIFT,
　　"We Are Never Ever Getting Back Together"

This book deals with emotionally difficult topics, including pregnancy, fertility treatment, serious illness of an elderly relative, ableism and ableist language, alcohol use, misogyny, homophobia, explicit and graphic sexual content, and vulgar language. Any readers who believe that such content may upset them or trigger traumatic memories are encouraged to consider their emotional well-being when deciding whether to continue reading this book.

PROLOGUE

October
Long Island

Rosie would have been delighted with the Southampton house party, Tom mused, leaning against the twin bolsters of his seat belt and the cold windowpane. He had the romantic idea that drinking made him maudlin, and he seized that excuse to wallow in thoughts of her. Rosie loved corny shit like lawn games and Cards Against Humanity. She'd loved going with him to cast parties. She would have liked the big spread of imported cheeses and fancy pickles they'd eaten, and she would have been thrilled to be introduced to so many interesting theater people at the seated dinners, and she wouldn't have told Tom to sit down and be quiet for the whole drive back, because she liked car games too.

More importantly, she would have made sure they left yesterday afternoon, before traffic got bad, and certainly before the hurricane arrived. But of course Rosie wasn't there, which was why things were going to hell.

Three hours into their evacuation, with the road west jammed with cars and the first bands of torrential rain already tossing the branches of trees to the ground, Tom started getting worried. He'd sobered up into regrets, for both the delay in leaving and his own drinking. He was from Florida. He knew better. He would never have messed around with a Category 3 hurricane on purpose, but he hadn't expected one on Long Island in late October, and neither had anyone else in the cast of the play whose run they'd just finished celebrating.

The car came to a sudden halt. The rain was falling so thick and heavy that Tom could barely see out the passenger window of the back seat, where he was crowded with two other members of the cast. The windshield was little better, even with the wipers on their maximum setting, so Tom saw only the brake lights of the car in front of them illuminating the gray dark.

"Shit," said Ximena, the production's female lead and the car's driver. "Road's flooded ahead."

She rubbed her stomach nervously. Tom knew that Ximena was a couple months pregnant, a fact that had presumably not come as a surprise to her or her wife, but which she was not widely announcing. Even if her father-in-law was one of the producers, she had to wait like everyone else for her role to be secured in the forthcoming Broadway transfer.

Tom craned his head to look over the dashboard. The car in front of them, a plucky little Kia Sorento rented by the show's marquee actor, was stopped just in front of a rapidly moving brown stream where runoff from an overpass was flowing across the street and down the embankment to their left.

As he watched, the brake lights faded when Boyd put the

car into park. There was no getting past the runoff, even for Boyd Kellagher.

Tom had been pleasantly surprised to land a big featured role in a well-funded Off Broadway debut even after he learned that the play was Boyd's vanity project. At thirty-four, Tom's stage credits were mostly regional, mostly supporting, and mostly undistinguished. Boyd Kellagher had only this single stage credit to his name, but he *had* acted in several multi-bazillion-dollar superhero franchise spectacles since being plucked from obscurity on the basis of his extraordinary physique and darkly brooding good looks. Boyd's decision to pick up some more traditional acting chops in the New York theater scene had catapulted this production into undeserved fame and success. Tom frequently reminded himself to be grateful; Rosie would have called his role a stepping stone. She would have been thinking about next steps already.

Tom peered out his window, squinting away from Boyd's car. He could see some dim lights through the trees, suggesting there were businesses or at least houses a few hundred feet away up the hill. They would need to ditch the cars before the main storm really hit.

Tom wiggled to get his battered denim jacket off, nearly knocking the actor sleeping to his left in the nose.

"Here," he said, offering the jacket to Ximena. "I'll get Boyd. You head out and start walking up the hill."

Boyd had sworn he was sober enough to drive, and Tom was sure two hundred pounds of muscle could efficiently metabolize a great deal of alcohol, but still, nobody had wanted to ride with him. It wasn't that they *disliked* Boyd, but he was like a big exotic cat raised in captivity: though he looked majestic, he was barely housebroken, he needed a lot of attention, and he always smelled kind of funny. So Tom and the other actors had crowded in with Ximena rather than ride with Boyd.

Tom sighed, imagining several more days trapped with Boyd in some emergency shelter or shitty motel. Boyd had decided that Tom was a *real actor* on the basis of his many years of scraping together a stage career and kept trying to corner him on their breaks to talk about Euripides when Tom just wanted to mindlessly scroll on his phone in peace.

Tom unlocked the car door and prepared to duck out into the rain to fetch the lead actor just as the brake lights in front of them flared back to red. He heard the engine turn over. Tom frowned. There was no place for Boyd to go. Ximena's car wasn't far behind him, and there was very little shoulder. In front of Boyd's car the road dipped; the water was at least a couple of feet deep and rising.

"Shit," Ximena said again, leaning forward over the steering wheel. She laid on the horn. "Don't do it. Don't do it, motherfucker."

Ximena was from Missouri, so she didn't know from hurricanes, but she surely knew about floods. She knew better than to drive through flowing water of any depth. Did Boyd?

"The water's too deep," Tom said, now really concerned. He fumbled for his cell phone, intending to call the big putz driving the car in front of them to tell him to wait, but he wasn't fast enough on the screen. Before he could connect, Boyd revved the engine and began to creep slowly through the water on the road.

"Boyd, stop!" Ximena yelled. Tom doubted Boyd could hear her through the storm though, and they all knew he didn't take direction well.

Tom hesitated with the door open and watched with morbid fascination, knowing what was coming.

Boyd made it no more than a dozen feet before the water rose above the level of the undercarriage, where it was sucked into the air intake and flooded the engine. The brake lights flared again, quickly followed by the cabin lights. The engine fell silent. Boyd's car was dead.

Rolling his eyes, Tom turned his attention back to his phone, thumbing through his contacts for Boyd's number. Boyd needed to bail out and be careful about it as he went through the floodwaters, which could knock him over even at only ankle-deep. Tom didn't want to have to carry the guy up the hill to shelter.

"Oh *shit*," Ximena whispered again, with additional feeling.

Tom jerked his eyes up, not understanding how the situation could be getting worse already.

The Kia was beginning to drift laterally as the water rose and carried it aloft, dangerously close to an embankment that dropped off ten feet into what had once been an empty drainage canal but was now a rapidly flowing stream.

"Get out now!" Tom immediately yelled, waving his arm, but Boyd either couldn't hear him or still wasn't listening. The car slowly, almost gently, drifted across the road and then began to slide down the hill. Ten feet over, it tipped sharply to the left, spun on one tire, and disappeared from view.

The other people in Tom's car, drunk as they were, had finally cottoned on to what was happening and started to scream.

"Holy shit, holy shit," Tom yelped, hand reflexively caught in his hair before he remembered to move.

He jumped out of the car and ran to the edge of the embankment, looking down in horror as he peered to see what had happened to the Kia. He spotted it at the bottom of the hill.

It wasn't as bad as it could have been—the car had landed nose first on the concrete lip of the canal, the airbags had deployed, and Boyd's arms were moving in front of the billowing white shapes of the airbags. He wouldn't have taken severe injury from the crash.

But the water was flowing around the vehicle, threatening to dislodge the car again and tip it into the growing stream. The black floodwaters were deep and white-capped from their turbulence, more than halfway up the body of the car already.

Even if Boyd wasn't already injured, he'd drown if he was still in the car when it was pushed off the slope it precariously rested on.

Tom tested the hillside with one toe, and it promptly gave way. He scrambled back a step. It had been a dry summer, and the water was running off the ground rather than saturating it, making the earth treacherous and unsteady. It would probably send him tumbling into the ditch before he made it halfway to the Kia.

Don't die doing something that gets you described in the papers as

"Florida Man." That had been Rosie's number one rule, first whispered into his ear as she prevented him from stumbling in front of a Boston trolley on the night they met.

Ximena ran up next to Tom, cursing in a creative mix of Spanish and English.

"I told everyone else to call 911," she said, breath coming ragged with alarm. "I told them we need a tow. Or a crane. How is a fire truck or anything going to get here, though?"

"It won't," Tom said immediately. Emergency services wouldn't—usually couldn't—come in the middle of a hurricane. The roads were impassable, and nothing could fly in this.

"I guess we—we—we need to get down there and rescue him?" Ximena's voice stuttered with fear.

Tom found clarity in the sudden rush of adrenaline. He turned enough to meet Ximena's wide eyes for emphasis. "What do you mean *we*? You're pregnant! You have a wife and a kid on the way. Get out of here." He pointed up the hill.

Guilt flashed across her face.

"That doesn't—I mean—are *you* going to climb down there?" she demanded. She gestured at the car. Boyd still hadn't gotten his door open.

"Of course," Tom blurted, looking at the smashed Kia. "I just—shit, I don't know."

He didn't want to die saving Boyd Kellagher, who'd gotten himself into this classic Florida Man situation all on his own. He didn't want to die at *all*.

That prime directive was only exceeded by the thought that it would be hard to live with himself if he stood by and watched a man die. Tom had managed to survive his lengthy history of big mistakes, bad decisions, and colossal fuckups, but he didn't think there would be any coming back from this one if he didn't climb down to the drainage canal.

"Tom?" Ximena asked, shaking his arm urgently.

Tom glanced down at his phone, which was still illuminated in his hand, screen displaying his contact list. How odd that the very next person in his contact list after Boyd was the one person Tom needed to call before doing something stupid and potentially deadly.

I can't die now. I was supposed to get Rosie back first was the delirious thought that bubbled up to the surface of his mind, so fragile it was hard to examine. But it persisted even through the pulsing fear of the moment. How had he let it get to ten years since he last saw her, when he'd always thought he was supposed to get Rosie back?

Acting before he could think too hard about it, he pressed her name with his thumb and lifted the phone to his ear, leaning over to shield it from the wind and rain.

"Hey, Rosie?" Tom said when the call unsurprisingly went straight to voicemail. Who knew if this was still her number, or if she maybe had his blocked. "It's me. I'm, um. Well. I might be about to die. And in case I die, I just wanted to say I've always loved you. And if I happen to live . . . I'm sorry for everything. I really am. I wish I had the chance to make it up to you. Okay. Bye."

Tom hit the button to end the call and handed his phone to Ximena, ducking his face away from her shocked expression.

"Get inside!" he told her, even though his throat was closing up from panic, both that he might actually die and that it had somehow been *ten years*. "Don't wait for us."

She nodded shakily.

When he was sure she was going, Tom rolled his shoulders back and focused on the slick ground ahead of him. He wiped all thoughts of the call he'd just made from his mind. He sent a small internal prayer to anyone listening in the sky.

And then he started sliding feetfirst down the hill.

1

Rose liked parties, but she loved holiday parties in particular. She liked everything about the holidays. She liked the little rituals: the decorations, the special meals, and the seasonal music. Hand turkeys for Thanksgiving. Flag cakes on the Fourth of July. "Silver Bells" in the grocery store before Christmas. She liked going out to her aunt's inn on Martha's Vineyard and falling asleep in the third-floor bunk room with all her cousins while conversation drifted up from downstairs.

When she was in third grade, she'd leaned in to Valentine's Day. She cut out two dozen red construction paper hearts, traced the edges with Elmer's glue and gold glitter, and personalized the valentines for each kid in her homeroom class, even the ones she didn't like very much. She added stickers and pom-poms and googly eyes. She did everyone's name in cursive with puffy paint by copying the letters from a calligraphy book, and she covered a shoebox in pretty wrapping paper to carry the cards in.

At the class party, the valentines had seemed well received

by her classmates. Her teacher called her a sweetheart. Rose felt good about what she'd done, and she collected the little cardboard Snoopy and Garfield cards she'd received in exchange to take home in her shoebox. But at the end of the day, when she was packing up her cubby, Rose happened to look in the trash. And there, creased and discarded, were her valentines, mixed in with the used paper plates and cupcake wrappers from the party.

When Rose was still bewildered and weepy about it that night at the family cookie exchange, her aunt Max came and cast a critical eye over the salvaged cards. Rose adored her aunt Max, a beautiful lady who always wore lipstick and smelled like Chanel No. 5 instead of cigarettes. It was Max who planned the perfect holidays and hosted the entire Kelly clan at her inn multiple times a year.

You should probably have done something with candy instead. And that glitter would have gotten all over their backpacks, she told Rose. *Of course they threw them out.*

While hearing what she'd done wrong had stung, there had been an undercurrent of relief beneath Rose's embarrassment. Her mistake was fixable. She could have done it right with lollypops and conversation hearts. The next year, she would. Max patted her on the head and coaxed her downstairs to the party, and Rose assumed that when she grew up, she, like Max, would know what to do about everything.

This year's holidays, coming right on the heels of the hurricane, had not been up to Rose and Max's standards. Max's inn had been caught in the fringes of the storm, and for the first time Rose could remember, they had not gone out to Martha's

Vineyard for Thanksgiving or Christmas. Instead of fine-tuning her stuffing recipe or coercing her toddler nephews into reindeer costumes for her personal amusement, Rose spent most of the season writing letters to the insurance company.

"Should we get started, do you think?" her aunt's financial adviser asked significantly when Rose's family was more than fifteen minutes late to his office.

"Have you tried the cornetti yet?" Rose evaded, shoving the box across the conference room table.

She'd brought two dozen assorted baked goods from the good Italian place on Salem Street for this meeting, because if you had to set a man trap for a Kelly at nine a.m. on the first Monday of the new year, you baited it with pastry. She was expecting her father, at least one of her uncles, and a reasonable quorum of her brothers and cousins. She'd brought pastries and made them binders just in case they hadn't had a chance to read her emails about the inn's repairs.

"It's nine twenty. The gym's going to be packed by the time I get there," Aunt Max complained.

"Water aerobics isn't until three," Rose gently reminded her. "I'll get you to your shuttle."

Max paused, momentarily perplexed. "Oh, right," she said. "I was thinking about pickleball. But it's January, isn't it?"

Max's delicate, dark Kelly eyebrows gathered in confusion. Looking at Max was like looking into the future, her iron gray curls the natural conclusion of Rose's black ones, her heart-shaped face the time-progressed image of Rose's own.

She'd survived a stroke the previous year. They'd caught it quickly, and she just had a little lingering weakness on her left side, but it had done a number on her short-term memory. So Max cast around the room, trying to establish what she was doing there with her niece and her financial adviser.

"Have you put on a little weight recently?" she asked Rose when the echoing silence of the conference room grew too loud for her.

Rose frowned over her full box of pastries, which she hadn't even been eating on account of the hazelnut filling. Max wasn't usually mean, and if she shared the family opinion that Rose ought to try being taller and thinner, she'd never before aired it. Some combination of boredom and disinhibition was making her pick at Rose today.

"No, I've always been this fat," Rose said evenly. Her family consisted entirely of short fat people; what did they expect her to look like?

Aunt Max huffed and shifted in her seat. "I wasn't criticizing you. I just don't remember you looking this stressed."

"That's because you have short-term memory loss," Rose pointed out. "And you saw me two days ago at dinner. Remember? We talked about all the storm damage at the inn. That's why we're here."

Taken aback again, Aunt Max crossed her arms.

"The inn's gotten to be such a wreck," she grumbled. "I never had the money to fix it up right. Wish Peter had left me his stocks instead, but those vultures at the Harvard alumni office had their talons in him. We shouldn't have to deal with this."

Once her opinions on her late husband's poor estate planning were aired for the umpteenth time and Rose dutifully nodded agreement, Max reached into her pocketbook, coming out with a section of the *New York Times*. "Of course I remember we're here to talk about the inn," she said grumpily. She ostentatiously unfolded her paper and flapped it open so that Rose could see the front page of the Arts section.

Rose clenched her jaw when she saw the article her aunt was reading.

"That newspaper is three months old," Rose informed her aunt.

"Oh? Well, like you said, I have short-term memory loss. It'll be new to me," her aunt said with purposeful sweetness.

Rose recognized the picture on the page because she couldn't mentally erase the image of her ex-husband's distinctive Greek-god nose smooshed up against the equally distinctive profile of Boyd fucking Kellagher.

As if she needed something else to deal with! This was the year Tom had to make the national news with his tongue in someone else's mouth!

If the *Times* article was to be believed, Rose had at least another year of news ahead of her about Tom smooshing faces with Boyd Kellagher onstage. And, hell, probably offstage too, based on the equally pervasive image of Tom dragging the movie star out of the floodwaters, the other man clinging to Tom's neck like a giant, chiseled damsel in distress. Rose did not want to see it again. Those photos gave her the same uncomfortable feelings as real estate listings for homes she could never afford or other people's holiday cards, pictures that made her quickly turn the page or close the card.

It wasn't that she begrudged Tom his first big Broadway role

in ten years. Or kissing Boyd Kellagher. Or even Boyd Kellagher kissing Tom. She was unsurprised he had a gorgeous boyfriend now. But if Tom was going to get everything he ever
wanted—love, fame, professional success—could Rose not get
just one thing? If not Tom, if not a family of her own, why
could she not at least get a couple of happy weeks of vacation
every year spent preparing extravagant meals and group photo
shoots in matching sweaters? It didn't seem like too much to
ask for.

"I've seen it already," Rose said, trying not to sound as
stressed as she felt.

"So handsome," Max cooed, and she could have been referring to either Tom or Boyd. "I always liked him."

"No, you didn't," Rose retorted, snapping at the bait before
she could stop herself. This was revisionist history. "None of
you did. You told me not to marry him."

"Telling you not to marry him is different from *liking* him.
I thought he was a nice boy. You should have waited for him to
grow up."

Tom's age had nothing to do with it. "We just ended up
wanting different things." That was her standard line on their
divorce, one that assigned no blame while obscuring the painful truth that Rose, specifically, had not been one of the things
Tom wanted.

"And you didn't even send us a wedding present," Rose said,
certain that would get her aunt off the subject.

Max raised her eyebrows, unimpressed. "I'm sorry, but we
all assumed you were in a family way and too embarrassed to

admit it before the wedding. I was going to get all your nursery furniture."

Rose stiffened her shoulders in familiar hurt because she'd known what her family thought, but nobody had ever given her the chance to set them straight. She hadn't married Tom because she was pregnant, then or ever, or for tax reasons, or to get him on her health insurance, or for any of the other reasons people had speculated about their marriage at twenty-two.

She'd married him because he'd asked her and because she'd loved him—she'd been utterly, stupidly in love with him—and she'd thought it would last forever. Which had made their breakup only a year later much more embarrassing than an unexpected baby would have been.

But that was a long time ago now. What was really embarrassing was that she was still having feelings about it at all, which she decided she would stop doing at once.

"Well, I wasn't. Obviously. And I'm happy he's finding success. He's a very talented actor, so I'm not surprised he's working with people like Boyd Kellagher," Rose said, getting herself in hand and saying the things the kind of person she wanted to be would say.

"Are you going to see his new play?" her aunt asked.

"It looks like I'm going to be busy over the next few months," Rose said dourly, checking the time again. Her family's tardiness did not bode well for their contributions to fixing up the inn.

She picked up her phone and scrolled to her father's work number at the tax preparation office he managed. He should have been here, not there, but she tried calling anyway. A new receptionist picked up the phone and sent a flutter of worry through her when he confirmed that yes, Derek Kelly was there, one second, please.

"Hey, princess," her father said when he reached the phone, sounding both wary and cheerful. "Can this be quick? You know it's not great for you to call at work, and it's tax season—"

"Dad!" Rose burst out. "What are you doing? You're supposed to be meeting with me and Max right now."

There was a pause. Her father's palm shifted awkwardly on the receiver.

"Did your uncle Ken not get a chance to talk to you this weekend?"

"No?"

"Ah. Well." Her father's voice trailed off. Rose waited for him to say more, but he didn't.

"You can still come now. It's only fifteen minutes if you take a cab," Rose said, looking worriedly at Max's financial adviser, who showed signs of bolting.

"I'm sorry you didn't know. And for your time this morning. But the boys and I talked about it over Christmas," her father said, still sounding deeply uncomfortable. "And we think you should sell the inn."

"What?" Rose said, leaning back in shock. "No. No. That doesn't make any sense."

Setting aside the problem that nobody had a big enough house for them all to get together if she sold it, the inn was an income-producing property. Or it was when it wasn't closed from storm damage. It was how Rose paid her aunt's bills.

"Yeah, it does though," her father insisted. "It's going to be a big old time and money suck for months, and it's just not worth it to haul ourselves out there every winter anymore."

"What do you mean not worth it? Everyone loves that place. It takes, like, a couple hours, doorstep to doorstep. And—"

"I know, but honestly, sweetie, can't you get back to Boston easier than Martha's Vineyard? Plus, your brother's the one with kids, and even he was saying he'd rather take them down to Disney next year."

Nobody had told her this. Nobody had breathed a single word of this to her. That couldn't be right—they just didn't want to help with the repairs.

"No. It can't be like it was this year every year—we were all crammed in at dinner, we barely saw the cousins—Dad. Dad, no. Come on. I made a schedule. I made binders. And if everyone pitches in just on the weekends, it'll only take a few months—"

Her voice was winding up higher and tighter, and she didn't like how young she sounded. She regrouped. Her father wasn't listening to her, which wasn't unusual, but he didn't like to fight either. She just had to hold her ground.

She couldn't sell the inn. She'd slept on the foldout couch in her parents' house this year, tiptoed through *their* space, carried hot casseroles on her lap through expensive cab rides, and none of it, not a bit of it, had felt like it should.

"I have to get back to it," her father muttered sheepishly. "Ken said he was going to talk to you. You should talk to Ken about the inn. It just makes more sense to sell and be done with it."

He all but hung up on her.

Rose jerked back in her chair, quickly looking for support from her aunt's financial adviser—the person who had walked her through all the insurance paperwork two months ago. His face bore sympathy . . . but not support. Nor surprise.

After he'd eaten her pastries?

"My dad talked to you about this," she accused him.

He cleared his throat. "Your father asked me to check what the inn would sell for without repairs, yes."

"It's got to be less than what it could produce if we fix it up. What did you say?"

"That it would simplify your aunt's estate significantly—"

"Her estate?" After she *died*? "She's sitting right here!"

Rose glared at him, eyes flicking to her aunt in distress. What a terrible ghoul this asshole was to be making plans based on the assumption Max would die soon. Max was doing fine!

Fortunately, Max had gotten bored with the proceedings and fallen asleep in her chair, face tilted down to her considerable chest, so she didn't hear that anyone was planning her demise.

Rose lowered her voice to a whisper and pointed a finger at the financial adviser. "It's up to me, right? I have power of attorney. I'm not selling it."

The financial adviser shoved a tissue box across the table, a practiced gesture he must have employed with many unreasonable women. Rose was prepared to be as unreasonable as necessary. She evaded his skeptical expression and looked down at her phone, pulling up group texts and calendar entries. Someone else had to see how important the inn was to Max and Rose. Fifteen different relatives she'd emailed, every single one of whom had gladly eaten Rose's steamed pudding every Christmas since she was old enough to look over the stove. She'd bought the pastries and sent the reminders. They would come. They were just late.

Three hours later, Rose staggered out into a Boston blizzard, blinking at the thin sunlight filtering through the snow. Nobody else had come. Nobody else had even called her *back*.

She'd never been this angry. Or, rather, she hadn't been this angry in a decade.

Thirty years of endless summer days on the back lawn, winter evenings in front of the fireplace, birthday parties and anniversaries and even Rose's long-ago honeymoon, and nobody else wanted to hold on to the inn? Nobody else cared? Where was the big family she'd thought she had?

Wondering if she'd somehow missed a message, overlooked an email, Rose stood in the knee-deep snow and searched through the electronic nooks and crannies of her phone. She checked her junk mail folder. Her spam texts folder. Her work email. Nothing. And then she called her old voicemail inbox, the one she'd quit using three years ago when she left her job in private wealth management for her current role at a nonprofit—she had too many old clients who thought she still solved their problems.

There was only one message, dated almost three months previous, and it made her whole body lock up in shock when she heard it. She nearly dropped her phone, one hand automatically scrabbling in her purse for her rescue inhaler, even if it wasn't her asthma that was closing up her throat.

Hey, Rosie? It's me.

She hadn't heard Tom's voice in ten years, but identifying it was the only effortless part of hearing his message.

I'm, um. Well. I might be about to die.

The message was rough and full of static. The roar in the background must be the rain. He'd left her a message just before that infamous picture of Boyd Kellagher's rescue was taken.

I've always loved you.

Rose's mind skipped right past that, as she'd long since decided that Tom meant something very different by those words than she'd originally thought. It was the next statement that caught her attention:

I'm sorry for everything. I wish I had the chance to make it up to you.

Tears threatened to spill out over her cheeks. There wasn't a way to make it up to her. He was supposed to love her for the rest of her life; tickets to his Broadway premiere weren't going to cut it as a substitute, and it was beyond her what else he might think he had that she wanted. Why bother being sorry now? Once again, he was too late.

However.

Didn't she need someone who knew how to swing a hammer? That was ironic. That was great timing.

Could she bust into his Boyd Kellagher–adjacent celebrity lifestyle and ask him to help pick out new siding for the inn?

Reseal a few windows? Air out the drapes? She was sure he hadn't thought about it at all, just like he'd never thought about what it would really mean to be married to her.

That was Tomasz Wilczewski—completely sincere when he made promises, totally incapable when it came time to live up to any of them.

Rose wiped her face with her palms.

I wish I had the chance to make it up to you.

She'd always let it go before. Every time he was late, every time he forgot, all the promises he made to her, even their damn wedding vows. She'd never held him to any of it.

It would serve him right if she decided this time she was going to make him live up to every single word.

It would serve him right.

2

New York

The blaring of the front door buzzer woke Tom up just before midnight. He'd passed out on the couch with the lights and TV on, which wasn't uncommon, nor was the blaring of the buzzer, but he wasn't expecting anyone.

Tom picked up his phone from the coffee table and squinted at the date and time. No missed calls.

The buzzing didn't stop.

"I'm coming, I'm coming," he mumbled. He stood up, winced at the pain in his back, and lurched in the general direction of the door. Today he'd worked a double shift at a fancy steak house downtown, which would provide a nice financial cushion before rehearsals started, but at thirty-four, he couldn't shrug off twelve straight hours on his feet with his waiter's apron.

He hobbled barefoot down the length of his hallway and two flights of stairs without bothering to put on more clothes. Anyone unexpectedly at his door at midnight didn't deserve to complain if they saw him in his skimpy boxers.

Tom threw open the front door of the building to admit a wintry mist of freezing rain, but that wasn't what had him rocking back on his heels. He made a wordless grunt of surprise, a soft, guttural *huh*, like he'd been slogged in the stomach. Shock sent him reeling to the side.

It was *Rosie*, shivering and wet on his doorstep, one hand frozen on the buzzer and the other clutching the handle of a roller suitcase nearly as large as she was.

He'd forgotten how small she was, even if he thought he'd forgotten nothing else. Tom was a couple inches short of six feet tall, so Rose Kelly was one of the only people on earth he towered over. His first sight of her in a decade was the top of her head, but that was a familiar view.

Tom put a hand on the doorframe to hold himself up. He could have used a little warning. A *lot* of warning. Rosie's reentry into his life ought to have been accompanied by an act's worth of foreshadowing and some kind of orchestral theme—maybe a mashup of the "Imperial March" and the bridal one.

He licked his lips, half wondering if he was hallucinating even though he couldn't recall imbibing anything stronger than half a strawberry White Claw after work today.

"*Rosie?*" he finally managed, sounding strangled. He cleared his throat. It helped a little that she seemed to be having just as much trouble speaking as he was. Two bright spots of color had appeared on her full cheeks, matching the tip of her nose and the rims of her eyes, which were still fixed on his bare chest. Her sweet and dainty cupid's-bow lips were parted as she took in the new topography of his chest muscles, then his entire bare body. He'd done nothing more than strip when he got home from work; his apartment was on the top floor and always boiling hot, even in January.

He wished he were wearing more clothes. Better underwear, at least.

His voice jarred her out of her reverie, and her gaze jerked up from his chest to meet his eyes.

"What's on your *face*?" she blurted, sounding horrified.

Tom rubbed his mustache automatically.

"I—it's for a role?" he said, feeling delirious. She'd never seen him other than clean-shaven, but then again, he hadn't even needed to shave every day when they first met.

This was like a dream. A pizza dream. His ex-wife showed up at his door at midnight, looking adorably disheveled, only to severely judge his grooming.

Rosie swallowed hard, visibly attempting to gather herself. She stuck a hand in the pocket of her sodden camel overcoat, fumbling for something, then opened her handbag. Her hands were shaking.

"I mean, um. I came to ask you if you meant it—"

"What?" Tom said, shaking the last vestiges of sleep out of his head. He was still holding the door open with his body, and his favorite bits—the ones protected from the wind by just one thin layer of threadbare cotton—were about to freeze right off. Rosie's black curls were nearly soaked to her head. This was all insane.

He carefully grabbed her by the upper arm and pulled her stumbling and half-heartedly protesting into the vestibule. He opened the door again to grab her suitcase and, without waiting for her agreement, began hauling it up behind him.

"Come in, at least," he said when he was half a flight in, his mouth belatedly catching up with the rest of his body.

He liked to think of himself as largely immune to the more toxic impulses of his gender, and where he wasn't, he was working on it, but within thirty seconds of seeing Rosie for the first time in a decade, a very primal set of instincts had kicked in. Get her into his cave. Get her wet clothes off. Keep her there. All of a sudden, the world had simplified.

Tom halted when he reached his open doorway, viewing his apartment with the same gaze he assumed she'd apply to it. Shit. It wasn't wrecked, but it wasn't how Rosie would have kept it.

He parked Rosie's bag next to the door, then stooped for the nearest stack of clean laundry, hurriedly pulling on a shirt before turning back to her.

"I, uh, I wasn't expecting anyone," he said.

"Of course not," she said, big blue eyes still wide and anxious as she hovered in the doorway like she might bolt anyway.

She'd cut her pretty hair; when he knew her, she'd laboriously straightened it every morning until it ran smooth down her back, then used a curling iron to put it into perfect waves around her face. Now she wore it just below her shoulders in her natural wispy ringlets, though it was frizzing from the rain.

"Let me take your coat," he said.

He'd never seen her this undone. Rosie was always so perfectly put together that all his associations with her current state of deshabille were erotic ones: times he'd smeared her lipstick down her chin or rubbed her hair into knots against his cheap pillowcase.

His knuckles brushed the soft fuzz of her white sweater as he peeled her coat off her stiff body. He wanted to press them against her to keep the small contact. She smelled like wet hair and expensive perfume, and he took a deep breath just to soak his lungs with her scent.

He propelled himself away just long enough to snatch a towel from his pile of clean laundry.

"Sit, sit, please," he said, gesturing at his couch and pushing the towel into her hand.

He grabbed the half-empty White Claw from the floor next to the couch and tossed it in the direction of the kitchen sink. "Can I get you something to drink?"

He knew he was stalling, but he was still trying to remember his lines. Over the years he'd imagined scenarios where he saw Rosie again—bumped into her on the sidewalk in Midtown, at a friend's engagement party, in the audience at his grand return to Broadway—but all the moving, charming, heartfelt speeches he'd composed for the occasion simply escaped him now.

". . . Yes, all right," she said from the other room, just short of a whisper.

He opened his liquor cabinet, which was also the under-the-sink cabinet.

But why do you have the palate of a fifteen-year-old girl whose parents are out of town? she used to tease him.

Better the palate than the musical taste. He always pushed right back.

Me? You're the one who likes doing it to Kesha. He remembered kissing her mouth and tasting the red wine he wouldn't drink.

Fifteen years later, he had only sour apple pucker and spiced rum.

He recalled that he had a bottle of Żubrówka in the freezer alongside twenty-five pounds of smoked salmon, part of Boyd's objectively thoughtful Christmas gift. Rosie was allergic to apple juice, the mixer he had on hand, so he just poured two fingers neat and rushed it back to the living room for her.

She had taken a seat on his big denim sofa and clutched the red throw pillow he'd been sleeping on to her chest, shield-like. He paused for a moment to fill his eyes with the sight of her: the small, round body, her porcelain-doll features. He'd caught only fragments of Rosie in the years since she'd left him, spotted around the edges of photographs taken at parties he wasn't invited to. It hadn't been nearly enough to make a full picture.

"Here," he said over a tight throat, offering her the drink.

She sniffed it and took an exploratory sip, her eyes widening at the burn of the alcohol.

"I could get you some ice—" he began to offer, but she shook her head. Her hand tightened on the glass before she tossed the whole thing back in one gulp. "Whoa. Easy there, killer," he said as she coughed.

That got a faint smile out of her when she handed the empty glass to him.

She took the towel and wrapped it around her hair, then tipped her head back to regard him, her gaze finally present and direct.

"Thanks," she said. "I needed that."

"I'm just sorry the place is a mess," he said ruefully, though she wouldn't have expected anything else.

"No, it's nice," she protested. "You have . . . furniture. You have good stuff."

Tom laughed. "You were probably expecting more of a ball pit concept?" She pursed that little flower bud of a mouth, unable to lie. "It's okay. You know, Adrian threatened to put me in an aquarium lined with cedar chips if I didn't get better at picking up after myself."

It was dangerous to mention their mutual friend—and also, obliquely, that Tom had slept on his couch for a year after Rosie kicked him out—but Rosie mustered half a smirk even though her posture was still rattled and uncertain. "As though Adrian wasn't always training to be someone's fancy little pet," she said.

Tom wanted to pick up his phone and text that cuttingly accurate observation to the group chat with Adrian and his girlfriend, but he was afraid to take his eyes off Rosie lest she vanish.

He'd been hovering awkwardly, but he took a seat at the other end of the couch, just close enough that his bare knee might brush Rosie's corduroy-clad one. He looked at Rosie's suitcase.

"Um. Do you need somewhere to stay . . . ?"

Many of his fantasies about finding Rosie again had revolved around her needing something implausible from him, like a date to a wedding full of assassins or maybe a kidney. *Anything for you, my love*, he'd sob as the surgeon drew on him with a Sharpie, and then the third act would explore the physical metaphor of organ donation in a satisfying way.

He had a hard time coming up with other explanations for Rosie on his doorstep in Inwood at midnight.

"Oh, no, I just got off the train from Boston," she said. She took a deep breath, as though preparing a long explanation, but her eyes landed for the first time on the painting hung behind the couch. It was a colorful abstract floral piece, and Adrian had given it to them as an engagement gift. It was one of the few things Tom had come out of the divorce owning. Rosie's face fell, and she ducked her chin.

"This was a bad idea," she muttered, more to herself than to him.

"What is it?" Tom said, stretching his arm out down the back of the couch in reassurance. "You came all the way here from Penn Station, you might as well tell me."

She popped her head to the side in a heartbreakingly familiar chiding expression before she looked down at her lap. "I came to ask if you meant it."

"Meant what?"

Rose reached into her handbag again, coming out with her phone this time. With a few clicks of her thumb, his recorded voice hissed through the room, startling and unfamiliar for the static and the distance.

Hey, Rosie? It's me.

She stopped the recording and looked at him expectantly.

Tom wet his lips. He'd thought of that message often for the first week after the hurricane, but when it went unanswered, he'd put those thoughts away for safekeeping with every other hurt that bore her name.

"Did you mean it?" she asked again.

Mean what? That he still loved her? *Like REO Speedwagon sang it: when I said that I love you I meant that I love you forever.*

"Yes?" he said, incredulous that it could really be that easy. It couldn't possibly be so easy to get her here as just calling her and telling her that. It didn't make any sense; whether they were in love had seemed very irrelevant to her reasons for divorcing him.

She must have heard the news. About the storm, Boyd, the Broadway run. In the press or maybe from Adrian or one of their other friends. Something to make her think he wasn't the same selfish jerk he'd been at twenty-two.

Rosie looked skeptical, catching his hesitation.

"I meant it," he confirmed, wiping his face clean and summoning more confidence.

"Okay. Okay, so, I actually do need something . . ." she said slowly.

Rosie was trying to work herself up to it. Oh God, it probably was a kidney after all. Rosie's health hadn't ever been great, what with the asthma and the dramatic allergen encounters, and maybe some exotic inflammatory reaction meant she needed a new organ?

Well, this was the reason he came with spares, he supposed. Hopefully the recovery period didn't take him too far into rehearsals.

"You remember the Windward Inn?" Rosie asked instead.

Tom blinked. "Of course I do. We went like ten times. And for our honeymoon."

She winced at that last word, but she continued. "So, in the hurricane—you know, the same hurricane . . . you remember the hurricane."

"Yeah, I heard it smacked Martha's Vineyard pretty good," he said, not sure where this was going other than not to the operating room.

"The inn got damaged in the storm. The roof and I don't know what else. My family thinks we should sell rather than try to fix it up," she finished in a rush.

Tom twisted up his mouth, trying to remember the place. His top concern, before their honeymoon, had been not getting caught sneaking into or out of Rosie's room, not the quality of the furnishings. And on their honeymoon—well, the suite's bed, walls, and floor had been pretty sturdy, he could confidently report.

But now that he thought about it, he could recall getting beaned by a chunk of ceiling plaster in the shower. Creaky stairs. Peeling paint.

"Yeah, it's kind of a shithole, isn't it?" he said cautiously.

Rosie went stiff. "It is not!" she protested. "It's a great building. In a great location. It just needs some cosmetic updates, and . . . and a few repairs."

From her affronted, worried look, Tom could begin to guess what she wanted, though he had no idea why she'd thought of him in connection to the project. His portfolio of useful abilities, which were mostly limited to stage acting and sexual prowess, did not include home repairs.

She twisted her delicate, ladylike hands in her lap with

another deep breath. "So I—I remembered that your parents used to be property managers at that retirement community outside Boca—"

"Still are," he cautiously confirmed.

"—and I thought, they probably had to handle a lot of repair stuff? I know you said you went with them on all their rounds during summer vacations . . ." She trailed off hopefully.

Tom swallowed hard. He had indeed spent most of his childhood trailing behind his parents as they went from one septuagenarian's apartment to another, but if he'd picked up anything along the way, it had been nothing more than a little Yiddish, a fondness for show tunes, and a good sense for which old folks kept bowls of candy for visiting children and which would smack him with a spoon if he touched their piano while *Wheel of Fortune* was on.

"Yeah, definitely," he lied. "All the hitting things with hammers. And unscrewing things. Screwing them too. I learned how to do all that."

When her face softened with relief, a nearly forgotten sensation of pain and tenderness twisted in his chest. Wanting more for her than he had to give. He wanted to tell her not to worry at all, that he'd take care of everything, but he also wished, even more fervently, that it would be the truth.

Shit. A kidney would have been easier to promise her. Maybe he could learn how to hang roof shingles on YouTube during the train ride out to the Cape?

"I mean, insurance will pay for some contractors. Most of what the place needs, hopefully. I've been writing a lot of letters. But it would be great if I could update the place a little.

You remember all the whaling swag my uncle left there—let's toss out all the harpoon guns before they accidentally skewer a toddler—"

She cut off when she began to speak very fast, her cheeks going pink again. She'd probably realized that she hadn't actually asked him yet, and she was having trouble making the request.

Well, Tom could sympathize with that problem.

"Of course I'll help," he said in his gentlest tone. "I meant it, after all."

Rosie looked up at him with red-rimmed eyes, her mascara gone clumpy with either tears or rain. Hope warred with caution in her expression.

He didn't like the caution, but he understood it. It was that hope he wanted to seize on, make real.

"It's the middle of the night," she said abruptly. "I'm so sorry. I'll text you about this tomorrow. I don't know why I came all the way up here—"

"Rosie." He dared to put a hand on her shoulder, got two seconds of soft warmth against his palm before she jerked away. He pulled the hand back slowly, pretended he hadn't done it, and cleared his throat. "It's fine," he said faintly.

She stood up, looking around for her coat as though she couldn't remember where she'd put it fifteen minutes ago. He could observe her visibly attempting to put some layers of mental distance back between them before she could resume the physical kind.

"Are you sure you don't want to stay?" he asked, and her eyes widened in affronted disbelief. "No, I mean, it's raining, and my roommate is traveling for work. You could have his room . . . or I could go back to sleep on the couch—"

"I'll get a car," she said, patting her handbag.

"At least borrow a jacket," he said. "Yours is soaked."

Without waiting for her agreement, he bounded into his room and rifled through his closet. He grabbed the first waterproof thing he found and returned to the living room to thrust it into Rosie's arms.

She thanked him genuinely at first, but then she turned the parka to check the size and saw the label.

"Wait," she said. "Is this real? Canada Goose? This is, like, a thousand-dollar parka."

"Is it?" he said, aghast. "Jesus. It ought to be illegal to charge that much. It's just a jacket."

Rosie hesitantly pulled it on. The parka fit her through the hips and bust, but the shoulders and sleeves were absurdly big on her. It made her look like a little kid in someone's hand-me-downs in a way that made him want to squeeze her hard. She cuffed the sleeves and rolled them up nearly to her elbows.

"I think they make them out of very special geese or something. Fancier geese than normal parka geese. Did you thrift it? Which place?" she asked shakily, zipping it up despite how poorly it fit.

He considered lying again, but since he often forgot what he'd told people, he tried not to lie very often.

"No, ah, it was Boyd's."

"Oh, wow," Rosie said, eyes widening. She covertly sniffed the fur around the hood.

Boyd who? she did not ask. So she had heard. She looked

around the apartment as though wondering if the man in question was hiding in his bedroom. Her face registered a number of new questions.

"I mean, people give him lots of free stuff they want him to promote. Clothes, cologne, watches, that sort of thing. And we're actually the same shirt size now, so he passed some extra swag to me," Tom said, aware that he was protesting too much.

"No, I get it," Rosie said. "That's really nice of him though." If anything, his disclosure seemed to have subdued her. She rubbed the side of her face, looking tired but no longer fearful. She took him in again from bare feet to boxers to rumpled T-shirt, then made a small, firm smile appear on her face.

"You look really good, Tom," she said, gesturing at him and the apartment both. "And I've heard nothing but good stuff. I'm glad. Really happy for you." Her tone had calmed.

"You look good too," he quickly said. *You still look like my wife.* "I mean, you always did though."

Rosie chuckled in response. "No, *I* look like a guinea pig that just went through a car wash, but thank you."

They were now doing the thing other people did when they met their exes in public. Little jokes before they could skid to the drink station on the other side of the room. He didn't like it.

"Okay, so, do you want to meet up tomorrow and go over the plan?" he asked, trying to prolong the interaction. "Do you want to go to dinner? Or lunch? Sometimes I work at a steak place in Washington Heights, and I can get us into a chef's table—"

If he couldn't keep her here, his caveman brain insisted he put a date and time on the next time he'd be with her.

"It's okay," she said, shaking her head. "I'll just text you. Thanks. Sorry again for the hour."

She hesitated, clearly considering the feasibility of hugging him or perhaps patting his arm but ultimately deciding against it.

She grabbed her suitcase and quickly let herself out, and Tom was as powerless to stop her as the last time they saw each other.

3

The next morning was a sodden gray with the previous night's chill, but Tom could practically hear the major-key orchestral theme following him down the street to Juilliard for a photo call at Ximena's alma mater. Before falling asleep, he'd worried that maybe he shouldn't have promised that he was going to be really helpful with the inn repairs. But this morning? It felt like the first day of an endless summer vacation. Everything was going to work out.

The big lobby was noisy and crowded with photographers and their equipment, and there was a happy background din made by Boyd's fans outside, who pressed their faces and handwritten signs to the glass windows. Tom was normally skittish near the people who followed Boyd around to take pictures of him, but today they merely seemed like the joyful chorus to his mood. *Hello, weirdos! Yes, everything is beautiful today.*

Tom checked in with the photographer and Ximena's publicist, kissed Ximena herself on the cheek, and stepped onto the set. He hoped the shoot didn't take too long—he wanted to stop by a hardware store afterward and osmotically absorb some construction knowledge before he talked to Rosie again.

Boyd rose from the makeup station when he spotted Tom, an out-of-character expression of uncertainty creasing his famous, Byronic features.

"You shaved!" he said. "Wait, are we not doing the mustache thing in the new script? Are we going back to the dick thing? I thought you said the dick thing was gross?"

Boyd looked vaguely like Tom if their height difference was ignored: dark hair and eyes, strong features, muscular build. Their play, *All's Well That Bends Well*, was an adaptation of Shakespeare's least famous comedy, and its central conceit was that Boyd, the real love interest, might be mistaken for Tom, the decoy boyfriend, in dim lighting. In the first version of the script, Ximena's character figured out the switch when she stuck her hand down Boyd's pants. She and Tom had both objected: the original play was vaguely rape-y upon any amount of scrutiny, and swapping the genders of the main characters didn't help. Also, shaming people with tiny dicks, even if Tom was very much not one of them, wasn't a great look. Tom had been told to grow a thick, seventies-style porn mustache as a compromise to preserve the plot beat.

"The dick thing was gross," Tom confirmed, taking a step back. "I'll grow the 'stache back before rehearsals start. It was just getting itchy."

If Rosie didn't like it, off it went. God willing, everything else she wanted was that easily handled.

"Oh, yeah, okay," Boyd said with a great deal of doubt, looking Tom up and down. "It was just, you know, a big part of your character. Did you get the fish I sent? Have you been sticking to the diet?"

Tom tried not to squirm under Boyd's scrutiny. "I got the fish. I've been eating the fish."

He'd eaten some of the fish.

Boyd's gaze was assessing. In the lead-up to their Off Broadway run, Tom had been obliged to spend several hours a day lifting weights on the ancient 1990s infomercial torture devices of a local gym in order to force his body into a facsimile of his Hollywood action movie colead's.

He wondered if Rosie had been at all impressed, what with most of him on display when he'd opened his door. Hopefully a little impressed? He needed all the advantages he could get.

"You could come to my training sessions now that I'm back in town," Boyd said, face brightening. "I started seeing a new trainer. He's not just about fitness. He's also a healer."

"Like, he's a doctor *and* a fitness trainer?" Tom said, trying to sidestep over to the makeup table.

"Not a doctor, no, he's not captive to western pharmaceutical interests," Boyd said earnestly. "He teaches your body to protect itself from toxins using natural feedback. Like, if you're dehydrated and bloating, you use frog venom to restore the balance." Boyd lifted his loose T-shirt up to display a trio of round, angry-looking welts like cigarette burns along his collarbone. "You do get frog face for like twenty-four hours after he applies the venom, but after that, all the water weight is—boom—gone."

"Uhhh," said Tom, looking around for someone to handle this imminent risk to the production's headliner. Boyd was a nice man, really, but so naive and credulous that it was a wonder no celebrity cult had scooped him up yet, and Tom was in no position to provide a good example before he got his own life sorted out. "Ximena, Boyd's burning himself with frog juice. Should he be doing that?"

"Oh, baby, no," Ximena said, catching on to Tom's imploring look and sweeping over to put her arm around Boyd's massive shoulders. Ximena was tall, Tom's height, with her black hair freshly styled into a spiky pixie cut and delicate gold hoops crowding her earlobes. "No frog venom. Have you tried drinking actual water? I'll get you some."

She pushed Boyd back toward the makeup artist, who sat him down to work on his foundation. Boyd's skin wasn't great—theater pancake would do that, but so would anabolic steroids, which he'd offered Tom before. If he wanted health advice, Tom's position was that no role was worth shrinking his balls or puffing into "frog face."

Ximena frowned and looked at her watch as they waited for Boyd to be made pretty.

"I was hoping to get out of here by eleven," she complained. "Lú wanted to tour another school during her lunch hour." Ximena's wife Luísa was a partner at a fancy white-shoe law firm and the child of Broadway producers; the dirty secret of this industry was that people mostly managed to stay in it via someone else's money.

"Preschool? Already?" Tom asked. Ximena wasn't even due till May.

"Preschool. This town is insane," Ximena said, pressing a hand to her forehead. "Lú was applying to day cares while my feet were still in stirrups at the fertility clinic."

They both fidgeted impatiently through makeup, but at last the photographer came over to tell them where to stand for light check.

"Why am I in Boyd's lap again?" Tom complained when he got his own assignment. It didn't make thematic sense in the context of the already incoherent play, but this was the third photo call since the hurricane to explore the visual concept of "Tom and Boyd *love* to cuddle." *Vanity Fair Mexico* had draped Tom across Boyd's naked, greased-up chest with instructions to simper when it had been Tom who'd hauled *Boyd's* lunatic ass out of a drainage ditch!

It was a bait and switch. Tom didn't even appear until the second act, his onstage romance with Boyd was nothing but misdirection, and their offstage relationship was nothing like the fangirls imagined.

"Because our friends outside love the idea that you call him 'Daddy,'" Ximena answered, nodding her chin at the crowd on the other side of the windows, although the question had been hypothetical at best.

"It's part of our brand now," Boyd agreed.

Tom was a little queasy at the idea that he was a part of Boyd's brand, much less a part that masses of strangers found sexually titillating.

"We should switch things up," Tom said. "Ximena's the oldest. Get in her lap and I'll stand behind you both."

Ximena shot Tom a dirty look, but hey, their characters got married in the last scene, this was her cross to bear.

Boyd shook his head. "*Daddy* isn't about age," he rumbled in his bass voice.

"*Daddy* is a vibe," Ximena agreed, crossing her legs and inspecting her manicure. "Get in his lap, baby bear."

"I can do the daddy vibe," Tom muttered darkly. If Rosie had arrived at his door looking for a guy who could swing a hammer, that was the vibe he *needed* to project. But nonetheless he took his assigned perch between Boyd's spread knees, wrapping the other man's arm around his waist and tilting his head to find his light. The girls outside went berserk, cheering and banging on the windows so hard Tom was afraid they'd break the glass. Boyd shot them a tolerant smile and patted Tom's stomach consolingly.

"Hey, do you have some time to look at the script revisions? It looks like they want to take my character in a different direction, but I want to make sure I understand the deeper implications," Boyd said as the photographer's assistant took some test shots.

"Ooh, I'd love to," Tom lied. He was sure there was nothing deep to be found. The story was bananapants fluff tied together with a few clever anachronisms. "But I'm actually heading out of town, and I probably won't be back till rehearsals start."

"Are you pursuing other artistic endeavors?" Boyd asked in his recitative way.

"No, my, ah, Rosie asked me to go spend some time with her out on Martha's Vineyard. We're going to replace the roof on her aunt's B and B." The idea of it was so new and precious that it felt like jinxing it to speak it out loud. But he couldn't stop an uncertain, giddy smile from spreading across his face, much to the photographer's dismay.

"Whoa, whoa," said Ximena. "Your ex? She finally called you back?"

"Yep," Tom confirmed, forcing himself to nonchalance and then, at the photographer's gesture, a wide-eyed pout. No, this was really happening. He could tell the world. "We're, well, I guess we're going to see if we can work things out."

"Wow," said Ximena. "That's pretty sudden, isn't it?"

"Congratulations," Boyd said, slapping him on the shoulder with his free hand. "That's fantastic. Happy for you. Love to hear it."

Ximena's expression was more skeptical. "I thought you guys hadn't spoken in years."

"Not until last night. She just got my message, I guess? And she's finally open to getting back together."

"Why now though?" Ximena asked. "Right before your big return to Broadway? I mean, I pity the woman who decides to be *your* groupie of all people, but you need to be worried about people who just want to get close to Boyd."

Tom nearly snorted at the idea of Rosie as a groupie. Or of Tom as close to Boyd in anything other than the very short-term sense that yes, he could smell what the other actor had eaten for breakfast. More fish.

"That's not Rosie at all," he said. "She's a normal person with an actual, normal life. And anyway, I'm the one who messed things up. This is only happening because I asked her for a second chance."

Ximena's expression softened, though Tom would have liked to see at least a little supportive skepticism of the idea that Tom had been the one who messed up.

The photographer cleared her throat again, and Tom was glad for an end to that line of questioning. For another few minutes, he obediently struck a variety of alluring poses over Boyd's trunk-like thighs. As soon as he was released, he bounced up onto his toes and shook out his muscles. Boyd sprawled out on his seat, waving at his fans.

Ximena stood up more slowly, rubbing her lower back and making a face like she needed to pee. But instead of taking care of that important function, she turned back to Tom to continue the interrogation.

"So, what did you do to this poor girl, then?"

Tom swallowed, freezing mid-bounce as Boyd tuned in to the question as well. But Tom still didn't have a ready answer. He'd been blindsided at the time. Rosie hadn't exactly given him an itemized return receipt, more a shouted list of emotions she was feeling as she tossed his clothes into the hallway.

Other people had confided their own theories:

His best friend had thought Tom was a bad roommate.

You don't clean anything until I yell at you, the last time you bought groceries you came home with nothing but lychees and cocktail shrimp, and every sock you own is on my living room floor, Adrian had yelled. *It's like living with a raccoon.*

Tom's parents thought he was a financial drain.

You shouldn't have gotten married until you could support a family, his stolid, responsible father had told him. *It shouldn't have all been up to her.*

But Rosie never expected me to make any money, Tom had replied. *That's why she took this dumb finance job in the first place.*

How much of the rent can you cover if you get a second job? his thoughtful, patient mother had asked.

I don't actually know how much our rent is? Tom had admitted, and his parents moaned.

Their mutual acquaintances seemed to think Tom had never deserved Rosie in the first place.

Rose's such a sweetheart, Conner Lynch had said. Tom had known him in college, and he was the only one of Rosie's co-workers Tom had known well enough to call and ask whether anything different was going on at her job. *Our VP is screaming at us all day long, but you still have her scheduling your callbacks while she's eating her little homemade lunch? She's wasted on you.*

You sound like you're just waiting to ask her out, Tom had accused him.

I mean. You're still technically married, right? Conner said after a hesitation. *So, like, not until she's ready to date again.*

Oh my God, fuck you, Tom had said, hanging up the phone.

Tom knew that people with anxiety often worried that everyone secretly hated them. He'd never suffered that intrusive thought himself. He'd felt great about his life at twenty-two. He was married to his soulmate, he had his Equity card in hand, he was living the dream . . . and then he discovered over the course of one awful week that everyone he loved did, in fact, think he was a bit of a shithead.

"We moved here after graduation," Tom explained to Ximena and Boyd. "And right away, I got cast as a swing in a revival of *Jesus Christ Superstar* when someone fractured his tibia. And I met a ton of people that way. So things were going great for me, but Rosie—okay, so it took me a long time to realize this. She was having a hard time at her job, and she missed her family and our friends in Boston. She was lonely, and we hadn't even been married a year, and I—"

"You what?" Boyd asked when Tom simply trailed off.

"I—nothing." Tom swallowed hard. That was really the extent of it. He'd done nothing about it. "I nothinged."

Tom hazarded another look at Ximena, who appeared to be waiting for more. But there wasn't. He hadn't done any of the specific terrible things that typically wrecked marriages; he just hadn't acted like much of a husband at all.

"But it's going to be different this time," he added. "Look, I know I fucked up. But things are different now. *I'm* different now."

Ximena and Boyd shared a pitying glance, one Tom caught as being about him.

"What's that look about, oh wise married lady?" he asked.

"She's your age, right? Thirty-four? And she never remarried, no kids?" Ximena asked.

Tom shook his head.

"So, she's hearing her biological clock tick. She's seen what the straight men of this city are serving up these days. And she's wondering if she made a mistake back then, whether she should have settled for you. Whether you might be better than the alternatives."

"What? No," Tom instinctively objected.

"There's nothing *wrong* with him." Boyd came to Tom's defense, an action slightly undercut by Ximena licking her thumb, leaning over, and swiping a smudge of eyeliner he'd missed off his cheekbone.

"I'm not saying you're defective," Ximena said to Tom. "But I think you have to be realistic about this. Are you okay being the guy who's just good enough in a pinch?"

Tom frowned at the other actor. Ximena seemed to think this would be a big hit to his pride. But he'd always thought he was lucky to land Rosie in the first place, a tiny, marvelous creature dedicated to making the world better for the people she loved.

"Yeah," he said. "Please. Let her settle for me. I'm *glad* every other option sucked more than I did."

A flash of surprise crossed Ximena's face. "Oh. Well." She shifted her weight, reassessing him. "So you're going to prove your devotion with home repairs?"

"Yep, that's the idea," Tom said, a little pissed at Ximena's lack of optimism. "I show her I can be a good little husband this time. I'm fully trained. I make breakfast. I run errands."

"But then maybe you should take her somewhere nice instead?" Boyd asked. "A place with a roof? Do you want to borrow my condo in Malibu? It has a beach view and a hot tub."

"Right, home repairs are super stressful," Ximena agreed. "Lú and I nearly strangled each other when we redid our kitchen."

"Nah, this place on the Vineyard is terrible, but she loves it," Tom said. "And she asked me to help her get it fixed up. She seemed pretty stressed about it, in fact, which means I get to swoop in to the rescue." It sounded like a sterling opportunity to demonstrate maturity! Financial stability! Core definition!

All the things Rosie had probably wanted in a partner and not gotten the last time around.

Ximena squinted at him. "Maybe you could find a swooping opportunity that plays more to your strengths than managing a construction project."

Tom was really getting the sense that she thought he'd screw this up. It would have been deflating, except that he knew Rosie perfectly and Ximena didn't.

"You don't understand. If there were an Olympic event for executive function, Rosie would be the world champion. She'll have everything already planned out," he said. "I'll just have to do the manual labor part, and then we'll work on our relationship. This is the perfect opportunity."

"I'm sure you're right," Ximena said, sounding as though she meant the exact opposite.

"When do we get to meet her?" Boyd asked guilelessly.

"Uh," Tom said. The last two people from his current life he needed to introduce to Rosie were the judgy pregnant lady and the guy trailed by strangers obsessed with his sex life. Tom wasn't sure how Rosie now imagined happy domesticity, but these two probably weren't part of it. And he still had to convince her that he was.

"I'll bring her to the premiere," he promised.

4

So you're getting back together with your ex?" Sloane asked.

"Absolutely not," Rose replied to the younger woman, hoping that would shut the line of questions down.

Rose had once dreamed of a big corner office from which she'd rule a vast financial empire on a Lucite girlboss throne or perhaps an Aeron chair (better for her back). Instead, a series of sanity-preserving moves sideways and down the finance career game board meant that she still waited for her paycheck to clear before she paid rent every month, but her theoretical boss cared much more about her love life than how she was going to manage the investment portfolio from a decaying B and B on Martha's Vineyard.

Rose's actual boss, the chairman of the family charitable foundation where she was the chief investment officer, was in Yellowstone on his honeymoon. Watching the bears or being eaten by them or something. His younger sister, Sloane, who was only twenty-three but seemed to think she'd been left in charge, had not just agreed to indefinite remote work but also offered to have her billionaire boy toy of the week drop Rose and Tom off on the island via his mega yacht. The price of transport, however, was being interrogated on Chelsea Pier while they waited for Tom to arrive. He was late.

"Then is this going to be, like, a hate sex scenario? Bang out the rest of your feelings?" Sloane asked.

Rose's phone buzzed in her pocket. Her friend was texting her.

> **Adrian: You're trying to work things out with Tom?**

Rose glared at the screen. Adrian's girlfriend, Caroline, must have snitched. Rose shouldn't have said anything at all, but Caroline was the only other person with remote access to the foundation's brokerage accounts if something urgent came up.

> **Rose: No!!! 100% no.**

Of course Rose wasn't getting back together with Tom. This was nothing more than two adults deciding to mend fences in a very civil, cordial, distant, adult way. She touched a thumb to her mouth to check on her lipstick. Today she wouldn't look like a drowned rat. She'd look like the polished professional woman she was, even though she was running on the fumes of only three hours of sleep.

Rose turned back to the young foundation director. "I don't hate Tom. We're amicably divorced," she said to Sloane, hoping that would keep everyone clear on her intentions.

But, of course, Adrian had thoughts about the situation. Thoughts he would insist on sharing.

> Adrian: Maybe wait until Caroline and I are back from her semester abroad to see Tom?

> Adrian: We could do a group date.

> Adrian: And I'll help with the inn when we're back.

Rose grimaced. Adrian had been not-so-subtly campaigning for Rose to make peace with Tom ever since she'd hired Caroline to start full-time in the fall—Caroline and Tom were close friends—but he'd probably imagined something like Rose and Tom sniffing each other through a closed door while Adrian and his girlfriend fed them treats and stroked their hair in a soothing way.

Rose was a big girl. She could be mature and reasonable. She could handle this.

> Rose: I'm not going to be dating Tom at all

> Rose: He has a serious boyfriend and I need the inn fixed before tourist season

She shoved the phone back in her pocket and looked up to find Sloane smirking at her. "I don't know why you'd ask for help from some guy you don't want to get back together with and don't want to sleep with," Sloane said. "I think you're *lyyy-ing*. By the way, you're wearing two different shoes."

Rose looked down and jolted because Sloane was correct and she was wearing one black ankle boot and one brown.

It wasn't like Rose was typically a stress zombie—anymore—but she hadn't been able to sleep after seeing Tom. And seeing way more of Tom than she'd anticipated seeing, down to his flimsy little boxers on his stupidly muscular thighs.

She didn't want to be like this. She wanted to be unmoved by Tom's naked chest and Tom's easy promises. Helplessly longing for Tom was too familiar a feeling and *not one she wanted to feel again*.

Her phone buzzed.

> Adrian: He doesn't have a boyfriend.

> Adrian: He didn't mention anyone at Christmas.

> Adrian: Caroline also says he's not dating anyone.

Rose entered her ex's name and Boyd Kellagher's into the search bar of her phone's browser, copied and pasted one of the dozens of tabloid stories that resulted into the chat, and didn't quite get the image of Tom's lips on Boyd's out of her retinas before she'd made a terrible face in front of Sloane.

"I'm sorry I'm such a mess today," Rose groaned, putting her hands over her eyes. "I swear I can still do my job. Just give me one more day to get my act back together."

"What, now you're worried about your professional reputation?" Sloane asked, sounding delighted. "I'm just, like, excited for you. I used to think you were kind of scary, you were so perfect. Just phone it in for a while, it's fine. Your marriage is more important."

"I can't phone it in," Rose protested. She was short and busty and named after a flower. Nobody ever took her seriously *unless* she did her job flawlessly. "Besides, Tom has a boyfriend. The only reason he's coming with me is to help with construction, and that's the only reason I want him there."

Sloane's smirk grew into a grin. She flicked long glossy hair over her shoulder and looked down the street, where a figure toting a large duffel bag had just come into view. Tom. Rose took a deep breath to brace herself, but Sloane elbowed her.

"Is that all you're worried about? The half-assing of your job, the finessing of the extraneous boyfriend? The boyfriend is not an issue. No guy volunteers to do home improvement projects for free if he doesn't at least want a round of weepy, nostalgic remember-when sex with you."

Rose scoffed to cover the sharp feeling in her chest. That was the last thing Tom wanted from her. Someone with Boyd Kellagher at home did not go out for a tightly wound thirty-four-year-old investment manager.

After the number her divorce had done on her, it had taken years before she'd begun to feel like she might be attractive to some people—in the right lighting, if she wore expensive lingerie, if the man in question was a boob guy and not a leg guy—but rose-tinted nostalgia glasses were not going to make her more appealing to Tom after he got a look at her in plain daylight. Which was fine, because she shouldn't care if Tom found her attractive now anyway.

"Holy shit," Sloane murmured, squinting to get a better look at Tom as he approached.

"What?"

"*Construction reasons* my ass. You didn't tell me he was hot," she said, voice emerging in a joyful squeak.

Alas, Tom was hot.

He was objectively hot, and not just cute in a floppy-hair-and-baby-fat way, like he'd been at eighteen. His thick dark hair was shining in the rare winter sun, long enough to brush his jaw. His eyes were shaded by a pair of expensive Wayfarers. His profile was classic and handsome, his chin chiseled, his smile broad and white. He wore a new black waffle-knit shirt and cheap, faded blue jeans, the former cradling his muscular new physique and the latter hanging from his narrow hips.

Rose closed her eyes, trying to remember that he had a boyfriend and she would be a bad person for ogling him, especially since they had days alone in close quarters ahead of them.

Sloane shoved Rose's shoulder with her palm, pushing for affirmation of her opinion.

"Why wouldn't he be good-looking? I did marry him in the first place," Rose grumbled, her cheeks heating.

Sloane's eyes danced with amusement. "Well, obviously. You're a treat yourself, Rose Kelly. But you're sure you don't want to think about keeping him this time around?"

Tom was just a few feet away.

"Even just for sex reasons?" Sloane stage-whispered.

Tom arrived in a waft of sunshine and cinnamon candy, then darted in to kiss Rose on the cheek. It was just a tiny contact, a brief impression of breath and fine stubble, but she didn't successfully swallow her noise of surprise, and Tom shot her a nervous look as he stepped back.

It startled her only because he'd never done it before. When Tom went in for a kiss, it usually involved a substantial amount of tongue and a situational amount of grab-ass. Even if, say, the elderly Rev. Fr. Gabriel Shea, SJ, was right there officiating their wedding.

But of course he should kiss her cheek. That was the sort of thing exes did if they were on good terms. He could have done that even if his boyfriend were right there.

Tom offered Sloane his hand instead.

"Tom Wilczewski."

He was clean-shaven and beaming, demonstrating a very masculine kind of beauty now—too rugged for what was currently popular in film, but overwhelming in person. It was why audiences loved him. They held each other's gazes, Tom grinning, Rose rethinking her decision to ask him for help for the thousandth time.

Did he shave because she hadn't liked the mustache?

No, that was ridiculous. Ten years ago he hadn't cared enough to *come home.*

Rose hesitated in a frozen pause, unable to speak because thoughts were tumbling through her head like stray socks in the dryer. Sloane saved her—she blinked a few times like she was trying to place Tom, then gasped, dramatically pressing a hand to her mouth. "Boydcat! No, Catboy. Tomboy! Tomboy."

Rose bent away in confusion, though Tom didn't seem surprised—only mildly embarrassed.

"You've heard about that, huh?" Tom asked.

"Oh, I've *heard*. I've *seen*. But you shaved your mustache? I have to tell the Internet."

"What?" Rose said, but Tom gave a wincing smile and rubbed the back of his neck.

"Yeah, it was for the role, but it'll be a while until we start rehearsing again, so—"

"What's a Tomboy?" Rose finally inquired.

Sloane delayed Tom with a gesture and turned to Rose, her face delighted. "Him and Boyd Kellagher! They have a ship name. They were all over Tumblr a couple months ago. There was a ship war with the Benny Boys. The people who ship Boyd with Benedict Cumberbatch. Or their characters."

Rose didn't understand half the words in that explanation, but Tom apparently did.

"You have a Tumblr?" he deflected. He curved his hands into parentheses. "Derogatory."

"Of course I have a Tumblr. A fashion blog." Sloane nodded in satisfaction. "Fifteen thousand followers. But, you know, I can't totally avoid the fan art. With *you*. God, the things I've seen you and Boyd doing—"

Tom gave a weak laugh, shooting Rose an uncomfortable side glance. "Oh man. You must have . . . seen some things. I know Boyd's fans can be . . . a lot."

Sloane turned back to Rose. "I didn't realize you were talking about Boyd Kellagher! Isn't he amazing?"

"Sure," Rose said stoically, because only a terrible person said anything catty about their ex's new flame. "I liked that movie where he blew up the moon."

And he seemed like a nice man whenever she saw headlines about him. Not just gorgeous but nice too. And it was cute that he and Tom shared a wardrobe. Probably cut down on laundry.

Rose pointed toward the marina behind them. Her phone was still going off in her pocket, but she ignored it. Adrian needed to mind his own business for once.

"We should probably get moving if we want to make it to the island before dark. Are you okay to leave for a while? Did you stop your mail? And take out the trash?" Rose asked Tom, trying to keep her tone gentle.

Tom's smile dimmed. "I did take out the trash. I'm pretty sure." He thought for a second, pulled out his own phone. "Let me just call a neighbor about the mail."

He walked away down the block to have a second think about his readiness for departure, his phone pressed to his ear.

Sloane gave Rose another incredulous look as soon as he was out of earshot. Rose was abruptly exhausted by the effort of keeping her face clear of her emotions. She would have liked to slouch and rub her eyes and consider having a few feelings about hundreds of people on the Internet imagining Tom and Boyd doing it, but she was determined to be unbothered by any amount of news about her gorgeous ex's gorgeous boyfriend.

"He seems really sweet," Sloane said when Rose didn't speak.

"He *is* sweet," Rose confirmed.

"But he didn't remember to take out the trash, huh?"

"Never did," Rose agreed.

Sloane gave her a wide-eyed, imploring look. She fisted her hands and propped them together under her chin.

"I didn't divorce him because he didn't take out the trash," Rose said, annoyed. "I knew this about him when we got married."

If Boyd Kellagher was really the dark, dominating fuck prince he played in the movies—or if he could afford a housekeeper and a personal assistant—she was sure the two of them were enjoying substantial domestic bliss. It wasn't like Tom didn't think the trash needed to go out; he just needed someone to tell him to do it.

"Okay, so what's the problem with seeing how things go, then?"

"Aside from his movie star boyfriend?" Rose suggested.

Sloane scoffed. "They're probably not exclusive. Boyd's got to be off filming most of the time. That's not how guys like that operate."

Rose checked her phone, cleared three missed calls from Adrian, and wrinkled her nose at his new texts.

> Adrian: Caroline says she just read the article and it doesn't have any pictures of Tom and Boyd together since last summer.

> Adrian: Answer your phone you coward

Adrian: That last was Caroline but please
don't fire her.

Rose put her phone on silent without responding. If Adrian thought that she was still harboring tender feelings for Tom, he needed to prepare for disappointment—Tom's theoretical open relationship, big stupid muscles, and willingness to do unpaid construction work at a moment's notice didn't matter at all.

"Okay, but even if they're not exclusive," Rose said, "the next problem would be *our* relationship. Trust me, the kind of issues we had are not the kind that go away with not seeing each other for ten years."

Sloane looked disappointed by this unequivocal statement. "I think you should give it a try. People can change a lot, especially after such a long time," she announced.

Rose elaborately shrugged to cover her discomfort, eyes tracking Tom's progress as he paced the block. He was apparently double-checking the trash situation.

Why would Tom change, when he had the exact life he'd always wanted? Rose was the one who'd obviously screwed up somewhere along the way.

5

When Sloane directed them to her boyfriend's yacht slip, Rose discovered that despite a decade in wealth management, she was still capable of being impressed by ostentatious displays of consumption. The yacht that would take them to Martha's Vineyard was a hundred-foot monstrosity, its three decks gleaming white and new in the sun, its wooden railings whispering that they hailed from endangered tropical rainforests, its custom leather banquette seats confiding that many nonbovine creatures had forgone their bumpy skins in their construction. It was a floating argument for higher marginal tax rates.

"Oh my *gawwwd*," Tom drawled, sinking into a crouch on the concrete pier, palms clasped to his cheeks. He hummed under his breath, a tune Rose hoped Sloane wouldn't recognize as the international communist anthem.

"It's nice, isn't it?" Rose said with purposeful nonchalance, resisting the urge to take out her phone and look up how much the yacht must have cost. Or to take a selfie in front of it. She never had anything good for the group chat.

She wasn't pretending for Sloane's sake, or for her boyfriend, who looked like the love child of Elon Musk and the last root vegetable at the bottom of the discount bin. But Rose was getting a little of her own back in Tom's reaction now. If he happened to think Rose spent a lot of time lounging on mega yachts, that wouldn't hurt anything. Sometimes her life took her interesting places.

Not that she and Tom were in competition. He was dating a movie star; he won.

A middle-aged man in an admiral's hat slid a window open near the bow and waved at them. Sloane blew him a kiss and bounded across the metal gangway to greet her billionaire boyfriend.

"This is *obscene*," Tom murmured, eyes following their host. "What did the guy do to make this much money? Sell a nuclear weapon to the fur seal cartel?"

"Tom," Rose preemptively warned him, though he wasn't too far off the mark. "They're being really nice to drop us off."

"They're always nice in person, aren't they? Very pleasant. Right before they order the AI war bots to destroy the low-income housing development."

"No, sometimes they're assholes from the get-go," Rose told him, thinking about all the coffee mugs that had been chucked in her general direction over the years. "But I'm sure these are the pleasant kind who support the arts, not the kind who murder people in Benoit Blanc movies."

"Fine. After the revolution, though, I call dibs on this thing for my turn at fully automated luxury gay communism," Tom said. Still balancing on his heels, he stuck out one hand and petted the hull with reverent fingertips.

Rose sighed, because handmaiden to the ruling class might not be the kind of job people dreamed about, but it was how she paid the bills. "Promise no more eat-the-rich talk until we get to Martha's Vineyard? Or at least make it clear you'll eat Sloane and her boyfriend last?" She squinted at the door Sloane had disappeared through, nervous that someone would overhear.

Tom snorted. "As if the resource that most needs to be re-distributed is this guy's dark meat. I bet he's gamey."

Rose finally laughed at Tom's unrepentant grin, feeling a tightness loosen in her heart. Like she'd told Sloane, there was a reason she'd married him in the first place. "I forgot what a dork you are."

"What, should I be playing this whole yacht scene cooler?"

"No, I actually liked that you never pretended to be cool," she said, rolling her eyes to cover her reluctant smile. For some-one whose career was predicated on the ability to slip into the skin of a leading man, Tom had never cared at all about his dignity, not if he could make her laugh instead.

"Oh, good. I'm still not cool."

"Not unexpected," Rose said, finally crossing onto the boat. "But please be charming until we get to Oak Bluffs?"

"I'll be charming," he promised, standing to follow her onto the main deck. There were at least a dozen crew members on the yacht who swarmed the pile of luggage, efficiently dragging it off to somewhere it wouldn't disturb the bleached perfection of the deck.

When nobody told her where to go, Rose shrugged and headed to a vacant group of lounge chairs with her day bag. Tom trailed after her, watching her stage her laptop, her thermos of iced coffee, and her boat snacks on a low table. He bounced on his heels, energy undimmed in the face of a nine-hour boat ride. "So, ah, how would you like to be charmed?"

Rose paused in the middle of setting up her workstation. She'd assumed he'd want to explore the rest of the yacht and give her a moment to collect herself. His interested, beaming regard was making her squirm with confusion. "No, not me. I already know all about you. Charm Sloane. When she gets down here, you can tell her and her personified daddy issues all your best Boyd Kellagher stories."

"What, you think she wants to hear more about Boyd?" he asked, sounding a little surprised. He unselfconsciously ran his hand through his thick dark hair in a classic leading-man stretch.

"Of course she does. I mean, anyone would."

"Anyone? Do you?"

"Yeah, why not?" Rose said lightly.

She had the idea that she could toughen herself up to this. The blisters were part of the process. She was *not* jealous.

Tom lifted his eyebrows. "Okay, I've got one. When he first joined the cast, he used Axe Dark Temptation bodywash. So much of it. Also the body spray. And the deodorant. We staged an intervention when it got unbreathable onstage. Even the bedbugs were fleeing the theater. Ximena Tejeda-Souza and I had to drag him to the bathroom and scrub him down with hand soap."

"Oh my God," Rose said, appalled. "Are you kidding?"

Tom smiled crookedly. "Yeah."

Rose made a noise halfway between a snort and a giggle in the back of her throat and pushed him right between his fancy new pectoral muscles. He reeled back theatrically, arms waving to make her laugh harder. This was a familiar groove to settle into, as easy as her oldest shoes.

The yacht sounded its horn and drew away from the pier, slipping into the Hudson. The sweet silt smell of the river gave way to a hint of brine as they slowly turned into the bay. Rose had been here for over a decade, but she still loved the sight of the city from the water. Tom stilled too, both of their heads tracking the Midtown landmarks as the yacht began to trace around the edge of Manhattan. The yacht could cross deep ocean, but for this short voyage they'd cling to the coast and navigate into Long Island Sound instead of chancing the Atlantic in winter.

They took their seats on a pair of teak lounge chairs flanking an enameled coffee table and stretched out their legs. The wind caught their hair, rubbing it across their cheeks. Tom had managed to get a tan somewhere, and it looked good on him; maybe he'd gone back to California with Boyd at some point.

With a casualness she was abruptly certain he'd practiced in his head, Tom reached across the table and put his hand on top of hers. Lightly, so she didn't feel the weight of it, just the warmth.

Rose didn't yank her hand away, but she stared down at the point of contact. A kiss on the cheek. Deprecating stories about his boyfriend. His hand on hers. Her heart needed to grow those protective calluses, and soon. *She* hadn't gone through a near-death experience. *She* hadn't even adjusted to the idea that Tom still thought of her at all. Her head went swimmy with the unreality of the situation. She used to dream about this: Tom turning to her, seeing her, looking like he cared. She might have believed it ten years ago.

"I missed talking with you, Rosie," Tom said, his voice very soft.

She ducked her face toward her lap, feeling her lower lip tuck in reflexively. That wasn't true. It couldn't be.

At her expression, Tom released her hand and pulled his arm back to his side of the table, leaving her wrist feeling tingly and exposed.

"Um," Tom said, tone now vaguely embarrassed. "We should probably do that, right? Talk?"

Rose sighed to anchor herself. "Right." She pulled out her day planner. "I'm sorry, but I need to send some out-of-office emails and instructions to the foundation's property managers right now. It'll probably take me like an hour. But then we can talk. I think the best place to start is the claims estimate, right? Have you had a chance to read that yet?" She opened her purse and found the binder that had the insurance paperwork in it.

"Oh," Tom said. His face was a muddle.

"What?" she asked. "It's okay if you didn't get to it yet. It's a long boat ride. I'll walk you through it."

"No, I read everything you sent. I just meant—yeah. Of course we'll talk about the inn stuff. But. Everything else too, right?"

"What else?"

"We never really did, you know," Tom said, when of course Rose knew that. "What happened, why, how you felt—"

"But why? You think we need to—for closure?" It was the only thing she could think of, and she supposed she might owe him that for his troubles here, but if she had to think back to how she'd felt as a scared and lonely twenty-two-year-old, she needed a fifth of whiskey and her therapist on standby.

"No, basically the opposite of closure," he said, deep brown eyes wide and concerned. "We're going to talk, and then we're going to work things out the way we should have ten years ago." Tom paused. "Isn't that why I'm here? We're going to work things out?"

No, she'd thought he was going to help her hang drywall in a suitably apologetic way, and then maybe once a year or so they'd exchange gentle yet emotionally fraught nods from across crowded rooms.

Remember when we thought we'd die holding hands in the same nursing home?

Ah, yes, we were young once, weren't we?

"You didn't seriously think we'd just pick up where we left off?" Rose demanded, even though it sounded beyond ludicrous to articulate. She'd thoug... there was zero chance Adrian or Sloane could be right about why Tom was here.

Tom laughed, the sound bright and startled.

"Um, no," Tom said. "Where we left off was you tossing my

clothes in the hall." He mimicked her voice. "*I hate you, you bastard, you ruined my life?*" His chin tilted as though he was waiting for her to acknowledge the accuracy of this recitation. She stiffened instead, unable to defend herself but unwilling to say he hadn't had it coming. "That was *not* a good place. So, no, not where we left off. Forward? Backward. Not sure which way. But someplace else."

Rose blinked at him, her cheeks turning to flame. "You mean you think we could be friends now?" she tried to clarify.

It sounded unlikely. What did he think they could manage? Drinks at their college reunions? Jointly plan Adrian's eventual bachelor party?

"Friends? I don't know. We were never really friends, were we?" he said cautiously.

Rose looked down at her lap, clenching her hands where they'd twisted together. "I used you think you were my *best* friend." That had been the worst part. There was only so much one kind of love could do to substitute for another, and loving her remaining family and friends even harder hadn't felt like it could ever fill the giant Tom-sized hole in her life after he left.

She swallowed, thinking about ice cream and cold beer and pickles out of the refrigerator, which was a trick to clear her throat when it felt too tight.

"I didn't mean it like that," Tom said after a moment, tone abashed. "Of course we were friends. And if I hadn't been such a dick, I would have tried to at least keep that, if nothing else. If that's all you want from me, I'll—I'll try. But can't you try too?"

"I don't know," Rose hedged. "What about you and Boyd?"

Tom made a face. "Is Boyd really a problem? What you've heard probably isn't even true, and uh . . . we were divorced."

Rose had not at all intended to suggest that she judged him for dating Boyd, but rather that Boyd might have some objection to Tom's ex-wife playing a recurring role in his life.

"Of course I don't have a problem with you and Boyd," she hurried to say. "Who would say no to Boyd Kellagher, even if they were still married?"

She was joking, but Tom looked even more uncomfortable.

"He's not *that* great," Tom muttered. "Not everyone likes him."

Rose snorted. "Come on. Everyone *does*. I will never have a relationship that is closed to someone like Boyd Kellagher, and I wouldn't expect you to either."

Tom now looked like he was about to cringe off the entire boat. "Seriously? That's how you'd want it?"

Oh, yeah, Rose couldn't make it between the break room and her windowless office without getting propositioned by a movie star who wanted to be one of her many boyfriends. "Completely serious," she drawled, covering the hurt with sarcasm. "Give him my number."

He did not appear reassured. "Well . . . monogamy is not the hill I want to die on. I guess . . . we can talk about that too? I'll get my head around it. Eventually."

It took her a moment to process that she might have accidentally tripped into some current drama with Tom's relationship with Boyd. Oh shit. Rose had no idea how people handled open relationships, never having voluntarily been in one, and she was the last person Tom ought to be taking advice from on the subject. She started looking for the exit.

His eyebrows gathered unhappily. "I know that face. What did I say? Babe, I get that this shit is complicated, but it only works if we agree on what we want. What do you want for us?"

Us? Us as in her and Tom?

Her ex-husband patiently watched her, as present and earnest as she'd ever ripped her heart to shreds wishing for before their marriage ended, and it only then snapped into focus that Tom really did think there would be an *us* involving the two of them in some configuration at the conclusion of this trip, notwithstanding his preexisting relationship with Boyd Kellagher.

Now approaching panic, Rose was prepared to fake an asthma attack to get out of the conversation, but as though sent by angels above, Sloane came clattering down the endangered redwood stairs, crowned with her boyfriend's admiral's hat and sporting a knit bikini under a stolen Mandarin Oriental robe.

"There you are!" she crowed. "Everyone's getting in the hot tub on the top deck. Everyone's getting stock tips. *You* get a stock tip, and *you* get a stock tip, and *you* get a deferred prosecution agreement if you turn them in for insider trading. Are you coming?"

Rose shot her a silent plea for assistance, telepathing as hard as she'd ever done in her life that she needed a rescue.

"Thanks, but I was just going to keep Rosie company while she works," Tom said, crossing a foot over his knee and adopting a patient posture.

Sloane looked back and forth between the two of them. She made a dramatic pout at Rose, who imagined Sloane didn't care to be the only woman in a hot tub full of billionaire bros. Rose put her palms together in supplication beneath the table.

"I guess . . . if Rose needs to work," Sloane said slowly, corners of her mouth turning down. "Then maybe we should give her a little space."

Tom rubbed the back of his neck. "I'm pretty sure that was one of the things I did wrong last time."

"Not at all," Rose lied through her teeth. If he'd comfortably ignored her for more than eleven years, he could give her some time right now, when she actually needed it. "Go have fun. Entertain our hosts. Sloane was just mentioning that she loves show tunes."

"I *dooo*. Can you sing anything from *Cats*?" Sloane asked excitedly. "I love basically anything Andrew Lloyd Webber." She winked at Rose, grabbed Tom by the upper arm, and paused with her fingers pressed into the muscle. She mouthed *Oh my God*, and Rose died a little inside. When Sloane recovered, she hauled Tom to his reluctant feet. "Just let me know when you want him back."

6

The yacht dropped the two of them off just before sunset in Oak Bluffs, on the northern tip of Martha's Vineyard. It was quiet and empty. The last snow was mostly melted, leaving the rocky cliffs brown and bare around darkened houses. Rosie coughed in the wet air, hand automatically smoothing over the inhaler in her purse.

"I'm not sick. It's just the humidity," she explained apologetically.

Tom knew that already. *Rosie, it's me*, he wanted to tell her.

He wouldn't have thought it was possible on a boat that only had three decks, but she'd managed to avoid him for the entire trip. He'd spooked her badly, and he didn't understand how. Had she not spent the last decade the same way he had, wondering how things had gone so wrong, wishing there were some way to make them right again?

But Rosie only mumbled a request that he stay with their bags before scurrying away down the block to the car rental shop.

Maybe he'd approached this from the wrong direction. There was no reason they had to start with some big relationship-defining discussion. If Rosie wanted to start on the scene where they held each other and cried, or even on the make-up sex, that might put her in a better mood than she seemed to be in now. Tom resolved to keep things lighter for a while. She was lovely today, in a floaty blouse over a knit skirt and tights, all of it hugging her curves. Rosie always looked nice to touch, but the cling of the fabric made his palms ache to press themselves against her.

She returned with a small four-door Honda sedan.

"We were supposed to have a pickup truck," she said, half in annoyance and half in apology. "For the construction stuff. But I guess they move a lot of the rental cars off the island for winter."

She fiddled with the radio, drawing mostly static and commercials as she hunted for music.

"Do you want to play Three Songs?" Tom asked, attempting his most appealing and least intimidating grin. It was her favorite car game.

Rose sawed her lower lip over her upper teeth, worried blue eyes darting his way before answering. "No, thank you. I think there's an NPR station."

NPR was in the middle of a long-form feature story about a scientist with scleroderma who had identified a new species of tube worm in her backyard. Somehow the story was also about grief and the history of Casimir Pulaski Day. Tom didn't doubt its literary merit, but he thought Rosie would have really appreciated winning a few games of Three Songs more. He had a lot of sets saved up for her.

There was little conversation as they drove to the inn, half an hour up-island. The last time they were here, on their honeymoon, they'd both been too young to rent a car. They'd hitchhiked from Edgartown with a vacationing family of five, and Tom had to sit on top of the suitcases in the luggage compartment, the two of them giggling and holding hands across the seat backs.

Do you remember when we were in love, Rosie?

It was winter now, and everything looked different. Tom couldn't recognize any landmarks until they arrived.

The Windward Inn was a sprawling, three-story, gray-shingled building on seven acres of land, built in classic New England cottage style. The white paint on the gutters and downspouts was peeling, and plywood covered several front windows. The entire effect was scabrous and injured, even setting aside the blue tarps on the roof.

As Rosie pulled up to the front of the circular drive, a flock of enormous brown birds scattered from where they'd been loitering near the unassuming entrance. There was a very dirty Prius parked at the other end of the drive, but it was empty, and the lights in the inn were off.

"Oh no," Rosie said, surveying some loose paper and other trash swirling nearby. "I think they found the grocery bags."

"What kind of birds are those?" Tom asked, eyes tracking the creatures to where they'd regrouped a dozen yards away to flap and hoot in a vaguely malevolent way.

"Wild turkeys," she said, climbing out of the car and glaring at the birds. "I've seen them on the island before. Guess they're hanging out here because nobody's mowed since the storm."

The inn was surrounded by tall, dead scrub grass. There was a little debris around the front drive, and one downed tree that Tom could see from his vantage point.

"And they're cannibals too," Rosie sighed, poking at what had been a paper-wrapped package of chicken thighs, torn open and mostly devoured by the birds. "Can you help me clean this up? There should be a bunch of garbage bags somewhere."

"Of course," Tom said, hopping out and wading through the scattered boxes and plastic bags. He popped open the trunk and began stashing the few things the turkeys hadn't been able to rip up. Sacks of mandarin oranges. Some unbroken eggs. Frozen bags of hash browns and microwavable broccoli. All Rosie staples. A few surprises.

"I thought you were allergic to fish?" Tom said, finding a partially eaten salmon fillet.

"I am," Rosie said after a minute. "But I—" She broke off.

"What?" Tom asked, spinning around to see her blushing.

"I happened to see a headline about the fitness routine for you and . . . Boyd. I figured maybe you weren't eating Cheez-Its for as many meals a day anymore. So I got you some fish and veggies."

Tom halted, chest swelling in a painful, enjoyable way. "You didn't have to get my groceries. Especially stuff you can't eat."

"I figured the least I could do is feed you as long as you're up here."

That was a little deflating, but Tom tried not to lose the

thread of gratitude. "I could have gotten the groceries though. I just did an Equity production. I'm not totally broke. And I can cook too."

"I thought you liked my cooking," Rosie said mostly to herself, her voice faint as she brushed through more garbage in search of salvageable food.

"I did. I mean I do—" While Tom was still filling trash sacks, he heard the front door of the inn open, emitting a barrel-chested man in chinos and sneakers from the dark foyer.

Tom hadn't expected anyone, but Rosie apparently had— she bounded over and threw her arms around the man's neck with a broad smile. Tom swallowed a surge of irrational jealousy—*Kill?*—before he recognized those pointy Kelly eyebrows on the other man's face. Then Tom was only slightly guarded, because Rosie's family had never been his biggest fans, and that situation was unlikely to have improved since their divorce. *Florida Man murdered by irate in-laws.*

"Do you remember my cousin Seth?" Rosie asked excitedly.

"Oh, yeah," Tom said, belatedly sticking his hand out. "Hey, Seth." He remembered that Rosie had fifty bazillion cousins and uncles, who all looked alike and were generally uninterested in talking about anything but sportsball.

"Um. You remember Tom. From when we got married. But—maybe you don't need to mention to anyone that Tom is out here helping me with this?" Rosie asked her cousin, who squinted without curiosity at him. "Things are a little complicated."

Ow. *Complicated.* His heart.

"Sure, no problem," Seth said, confused.

"Seth works for the property management company that does all the day-to-day operations for the inn," Rosie confided to Tom, although no property management was in evidence at the moment. "They've been off-site since the storm, but as soon as we get the repairs done, they'll open it up for the summer."

Seth scratched his neck and shifted his feet. "Maybe. It's in bad shape, Rosie. We can't get back in until you've got a certificate of occupancy, and it's real run-down—I just took a peek inside and I see, like, *months* of work. I heard from my dad you're thinking of selling? That might be smart."

"Selling? I'm not selling." That set Rosie completely off. As Tom collected the remainder of the groceries, she held forth on the extreme wrongness of Uncle Ken's suggestion, all her plans for the inn, the binders and Pinterest idea boards she'd already created, and why the inn would be better than ever by the summer season. Rosie was magnificent when she was passionate about something, all flashing eyes and speaking hands.

"Uh," said Seth. "I guess you'll just let me know if you need anything, then? And you'll tell me when I need to get the inspection scheduled with the county?"

Tom thought this was a bit of a non sequitur—the many things the inn needed were obvious. And the other man was already edging back toward his car.

"Aren't you staying?" Tom asked. It wasn't even seven o'-clock. Rosie looked surprised too.

"Oh, no, I've been here for a little bit," the other man said evasively. "I just wanted to get an idea of how long it might be before we could start up again."

"Okay, well, when are you coming back?" Tom asked.

Seth smiled in a conciliatory way. "You see, we're not actually insured or bonded for any kind of repair work. We only do routine maintenance. We can't do any construction or painting or anything like that. It would be illegal."

Rosie seemed to accept this explanation, but Tom frowned at him. Tom was not licensed or *bonded* or even into that kind of thing. "What about in, like, your free time?" he asked.

"I wish I could, but, you know. We just had a baby," Seth said, not even considering it. "My wife would kill me if I took on some kind of construction project."

"I know," Rosie said softly. "How's the baby? It's Harper, right?"

"Amazing," said Seth. "So busy. Thanks for the play gym, by the way." He lifted his phone so they could see his lock screen, which depicted a chubby toddler of at least one year of age. He looked between Tom and Rosie. "I've got to get home, but if you guys need a break, just give me a call. Come have a drink down-island or something."

They waved him off, and he got back into his car, speeding away quickly down the drive with a half-hearted wave. There were no other car sounds once he was gone—just the distant gobble of the turkeys and the faraway noise of the ocean. Tom felt an immediate sense of foreboding when he looked back at the darkened inn.

"It was nice to see him, wasn't it?" Rosie said wistfully.

"Uh-huh," said Tom, who didn't want to disagree with her, especially since he'd half expected the first of Rosie's male relatives he encountered since their divorce to take him out behind the woodshed a bit. Though he was also not sure there had been anything nice about the guy showing up only to not lift a single finger.

Rosie sent him a hurt look at this lack of enthusiasm.

"Babe," he said, defending himself. "We don't have to get started tonight. You wanna call him back? I'm all for going out and getting a drink instead. Instead of any of it."

On firmer ground now, Rosie sniffed and firmed her mouth in an expression he used to kiss off her face if it was directed at him. She turned on the flashlight feature in her phone and marched up the front steps. She pulled the sanitation notices off the front door and stuffed them into her purse.

"No," she said haughtily. "They'll come when it's all cleaned up. Which we should do now while you're still here to help."

7

Tom's first impression of the reception area was that it was very cold. The second was that it was very dark. And the third was that it smelled bad: a damp, musty aroma of wet and creature.

Tom's housekeeping was notoriously lackluster, but he didn't think he'd ever been responsible for a smell like that. He winced and wedged the front door open to encourage more airflow. Rosie gasped and lifted the neck of her pretty silk blouse to cover her nose.

Tom couldn't see an obvious source of the smell. But it was dark. He fumbled with the switch panel near the door, which didn't turn any lights on.

"The power's not still out, is it?" Tom asked.

"Richest county in the state. I'm sure it was back within a couple days," Rose said. "Maybe a fuse blew in the storm."

She coughed into her blouse. Tom suppressed the urge to rub her back, a thing that didn't actually help her when her asthma was flaring up but had always made him feel better about it.

"Do you know where the box is?" Tom asked.

"No." Rosie took several steps back, lingering in the doorway.

"Do you want to stay here while I go look for it?" Tom offered.

Rosie briefly closed her eyes, then cleared her throat. "No. Obviously, the monsters would eat you first."

Tom wanted to squeeze her for her bravery. Rosie hated mess, hated bugs and dirt, and hated scary movies and the dark. Her music was pop, her entertainment upbeat, and her beauty routine lengthy. But her aesthetic preferences weren't a personality trait—she crushed her foes in size-five heels.

The reception area was clear of storm debris except for the sheets of plywood nailed over the windows. The storm hadn't been strong enough to break the glass, although the entrance was along the east side of the inn, and Tom would expect most of the damage to be on the south and west sides of the building. But there was evidence everywhere that people had picked up and left quickly.

"It's giving low-budget horror movie set," Tom announced as they investigated the sitting room. The decor hadn't changed at all since he was last here: heavy, dark wood paneling, pictures of sperm whales, scented knickknacks. It looked like it was home to a nineteenth-century whaler who also made a lot of impulse purchases at the mall. *Moby-Dick* meets Yankee Candle. "You could always rent it out for nonunion productions. You know. Film students. Porn."

Rosie didn't laugh, but the corners of her mouth twitched. "I was actually thinking it reminds me of Pripyat. The city by Chernobyl. Where they have all the endangered animals wandering around the abandoned buildings because people can't live there anymore?"

"I saw that documentary too!" Tom said, pleased. "*The Zone of Alienation*. I kept hoping for a fox with two heads or something."

"If we see anything with two heads, I'm burning this place to the ground," Rosie said shakily.

Tom got the sense that she was avoiding the kitchen, but eventually they cleared all the other rooms. Rosie hesitated before pushing that door open, but she gathered herself and pulled it wide, ducking her head preemptively.

The smell assaulted them as soon as they looked in. The chill meant there were no bugs, but Tom winced at the sight of the countertops as the light of Rosie's phone illuminated the area.

"Jesus Christ." He coughed through the reek of trash. "Did Seth just leave everything here?"

It was hard to tell in light of the time elapsed, but it looked like someone had laid out breakfast for two dozen then simply walked away from it. There was the desiccated bone of a spiral ham on one counter and the rinds of several melons still visible amid a pile of what looked like fruit decay experiments.

"I guess they felt like they couldn't come back after the storm shut it down?" Rosie half-heartedly defended her cousin's company, though her face had fallen.

The trash cans were full and unemptied, and dirty dishes were moldering in the sink. When Tom turned a faucet, no water came out. He crouched to peer under the sink, but it looked as though the pipes hadn't frozen at least, despite the lack of heat to the building.

Tom had worked in food service long enough to have a cast-iron stomach in the face of the worst of smells, and it would take more than a few mice and some rotten food to put him off, but Rose looked pale and green. She pressed her hands to her cheeks as she took in the piles of organic waste.

Even though they'd lived less than five miles away, Rosie hadn't invited him home with her until Easter weekend of their freshman year. He'd thought she might be embarrassed of him, but her family home, with its full ashtrays and stained carpet, had done a lot to rewrite his idea of the kind of people who produced someone like his Rosie, who ironed her pillowcases and mended the rips in his blue jeans with embroidery stitches. She had to hate this.

"Hey," Tom said, finally giving in to the impulse to rub her back. *You can't fool me, Rosie.* He knew that the taller she stood up, the more vulnerable she felt. "I'll toss a bucket of bleach on this and it'll be fine. I've seen worse than this at kitchens I've worked in."

"Which ones?" Rosie asked, voice wobbly. Her gaze bounced around the various health and safety violations.

"Don't worry, I'll only take you out to places that are too nice to hire me," he promised. He held his breath, but she didn't reject the idea out of hand.

Instead, she drifted toward the walk-in refrigerator as though planning to open it, but Tom intercepted her, seizing her by the shoulders and turning her toward the door. She didn't need to meet whatever intelligent life had blossomed in a low-oxygen, high-nutrient environment over a few months with no power. He marched her back out of the room against her weak protests.

"I need to make a list of what needs fixing," she said.

"Everything needs to be thrown out and all the surfaces need to be disinfected. That's it," Tom said firmly.

Rosie squeezed her eyes shut for a moment, then nodded. Tom would have suggested they take a moment outside, but she turned and proceeded up the main staircase.

"Let's just get it over with," she said.

There were a dozen rooms on the second floor, all doors shut on either side of the long hallway. The first two rooms they checked were full of stale air and dust, but there was no obvious water damage until they checked one at the end of the hall. One pane of the original window had popped out, and the ceiling and floor were discolored where rainwater had flowed in from above and through the window.

She took out a checklist and handed him a binder of his own. "I don't think anything structural needs to be fixed in the dry rooms. Can you check the rooms on the other side of the hall?"

Tom nodded, beginning to sing under his breath. Following Rosie's lead was as easy as it had ever been. He poked through musty rooms, a couple of which had been slept in since they'd last been cleaned, but as everything in the whole place needed to be laundered, that wasn't much of an issue. He wrote down *clean everything* on his paper just to look productive.

"Zombies," Rosie said when they met back up in the hall.

"Hmm?" Tom said, having momentarily forgotten what he was doing.

"You're doing three songs about zombies. You should have saved the Cranberries for last though. Dead giveaway."

Her face was neutral as she delivered her verdict—and a pun he was sure she'd intended—but Tom barely suppressed a victorious smirk. *There you are.* Rosie was excellent at Three Songs. He bet she'd gotten it after "Thriller."

"Anyway, let's check the suite, then we can bring our bags in," Rosie said, looking more settled. "You can pick whichever room you'd like. I figured I'd take the suite, if that's okay."

There was only one suite at the inn, which featured a kitchenette, a living room and dining area, and an en suite whirlpool hot tub. On their honeymoon, Tom had considered it serious luxury.

He was swept up in the memory of opening the door eleven years ago: trying to convince Rosie to let him carry her over the threshold, Rosie not sure her dignity and his upper body strength would allow it. God, he'd felt like a superhero. Twenty-two and married. He'd thought they could do anything.

The funky smell was stronger when the door opened, putting him back in the present, where their left hands were bare and Rosie was keeping a careful distance between the two of them.

"Oh no," Rosie said, pulling her blouse back over her nose. "What are the mice even eating in here?"

The big four-poster bed was unmade, and there were mouse droppings visible on the turned-over bedspread.

Tom looked around for what had drawn the mice, but couldn't identify anything amiss. There was a big dark stain in one corner near the door where the ecru shiplap was discolored, so he approached and put his hand against it. The damp surface felt almost warm to the touch.

"Is that where they're getting in?" Rose followed up.

"I don't see a hole," Tom said. "And I don't see where the stain is coming from. Weird that it's not by a window. Maybe a pipe burst in the wall?"

Rose looked at him expectantly, and Tom remembered that he was supposed to be handy on this trip. He'd bought a multitool at a hardware store yesterday, and he took it out of his pocket as though he knew what he was doing.

I don't perform traditional masculinity for just anyone, Rosie. Please be impressed.

"I'll just open it up and take a look," he said authoritatively, flipping out the penknife attachment and slipping it into a crack in the shiplap. The panel, floor to ceiling, lifted easily.

He was checking out of the corner of his eye to see if Rosie was turned on by this display of competency, so he heard her gasp before he turned back to the open panel and saw that he'd literally lifted the lid on an enormous, swarming hive of bees.

The entire wall was riddled with golden honeycomb and, more problematically, a moving carpet of brown bees, thousands upon thousands of bees. Bees that probably did not appreciate someone opening their hive up with a penknife. The faint sound of buzzing turned into a near roar.

Rosie and Tom both screeched and jumped away from the wall, which took them toward the middle of the room. The bees poured out, buzzing and pissed, the cloud growing and obscuring the exit. They'd probably just woken up and were, like Tom, taking a moment to figure out what had gone terribly awry. There was an imminent collision of two civilizations: *Oh shit, people*, thought one group. *Oh shit, bees*, thought the other.

Rosie made a wordless squeak of panic, a sound he would have found adorable under other circumstances.

"They won't sting us if we don't mess with them," Tom said, repeating his mother's advice by instinct.

"We just broke into their house while their kids were sleeping!" Rosie pointed out in a furious whisper. She pressed up against Tom, trying to get behind him as they scooted backward to the opposite wall. "Oh my God. If I die here, don't bury me at Mount Auburn, because I swear to God I'm coming back from eighteenth-century Catholic hell to haunt the crap out of my dad for not helping."

"Are you allergic to bees?" Tom demanded.

"I don't know! I've never been stung." Rosie hid her face between his shoulder blades. "But I'm allergic to *everything*."

"Where's your EpiPen?" Tom asked, frozen in place as the bees began to expand into the rest of the room.

"In my purse. In the car. God," Rosie mumbled against his back.

The tightness and fear in her voice finally spurred him into action. He'd only seen her use her EpiPen once before, their freshman year, when she was caught unawares by the shrimp in her soup. The experience had been embarrassing for her, terrifying for them both.

I only get one Rosie, and if she breaks, I don't get another, he'd said when she asked him not to call campus EMS.

Tom took a step away from her to strip off his parka. Then he turned and draped it over her, pulling the hood over her head as though he were dropping a cover over a birdcage. When he was sure he couldn't see any skin, he wrapped his arms around her and hauled her out of the room, straight through the cloud of angry bees.

At least three of the little bastards got him on his fingers and the back of his neck as he rushed down the hall, pursued by some of the swarm. He didn't stop when he got to the stairs. He lifted Rosie off her feet by the waist so they could stumble, slide, and fall down the spiral stairs to the main floor.

He carried her straight out the front door and didn't set her down until his feet crunched on the gravel of the front drive. His chest ached from the effort and the sudden adrenaline, but exhilarated victory coursed through his veins as he pulled off the couple of bees that had gotten him.

It was dark and cold outside. They wouldn't want to fly around out here.

Tom checked his parka's sleeves and hood for stowaways before unwrapping Rosie. He was prepared to be celebrated for his daring and bold initiative, but when he pulled the fur ruff over her head, Rosie's face was bright pink, and tears were streaking down her face. Her tight, bunched shoulders shook.

Tom instinctively looked around to see if anyone was nearby—Rosie *hated* anyone seeing her cry—but his brain quickly caught up with bigger concerns.

"Did one get you?" He gasped. "I'll—I'll grab your purse. You have your EpiPen? I'll call 911. How far is the hospital?"

Rosie loudly sniffled and wiped her face on the sleeve of her pretty blouse before she answered. "No, I didn't get stung."

Noticing how cold it was outside, Tom used his grip on her shoulders to gently pull her a few steps closer to the car, letting go of her only long enough to open the door and guide her into the back seat.

Tom slid in next to her, heart hammering through his chest. She bent over with her forehead against the seat in front of her, shoulders shaking.

"Rosie?" he asked tentatively, pulling the door shut. "What is it?"

Tom curled his arm back around her shoulders, part of him exulting *Finally!* because she still fit perfectly there, although he hadn't thought it would take this long or involve so many bees.

She didn't answer, but she shook her head. Her breath came in tight gulps. "It's such a mess." She sat up, fumbled for her purse, then took a puff from her rescue inhaler. That was twice he'd seen her use it today; that wasn't a good sign. "Maybe I *should* just burn it down," she mumbled. "That would take care of the bees."

"Sure. It didn't look like the grease trap had been cleaned in a while," Tom said, striking an encouraging tone. "I could make it look like an accident. Is there fire insurance?"

"See! You're already thinking of bailing," Rosie accused him, pulling away.

"I was trying to be helpful?"

Rosie's face twisted in dismay. "I'm just—oh God. This is going to take so long. And I'm going to have to do it all by myself."

"Um?" Tom said, mildly outraged. Here he was, and he thought he'd been pretty studly so far. But maybe that wasn't the point. Maybe the point was that it was going to *suck* to fix everything. "You don't have to. You could sell it, like your cousin said." Rosie was quiet, apparently thinking about that.

"We could just go," Tom urged her. "We could make the last ferry, get to Boston tonight. I have a key to Caroline and Adrian's place. We could fly out of Boston. You wanna go somewhere else for a long weekend? Somewhere sunny?" Actually, the sun wasn't Rosie's friend. "Or snowy, now that I think about it? Anywhere. Boyd's condo in Malibu?"

She turned to him, tears welling up. "You don't have to stay," she said. "This is—I know you can't have this much spare time. You can't have thought it would be this bad."

"I'm not saying I want to go—babe, if you want to fix this shithole up, I'll help you do it," he insisted. "I said I would."

"Don't," she said, voice still shaky. "It doesn't actually help, you know? If you say you'll do something and then you don't. Don't you have rehearsal? And, like, a life?"

He hadn't spared a single thought for the godawful play since stepping out his door that morning.

"Not for months," he said, unable to recall the exact date. "I'm just saying, is this what you really want? Why do *you* want to mess with this disaster site? You don't even own it. I can't imagine Max expects you to put your life on hold this long."

She gave him wide, affronted eyes. "This is my whole

family's place. This is where we get together," she insisted, despite the pressing lack of any other Kellys on site to provide any assistance. "I was going to bring my kids here."

Tom froze. "What kids?"

Rosie made a wordless noise of hurt in the back of her throat and pushed the door open on the opposite side of the car. "The kids I was *going* to have."

Well, that was a kick in the teeth.

At least you didn't have any kids was a not-helpful thing people had told him after their divorce. Like he was supposed to be grateful for the nonexistence of people he'd planned on existing, tiny humans whose faces and names he knew Rosie had already imagined.

If she hadn't kicked him out, they could have had kids by now. They could have done any of the hundred things she'd told him they'd do.

Why hadn't she had kids, if that's what she'd really wanted? She didn't get remarried, didn't have kids, didn't even move out of New York, which they'd only lived in to support his supposed Broadway career. If she'd changed her mind, he couldn't blame her—they'd been so young—but that wasn't *his* fault. He'd been on board for all of it.

Before she could get out of the car, Tom reached out to cup the back of her head so that she had to turn and look at him.

"Look, I'm *here*," he said. "And I'll stay till it's done. That's what you asked me to do, right? Let's just do it."

She sighed unhappily. "Tom. That's what you said about our wedding. And I ended up planning the whole thing."

"I—" He couldn't really remember what had been involved in wedding planning to negate that proposition. It hadn't seemed like a lot? There had been a ceremony in the college chapel, then lunch with a couple dozen family and friends at an Italian restaurant. Had she wanted more?

"This is different," he protested. "I can get the roof done. And everything else. You know what? I can handle all of it. Everything the place needs. Babe. It'll be okay. I'm not going anywhere. I'll do the whole thing."

"The whole thing?"

"Yeah. I'll take over. You've got a real job, right? I don't have anything I have to do until rehearsal starts."

"*You* are going to pick out carpet samples. *You* are going to make sure the wallpaper matches the linens," she said doubtfully.

And why would she doubt his ability to do that, only because he never had? He wanted to do it all for her. He wanted to be the one who bravely ordered bolster pillows and paint swatches. He wanted to defeat the bees in her name. Knowing what to do for her was very fulfilling, a satisfaction that had grown rarer and rarer before vanishing from his life entirely.

"Fine. You got me. I'm already planning to half-ass the window treatments," he said. "Like, do the middest possible job picking them out."

Instead of laughing, which was what he'd wanted her to do, her big blue eyes searched his face as she transparently wondered whether he was going to flake out on her.

"Why though?" she said. "This is—I don't expect you to

understand. This is what I decided I was going to do with my life after you and I broke up. This isn't anything you promised me."

Answering that was easy.

"Because I meant everything I said."

The way her eyes widened, the doubt on her face—that was hard.

8

So, the bunk room has a hole in the roof the size of a squirrel. Relatedly, it has squirrels," Tom announced when Rose returned from picking up a sack of burgers for dinner, feeling exhausted and dispirited. "And the bees are still a little worked up on the second floor. But! I found us an awesome place to stay, right across the street."

He was glowing with his success, his smile conspiratorial and welcoming.

"Those cottages over by the bluffs? Aren't they pretty expensive?" Rose asked, wishing Tom's mood would rub off on her.

Seth had texted her the names of three local Realtors. *Just in case!* The rest of the family had reacted with crying-face emojis to her pictures of the water damage at the inn, but still nobody had committed to coming out to help, even just for the next weekend. Max, who thought she was funny, had sent Rose a link to a beeswax crafts store on Etsy.

"Off-season rates," Tom said cheerfully. "And insurance should pay for a hotel, I think. At least until the bees are gone.

I read the policy." He made these announcements in a tone that suggested that Rose should be very impressed. "You don't think it sounds fun to stay at a nice little cottage, get reacquainted, relax, and put on some HGTV?"

Rose put her knuckles over her mouth. In the abstract, that sounded exactly like her idea of fun. But she'd woken up this morning thinking today would go one direction, and it had zigged and zagged so much she wasn't sure which way was up.

"You're going to love it," Tom wheedled. His face had lit up with the pleasure of a small adventure. "It's got Rosie written all over it."

The cottages were the kind the island was known for—cedar shingles and white trim, cozy and inviting even with the hydrangeas dormant and the rocking chairs sitting empty on the small porches. Rose had walked by them many times on the way to the bluffs but had never gone in.

Tom led her to one at the very rear of the complex. Pausing to favor her with a devilish grin, he pushed open the unassuming door and flicked on the lights.

Rose gasped, because Tom was right. She adored it.

Most of the vacation homes on Martha's Vineyard featured a classic nautical style in understated white and navy. WASPy. Boring. But the owner of this cottage had leaned toward a more maximalist aesthetic, with a strong dose of Palm Beach. Rose would never have imagined the interior.

The room was dominated by a magenta chandelier with shell ornaments. The wood floor was painted peony pink, and the appliances and furnishings matched it. Rose-colored toile on the love seats. Blush velvet on the curtains. Fuchsia on the printed rug. It was like an enveloping hug from a roll of cotton candy. The first pleasant surprise in a long day of shocks.

"You love it, right?" Tom said, lifting his eyebrows at her. When Rose choked on the appropriate words of gratitude, he brushed a kiss to the side of her temple as though she'd managed to say thank you anyway, which didn't help her find her footing. What was Tom doing? What was happening? Who was this person, and where had he been when she'd needed him ten years ago?

As Rose was specifically thinking this was all too good to be true, she spotted signs that the cottage had been closed up for the winter: open cabinets under the sink in the kitchenette, drawn curtains, a stone-cold water heater. The air was a little stale too.

"How'd you get in touch with the owner?" she asked as Tom busied himself with putting away groceries.

"Just booked it online," he said cheerfully.

"Huh," Rose said. "Did they have a lockbox?"

Tom nodded at a window. "Not exactly. But it was unlocked."

Ah, there it was.

"You broke in?" Rose asked, trying to summon some outrage over the trespassing. It wouldn't come, probably because she'd been inciting him to arson an hour ago. "Is this a felony?"

"Raise your hand if you've never been arrested." Tom stuck his arm straight up in the air and waved at her.

Rose narrowed her eyes at him. "I was only arrested because you ran faster than me."

"Yeah, keeping up a good speed is pretty much the prime

directive of streaking." He laughed. "Don't worry, baby, you've still got two strikes left."

"I wish you knew less about me," she said, flustered by the mention of a rare college indiscretion. She walked to the window to check whether she could see the road. She couldn't. So maybe nobody would notice them breaking and entering.

"Anyway, it's not breaking in if I have a reservation. Why don't you sit down and eat some food? Here, you want a beer?" he asked, pulling one out of the refrigerator and pressing it into her hand. He found the remote and turned the TV to entertainment news. Rose wasn't entirely mollified.

"You made a reservation for *tonight*?" she pressed, still suspicious.

Tom sucked on his pouty lower lip, thinking. Her stomach sank.

"Tom."

"Well, we have a reservation for either January 5 or May 1 of this year, but American dates are so confusing to me," he said, slipping into a deep Polish accent. "Why do you people put the month in front of the day? Makes no sense."

She fought the urge to laugh. "You've never even been to Poland."

"Nie mówię po angielsku, nie rozumiem cię."

"You barely speak *Polish*," she corrected him, cracking a smile in spite of herself.

"Like anyone who comes to check on us will know that! And anyway, I couldn't find anywhere else with open rooms tonight. Do you want to sleep with the bees?"

"No," Rose admitted. "Where are you going to sleep though?"

She looked around the cottage. There were a pair of love seats in front of the fireplace and a chaise lounge facing the entertainment center, but only one bed: a king tucked into a loft over the living area.

Tom's small disappointed frown said that he'd thought there was some chance they'd both end up there, when Rose was one more casual forehead kiss away from having a giant snotty emotional meltdown about how confusing this was.

"I guess I'll sleep on the chaise?" he said, making that eventuality sound distant and unlikely. He rummaged through the cabinets and pulled out a stack of plates for the fast-food burgers she'd brought home. "Sit down and put some food in your face, babe. You look like you're about to fall over."

She felt like it. She felt like she'd fallen down the stairs.

She wasn't handling this well. This was not the grace and sophistication and gentle forgiveness she'd expected to offer him. But Tom also wasn't what she'd expected.

Maybe he'd changed. Maybe he wasn't the same person he had been at twenty-three. That thought was more painful than Tom's frequent displays of familiarity, because *she* hadn't changed. Sometimes she thought she would have liked to—it would have been convenient to want different things—but it felt sad and awkward to show up here as essentially the same person he'd left.

Maybe Tom hadn't finished growing up when she had. There were moments when he seemed like a complete stranger. It was startling, because she liked what she saw. It was just harder to understand what he wanted from her now. She'd thought he just wanted to make it up to her, but the way he looked at her, the way he kept touching her . . . Maybe she could figure out some way to navigate his movie star boyfriend and his Broadway lifestyle. She'd thought their lives were going to be a big adventure together. Maybe it was on her to figure out how to meet Tom where he was.

"We need to relight the pilot light for the water heater. It's cold," she mumbled around a mouthful of french fries.

"Right, right," Tom said from the second love seat, patting at his pockets and coming out with a lighter. Which he should not have had on him.

When Rose glared at it, he held up a hand to fend off her remonstrations.

"I don't want to hear it," he said.

"*Tom.*" She dug in.

"I would never smoke around you. You've got asthma."

"You should quit," Rose said firmly.

"Why, is it bad for me?" he asked with pretend innocence. He blinked his wide brown eyes at her like he was playing the ingenue, but there was an edge to it.

"It'll ruin your voice, it's bad for the environment . . . I can't believe you started smoking."

Tom got to his feet and shot her a look of mild reproof.

"Maybe not every single coping mechanism you'd pick up if the love of your life tossed *you* out on the street would be a healthy one, huh?"

Rose closed her mouth over a shocked breath, waiting for him to take that back. Obviously, she hadn't been the love of his life. Obviously, she hadn't tossed him out *on the street*, because he'd been sleeping somewhere else for the week before he left for good.

Tom stalked across the room and stood in front of her, pressing into her personal space. He put his hands on his hips, right over the loose band of his jeans, and stared her down, looming in a way that somehow emphasized the breadth of his chest. She was treated to the sudden, intrusive memory of that chest pressed against her cheek, the solid weight of his body. Heat suffused her face as she struggled to meet his heavy-lidded stare. He was standing too close, but that was probably the point he was making. She didn't have any claim on him.

"Why smoking though?" she said weakly.

"Couldn't afford coke, and sniffing glue would have freaked Adrian out," Tom said, expression deceptively mild. His jaw worked.

"You can't live your life without freaking Adrian out. He's the most reactionary artist I know," Rose said, backpedaling with all her might.

"That's what I keep telling him." Tom let her off the hook with a knowing twist of his mouth and took a step back. She felt like she'd been the one smoking unfiltered Marlboro reds when he moved away. Tom's force of personality was giving her a contact high.

"Anyway, I quit smoking cigarettes three months ago. Just have the lighter out of habit," he said.

He went to ignite the pilot light with his cheap Bic lighter, leaving it on the floor by the water heater. Then he straightened and looked at her with patient, steady expectation.

He'd tried to talk to her. About the things they both wanted. She was afraid she'd been unfair to him.

"Tom, I—if I haven't said it yet, thank you," Rose said. "And

I'm sorry if I've acted less than grateful about everything. I'm glad you came."

His face gentled. "Don't worry about it. I know this is a lot for you. Not just me, but the big construction project. I'm sorry Seth wouldn't help."

"Yeah. But I'm going to try to stop . . . stop thinking I ought to know how this goes. Stop making any assumptions about you, really. You obviously know how to handle your own life. I think this is going to be good for me, actually. I need to learn how to let go of . . . a lot of stuff. Every time I've tried to make a big plan and force everyone else to go along with it, I've fallen flat on my face. I need to stop."

Tom frowned. "Well, I'm not sure if that's the primary lesson, actually—"

"No, I mean, I think working with you will go a long way toward helping us figure out a way to . . . you know. Meet where we are now. I don't know what I would have done if you hadn't come to bail me out," she said. "I'm sorry for getting on your case today."

Tom had been nothing but kind and helpful. She needed to stop judging him based on who he'd been to her a decade ago. This was a man who was actually living up to his promises— one who'd dropped everything, volunteered to take over a big dirty job, and lodged her in a cute little pink cottage. He was doing this his own way and doing it better than her.

"So," Rose said, shoving her tote bag full of binders and folders into the corner. "You're in charge. We're going to do this your way. What's first?"

Tom rubbed his jaw, scratching his cologne-model five-o'clock shadow. He looked over his shoulder, in the direction of the inn. He wet his lips, shifting his weight.

"Yeah, why don't you just relax here for a while? I'm going to fill a few bags of trash at the inn, check on the bee situation, and, um, make a few phone calls."

Rose winced. She'd thought she'd just given him an opening to talk. But of course he hadn't spoken to his boyfriend all day, and no matter how confident a man like Boyd might be in his relationship with Tom, and how little a threat Rose might pose to it, he probably wanted to hear from Tom.

"Of course," she said, pushing her knees together.

Tom took two steps toward the door, hesitated, then came back to where Rose sat on the couch.

Her expression must have been wary, because he telegraphed his motions as he reached out to brush one careful thumb along her cheek. The gentle, reassuring touch felt better than it had any right to. As if he could read her thoughts, he sighed, his own expression troubled.

"I should have done this years ago," he said.

"Done what?" Rose asked.

"Anything," he said with a little half shrug, like he hadn't really been speaking for her benefit.

Tom paced the entryway of the inn, feet scuffing some remaining debris. He'd filled the existing dumpster; he needed to find out how to order a new one. He'd opened a bunch of windows to let the trash smell and the bees out, but snow was in the forecast for the next day; he needed to go through and shut them.

He was panicking.

Tom knit his fingers on top of his head, mind flitting from necessary task to necessary task like a bug trapped in a porch light. He groped for focus.

"Fortunate Son." "Alice's Restaurant." "WAP." Three songs about cleaning up.

He knew a lot of songs, but he didn't think he knew enough to keep him on mission long enough to fix this place up. Things would slip through his fingers, he'd lose track of time, he'd get overwhelmed, and then there'd come some neck-snapping moment of reckoning. Like the time he'd absentmindedly buzzed a pleasant middle-aged lady into the lobby of Adrian's apartment building, only to discover that she was there to serve him with divorce papers.

How are you going to handle this one, Tomek?

With jittery hands he pulled out his phone and called the first responsible, available adult he could think of.

"Come on, come on," he muttered at the phone.

Ximena picked up on the last ring, her voice muffled.

"Hey," she said. "I'm about to head into prenatal yoga, can it wait?"

"Um," Tom said, because he wasn't sure it could wait. He had no idea how long it took to order furnishings, how long it took for that stuff to arrive on Martha's Vineyard in winter, and how long Rosie would give him to finish the work before she pulled the plug. "Do you have a minute?"

Ximena sighed heavily, as a celebrated, Tony-nominated actress had every right to when her flaky younger friend began unexpectedly imposing on her charmed existence. "I'll go sit in the break room."

As soon as the background noise of other parents faded, Tom began to babble at her, detailing the trip out here, the state of the inn, and his conversation with Rosie this evening. As he moved through the inn, shutting windows, his eyes kept falling on things that would need to be replaced or repaired.

He didn't know how to do this. He'd never done anything like this. He should never have told Rosie he could do all this.

"Calm down," Ximena said. "You're stressing *me* out, and stress is bad for the baby."

"No, you don't understand, panic is a great way for me to get things done," Tom told her earnestly. "Basically that and spite? Those are the only fuel this machine accepts."

"Are you going to panic until everything's done? No? Well, then, I think you should just go to your ex, level with her, and apologize for wasting her time. If she's a reasonable person, she'll understand that you can't spend the next six months playing Chip and Joanna with her when rehearsals start in three."

"Six months!" he yelped.

"Yeah, have you ever ordered furniture? Even stuff like rugs can take weeks to arrive."

"My furniture is all thrifted," Tom said. He put his palm against his forehead. "Ximena. Please, you have to help me."

"I *am* helping you. I'm sure she doesn't want to set you up to fail. Maybe you could just help her pay someone else to do the interior—"

"You know how to do that stuff. I've been to your apartment. It's gorgeous. It looks great."

"Yeah, because Lú hired a decorator," Ximena said, sounding amused.

"But you have good taste," Tom begged. "Can you just come out here for a little while and tell me what stuff I need, even? Just tell me what to do, and I'll do it."

"I'm in my second trimester, and your inn is full of bees," she pointed out. "This isn't going to work. Besides! What are you going to do if rehearsals start while you're in the middle of this disaster?"

Tom chewed helplessly on the inside of his cheek. From this last window, he could see the lights on in the cottage he'd left Rosie in. She was less than a thousand yards away, and she'd probably put on fuzzy socks and soft, stretchy pants that clung to her ass and that lip balm that smelled like vanilla.

When he was twenty-two, he'd thought there would be unlimited opportunities to see Rosie getting ready for bed, and he'd missed it more often than not. He'd taken the worst, least scenic, longest detour imaginable from the life he could have had, and he just wanted back on the interstate. He didn't want to be in this fucking decrepit inn; he wanted to be over in the cottage, watching *Entertainment Tonight* with his head in her lap as she put three specific types of lotion on specific delicate parts of herself.

But the only clear path to that position he could see led him through this impossible task first.

"I won't do the show if I can't get this done first," he said. "I swear I won't, so you've got to help me."

It was almost blackmail.

"You can't pull out of a lead role on Broadway, Tom, Jesus Christ."

"I haven't signed anything! It's not pulling out—"

"They're writing you new lines! They are planning promotional T-shirts with your face on them! You barely have a professional reputation to wreck, but if you tell the producers you're out at this point, I'm pretty sure that would do it."

Tom leaned forward and rested his forehead against the clammy wood of the doorpost. "I know, I know."

"Just tell your ex you can't do it," Ximena insisted.

"I can't tell her no. If I have to choose between another ten years in regional theater or another ten years where Rosie's not speaking to me, I know which one was easier to live through the last time," Tom said. That, at least, felt crystalline clear when he spoke it. If Rosie watched him make a giant hash of this, at least she'd see him *trying*.

Ximena groaned dramatically.

"Okay, let me see what I can do," she grumbled.

"You'll come over here?" Tom asked, hopes rising.

"I'll come by for a weekend once it's bee-free and you've got somewhere decent for me to stay," Ximena said sharply. "But I'll see what I can do from here right now. Jesus, you asshole, you had better buy me the biggest bouquet of flowers you can find as soon as you get that next Equity check. I mean, entire rainforests had better disappear from the size of that thing."

"I will," Tom promised, grasping for the thread of hope,

even though Ximena hadn't promised anything specific. "The size of a Thanksgiving Day float."

He felt only a little better as he hung up the phone, but at least he'd done something. Doing the first thing was often the hardest part.

9

Rose had decided to be asleep when Tom got back to the cottage. Easier said than done, even though she was running on fumes. Her brain felt like it was downloading a decade's worth of software updates on one bar of cell service.

When Tom came in, his steps more confident than when he'd left, Rose shut her eyes to a crack and positioned a pillow over her head. Avoidance was not a healthier coping mechanism than smoking, but with lungs like hers, it was the one she had.

Tom climbed the ladder to the loft without unnecessary noise and peered into the bed nook. Rose held her position, curled in the center of the bed, pretending to be asleep. He must have bought it, because he slid back down the ladder and went to check the water heater with a hand on the tank. Apparently satisfied with the temperature, he began to strip.

Off went the black waffle-knit T-shirt, tossed to the couch.

Off went the blue jeans, discarded in a puddle on the floor.

Rose wanted to be a good person. She paid her taxes to the

penny. She volunteered. She donated. She generally tried to treat people as she wanted to be treated. Voyeurism was wrong.

However, she didn't think Tom would mind if she looked at all that sun-kissed skin he'd just exposed—in fact, he'd probably be flattered at the bolt of heat the sight sent zipping through her body. Tom was anything but shy. If he was putting on a show, he wanted someone to watch. So she looked. Tom had a soft spread of dark fuzz across his chest and trailing down across his stomach, and she knew what it felt like under her fingers, but she imagined pressing down and feeling nothing but solid muscle coiled underneath.

Rose expected him to go after his socks next, or perhaps move closer to the shower stall, but Tom slipped his thumbs under the frayed band of the boxer shorts that already concealed very little of the muscular shape of his thighs and leaned forward to slide his underwear off.

Oh God. She was going to spontaneously combust if she kept watching.

Rose sat up and tossed a pillow down at him.

"Modesty, Tom," she said in a rebuke that would have been more convincing if her mouth had not been so very dry.

Would his boyfriend really not care if anything happened? Was that what they'd hammered out on the phone just now? Maybe she'd feel better if she actually confirmed it with Boyd somehow.

"So you *are* awake," Tom said, grinning cheekily up at her. He caught and held the pillow just at waist height, so she was not longer confronted with a view of the forbidden mountain, so to speak, but he cradled the pillow in his hands as though preparing to toss it right back at her.

"I'm awake now," she said, jerking the covers up like she was ready to go right back to sleep, but she probably undercut this posture by staring directly at the pillow.

"It's nothing you haven't seen before," he said very innocently.

He knew it was a different view from before. He was fishing for compliments. *Yeah, it's really nice, Tom. You must have worked really hard. I bet you could support my body weight on like five different muscle groups. Though your cock is still very good looking too; I'm glad you didn't go too porny with the manscaping.*

If Rose had been running on full steam, she would have made sure to sound snarky and aloof when she replied.

"Gah," she said instead, rubbing her face with her hands and peeking at him through her fingers. "Please put a towel on. I can't right now. No striptease until I've slept."

Tom made no move to cover himself, tipping his head back to laugh at her instead. "Babe, I could accurately describe the location of every single freckle on your body. You're bothered by some nonsexual nudity?"

Oh, he was definitely *trying* to mess with her. He wasn't letting this go without specific feedback, but she was going to expire if she let herself think about it.

So she tossed a second pillow at him. He retaliated by dropping the first one.

"I'm just taking a shower!" he insisted, hand pressed between newly defined pecs instead of over his heart.

"It's nonsexual nudity?" she asked, unconvinced.

Tom's expression grew even more delighted. He squared up his hips and spread his feet as though trying to stand on full display.

"Why, does it feel sexual to you?" he all but purred.

Rose was running out of pillows, but she hurled another just to make her point.

Tom finally turned to get in the shower, which shifted him out of her direct line of sight but instead gave her a view of all the muscles down his back, as well as the round ass that—

She still had one pillow left. Maybe she could smother herself with it. Or at least starve the horniest of her brain cells of oxygen.

"Do you remember when I was in *Equus*, our senior year?" Tom shouted up at her.

Of course she did. He'd been so good in it—he'd played the main character, Alan Strang. She'd cried at every single performance. But that probably wasn't what he was referring to—he was reminding her that most of Boston had seen his kit when he'd appeared naked onstage. That had *actually* been nonsexual nudity.

"Oh my God. Yes. I can't believe Adrian didn't tell his girlfriend you'd be naked in that play," Rose said, speaking toward the ceiling. Served Adrian right for dating a snotty French literature major who'd offered Rose highly unnecessary diet tips. Tom and Rose had made Adrian dump her soon afterward.

"She never looked me in the eye again. Every time she came over, it was like I had a bull's-eye painted on my crotch."

Rose could perfectly visualize the scene at the big house in Somerville they'd rented that year. Adrian's love life had been a chief medium of entertainment: all his girlfriends had been terrible. Tom and Rose had been the smug, judgmental couple lifting scoreboards over breakfast when he brought someone new home.

It was nice. They'd been happy. It was the closest Tom and Rose had ever gotten to domestic, even with three other roommates and their hookups and random houseguests cluttering the space. No, actually, Rose had been thrilled to make like a 1950s housewife between interviews and her scanty senior schedule, baking custard pies and elaborate casseroles for ten people.

When she looked back on it now, it was with a faintly embarrassed lens on the memories. She'd thought the rest of her life would be like that, when it was obvious in retrospect that she, like everyone else in the world, had just had a good time in college, and she ought to have savored the experience as a temporary joy.

"What was her name?" Rose asked. "Ellen? Elena? She tried to say it was Hélène for a while, but nobody bought it."

She heard the water turn on.

"It was Helen! And God save you if you called her Ellie," Tom called from the bathroom. The shower door clanged shut.

Tom would be in there until the hot water ran out, so Rose could go to sleep now. She used to tease him about his long showers.

It only takes like five minutes to jack off. What are you even doing in there?

Thirty minutes of aftercare, Rosie, because I'm treating myself right.

But really he just liked to sing and practice his lines and let the water run over his back and wrinkle his toes. Rose could hear him singing now: a little scatting as he worked his way up to the falsetto chorus in "Smooth Criminal."

She sighed and put her last pillow over her head. It wasn't a terrible pillow, but it was ineffective at blocking her awareness of Tom in the shower. Wet. Naked. Lonely? No, Jesus Christ, Rose Kelly, keep it together. He's fine taking a shower alone, and you haven't cleared anything with his boyfriend.

Thoughts of little drops of water sliding down Tom's hip bones were easier to focus on than Tom's singing. She'd missed his singing. He had a wonderful, rich baritone, and several of his professors had tried to push him toward music instead of theater, since he played the piano as well as he sang. But Tom didn't have the patience to compose, and he only practiced if he had an appreciative audience for his Broadway standards and Beyoncé medleys.

Tom's music was supposed to have been the soundtrack to her life.

As Rose breathed into the mattress, Tom followed "Smooth Criminal" with "The Weight" and then "Tomorrow." Rose laughed when she got it, even if it was pained.

"Three songs about girls named Annie," she called.

"You're so good at this!" Tom called back.

That had been an easy one, but Rose finally rolled onto her back and looked up at the close, floral-stenciled wood ceiling. She was very awake.

Since Tom was giving out free tickets to the show, Rose propped her head on her arm and watched as he got out of the shower and toweled off with slightly more modesty than he'd shown during his entrance.

He did a little shrug when saw her looking—not in a vain way, instead almost apologetic.

"Just so you know, this is for the play," he said, apropos of nothing, with a wave at the defined plane of his midsection. "You might want to take some photos. I probably can't keep this up after the Broadway run wraps."

"Too time-consuming?"

Tom would go to three dance classes in a row if he had the time and money, but as far as Rose knew he'd never set foot in a weight room.

"Yeah. Hours a day. I've hated every second of it. And, God, I miss eating cheese." Tom looked at her expectantly, as though he were waiting for her permission. As if she'd ever tell anyone to give up cheese.

It was also none of her business what Tom did with his body, not just now but ever, so Rose shrugged. "I bet cheese misses you too."

Apparently encouraged, Tom stepped into his boxers and concluded the display by pulling on a faded T-shirt advertising a Pokémon movie. Not one of Boyd's cast-offs. She'd given it to him for Christmas their sophomore year.

How was she supposed to wipe his slate clean while still burdened with knowledge of where Tom's T-shirts came from or the little shuffle he did with his feet when he was trying to remember where he'd left something? She knew too much

about him. He knew too much about her. She could still recognize the charming man who'd left her. And she was still very
much the same person who'd been so easy to leave.

Rose heard Tom puttering again in the bathroom. She knew
what he was looking for.

"You can use my toothpaste if you didn't bring any," Rose
said without turning over. "But not my toothbrush."

"Too late," he said around it.

10

It was after midnight, and they were both still awake. The cottage was tiny, and the quiet was echoing in contrast to the city noises Rose was accustomed to. She could hear Tom shifting on the love seats he'd pushed together every time he turned over or rearranged a pillow.

There were fifty different obstacles to sleep, even up in the luxurious king bed. Rose stared at the ceiling, wondering if she was being silly to enforce trivial social norms like not sharing a bed with the ex she hadn't seen in a decade.

She didn't do this. Nothing casual. Nothing without thinking about it first. Not without thinking where it might lead. But she wasn't some kind of Victorian. She wouldn't have made Adrian sleep on the love seats. What was she worried about? That Tom might think she was easy? He already knew the exact extent to which she was easy.

"Are you awake?" she whispered into the still, pink room.

"These are really small love seats," Tom immediately said in a normal, though annoyed voice.

"Is there any chance you can keep your hands off my boobs if I let you sleep in the big bed?"

"No better than even odds."

Rose huffed in amusement because at least he got points for honesty.

He must have sensed her hesitation, because he pleaded, "It's a really big bed." Before she responded to that, he was already standing up, the pillows she'd tossed at him clutched in one hand.

"You can sleep up here if you promise to be good," she decided, though she thought she might have already lost control of the situation.

Tom climbed up the ladder one-handed, hauling the pillows back to the bed. He paused at the top to survey the situation, a sleek, satisfied expression evident on his features even in the dark.

"I can be good," he assured her in a tone suggesting that this contract had very few covenants and definitions. *Good* could mean many things.

She politely withdrew to the far side of the mattress to make room, but Tom flipped the duvet down and walked on his knees into the center of the bed.

"Jesus, babe, you're going to give me a heart attack," he said, looking down at her sleepwear with heated appreciation.

Feeling both flattered and exposed, Rose tossed her head as though she'd expected his reaction.

It wasn't lingerie, or what she thought of as lingerie, because it covered her from neck to knees. She owned really good lingerie, but it wasn't for sleeping in. No, here she'd found a line of satin pajama sets she liked and bought one in every color. She matched the decor in petal pink tonight, so she preened a bit, turning her head so that Tom could notice that the scrunchie she'd used to pull her hair back matched the pajamas. She tried not to wonder whether he was admiring the shape of her breasts through the thin fabric too, because that was out of her control.

"You always had the best little outfits," Tom said contentedly as he dropped down next to her, making the mattress bounce under his weight. He was right next to her. Was he under the impression there might be spooning?

"You said you'd be good," she whispered when he pulled the duvet over them both.

"I'm going to be *very* good," he whispered back.

He scooted closer so that his chest was pressed against her shoulder blades, the heat of his body barely dampened by one layer of thin cotton and another of satin.

"I, um, I meant it about the hands and the boobs," Rose said when he cupped her upper arm, palm curled under the edge of her sleeve.

"I would *never*," he replied, but he curved his body around hers, the arches of his feet batting familiarly against the soles of her own, his breath so close she could feel it against her neck. It was too close. She wound against the pull of Tom's body, heart rising and pounding in her throat.

She couldn't pretend it was anyone else. Her body would have known him even if her mind had not, this position still encoded into muscle memory. Good memories, all of them. But inescapable. They had easily shared a thousand nights of comfort and body heat and sex, even allowing for the objections of their roommates and the nights he hadn't come home.

The first orgasm she'd ever had with another person had happened in this position: the two of them crammed into a twin bed, Rose's faded heart-print sheets from home kicked down by their feet. Tom had put his hands over hers, *Show me*, because he didn't know what to do yet, and she didn't have the words to explain it to him. Her body had seemed so complicated to the both of them, especially compared to the very straightforward, predictable way his responded to her. They'd solved that mystery with tentative fingertips, found every point that sparked pleasure on her body, and Tom's hands had grown confident when he put them against her.

That was the way he still touched her now: like he knew what to do with her. She didn't doubt, with mind or body, that if he slid his hand over her hip and pressed it between her legs, he would have her gasping his name in moments. She'd feel him hard against her thigh and his mouth against her shoulder, then his whole weight pressed against her body to roll her over onto her stomach. She knew exactly how it could happen.

"Slow down," she said.

"Am I doing anything you want me to stop?" Tom asked. And she realized his hand hadn't moved—it was still resting chastely on her arm. His hips weren't even flush against hers.

"No, I—actually, I'm fine." She was embarrassed. Impressive— they'd gotten to third base entirely in her head, and he was just trying to go to sleep.

"You sure?"

"Yeah. It just felt like—never mind."

It wasn't like he'd announced that he wanted to sleep with her. Maybe he didn't.

"I didn't think I was getting laid tonight," Tom said, sounding smugly amused.

"You are absolutely not getting laid."

"That's fine," he reassured her. He rubbed her upper arm with tender familiarity. "You made me work for it last time too."

This pronouncement was so dignified and also so ahistorical that Rose stiffened and craned her head back to glare at him.

"What? Oh my God. I did *not*."

She did not. She was not someone who had ever, would ever, make a man *work for it*. She liked sex. She just didn't believe in having sex with someone she wasn't serious about. She had sex with men she was contemplating a future with, whether that happened on the third date or after three months.

"Okay," Tom said, making it sound like he was humoring her. Rose rolled to her back and narrowed her eyes at him.

"We met at freshman orientation. I was sleeping with you by Halloween. It was six weeks, *max*."

They'd been *virgins*. And Rose had needed to dump her high school boyfriend, figure out birth control at a Catholic university, clear out her roommate for a whole night—it had happened super fast, all things considered.

Tom paused with the air of a man doing complicated mental math. "Maybe you're right." Even in the dark, his expression was beseeching. "But six weeks felt like a very long time." Rose jammed an elbow back toward his stomach, and he grunted dramatically. "Six weeks would still feel like a very long time!" he protested. "It would feel like a long time to anyone!"

"What if I told you there will be no sex for you at all on this trip?" Rose demanded. She wasn't sure whether there would be. She was letting go of expectations.

"Don't say things you're just going to have to take back later," Tom said, undeterred. "There's not much to do here in the winter. Don't take sex off the table when it's too cold to play horseshoes or lawn darts."

He caught her elbow before she could jab it into his ribs again and wrapped her arm around her stomach instead.

"It's okay, babe," he said. "I don't mind working for it."

"I just want to go to sleep," she pleaded.

Tom paused as though rifling through a mental tool kit. Then he rearranged the pillows under their heads. "I get it. You can go to sleep. I'll be good. Just relax." He pulled back just far enough to put both his forearms against her upper back. She made a noise of confusion, and he shushed her. It wasn't clear what he was doing until he put his hands on her shoulders and dug his fingers into the muscles there.

Tom held on to her shoulders and let his thumbs work little circles up and down her neck. The stiffness began to trickle out of her body, minute by minute. She went quiet, caught between the pleasure of it and the boundaries she hadn't yet decided where to place. She supposed a shoulder rub was allowed. She probably deserved a shoulder rub.

Her guard wasn't quite down when he bent his head to the back of her neck again. If he was going to kiss her there, that felt like an escalation, so she teetered on the edge of a protest.

He hadn't kissed her yet. It ought to *mean* something if he kissed her after so many years.

And then it wasn't his lips on the back of her neck but the tip of his nose, pressed into the downy hairs at her nape. He inhaled deeply, the unexpected intimacy of it tightening her chest.

Before she could decide how she felt about it, Tom reached up to pull her hair loose from the band, letting his fingers slide up into her hair and prompting a very embarrassing noise when he began to stroke her scalp with soft fingertips.

The novelty of it was instantly gratifying, nearly as much as the wonderful sensation of his hands in her hair. He hadn't done this before. She would have loved it if he'd done this before, but it hadn't occurred to him to do it, and she hadn't thought to ask. Someone else had taught him to do this.

That last thought felt like it could have had some hard edges, but it didn't. She was thirty-four. She no longer expected to be anyone's first anything. People her age came to the table with a lot more history. She'd gone out with people who had kids and dogs and divorces. She was nothing but lucky to get this expert pressure along all the tense spots on her head, places she hadn't even known about.

"Don't ever stop doing that," Rose mumbled even as her eyelids got heavy.

"Okay," Tom readily agreed. "Every night, if you want."

"I want," Rose said. "But your boyfriend will probably demand some kind of schedule."

It was a throwaway line—she wanted to go to sleep, not have a complicated discussion about their limits, because Rose was a normie, a square, and she needed to check out Tumblr or wherever people learned how to navigate the boundaries set by their head-scratcher's main boyfriend before she got into it. *I could be cool about this,* she supposed she was saying.

"My what?" Tom said.

"Your boyfriend." Maybe that wasn't the right word. She didn't know the open relationship terminology. She didn't think Boyd was his partner, because she didn't think she believed in long-term commitments that opened not just for sex but for regular head-scratching arrangements with ex-wives. Though what did she know, really?

Oh look, she was awake again. "Boyd," she specified and rolled over. Tom, still sprawled across most of the pillows, looked honestly confused.

"Boyd's not my boyfriend. He's not my anything."

Rose frowned at him. "Okay."

Tom propped himself on his elbows, blinking rapidly.

"You don't believe me," he said.

She wasn't sure she did.

"There are photos of the two of you kissing in a national newspaper. Sloane said there are fifty bazillion pictures of you on the Internet—"

"Because we're in a production together, and his fans are weird."

Rose searched Tom's face for signs of deception, finding none. But he was a good actor. "Really?" she said doubtfully. Tom and Adrian were very good friends, roommates over multiple years, and yet Tom had never shown up wearing Adrian's clothes. "Seriously? You two never . . . ?"

Jesus, why *not?*

Tom looked down at the pillows, rearranging them with atypical delicacy. He didn't meet her eyes.

"Okay, well, you see how that's a different question, right?"

That was actually a hilarious response to a straightforward inquiry.

"No! I mean, I could tell you, but do you actually want me to?" he asked. "I guess wanting to know if I've got something going on with him is fair—and I *don't*—but do you really want to know what I was doing before you showed up on my doorstep? I don't mind telling you everything, but do you want to hear it?"

Rose typically skipped that conversation, but a small, bitter part of her pushed her to continue.

"Yes," she said. "Sure, go on. Anyone more famous than Boyd Kellagher? Anyone else I've heard of?"

"If I—if I tell you, are you going to do the same?" Tom asked, a tense little line appearing on his forehead. She couldn't tell if he actually wanted to know or just thought this was a trump card to avoid admitting to what was surely a good decade-long fun run.

"Me?" Rose said, pressing a palm against her chest and looking at him with wide, concerned eyes. Two people he'd never met, one he had, none of them any of his business.

Annoyed, she screwed up her mouth and then looked away with a deliberate expression of frustration. As though deeply unwilling to admit it, she dropped her shoulders. She wasn't an actress, but she'd gone to a *lot* of rehearsals.

"So I actually haven't—yeah. Since you. I just didn't—it

didn't feel right. I couldn't." She sighed with what she hoped was convincingly tragic, celibate resignation. "I took vows, you know." She held the position for thirty seconds before she peeked at him.

His jaw had dropped. He was staring at her with four different emotions warring for top position on his face: Panic. Guilt. Disbelief. Awe?

Then she rolled her eyes at him.

He grabbed a pillow and held it out as though he was going to smother her with it. Rose snorted, falling back on the bed.

"I was trying to be considerate," he growled.

"No, you were trying to cover your ass," she said. "And you don't have to. I don't care if you've filled out your entire Pokédex."

"Except that you *do* care, or you wouldn't have brought it up in the first place!" he said heatedly.

He had her there. She inelegantly conceded the point, gathering up the pillow to her chest. "I thought Boyd was your boyfriend," she admitted. She fell back on the bed. This wasn't working. She was never going to sleep. She didn't know how she'd sleep with Tom on the same *continent*.

Tom's lips thinned. "I'm not a cheater, Rosie."

"Okay," she said. Nobody would dare cheat on one of the most famous movie stars in the world. She hadn't thought that. She'd thought they had some kind of open relationship.

"Not just now, but ever. I've never cheated on *anybody*. Including you."

"Okay," Rose repeated, trying to scoot away from the conversation she now regretted starting. Wasn't it past everyone's bedtime now? Certainly hers.

"Do you believe me now?"

"Sure," Rose said, just wanting the conversation to be over.

Tom scooted to the opposite side of the bed and raked an agitated hand through his thick, tousled hair. "Really? Because some of our friends—well, I guess the ones who turned out to be *your* friends—seemed to think I had. I heard about it a lot, in fact."

His face was so righteously aggrieved that Rose felt her own anger rising. She'd had about enough of his subtle insinuations that he'd been so hurt and wronged when she threw him out. Fine. They were both awake now. Nobody was sleeping tonight. They were doing this now.

"I never told anyone you cheated on me." That was one of the grounds for a contested divorce in New York, so she'd had the opportunity. "I just said that you'd basically stopped coming home, and I had no idea where you were or what you were doing for days at a time. Which was true. What was I supposed to think? Honestly."

She groped around on the floor for her phone. She needed to get out of here.

"I never, *ever* would have cheated on you," Tom said, and he was standing now, or trying to, but the ceiling was too low for that, so he was just looming uncomfortably. "If I was gone overnight, I was just passed out in the green room at La MaMa or on someone else's floor because I didn't want to come home drunk."

Rose gave him a long look, wondering whether he might happen upon some realizations as those words emerged from his mouth. Ah, there were her socks.

"Okay, yes, I can see now that that was . . . not great," he said, motioning as though he'd put that thought away to the side. His tone was only slightly less aggressive. "But I never cheated. The day you filed for divorce, I'd never been with anyone else. I never *looked* at anyone else. Why would you think that?"

Rose took note of the flag he planted—the day she filed for divorce, not the day a year later when he finally signed the papers—but it wasn't as though she hadn't been seeing other people by then too. So she took him up on his more important point.

"Oh, come on. You didn't even notice when *we* stopped having sex, and you like having sex more than anything except dramatic solo numbers. Of course I thought you were cheating on me." She crawled toward the ladder.

Tom snorted incredulously. "Believe me, I *noticed*. But you were working a hundred hours a week and managing both of our entire lives. Was I supposed to complain that you weren't finding time to have sex with me too?"

Rose put her feet on the top rung as exhausted tears began to prickle in the inner corners of her eyes. "Complain? I couldn't tell if you cared at all. And I—I couldn't live like that. You stopped looking at *me*."

That he was cheating on her had been the good story she'd told herself. A reason he didn't notice how unhappy she'd been, because he was too guilty to look. She'd already decided to for-give him for cheating on her.

The bad story was that he'd just fallen out of love with her; she didn't know how to forgive him for that.

Tom sucked in a surprised breath and held it. If Rose knew him, this was the moment he bolted. Tom wanted everything to be fun and easy and pleasant. Any sign of distress was to be immediately soothed away, and if it couldn't be soothed, it was to be avoided.

That was why she had her feet on the ladder. Either he'd take himself out, or she'd leave.

Indeed, Tom looked at the door. Off he'd go, and then they'd never speak of it again, if they even spoke again. But then he set his jaw and met her eyes, and although his own were wide and scared, he held still.

"We should have had this fight," he said.

Rose sighed and climbed down to the bottom of the ladder.

"Where are you going?" he called.

"I need to sleep," she begged him.

"We should have had this out," he said. "Baby, please. Tell me what you wanted me to do. I didn't know what you wanted me to do."

Maybe he was right and maybe he wasn't. They'd never know because they hadn't fought about this. Or, rather, they'd had *one* fight, and then Tom never came home again.

"Rosie," he called down when he saw her gathering her clothes. "Seriously, where are you going?"

"I'm going to sleep in the car," she said.

Tom turned around and slid down the ladder like a fireman, just hands and insteps on the poles. It was physically impressive, but for the first time since that morning, he wasn't trying to show off.

"Come on," he said when he turned around, face still wounded. "You think you're better off not knowing I was going to be faithful for the rest of my life, and I never get to hear you say what I did wrong?"

Rose curled her hands into tight fists, arms rigid at her side.

"You can't have it both ways," she said. "You can't tell me *Baby, I've changed* while you're still trying to prove things should have worked out a decade ago. They didn't work out! We got divorced! You broke my heart into tiny little pieces, and that *happened*, even if you think it didn't have to."

Tom's mouth pressed into a thin, flat line as he considered that.

"Just come back to bed," he finally offered. "I'll stop."

Rose shook her head. "No. You're either the guy who broke my heart, or you're someone I just met. And I don't sleep with either of those guys."

He took a deep breath and let it out. He was disappointed, but not dejected.

"Okay," he said. "I'll go, then." He stooped for his pants, which he'd conveniently left in the middle of the floor.

"I'm not trying to be mean," Rose said. "I'll fit in the back seat. You won't."

"Nah," Tom said, one corner of his mouth curving up. "I'll go across the street to one of the clean-ish rooms. I got the lights on and the bees corralled in the suite."

"What?" Rose looked around their stolen little pink cottage. Not that she was sure she would have left it if she'd known. "Why didn't you tell me?"

He shrugged apologetically, shoved his bare feet into his shoes. He took his coat off the hook where she'd hung it. "Why do you think? You were over here." He gave her a tired smile. "And I wanted to be over here with you."

11

It was overcast the next day, with a steady drizzle threatening to turn to snow. Tom was fuzzy-headed from lack of sleep. Even dousing his room in Febreze had failed to completely cover the musty odor that pervaded the inn, but it was his urgent, itchy sense of things left undone that had kept him up.

His only real sense of time was *now* and *later*, and he'd learned that *later* usually meant *never*, so when something absolutely had to be done, he wanted to do it *now*. He wanted to finish having it out with Rosie *now*, tease out everything else he'd done wrong *now*, start fixing things *now*.

I stopped inviting you to come out with me because you always had to work and I felt like I was rubbing it in your face that I got to have a social life. Bad call?

I know you were dating that douchebag Brent from our geology seminar before our divorce was finalized because when you dumped him he fucking texted me about it like he wanted

*to form a sad little club. Nevertheless, I forgive you, because
you apparently dumped him in a Duane Reade.*

*In the future, if you are overworked and unhappy and I have,
for example, just watched you shred an entire rotisserie chicken
with your bare hands like it said something nasty about your
mother, would you prefer that I offer to have vigorous, life-
affirming sex with you amid the wreckage of its carcass instead of slinking out the door so that you can finish your
meal-planning in peace? It's no trouble.*

His body felt driven like a motor, and it took all his restraint
to channel that into productive work at the inn rather than lurk
around the pink cottage he'd rather be in. Rosie didn't appear
until midmorning, wearing a long, puffy black parka over a red
knit dress, which made her look like a little round songbird.
She looked calmer this morning, back in order.

"I have really appalling news," she said, shuffling her feet until she stood right in front of him, peering up through curling
eyelashes. "I slept and ate, and now I feel better." Tom let out a
relieved breath because he hadn't been sure what her temperature
on him was going to be that morning. Her little rosebud mouth
tilted up, and she gathered his hands loosely in hers. He relaxed
at her touch like he'd shed the weight of entire continents.

"I hate it when that happens," Tom deadpanned, squeezing
her hands back.

Her eyes flicked up toward his face and away. And it was
sweet, the way she did that, but it tore his heart in two directions. He wanted to kiss the hesitation off her mouth.

"How's the inn this morning?" she asked, looking around the foyer.

"Um, I've been working on the bee situation," he said, not sure if she was checking on his progress. He'd learned that his options for dealing with the bees were, one, allowing an exterminator to pump the walls full of a poison gas that had also been employed in several Geneva convention violations or, two, contracting with a painfully earnest white woman whose Instagram portrayed her scooping bees out of car trunks with her bare hands to a soundtrack of early Taylor Swift anthems. Neither could commit to an arrival window narrower than eight a.m. to eight p.m. the next day.

Rosie frowned in concern, eyes tracking the multiple problems visible even in this room, which had no storm damage. Her shoulders bunched.

"Tom, I—I think I made some unfair assumptions about you. Not just yesterday, but ten years ago. I am not at my best when I'm sorting through a giant mess like this. I become part of the mess." She hesitated again. "Maybe we should hold off on clearing the air until we're back in New York and can go to—"

"Marital counseling?" Tom suggested, perking up.

Her eyes rounded at him. "—dinner," she finished, voice fainter.

"Oh." He supposed dinner would be better than nothing. And it would be good to give Rosie a glimpse of his normal, Boyd-free, Rosie-friendly life at home, since he wanted to coax her back into it. "But what would you do?"

She sighed. "I'd stay. I would have come out here even if you couldn't. I know it looks terrible now, but—okay. Just after our divorce was finalized, I was . . . pretty low. It was right before the holidays. Max had me come out here for three weeks with my dirtbag teenage brothers and a couple of my younger cousins. And we did a big Christmas. You know, the whole twelve days, big white elephant party for her friends, homemade fruitcakes and new stockings for the babies, and I—I felt better. Like even if my life wasn't going to look at all like I'd thought it would, I'd be okay. Because Max had a wonderful time. The whole family did."

"Yeah," Tom said softly, because he got that feeling.

Rosie bit her lower lip hard, but she didn't let go of his hands. "I wish everyone else wasn't too busy to come out and help, but, you know, most of them have kids now, or a lot more going on at their jobs than I do, so . . . it's just on me, I guess."

"And me," Tom insisted.

With all the yearning and hurt and anger that had been tied up in thinking about Rosie for years, he'd forgotten what it was like to hold her hand and feel like he could stand between her and the entire world. He wasn't going anywhere she wasn't. Not when she'd already told him she'd like to see him actually accomplish something for once.

He knew he could be a better partner this time. He just had to finish this before he got the chance.

He took a deep breath. "I think we cleared the air enough already. And, you know, I'm used to living in a giant mess. I'm amazing with mess. You can count on me."

"Oh good," she said, expression brightening. "Because I am actually so glad not to be in charge of the bee stuff." Her face relaxed into a real smile.

She did an adorable little bounce of her knees, releasing his hands to curl her own into excited fists. She smiled up at him, pretending to jab at the air in a one-two punch. "What did you have planned this morning? You wanna go into town to look at wallpaper with me?"

Wallpaper wasn't at the top of the list of things he wanted, which contained higher-ranking items like *I sleep in the big bed* and *Someone with a clue about construction comes and tells me what to do*, but he supposed it was on the list.

"Yeah, I'd love to go check out some wallpaper with you," he said earnestly.

I t was raining hard by the time they got into town, but there were still workers out stripping the gold wire ribbons and lighted artificial greenery from the street lamps and store awnings, heedless of the precipitation as the holiday decorations came down on schedule.

Rosie handed Tom a battered umbrella emblazoned with the name of a multinational consulting firm before cracking the car door and unfurling a much nicer umbrella in poppy-red polka dots. It matched her dress and rain boots, and Tom would have told her she was the sweetest thing he'd ever seen if he'd been certain that was allowed. As it was, he scurried after her to the wallpaper shop, a charming little shingled storefront just off the main drag.

As the doorbell rang in the wallpaper shop, Tom felt as though he'd picked up the script for a different version of himself, a man who hadn't wrecked his marriage and was walking in with his wife of twelve years. His mind jumped to fill in the character details in this new role: Did he have the six kids he'd never been sure Rosie was joking about? Did they still live in New York? Did Rosie bring her embroidery hoop to his rehearsals and sit in the third row, stage left, until they broke for the evening, or had he quit theater a few years back so he could coach peewee soccer and order pizza if Rosie had a call with Hong Kong?

He had to blink rapidly so that he didn't stumble into a display counter.

The only employee in the shop, a middle-aged man in chambray and suspenders, was on the phone when they entered, so Rosie nodded at him and drifted to the far corner, lifting a book of samples at random. She flipped through a few pages before she replaced it and took another.

"Do you have an idea what you're looking for?" Tom asked.

Rosie trailed her fingers along the texture of one page and shook her head. She browsed through almost a dozen books, finally finding one that interested her. She took it to a table and unfolded a pale green paper that was festooned with tiny woodland creatures doing bucolic, vaguely British things, like wearing funny hats and gardening.

"That's cute, isn't it?" Rosie murmured, fingertips brushing a hedgehog with a picnic basket and a deerstalker hat.

Tom nodded.

"Or there's this one. Look, it has bees. Friendly bees."

"An alternate history of the place," Tom said, playing along.

"I could put it in the suite. But Max would say it's too sentimental."

"I'm pretty sure Max would be okay with whatever makes you happy," he pointed out.

She paused with her hands on the pages. "Maybe. There's just this part of me that thinks that there is a right wallpaper. A perfect one. And if I find it, my family is going to be thrilled. They're going to see this perfect wallpaper, and they're going to love it, and they'll love being here . . ." Her voice trailed off.

Tom didn't quite understand the hurt in her voice, but he knew she didn't deserve it.

"Babe, nobody loves you for your taste in wallpaper."

Rosie frowned like he'd missed the point. "I know this intellectually," she said.

"No, people love you because of your amazing rack," he said.

She hadn't been expecting that, and she snort-laughed through her nose, bending over to hide her face from the store staff.

"I do have great tits, don't I," she said in a slightly less aggrieved tone.

"The best," Tom said loyally.

The shop clerk finished his call and came over to quiz Rosie about the project. Tom zoned out a little as the clerk weighed in on the many options available to the modern wallpaper enthusiast. Something struck him about the way the guy was looking at him though, and it took Tom a moment to put his finger on it.

The clerk was deferring to him. This wasn't the reaction Tom usually got from store staff, especially in nice places, but, then again, he was wearing Boyd's thousand-dollar jacket, he was on Martha's Vineyard, and he was accompanied by polished, shiny Rosie.

Maybe he could pull off this performance.

"I think this paper will be too cutesy for a big room," the clerk told Rosie, cutting his gaze to Tom.

"We'll see," Rosie said, eyes narrowing.

She flipped to the next page of the sample book, which was printed with abstract white birds, like gulls or albatrosses, on a bright yellow field.

"I like this," she said to Tom, looking up through her eyelashes at him. "We could replace the shiplap in the suite, maybe paint the floor and trim white? And do white linens on the bed?"

"That would be pretty," Tom said, not just because he could tell she liked it, but because he had not lasted as long as he had in theater without learning how to execute the creative visions of better-informed people than himself.

The clerk made a small noise of disagreement in the back of his throat. He put his hand on the sample book as though ready to take it out of Rosie's hand.

"You don't want that," he told her. "Bird prints are very dated."

"Do you have it in stock though?" Rosie asked.

"No, maybe you're too young to remember, but *put a bird on it* was a thing a few years ago. Nobody wants bird prints anymore. It's not on trend. We're doing a lot of geometric prints right now."

"I like birds," Rosie said with a stubborn tilt to her chin. She pulled the book away, but the clerk didn't let go. "What, will you not sell it to us?"

Tom had done enough improv exercises to recognize a *yes, and* moment when he saw one. "Yeah, if she wants birds, show us some more birds," Tom said, subtly aligning his body with Rosie's.

"I like this one," Rosie said.

The clerk put his hand on Rosie's shoulder, which made her back go absolutely rigid. Rosie was only five feet tall, which many people took as license to treat her like a child, and patting her around her head or shoulders was a good way to lose a hand.

"You can buy something fun without going twee or saccharine," the clerk confided. "Wallpaper is too important a decision in a decorating scheme to pick on impulse."

Rosie jerked the book to her chest and glared.

"Maybe I *love* twee and saccharine. Maybe that's my decorating scheme. Maybe I want to fill the entire suite with my collection of Precious Moments dolls."

The clerk looked over Rosie's head to meet Tom's eyes in a silent plea for help. *Make your woman be reasonable*, his face said.

Tom audibly scoffed at the idea that he'd weigh in on the clerk's side. Were there men who publicly disputed their wives' takes . . . on wallpaper? If so, how was it that these men were still married and Tom was divorced? He was a dumb motherfucker, but he wasn't *that* dumb.

"I think Max would be happy if we doubled down on birds," he suggested. "Owl clocks over reception."

"Birdcage planters by the front door," Rosie replied.

"Flamingo print on the chaise lounge."

"Wingback chairs by the fireplace."

"Roosters in the kitchen."

"You do love cock." Tom grinned down at Rosie's flushed cheeks and dangerous expression.

The sales clerk's face was both horrified and uncertain as he tried to determine whether Rosie and Tom were lunatics or just doing a bit, but he must have decided on the former, because he backed two steps away.

"Makes all the design decisions easier if we just default to *bird*," Rosie said. She looked back at Tom. "Right?"

"Baby, if you wanted to set the world on fire, I'd hand you a match. You want to cover the place in birds? That's not even illegal. Let's do it." He watched a flash of gratification cross her face before she looked back down at the wallpaper samples and rolled her eyes.

"Drama queen," she muttered, but Tom marked the way the corners of her little curling mouth turned up before she ducked her head to her chest.

I got my lines right in this scene.

12

The temperature had dropped further and it was raining hard by the time they got back to the inn. Rose formed a tentative afternoon plan of sitting next to the fireplace and running search strings consisting of various products plus *bird* so as to tick off as many procurement tasks as possible before she lost her nerve.

She'd asked Tom to drive back because the change in weather was making her cough more. Now his left hand was on the wheel and the right was resting on her knee. She thought about objecting—especially since his fingers slid up along the inside of her thigh when he made right turns—but he'd focused so hard on the placement of his hand that he nearly ran a stop sign, and that gave her a little tumble of butterflies in her stomach. It was nice to feel worth the effort. To feel desired.

She hadn't made him work for it last time, whatever he now told himself.

I have no idea what I'm doing. I always thought my first time would be with some experienced guy who'd tell me what to do, Tom had confessed, a little wild-eyed when he'd realized what Rose had planned.

We could see if that slutty ginger across the hall will come give us some tips, Rose had teased him.

He's tragically straight, but maybe if you asked instead of me?

So even though Rose had been working off a Catholic school education—*Don't do it, you'll die*—she'd been put in charge of whether and when they were having sex, while Tom just got to be sweet and trusting and happy to be getting laid. But she'd been encumbered with fifty different hang-ups and contradictory expectations of her own: be sexy but not slutty; be adventurous but not dominant; blow his mind but make sure you come too!

No wonder it ended up being just one more thing they didn't talk about, just like she hadn't *asked* if he was dating Boyd Kellagher.

She didn't know what she was supposed to do now with Tom, who was single; Tom, who was *here*; Tom, who said he wanted her. But it might be nice to figure it out together this time. Start fresh.

Let's pretend you're absolutely dying to touch me. Let's pretend you're a construction worker here to tighten my screws. Let's pretend I'm not your college sweetheart. Let's pretend we just met and you think I'm beautiful.

Rose looked out the passenger window and saw a white cargo van parked in the front drive. Tom hadn't mentioned any contractors appearing today. Rose decided to be unbothered about that. She was just a lady riding in a car with a handsome man. *Tom's in charge of all the repairs plus getting me into bed.*

His hand gripped her thigh before he let go of it, and for the first time, Rose felt a little bit like she was on vacation.

A weather-beaten man in a poncho ducked out to meet them as soon as they parked.

"Heya, I'm the glass guy, here to see about some broken windows?" he addressed Tom.

"Oh shit," Tom said, smacking his forehead. "Sorry, I forgot that was this afternoon."

"I tried to call you, but it went to voicemail."

"Yeah, sorry," Tom apologized again. "My phone's dead. Sorry if you had to wait." He shot a worried look at Rose, as though she was unaware of what he was like.

She stopped and mentally kicked herself at that uncharitable thought. All Tom had done so far were all the things she'd wanted from him when they were married.

"No worries about the wait," the contractor said, regarding Tom judgmentally. "I caught up on some invoices. I was calling mostly because it looks like you've got a little flooding going on around back, by the pool."

Tom and Rose looked at each other in mutual consternation. She had no concept of pool maintenance, and she assumed he didn't either.

"Thanks," Tom told the window guy. "If you're okay going up to the second floor by yourself, I'll, uh, see about the pool. Careful of the closed doors—some of them are holding back our bees."

Rose and Tom sloshed through puddles as they hurried around to the back patio. The inn's pool wasn't large, but it was located close to the foundation of the inn, and the water level was almost flush with the deck. From there, the ground sloped down a few feet to the inn and the fire exit of the basement, where Max had once run a small pub.

The pool was dark and fetid with months' worth of rotting vegetation. A broken tree branch extruded on one side, and smaller clumps of broken twigs dotted the opaque surface. Rose had caught a glimpse of it out the window and placed it firmly in the *Deal With Later* category of unpleasant tasks. It was obvious that it needed to be drained and cleaned, but nobody was going to be swimming on Martha's Vineyard until June.

"I bet the drain's clogged with leaves," Tom said.

"Is there someone we can call?" Rose said, eyeing the water level with trepidation. If it kept raining like it was, the window guy was right—water would flow down into the basement.

"Nobody'll get here soon enough," Tom said morosely. He looked skyward as though asking for strength.

"Maybe I could fish some stuff out with one of those basket poles," Rose said, looking for a storage shed.

"Nah." Tom sighed. "I'll do it."

"Do what?" Rose said, but then Tom bent over to untie his laces. "Wait, what? No."

Tom lifted his head long enough to give her a tight grin. He stepped out of his shoes.

"No, Tom, what? You can't go in the pool."

"If I die, please remember I always loved you. I meant everything I said. I think you know how the speech goes now."

"No," Rose said more firmly, moving between him and the pool. "It's almost freezing out here."

"I did the Coney Island polar bear plunge last year. It'll be fine." He unzipped his jeans.

"Put your clothes back on," Rose said, beginning to feel real panic. "Tom! I mean it. You're not going in the pool. Anything could be in that water. This is a Florida Man moment. I am playing a Florida Man card. Tom!"

"I've got it, babe," Tom said, shucking off more of his clothing. "I'm a very good swimmer. Didn't you see me on the news?"

He wasn't listening to her, his attitude growing downright cheerful as he stripped to his boxers and attempted to maneuver around her spread arms.

Rose's warnings grew more fervent, a rapid, unheeded litany of *No, Tom, no, you are going to get diphtheria, you are going to get hypothermia, you are going to stab yourself on a bunch of rebar and need fifty tetanus shots, Tom, no, stop I mean it, Tom, I am not going to have sex with you if your dick touches that stuff in the pool, no, Tom, Tom, TOM!*

He slid into the water feet first, yelping when the oily, freezing sludge enveloped bare skin up to his neck.

"You are going to get an ear infection and die," Rose told him, hands pressed to her temples. Tom felt around in the water with one tentative outstretched foot, wincing when it impacted something. "Tom! Get out right now before you drown."

"C-could you bring me a couple towels?" he asked through teeth that had begun to chatter violently. "I'm going to need them in a second."

Rose growled, closing her eyes and lips over the many bad

words she wanted to call him. "Don't die before I get back, because I am going to kill you," she told him instead.

The towels in the inn could be full of mice and bees and God knew what else. She'd have to get them from the cottage. She turned and jogged for the front of the inn. God damn him. She hated running.

She was breathing in pants and gasps before she even made it back to the cottage, and she didn't have time to catch her breath before she grabbed the entire stack of towels from the bathroom. She walked to work every day and made it a point to take the stairs, so she hadn't thought her cardiovascular fitness could be *that* bad, but her asthma had been acting up, and she felt dizzy and lightheaded from the effort of making her lungs expand by the time she got back to the pool.

She spun around, looking for Tom. Had he gone inside? No. His clothes and shoes were still in a pile on the ground, getting soaked by the rain.

"Tom?" she called wildly. The rain was disturbing the surface of the pool, but she couldn't see anything under the water. "Tom?" she called louder.

She'd been gone less than five minutes. Oh Christ, what if he *had* gotten caught on something?

"Tom?!"

She kicked off her boots in a panic and shuffled right to the edge of the pool, staring down into the black water. She could barely swim. The water would be over her head.

She was leaning over the surface, eyes frantically scanning the depths, when two events happened in exact unison: first, to

Rose's right, Tom's shaggy head popped up from under the water as he victoriously thrust a rotting oak branch into the air, and second, to Rose's left, a burst of light and sound like a flashbulb going off surprised and stunned her.

So she fell in the pool.

The shock of the cold, fetid water made her instinctively scream on impact, even though she should not have opened her mouth immediately after having fallen into a pool full of decomposing leaves and storm debris.

She choked on sludge, and her arms and legs kicked out uselessly for purchase. Before she could work through the panic, Tom grabbed her by the sleeve and pulled her upright. The next thing her hands hit were his chest and the side of the pool, and with these two anchor points, Rose got her head above the surface.

"Oh God," Tom said, but the asshole was barely able to breathe through his loud howls of laughter.

Rose coughed the worst things she'd ever tasted out of her mouth, determined to get her airway clear if only so she could tell Tom, with her last words, how much she was going to murder him, but she couldn't stop wheezing. She weakly smacked him on his bare chest instead. He laughed harder. She tried again, but she didn't have any leverage, and her palm only bounced off the muscle. She let go of the side of the wall, delirious anger telling her that if she drowned while strangling him it would be worth it, but she nearly slipped beneath the water again.

Tom's sputtering laughter was cut off at the moment when someone else grabbed Rose from behind, under the arms, and hauled her out of the water. This latest insult made her throat close completely with surprise, because she was dangling in midair like a misbehaving kitten, the water making her clothes twice as heavy on her flailing body.

There was another flash of light, stunning her for a second time. She was suspended by her armpits, the tips of her toes just barely touching the ground, breathing with difficulty. She couldn't get her legs under her. Her lungs were seizing up.

"Oh my God, Boyd," Tom said, sounding both horrified and deeply annoyed. "Get the fuck off my wife."

13

- - - - - - - -

"Y ou're welcome," Ximena told Tom after patiently listening to his angry, panicked update.

The rain had shifted to snow in the late afternoon, so Tom was able to stand outside the cottage and yell into his phone without disturbing Rosie's recuperation inside.

"No! I'm not thankful," Tom sputtered into the phone. "I asked *you* for help. Not Boyd and his camera crew. Boyd is not help. Boyd is a *hazard*. What am I supposed to do with him?"

Boyd had peppered Tom with a variety of questions about the repairs while Tom was in the middle of evacuating Rosie to the cabin, and only the presence of many recording devices had prevented Tom from telling Boyd to get back on the private plane he'd borrowed and fly it directly into the sea.

"Oh, come on, he's a trouper," Ximena said airily. "And he said he hung drywall for a couple of years in his teens. I'll supervise him once I get out there."

Tom growled despairingly in his throat and hung up the phone.

Any hope he'd possessed of demonstrating to Rosie that he had his act together was greatly diminished. As were his hopes of convincing Rosie, or anyone who had access to the Internet, that he wasn't screwing Boyd Kellagher.

Rosie was beyond pissed at him. She wouldn't even speak to him. Again.

Tom knocked on the door of the cottage. He'd prevented Boyd from carrying her back here, even though she was wobbly on her feet and wheezing badly. Then he'd gotten their wet clothes off and Rosie clean in the most respectful joint shower he'd ever participated in, but she'd tossed him out as soon as he got all the pool scum out of her hair.

He didn't know what he'd do if she didn't let him in now. He supposed he wouldn't blame her if she still wasn't talking to him.

"Rosie? It's me," he called again. He heard her coughing inside, but she didn't tell him to come in. After he waited a few more seconds, he pushed the door open anyway.

Rosie was up in the loft along with every blanket in the cottage. When she didn't yell at him to get out, he climbed up the ladder and hesitated at the top. She was curled in a ball on the far side of the bed, shivering.

When she saw him, she pulled the covers over her head.

Tom scooted to her side on his knees and bent so that his forehead was pressed against the mattress near her chest. "I'm sorry," he mumbled.

She was still wheezing, even though her inhaler was on the nightstand next to her.

"What are you sorry for?" Rosie asked, voice inscrutable.

"Um. I'm sorry you fell in the pool because I did a Florida Man thing," he said.

"Yes. And what else?" she asked.

"I'm sorry the photographer took pictures of you all wet," he said.

"The *Vogue* photographer. With fifty thousand Instagram followers," Rosie said.

"Yes, him. Boyd said he's leaving tonight," Tom said.

"Okay, and what else are you sorry about?"

"Um. I am sorry Boyd's here." He took a deep breath to prepare for a long explanation, but Rosie popped her face over the covers and glared at him.

"Yes. That. *That* is what you should be sorry about. I can't believe I believed you."

Tom tightened his shoulders and braced himself. He should have thought harder about the potential downsides of saving Boyd's miserable life.

"Okay, yes, I am sorry, but I didn't know he was coming. Ximena was supposed to come instead, but she told him I needed help out here and—and I'm sorry I didn't tell you either of them was coming."

Rosie banged her tiny, ineffectual fist on the mattress.

"You didn't have to be sorry, Tom! You didn't have to lie to me! You know what, don't be sorry he's here. Be sorry you lied."

He swallowed hard. "I didn't lie to you."

She met his eyes, and her own were pink and watery.

"Look me in the face again and tell me you have nothing going on with Boyd Kellagher," she said.

"I have nothing going on with Boyd Kellagher!" he said, leaning over her and grabbing for her hand. She snatched it away and shook her head in slow disbelief, expression only darkening.

"Get out," she said.

"No, no, wait," he said frantically. "Look, I went home with him *once*, when I'd only known him for three days, and the paparazzi happened to catch me leaving his apartment. That is *it*."

"I don't believe you," she said, shutting her eyes. "I shouldn't have. I knew better."

"Go through my phone," he said. "Ask anyone. Ask my roommate. Hell, ask Adrian. It is *just* a bunch of weirdos on the Internet who want to see us together—"

"Forget the fan stuff. Forget the photos. He is *here*, Tom. He chartered a plane and flew to fucking Martha's Vineyard in the *winter* for you."

"Because he's got boundary problems and no social skills, not because he's my boyfriend," Tom insisted.

"Don't talk about him like that. He didn't do anything wrong. It was not a problem that you had a boyfriend. We're divorced! Remember?" Rosie gritted out. "It is the lying about it that I can't handle. The not telling me about it that I can't handle."

Tom clenched his jaw so hard it hurt, because, of all the things he'd done wrong, she couldn't get him for that. There were plenty of things he didn't like about himself, but the part of him that was capable of loyalty was the part he *did* like. He didn't cheat or steal or betray confidences. He liked it about himself that he'd only ever loved Rosie. She was angry about the wrong things.

"I know when I have a boyfriend, Rosie. It doesn't happen by accident. See, we sit down and talk about our expectations, our feelings, things we are *worried* about. You know, all the things you won't do with me—"

"Oh, do not give me that crap!" she burst out. "*You* are the common denominator here, and I happen to know exactly how you could give Boyd the wrong idea about how you feel about him. I really know."

She swallowed hard again, and Tom saw that she was holding back tears.

"I really know," she repeated.

Tom's chest was tight and complaining, and it wasn't because he'd jumped in a freezing pool and run around wet in the snow. He'd gone from hoping Rosie was right about him, back when he couldn't believe someone like her thought he was a keeper, to hoping she was wrong.

He braced himself by his elbows on the bedspread. "When did I ever do that?" he asked. "When did you have it wrong? I've only ever felt one way about you."

She wrapped her arms tighter around herself and didn't respond. But another spasm of coughing soon rattled her chest.

Tom grabbed her rescue inhaler off the nightstand and tried to unfurl her enough to take it, but she waved him away.

"I already took it twice," she said.

"Where's your nebulizer, then?" he asked.

"My albuterol is expired."

"Does it still work?"

"I'm not breathing in expired steroids," she snapped.

Tom steadied himself. "I'll pick it up at the pharmacy," he offered.

I only get one Rosie, and if she breaks, I don't get another.

"It's almost five. All the pharmacies will be closed. I'll get some tomorrow."

"What if you get worse overnight?" He remembered the spring of their freshman year, when everyone had gotten the flu, and Rosie'd come down with the flu, bronchitis, *and* pneumonia. He'd dragged his mattress into her dorm room and slept on the floor for a week because he'd worried about her breathing. "I'll go to a twenty-four-hour pharmacy," he decided.

"There isn't one on the island."

"I guess I'll take the ferry, then," he said, backing away toward the ladder.

Rosie's eyes flew open with surprise. "No, you don't have to do *that*," she said, not very convincingly. "That's at least a three-hour round trip from here. And what if you miss the last ferry?"

"I'll drive fast."

"It's snowing."

"Then I'll drive slow," he said.

"That doesn't make any sense! I'm fine. I don't want you to do it."

Tom exhaled in exasperation, because obviously she *wasn't* fine and she *did* want to breathe.

"And you call *me* a liar." This was never going to work if she wouldn't even be honest about what she wanted.

"What?" she cried. "I'm saying you don't have to go."

"I dove into a flood for Boyd, and I barely *like* Boyd. You don't think I'd take a little boat ride to get your medicine?"

Rosie didn't say anything, but the tremulous expression in her wet, bloodshot blue eyes was answer enough.

Tom got his boots on and climbed back up the ladder. He went to her bedside and cupped her face between his palms, holding her still when she tried to pull away. "Baby, I love you. I'd *swim* if I had to."

Her lower lip quivered, and her face was uncertain.

On a wave of righteous anger—at Boyd, at the decade they'd wasted, even at Rosie for not hearing everything he wanted to tell her—he curled his fingertips into her soft, damp hair, weaving them in so she couldn't pull away until she heard what he had to say.

"I've been crazy about you since the day I met you, and the worst mistake I ever made was walking away instead of fighting it out with you. I'm coming back tonight with your medicine, and I'm not leaving again until we work this out. You'll have to get one of those vaudeville stage hooks to drag me off the island. Okay?"

Rosie put one palm on his chest as though not certain whether she was going to push him away or hold on tight. She was still breathing faster than he liked. He'd shocked her with that, maybe more than when his supposed boyfriend had showed up to collect him.

"Your threats are more convincing than your promises," she said.

He huffed out a short laugh. "Yeah, okay," he said, releasing her and climbing back down the ladder.

She followed far enough to lean out over the platform.

"Are you going to make him leave?" she asked.

"Do you want me to? I will," Tom said, since he hadn't decided yet.

She shook her head. "I'm not interested in publicly battling Meteor Man for your love."

Tom opened the door to go. "Well that's up to you, babe, as long as you know that you'd always win."

Rose intended to stay up until Tom got back, but she must have fallen asleep despite all the lights she left on, because she woke up in the dark when Tom slid the elastic band that secured the nebulizer mask over the back of her head. Confused, she made a sleepy noise of protest.

"Shh, it's okay, you don't have to wake up," Tom whispered. He turned the machine on, and its familiar hum oriented her as the sticky-sweet mist of the medication began to flow into the mask. "Just sit up a little."

He gently tilted her up, and she heard the rustle of the covers and felt the dip of the mattress under his weight, but she didn't get alarmed until she felt his bare skin brush against her arm.

"Wait, are you *naked*?" she demanded, lowering the mask.

"I'm wearing underwear," Tom said defensively, scooting into bed behind her and arranging her so she was lying back against his chest. "I had to take the rest off. It's as hot as the surface of the sun in here with the fireplace on."

He pulled the mask back over her face and settled in, his arms clasped loosely over her stomach and stiff body.

If she had a lot of self-respect, she'd tell him to get out of her bed now. He didn't get extra credit for fixing disasters he'd created. Even assuming he was telling the truth about Boyd, Tom had spent the past three days turning her world upside down and shaking it. This wasn't the help she'd asked for!

But she was comfortable.

Those new chest muscles of his made a perfectly functional backrest, it turned out, and also, there was the added benefit of being able to breathe for the first time in several days once the medicine started kicking in. Tom might have complained about the heat, but Rose was always, always cold. Adding his body heat underneath the stack of blankets she'd burrowed into meant she was finally at what she considered a reasonable sleeping temperature.

Rose couldn't remember the last time she'd felt like this—warm, safe, coddled. The steady rise and fall of Tom's breathing against her back felt like medicine, just as much as the mist flowing through the machine.

It didn't mean anything had changed, she told herself. Tom had always been better in a crisis than expected. He'd always been good when she was sick, or when her childhood cat had run away under suspicious circumstances, or when she'd had a fight with her mother. That he was exactly what she needed in this moment didn't mean he'd be what she needed on an ordinary Tuesday evening, and her life was going to be made of a lot more ordinary Tuesday evenings than snowy nights when she needed medicine from the mainland.

Still. He was here. He was the only one she could even imagine being here. That was something.

She dozed until the liquid chamber sputtered on empty and Tom flipped the nebulizer off. Rose tensed, not really interested in moving but not sure she ought to be sleeping on Tom's chest either.

"You seem warm enough now," Tom said with watchful nonchalance, rolling over to flip off the light. "Do you really need all these blankets?" His tone was innocent, even though he was making a patent play for promotion to the bed.

"I'll get cold later."

"I'm sweating," Tom complained, flapping the covers to air them out.

"Maybe you'd be more comfortable staying in the inn with Boyd," Rose deflected, hands protectively clutching her pile of blankets.

"No, I'm fine," Tom backpedaled.

"I thought you were hot."

"It's not *that* hot." He paused. "Unless . . . are you going to make me sleep on the love seats again?"

"Are you leaving if I say yes?"

Tom craned his neck to give her a disappointed look. "No, I'm staying regardless because you're going to need another breathing treatment in four hours."

Rose chewed on that. When she didn't roll out the welcome

mat for the bed, Tom sighed and sat up. He slid his legs off the mattress, then reached for the covers as though he'd peel her hand off them.

"I guess I just need one if I'm sleeping downstairs," he said.

She held on to the blanket stubbornly.

"Rosie," Tom chided her. "You can't have them all. It's time to compromise. Give me a blanket or make some room."

Compromise. He had no idea. She did nothing but compromise! Her entire life was one big compromise between the things she'd wanted and the things she actually expected she could have now.

If she let him back into the bed, it would be wonderful, for tonight at least. She'd pillow her head on that dreamboat chest, luxuriate in his warmth and comfort, and wake up feeling safe and rested.

The thing was, if he slept here tonight, then he'd think her bed was a place he was allowed to sleep. Which would make it into his choice whether he slept there or not. And the very smallest Rose had ever felt was the first night Tom hadn't come home. If there were going to be nights in the future when Rose's bed wasn't the place he most wanted to be, she didn't want to know about it.

She couldn't start sleeping next to him again when she didn't know how to stop sleeping next to him.

So here was the compromise she thought she could live with: she slid her hand onto Tom's arm to stop him from leaving, letting her fingers trail up the taut swell of muscle. It took him a moment to realize what was happening, but the flash of gratification on his face was flattering. He flipped the top two layers of blankets so they were doubled over her body, then sat back down next to her with hesitation and expectation warring for top billing on his face.

Rose closed her eyes before she kissed him.

She'd thought about this ever since he asked her what she wanted back on the boat, and she'd worried even as she'd wanted him. She didn't know whether it would be the same or different to kiss him again, and she didn't know which she was afraid of. If it was the same, would it take her back to who she'd been at twenty-two? Desperately unhappy, trapped, lonely? But what if it was different, or she was bad at it now, and it only proved that she had no business kissing someone like Tom?

She shouldn't have worried. It was a little awkward because of the angle and the pile of covers, and Rose couldn't smell or taste anything but the sweetener the manufacturer put in the albuterol to cover the bitterness of the medication. But first kisses were often awkward, and Rose had known that even before she met Tom. It felt like a first kiss: sweet and uncertain and promising. They feinted a bit, hands opening to find spots to press themselves, lips parting and retreating as they explored familiar contours on the other. Then Tom threw himself into it as much as he ever had, planting his forearms on either side of her head and rolling over her so that he could capture her whole mouth against his own. His weight was anchoring, but his heart pounded against hers. He was nervous too.

He would have deepened it if she'd let him. He would have stayed and wrapped that beautiful, warm body around hers all night long. But instead, she pulled away after a hundred unsteady heartbeats. Tom hadn't been her first kiss. She'd never know if he would be her last kiss. Maybe she could live with that—some days he would be in her life, and some nights she'd kiss him, and she wouldn't plan on either.

Tom lingered over her with his eyes closed and a blissful expression on his face until she peeled off the top blanket and pushed it against his chest. This much she could live with.

"Thank you," she said. "Good night, Tom."

14

Rose was a little surprised that Tom was gone when she woke up the next morning. Not disappointed, no, because that would have been a ridiculous way to feel after she'd made him sleep on the love seats.

Even if she'd kissed him too.

She took the last cup of coffee out of the pot he'd left on the burner, nudged his dirty clothes into a pile by his suitcase, and checked her phone for messages. Before the pool incident the day before, she'd sent pictures of the wallpaper samples to the family group chat, but all she had in response were two pity thumbs-ups from her mother and Max, and the conversation had moved on to the Pats game that afternoon. She supposed the birds were in without objection, but that was almost disappointing too.

She nearly missed the note Tom had left in the fridge with a peeled orange on a plate.

Off to do construction things & look good doing it. Don't worry about anything. Take it easy today. ♥ *Tom*

There were work vans parked across the street at the inn. Rose caught a tiny flutter of hope warming her heart from the note and the evidence of repairs to come and paused to savor the feeling. Maybe she could do this. Maybe *they* could do this. She'd never thought life with Tom was going to be free from the occasional disaster. She'd thought it was going to be an adventure. She'd thought they were going to be in it together.

Rose had to pick her way through piles of melting snow and ice to get across the road to the inn, and thus she nearly stumbled into two young women stationed at the end of the driveway. The girls—teenagers, or maybe twenty-year-olds—gave her twin looks of appraisal from her red snow boots up past her black parka and the French braid she'd corralled her hair into. They then dismissed her, turning back to the inn with their phones in hand. They were waiting for something.

"Can I help you?" Rose asked politely.

"We're allowed to be here. This is a public easement," said the first, a mousy blonde with her long hair flat-ironed within an inch of its life. Her confident statement had not necessarily addressed Rose's question.

"It's . . . a driveway," Rose corrected them.

"Tom Wilczewski made us leave the property," explained the second lurker, a South Asian girl with a faint British accent. She nervously shifted her transparent plastic retainer over her top teeth as she spoke. "But he can't make us get off the pavement."

Rose looked at them in confusion.

"Why are you here though?" she asked.

"Boyd Kellagher," said the blonde at the same time the dark-haired girl said, "Don't *tell* her if she doesn't know, Snowy."

Oh. A couple of Boyd's fans. Rose eyed them with new interest. They didn't look like her idea of Internet weirdos, though she didn't know what she'd expected them to look like. And she didn't know why Tom wouldn't let them on the property. As long as they weren't trying to, like, nonconsensually drain Boyd's bodily fluids, she would have been inclined to let them in to meet him, assuming Boyd was still there.

After dripping all over the man's expensive shoes the previous day, Rose could see the advantage of bringing some distraction with her if they were reintroduced today.

"Who are you two exactly?" Rose asked.

After silent communion with each other, the blonde introduced herself as Snow Wolf. The brunette, without a trace of hesitation, proclaimed herself the Great Puffin.

"Your parents really wrote that on your birth certificates?" Rose asked skeptically, because the girls were well dressed and glossy in an upper-middle-class way, and they were probably called things like Amy and Sita.

"You can't use your real name in fandom," the Great Puffin scornfully informed Rose, although she was not *in fandom* but, rather, on Rose's driveway.

"Yeah. I run the Tomboy Updates accounts. That's, like, thirty thousand people following me. I can't use my real name, obviously," said Snow Wolf.

"You didn't stalk Boyd here from New York or anything?" Rose clarified with some rising alarm.

"We're in school in Boston, but Snowy's from here," said the Great Puffin. "After we saw the pictures from yesterday, someone in our Discord used Google Earth to ID this nasty hotel. So Snowy and I came over to figure out what's going on."

"It's not nasty," Rose immediately told them. "The pool just hadn't been cleaned in a few months. It's fine inside, where Boyd's staying."

Snow Wolf scoffed. "He isn't *staying* in this shithole, obviously. We're trying to figure out if Tom or Boyd are doing some test shots for the Greta Gerwig zombie project that's supposed to start this fall."

Rose narrowed her eyes, mentally uninviting them from the inn if they couldn't say anything nice about it. They could practice for a career in the Pinkertons somewhere else.

"Oh my God," said the Great Puffin. "Wait. Are you the lady Boyd saved from drowning yesterday?"

Both girls gasped dramatically and scrolled through their phones to compare Rose with whatever horrible photos Boyd's camera crew had now put online forever.

"Boyd did not *save* me," Rose said, crossing her arms and glaring.

"How do you know him?" Snow Wolf demanded.

"She's probably just the pool cleaner," the Great Puffin said.

"I own this place," Rose told them. "And you should probably leave."

They scoffed.

"Nuh-uh," said Snow Wolf. "I did my research. This inn is owned by Maxine Kelly Steagall, and the online property tax records say she's claiming a senior citizen exemption. You're not, like, *that* old."

"If you're this good at research, shouldn't you two be, I don't know, violating someone's civil liberties for profit instead of stalking a movie star?" Rose demanded. "Pictures of him can't be worth that much. I *am* in charge of this place, and I'm not letting any paparazzi in."

"We're not paparazzi. This is just our hobby," Snow Wolf said, taken aback.

"We're just Tomboy fans," said the Great Puffin, big brown eyes going earnest and impassioned. "Do you work here? Could you let us in?"

"I wrote a 150k hockey AU longfic about Tom and Boyd. We just want to give it to them," said Snow Wolf.

"I did the art and the binding," said the Great Puffin, blinking at Rose beseechingly.

Rose softened at this. Tom didn't seem to think much of Boyd's fans, but Rose had written a very embarrassing letter to Orlando Bloom as a tween and not sent it only because she didn't have the spy skills of these two and hadn't known his address. And the way the Great Puffin was clutching a large binder to her chest did remind Rose a little bit of her younger self.

"Maybe I could give your . . . longfic? . . . to him. And see if he wants to come take some selfies later," she offered.

"Tell us who you actually are first," the Great Puffin demanded.

Rose wrinkled her nose at the suspicion and lack of gratitude.

"So I'm . . . well, I don't know Boyd. Yet."

"Ugh!" The girls threw up their hands, disgusted at Rose as a waste of their time.

"Wait," Rose protested. "I do know Tom. I'm his ex-wife."

But this only made them roll their eyes in disbelief. "Like you could pull Tom Wilczewski," said the Great Puffin, unaware that Tom had at one point promised to have several babies with Rose. "And anyway, he's out here with Boyd. His true love."

Rose gave her a flat stare. Even allowing that the two fangirls were not going to be receptive to any information suggesting that Tom and Boyd were not themselves headed for domestic bliss, this wasn't flattering to Rose.

"You got me. I'm actually here for Boyd too. He pays me to hit him with a sweep broom and tell him he'll never be as buff as Adam Driver," she told them disdainfully. "You'll understand when you're older."

That sent the girls into fresh fits of eye-rolling and demeaning glares.

"Funny," said the Great Puffin with maximum scorn. "You should be on Wattpad."

Rose sneered back and jerked the binder out of the girl's arms.

"I'll give this to Tom. Who I have, multiple times, *pulled*. Maybe he'll pass it to Boyd," she said as she swept away with all the dignity she could muster after an encounter with the youths.

It wasn't a good enough parting line. The girls were still glaring at her.

"And you're wearing mom jeans," Rose informed them. That was better.

She let herself inside the unlocked front entrance of the inn and saw more evidence of repairs. Butcher paper laid out on the floor, heavy footsteps echoing from upstairs. The lights were on, the windows were open, and she smelled nothing worse than dust. Encouraged, she set the binder down on the big round table at the entryway and took a couple of steps up the stairs.

"Tom?" she called.

After only a second or two, she heard jogging footsteps, and he popped his head over the top landing.

"Oh hey!" he said, looking tight-lipped and harassed. "How are you feeling this morning?"

"Much better. Is everything okay over here?" Rose asked.

"Um, everything is fine. I'm glad you're feeling better. The tape and bed guys aren't going to leave after all."

Rose frowned at this non sequitur. "Why would the tape and bed guys leave?"

"Well, they were worried about the bees."

"What's going on with the bees?" Rose asked, taking an instinctive step down the stairs.

"The bees are also fine," Tom said vaguely, casting a nervous glance back over his shoulder. "The bee removal lady definitely knows what she's doing."

His tone suggested less than one hundred percent confidence in every previous statement.

"Where's Boyd?" Rose asked.

"Out back somewhere," Tom said, nose wrinkling. "I'm not

sure. He might go home today. Don't worry about it—I have everything under control."

"Literally everything you just said makes me worry," Rose informed him, mind already sketching out unfortunate scenarios involving drywall, bees, and *People*'s third-sexiest man alive for the year 2022. "Do you want me to look over any of the estimates you got?"

"You don't think I can hire a repair guy on my own?" Tom demanded.

"I could at least help you come up with a schedule? You know. Who'll be here when."

Tom's shoulders hunched. "You're assuming I don't have a schedule."

"Do you? Can I see it?"

"It's a mental one."

"Uh-huh," Rose said.

"I do have one! Today it's something like . . ." Tom hesitated, transparently coming up with a schedule on the fly. He straightened and found his mark. "Ah, bees, roofers, drywall, *lunch*, painters, wash the sheets, take down the curtains, bleach the kitchen, and then it'll be time for the season premiere of *Drag Race* and dinner. There."

"Is that all?" His schedule sounded ambitious, to put it lightly. She didn't want to make any more negative assumptions about him after being spectacularly wrong several times so far, but she also didn't want him to feel like she expected him to do everything himself.

Tom peered at her thoughtfully, crossing his arms and tapping his lips. "Well, I could add sex after *Drag Race*, but only if you really want to, because I'll probably be pretty tired by then?"

Oh. Her eyes widened as Tom began to grin at her in a proprietary way. "That, um. I just meant that sounded like a lot."

"Ouch," said Tom, smiling wider, because she'd neatly fallen for his line. "Can we make out on the couch after *Drag Race*, at least?"

Probably. She let a tentative smile round out her cheeks. She actually thought that out of everything Tom was doing for her today, she'd appreciate making out on the couch after trashy TV the most.

"If you play your cards right," she said, taking another step up the stairs before Tom held out a hand to stop her.

"Babe, the second floor is full of dust and bees and who knows what else today. Nothing good for Rosies. I swear everything is okay. Really. Everything is fine. Why don't you just hang out at the cottage this morning?" he said.

A blonde woman in Crocs and tattered jeans appeared at the top of the landing with her two palms cupped together. "I found the queen," she announced to Tom in a whispery voice and began to spread her fingers. Tom shot Rose a look of mild panic.

"I'll be outside if you decide you need anything," Rose said, and she left.

Rose was now at loose ends. She was probably allergic to the bees, and for all she knew, one mistake would send her to the ER looking like a blistered cherry pepper. So she couldn't stay in the inn. Tom seemed to have made huge progress in task management from the days when she'd had to hand him his homework assignments one by one, so he didn't need her help with the demolition. And even from Singapore, Caroline had neatly picked up the weekly reports that were the most time-consuming part of Rose's job. These were all good things.

Still, Rose was feeling a little adrift as she backed all the way down the stairs and went through the kitchen to the back patio.

When she'd dreaded taking over this renovation, she'd dreaded doing it *alone*. She didn't mind doing it for her family. She loved them. She'd just wanted to do it *with* someone.

If all she'd done yesterday was choose the wallpaper in one room, she'd gotten to do it *with* Tom. She smiled as she remembered the shopkeeper's face at Tom's wildly inappropriate jokes. She'd expected to want to strangle him on this trip. And sometimes she did. But at other times . . . she thought she was looking forward to kissing him again.

Bolstered by this emotion, she managed to text the family group chat again, hoping to gin up some interest in the renovations. Even if they hadn't displayed any interest *yet*, she felt like it was on her to at least keep trying.

> Rose: I'm going to rake up the bocce ball courts today! Remember the year we did a tournament?

She squinted expectantly at the screen. It took a few long minutes before anyone replied at all. Only her brother and

Seth: Lol. Too bad my kids only play Minecraft! and How's the drainage? The realtor thinks the back five acres could sell as a separate parcel, respectively.

Rose couldn't bring herself to reply to either of them. She closed her eyes and tamped down her rising sense of disappointment as she shoved her phone back into the front pocket of her jeans. She didn't know what she'd expected. It was probably hard to imagine playing bocce ball when it had snowed the previous day.

She trudged through decomposing leaves toward the deck but stopped when she noticed movement in the scrubby woods out behind the property.

"Hello?" she called. In response, she heard a distant gobble. "Oh crap." She immediately cast around for a loose branch or something to fend off the wild turkeys if they attacked. She'd just picked up a decent-sized rock when she heard someone—a human person—call her name from deeper in the brush.

"Um, yes?" she replied, finally seeing a set of giant footprints in the slushy snow. She could guess who they belonged to. "Boyd? Boyd Kellagher? What are you doing back there?"

It took her another moment to spot him in the underbrush. Her brain hadn't immediately registered his shape as another human, since he was squatting back on his heels, and also, he was so *big*. She hadn't appreciated it while she was dangling like a drowned possum from his grip, but his thighs were like telephone poles and his hands were like construction cranes. *Big!* her mind exclaimed, like it automatically said *Horses!* when she saw horses or *Oh no!* when she saw a rollover accident.

"I'm considering the motivations of the turkey," Boyd

replied in the tone of someone who was used to having his every utterance considered as though it made a great deal of sense.

"The big one who keeps tearing things up on the porch?" Rose asked, picking her way over to the movie star.

"Yes," Boyd said. He lifted an arm and pointed back into the trees, where a large, round shape paced and flapped its wings with agitation. "The tom. Not Tom, capital *T*. The tom turkey. He's very distressed. There was an incident of violence earlier. Tom, capital *T*, was pecked."

Up close, Rose could see why Tom had been cast opposite Boyd. The two of them looked similar enough that her mind kept moving from feature to feature, marking the commonalities. It wasn't just the muscles. They both had strong noses and full mouths. The long, shaggy haircut they were both currently sporting softened the severity of Boyd's features and hid Tom's big ears and fuller cheeks. Maybe they went to the same barber.

Boyd turned his head to look up at her with soulful brown eyes. "Tom yelled at both of us," he said with enormous, dignified sorrow, like a sad granite outcropping.

It took Rose a moment to work out that Boyd meant himself and the turkey, not himself and Rose.

"Oh," she said, feeling vaguely as though she ought to apologize on Tom's behalf, even though she'd been rightly furious the day before at being manhandled and photographed against her will. "It's been . . . a weird couple of days. Tom's not usually a yeller." Though that had been a different relationship and a long time ago.

She expected that thought to hurt, especially while looking right at the big handsome man who'd slept with Tom at least once, a lot more recently than she had. She'd expected to feel jealous if she ever talked to Boyd about Tom. Instead, she had only a big rush of fellowship and sympathy. Didn't she know better than anyone else in the world what it felt like to be in a fight with Tom? It sucked. *You tried to do something for Tom and it blew up in your face? Do I ever have a story for you, buddy.*

"The tom turkey is concerned that we pose a threat to his hens," Boyd said, swinging his gaze back to the trees. "I'm going to offer him some food." He stuck his hand in his windbreaker pocket and brought out a wrapped energy bar.

"Maybe we shouldn't feed him?" Rose said. "Won't that just encourage him to, um, stick around?"

"He lives here," Boyd pointed out, blinking at her in soft confusion before sighing and putting the energy bar away. "Tom told me to deal with the turkey," he said mournfully. "But I don't know what else to try. I don't want to hurt him."

It would have taken a heart of stone not to be touched by a giant man devoted to nonviolence. "Of course you don't have to hurt the turkey," Rose exclaimed, even though she'd roasted many of the turkey's distant relatives over the years and would shed no tears for him if he met the same fate. "I'm sure that's not what Tom meant." She was sure that was exactly what Tom had meant.

Boyd pursed his lips, distressed. He rubbed his mouth with one bear paw–sized hand. "He saved my life, you know."

"I know," Rose said. "He can be kind of amazing sometimes. Makes the other stuff hit harder though."

"I'm sorry about the pool yesterday," Boyd said. "I was just trying to help."

"I know," Rose said again, because now she felt she did.

"And we're really not together. I'm sorry you thought that," Boyd added. His shoulders sagged. "I'm not even sure he likes me."

Rose wasn't sure how to be sorry about that, though she felt like she'd be a better person if she did.

"Do *you* have anything that needs to be done?" Boyd asked hopefully. "Tom told me to stay outside. When he was yelling. Even though anyone could see the drywall was rotten and needed to come out and I was just saving him time by pulling it out."

"I'm not sure," Rose said. "Tom took my binder of construction plans."

"There's a plan?" Boyd asked, perking up.

"It didn't get that far. It was more of a vision."

Boyd looked greatly impressed. "Of course," he rumbled. "Of course you have one. Tell me about your vision."

Rose hesitated. The man's face was nothing but sincere, but how could she say she wanted the inn to be charming and beautiful, the kind of place where she'd bring her husband and kids and family, without getting deep into how, actually, she didn't have a husband or kids, and her family was all AWOL too?

"So, one of the things I meant to do was work on the basement pub," she told him instead. "The inn had a beer and wine license, but it got so little traffic that it was losing money on the permit fees. I'm not sure what's a better use for the space though."

Boyd nodded vigorously. "You are still in the inspiration phase."

"I . . . guess I am, yes."

"We need to nurture your inspiration," Boyd declared. "Are there other pubs on the island? Vineyards? Wine bars?"

Rose blinked. "I'm sure there are. Yeah." Nobody actually grew grapes on the Vineyard, but people liked local wine anyway.

"We should visit them. And take notes. And form a complete idea of the character of the pub," Boyd declared. He stood up, and Rose had to take a tiny step back to absorb his full height.

Big! Big like a desert rock formation! Big like a marine mammal!

Rose swallowed and tried to get herself together. "I don't know if we should." She gnawed on the inside of her cheek, because it would be pretty weird to go off for the day with Boyd, regardless of whether he was in love with her ex-husband or just following him around out of some misguided idea of life-debt, the Chewbacca to Tom's Han Solo.

Wait, Boyd Kellagher wanted to go day-drinking with her. If there was ever a time to stop thinking and go with it, it was now.

"This sure sounds like a legitimate way to plan a basement renovation," she decided. "But it might take a little while to find a taxi willing to take us anywhere."

"I can drive," Boyd offered. Then he frowned. "No, I can't. Tom said I was under no circumstances to drive you anywhere." His big gloomy face creased in consternation. "Tom doesn't think I'm a very safe driver."

Rose caught herself before she could commiserate on that too. Yeah, almost getting him drowned just once would probably have Tom holding it against Boyd forever.

And then she had an idea. She knew two people with a car and not enough to do who would probably look *very* impressed if Rose came out with Boyd and a drinking agenda. Tom would probably not approve, but it sounded like he would be very busy with renovations today.

Her brother texted her again.

> Davey: Hey think I left a pair of snow boots in the bunk room could you bring them with you next time you're in Boston?

Rose wrinkled her nose at her phone. Why were her ex and *his* ex more invested in the success of this project than her own family? Well, she wasn't going to sulk around feeling abandoned. She was going to get blitzed with a movie star and his groupies.

"Boyd, I'd love to introduce you to a couple of your fans," Rose said. "They seem really good at research and inspiration."

15

By the time the bees were collected, contained, and expelled, Rosie had vanished. And although Tom had not found a roofer by lunch, he decided to reward himself for the morning's effort—which had, after all, included several bee stings and difficult conversations with Boyd and his delusional groupies!—by walking back across the road to parse out exactly where Rosie's boundaries lay between kissing him and letting him sleep in the big bed. But she wasn't there.

When he texted her, her response was uninformative and yet terrifying: Went into town with Boyd.

So Tom spent the rest of the afternoon on the phone with potential contractors, frequently looking out the front window of the inn toward the dark windows of the cottage across the street, waiting for Rosie to come home like Jay Gatsby monitoring the dock light at East Egg.

He didn't see lights on in the cottage until almost six, and he immediately called it quits for the day. At the bottom of the main stairs, he happened to stop, look right through the kitchen doorway, and spy Boyd with the two nutjobs he'd tossed off the front lawn this morning. They were looking at a laptop on the island countertop, pointing and discussing something in low voices.

Tom froze, wondering if they'd noticed him. Boyd was difficult enough to deal with, but Boyd and his fans together were nearly insufferable. Maybe he could edge out of the inn without any unpleasant interactions.

Still—

Right, he was playing the responsible adult now.

"Uh, those girls look real young, Boyd. Do their parents know where they are?" he called.

Both girls turned to glare at Tom, as though *he* were the pervert for thinking that maybe Boyd shouldn't be left alone with two possible minors.

"We'd never try to get between the two of you," the blonde said haughtily.

"And neither of us would allow anything *inappropriate* in light of the *power dynamics*," the South Asian girl declared.

"It's okay, I know they're fans," Boyd said, blinking innocent brown eyes at Tom and pantomiming his hands in the air. Tom and Ximena had previously had a conversation with Boyd to the point of *Don't show your penis to any groupies*, so that was a good acknowledgment. "They're going to help with Rose's design vision."

"Rosie wants them here?" Tom clarified, eyes widening.

Everyone nodded, but Tom frowned. Weren't Boyd's fans responsible for most of her incorrect ideas about him and Boyd? Did Rosie really want to be exposed to more of that?

Near the door, Tom spotted a large binder on the front table. Thinking it might have been left there by Rosie or one of the contractors, he picked it up.

Inside the binder were several folders and a hand-bound leather book. The lowercase title of the book was embossed in gold foil on the cover: **you're the one (who tried to burn it down)**. Although he should have known better, Tom flipped to the title page, which declared the book to have been composed by Snow Wolf for the Great Puffin. All rights were reserved to Boyd Kellagher, Tomasz Wilczewski, and the Toronto Maple Leafs. The author specifically and emphatically disavowed any infringement of the Maple Leafs' trademark on the second page. The third page contained excerpted lyrics from a Phoebe Bridgers song. The fourth page contained a highly stylized, anatomically suspect, and beautifully colored illustration of Boyd and Tom engaged in a ménage a trois with a hockey stick.

"Jesus fucking Christ," muttered Tom. He slammed the book shut. Casting a baleful look at the kitchen, Tom hurried out of the inn. It seemed likely that Rosie had spent the whole day with Boyd and his groupies, and God only knew what she'd heard about him. *I am not dating Boyd. I am not sleeping with Boyd. I have never had carnal knowledge of a hockey player, let alone a hockey stick.*

"Rosie?" he called cautiously as he approached the cottage. He was braced for anything.

"Come in!" she responded, sounding reassuringly upbeat.

The scene inside hit him right in the heart.

Rosie was curled up on one of the love seats in her pajamas—dainty baby blue satin this time. Her face was flushed, and her curly hair was wet from the shower and combed loose across her shoulders. She'd acquired a breakfast tray and set out a wedge of brie, an open jar of raspberry jam, and a package of fancy water crackers on the coffee table. In semicircular array around the cheese plate, she had a big bottle of Evian, a glass of white wine, the TV remote, her embroidery hoop, and a stack of home design magazines. The TV was playing last season's *Drag Race* finale.

Oh, it was just the scene he thought he'd come home to every night for the rest of his life: Rosie with her little snack, her little drink, and at least three ongoing projects. Tom halted in the doorway, mouth trying to pull in multiple directions as he felt joy and piercing regret at once.

"Are the bees gone?" she asked, eyes flicking to the Band-Aid on his neck.

Tom grinned. "The bees are all gone." He felt like a Spartan warrior coming back from battle, and Rosie looked like a hero's reward: the satin of her top was stuck damp to her skin where her hair had soaked it, and the shape of her breasts and the points of her nipples were visible through the thin fabric.

He dropped onto the love seat, wedging himself in next to her. She wrinkled her nose, probably because he was filthy from construction grime while she smelled like shampoo and wine, but she scooted to the side to make more room and gestured that he was welcome to her tray.

Tom knocked his denim-covered knee against her bare one, admiring their legs stretched out next to each other, then helped himself to some of her cheese board.

"Did you have an okay day?" he asked through a mouthful of crackers.

"A really good day," Rosie said.

The way she smiled was familiar, stirring up a swirl of old memories. For a moment, Tom thought maybe she looked younger with her hair combed out and no makeup on. It took another moment, and a tilt-turn jolt of guilt, before he realized that no, this was just what Rosie looked like when she was happy, and it had been a while since he'd seen that.

She knocked back another sip of wine. "We were so productive. We made tons of progress."

"We?" Tom asked.

"So it was mostly me and Puff, because Puff's got the artist's eye. But it was Snowy's idea that we should remodel the basement space with a stage. And then she found a used karaoke set for sale *on* the island, and Boyd offered to buy it for us right then. Isn't that wonderful?"

Oh yeah, wonderful for Boyd, Tom thought sourly, who'd gotten to spend the day with Tom's wife while Tom got stung by bees and ghosted by roofers.

"Puff and Snowy?" Tom asked, shoving away his jealousy.

"Two of Boyd's groupies. I decided to put them to work as long as they're lurking on my lawn making fancams or whatever."

"I don't suppose those are the two Michelangelos who drew me in a three-way with Boyd and a hockey stick?"

Rosie blinked several times in astonishment before recovering. "You know . . . I didn't ask what the story was about? A hockey stick? Wait, don't tell me any more. They're entitled to their hobbies."

"But do I need to have a talk with Boyd?" he wondered.

"About?"

"The girls," Tom said warily. "And their pornographic hockey dreams. Like, for liability reasons."

"Oh! No. Not at all. He was very professional with them." Rosie gave Tom a chiding look. "He's so nice, Tom."

"Of course," Tom said. Because, sure, Boyd was very nice. He was just a movable disaster.

"And he's afraid you don't like him anymore."

"I like him just fine," Tom insisted. He'd worked with worse people, even if Boyd was the only one who'd almost gotten him drowned.

"And he looks up to you."

"Me?" Tom laughed. "What, he's impressed by my many credits in the chorus? The cereal commercial I shot five years ago?"

Rosie shoved him with her shoulder. "No, you know. You've been in theater your entire adult life. And he's just started. He never had any formal training at all. So, like, you could be conscious of that when you talk to him—don't be too hard on him. Don't yell. I think you hurt his feelings this morning."

Tom snorted. "You think that just because I read some Brecht fifteen years ago, I'm in a position of authority over *Boyd Kellagher*?"

"No, I just—give him a chance," Rosie said, eyes wide and sincere. "He really wants to do something nice for you. He knows you both could have died."

"Huh," Tom said noncommittally. "So did he actually help today, then?"

"Mm," Rosie agreed. She settled into a more comfortable position as the TV turned to a montage of the current season. And then she launched into a convoluted explanation of her design dreams for the basement pub. She imagined the space lightened, brightened, set up to accommodate wedding receptions or anniversary parties, with a small stage for a four-piece band or karaoke performances. She alluded to a mood board and a new business plan.

It sounded like an awful lot of work to Tom, who still didn't have the roof situation under control, but Rosie was glowing and hopeful in the way she described it, and, God, at some point she'd stopped looking like that, even though this was his favorite Rosie of all Rosies: Rosie on a mission.

She halted in the middle of a lengthy exposition on the pros and cons of various flooring materials and seemed to catch herself monologuing, or maybe she'd caught the force of Tom's besotted, bittersweet attention.

"Um, so," she said. "I think I can make it work with the budget since Boyd's buying the sound system. Which is amazing of him. We should get him a thank-you card."

"Okay," Tom gracelessly agreed.

He thought he would have liked buying things for Rosie, if he'd ever been anything but broke, but then it occurred to him that he actually did have a gift today.

"On the subject of presents," he said, standing up and lifting his eyebrows.

He fished in his backpack and offered a Tupperware to her.

When she was slow to accept it, he knelt next to her and made more of a flourish to present it.

"Um." She hesitantly opened the lid. "Oh no. Did you pull that out of the walls?"

He had a whole entire honeycomb in the bowl, shaved by the bee lady so that it oozed raw honey. Tom stuck his finger into the goop and then obnoxiously sucked it clean just to make Rosie shriek.

"You know those bees ate nothing but trash for months," she squealed, scooting back. Tom followed her onto the love seat. Something about the jerky way she'd scrambled away triggered memories.

"Are you *drunk*?" he demanded, equal parts delighted and affronted. He'd really missed out today. "Oh my God, you are."

"I'm not drunk. Anymore," she said, blushing furiously. "We were researching wine bars."

"Is that what you call it?" Tom grinned at her. She was pink and embarrassed and beautiful with it. "You should have told me you were getting started. I'd have quit earlier."

He stuck his finger back in the dripping honey and offered it to her. When she shuddered away, Tom sucked the honey from his finger and bent down to kiss her. He got one bare taste of her vanilla lip balm and wine-scented mouth before she pushed him away with another delicate squeal and flailed her hands at him.

"What?" Tom demanded with mock innocence. He put the Tupperware on the coffee table so he could catch her hands and loom over her.

"I don't want any of your trash honey," Rosie insisted with tipsy dignity.

"You *looove* my trash honey," Tom sang. "It's the sweetest."

"It's trash spit out by bugs."

"I'm sure they were eating the clover next door too," Tom said, leaning in to kiss her again. He got more of her this time, her mouth hot and wet against his for three heady seconds before she ducked her chin and pushed back with her hands.

"Don't give me salmonella poisoning," she said.

"The bee lady said it was perfectly safe."

"The bee lady, who was taking them out with no protective gear and no smoke?"

"C'mon, Rosie, try the honey," Tom said. "This is a moment of victory. You defeated the queen and drove her from your lands. Hear the lamentations of the bees as you eat the winter stores they were saving for their children."

She snorted but kept her arms straight. Tom linked their fingers and balanced over her, letting her have the illusion she was holding him off.

"I'll try the honey, but I'm not kissing you to do it," Rosie said.

"Why not?" Tom said, wounded.

"We don't have a kissing relationship," she said, tilting her chin up stubbornly. "You can't just come in and kiss me whenever you want to, all casual-like."

Tom exhaled in disappointment. "So, wait, I can't kiss you at all? Or I can only kiss you sometimes?"

Rosie gave him a heavy-lidded look of feminine secrecy.

"That situation is subject to change. You'll just have to check whether it's a day I'm interested in kissing you."

Tom let go of her hands long enough to scratch the back of his neck in performative consternation.

"Well, you're the boss, of course, but I think all the fucking we're going to do will feel real unfriendly if it's on a day you don't feel like kissing."

Rosie bent her head back and cackled before she caught herself and remembered to glare at him, her mouth twisting from the effort of holding back her smile.

"Why do you think I'm going to sleep with you, when I just told you we don't have a kissing relationship?" she demanded.

"Well, here we are, in this nice snowy cottage with a big bed," Tom said, thinking hard, "and you're wearing some very attractive pajamas, and you smell like vanilla and expensive wine." He ducked his head and stole another kiss off the corner of her pursed lips. Rosie swatted him, and he took her hands back in his. "And, um, I can tell you're not wearing a bra."

If he could just lower himself a few more inches, he'd be able to feel her breasts against his chest, their bodies separated only by one thin layer of satin and his clothes, which were dirty and ought to be removed anyway.

Pinned, Rosie tossed her hair over a shoulder, now obviously pleased. "I do sound really fuckable," she agreed. "But *you* just showed up with sawdust in your hair and your mouth full of trash honey."

The obscenity in her mouth sent a rush of heat directly to his cock, and he spread his knees, planting them to bracket hers. He became pleasantly aware of the way her wrists in his hands felt, of the soft fragility of her skin under his fingers.

"I could shower," he murmured, pressing his lips to the corner of her jaw.

Rosie slitted her eyes at him, her expression considering.

"I've been drinking," she said with a trace of regret.

"That's a self-resolving problem," Tom said. "Because after my shower and the *Drag Race* finale and a couple hours of foreplay, you'll be plenty sober."

"Is that how it works? I don't really do casual sex," she confided.

"It doesn't have to be casual," he said. He hadn't thought of it that way.

Rosie squirmed beneath his grip. "I especially don't think you and I could have the serious kind."

"We had a lot of extremely serious sex within five hundred yards of this exact spot," Tom pointed out.

"You know what I mean. That didn't end well." She sighed heavily, looking away as he lowered her wrists. "Am I the only one who finds this tricky to navigate?"

She seemed to expect him to back away, but he didn't. There were definitely some tricky parts, but not this—this had always felt very simple to him. Wanting her.

"What are you worried will happen?" he asked.

She fixed slightly bloodshot blue eyes on him and tried to focus. "You know. I'll get hurt. You'll get hurt. We'll wonder why we thought things would work out any better this time."

Was that all? Fear of future regrets? Tom could report that

regret was nonfatal, even when it felt otherwise. It wasn't regret that had kept him from anything he wanted in his life. Regret wasn't something to fear. Regret had pointed his way home. Regret had brought him here.

"Babe," he said softly. "Are you really sorry for any of the days when I kissed you?"

Rosie wet her lips, thinking, then shook her head. No. Everything they regretted had happened on days he hadn't.

"Well, since I already kissed you once today, we're clear till midnight," he announced.

He knew there were some logical flaws in that argument, but she gave him a brief smile before he pressed his mouth to hers again. This time, when his lips begged hers for more, she opened to him sweetly, and he got to absorb the hot wet of her mouth and the intoxication of her scent with all his senses. He clutched her tighter, savoring the soft, warm weight of her body against him. Rosie finally slid her hands into his hair, which was full of dust and needed cutting, but the tug of her fingers took him back to other times, other beds where he'd held her in the same position: an extra-long twin in the Boston College dorms, the salvaged IKEA full they'd shared their senior year, the big four-poster king in the suite at the inn.

He dipped his head to the wet satin clinging to her front, mouthing her skin through the fabric. The water stain didn't go down quite far enough, so he pressed his tongue against her nipple through her shirt before sucking it into his mouth. He was rewarded with a sharp inhale and the lift of her hips, but before he could pursue that movement, there was a noise from the other side of the room. A knock.

Tom didn't stop, because he didn't care about the noise at all. He didn't care who was at the door: it could have been the pope and Bernadette Peters together with a flat tire break-down, and he'd tell them to take a hike. He had Rosie back in his arms.

But Rosie noticed it too, and she pushed him off her.

She sat up and adjusted her shirt. As her front was barely decent, she wrapped herself with a throw blanket and called, "Come in!"

Boyd hesitantly opened the door and stuck his head into the cottage.

"Hey," Boyd rumbled. He looked at Tom—who anyone could have perceived to be half-hard and *in the middle of something*—cringed, then turned his attention to Rosie. "Just wanted to see if you still wanted to order pizza. The Great Puffin said she's hungry."

Rosie's eyes lit up. "Yes. Pizza sounds amazing."

Tom made a noise of protest. "I was going to cook tonight." Shakshouka. Cheap, healthy, and it only got one pan dirty: an appeal to a very basic caveman standard of *I can provide suste-nance for you and your offspring; please let me back in the cave.*

"Do you have enough for Boyd and the girls too?" Rose asked.

"No," Tom replied, surprised at her eagerness to keep them around. He wasn't feeding someone who lived on entire, unsea-soned salmons and rotisserie chickens, much less his pornog-raphers. Why was she so interested in their company?

"Okay, you and I can do dinner tomorrow, then," Rosie told him, ignoring his disappointed grimace. "Did you check to see whether anyone delivers out here?" she asked, turning back to Boyd.

"I can go pick it up," Boyd volunteered.

Tom sat up. "Were you drinking too?" he demanded.

Boyd's big shoulders bunched defensively. "Not very much," he said. "It's tiny glasses of wine at the tastings."

Tom sighed, trying to convey to Boyd his annoyance. How had he ended up in charge of Boyd *and* a set of hotel renovations, when all he'd wanted to do was get Rosie alone somewhere for a few days? "You promised me *no driving* if you had anything to drink at all," Tom said firmly. "Go back to the inn. I'll get the pizza. And tell the kids they have to scram after dinner."

Boyd bobbed his head in an agreeable, submissive way and closed the door. Tom snarled and stood up, thinking about baseball and hunting for his socks.

"You could be nicer to him," Rose said. "He was a big help today. And he's going to tape all the crown moldings tomorrow. And he bought that sound system—"

"I'm getting him pizza!" Tom interjected, shoving his feet into shoes. What, did she want him to kiss Boyd on the mouth for her?

Rosie rounded her eyes at him, seeming to detect his plunge in mood.

"I'll pay for the pizza, at least," she said. "Since I invited him and the girls."

Tom tried to demur, but she rolled off the love seat and went to her purse. She fished a credit card out of her wallet and tried to press it into his hands, only seeming to think the better of it at the last minute. Her eyes widened with a flash of apparent panic, and she jerked the card back toward herself.

This double take caught Tom's attention, and acting on instinct, he intercepted her tipsy, uncoordinated hand and snatched the card from her fingers. Rosie made an abortive jump for the card as Tom held it up over her head, out of her reach.

"It's not what you think," Rosie blurted.

Tom turned his back to her so he could bring the card protectively against his chest and read it.

"I'm not thinking anything," Tom temporized. He supposed there could be a lot of reasons that Rose's credit card was still in the name of ROSE K. WILCZEWSKI, and all of them were appealing ones. He turned back and smirked at her, card pressed flat against his chest. No, maybe tonight wasn't ending on a disappointing note.

"Lots of women don't go back to their maiden name when they get divorced," Rose said unevenly, her face turning bright red.

"Uh-huh," Tom said. "I can see why you'd want to hang on to Wilczewski, especially." He grinned wider.

"It's not a weird name," Rose said.

"That's what my grandmother from Łódź told me," Tom said, taking a step closer to her.

"I only kept it because people at my first job would have made really terrible R. Kelly jokes if my email address had changed," she insisted. "I just didn't want to call any attention to it."

"Makes sense to me," Tom said, placing his hands on her

shoulders. This was amazing. He couldn't wait to tell his parents.

"And I use my maiden name at this job," she said. "On everything except legal documents, actually. I may still do the name change thing."

"Sure," Tom said, beaming now. Rosie was not the sort to put things off. Something had kept her from taking that last step and erasing the evidence that she'd ever been married. He dared more commentary. "I just think it's charming that you always planned to be Rose Kelly Wilczewski for the rest of your life."

Rosie's lips thinned in distress. "I didn't."

"What?" Tom asked.

She shot an unhappy look up at him, then glanced away again. He waited for her to explain, but she only did it reluctantly.

"I didn't think I'd be Rose Wilczewski for the rest of my life. I didn't think I would be at this point, even." Her shoulders bunched, and she sighed. "Shows how good I am at planning how my life should go. I thought I'd do the exact same thing I couldn't handle the first time, then ended up doing nothing at all."

It took him a moment to work through that, plus why she'd expected him to be upset. When would she have changed her name? Oh.

She'd thought she'd get remarried and take some other guy's name. She just hadn't wanted to go back to Kelly in the interim.

Tom had worried about that. He'd never stopped worrying

about it, actually. That someday Adrian would take him out to get stone drunk on a flimsy excuse, then drop the news that Rosie was marrying someone else. Tom thought that news would have prompted him to action in the same way the hurricane had, but this opportunity was surely a lot neater than hiring assassins to knock off her fiancé.

She ducked her head like she was embarrassed, and he cleared his throat. He waved the card between two fingers. "I'll go buy the pizza. Do you want to get dressed and meet me over at the inn?"

"Sure. I should probably move over to the inn suite if the bees are gone? I could pack up?" She made it a question.

Tom shook his head. "I wouldn't. It's still a mess. And there's lots of construction to come. Let's stay here for now." Like hell he was letting Rosie sleep *farther* from him tonight.

She agreed easily. Very easily, he noted as he put shoes on and headed for the door.

He liked to think it was the same reason she hadn't ever changed her name. She still wanted what she'd always wanted. Some part of her still thought he could give it to her. And the part of himself he liked best still thought he could too.

He still liked the idea of Rose Wilczewski, for the rest of their lives.

16

They're multiplying," Tom said, peering suspiciously through the inn's open front door the next morning. Snow Wolf and the Great Puffin were still there with Boyd, now accompanied by several other young people with laptops, tablets, and large iced coffees. Almost a dozen of them, ranging in age from late teens to midtwenties, none of them answering to names known to the Social Security Administration. "Like . . . gerbils. Stuffed animals. *Gremlins.* You know? Did you ever see that movie? You got the little creature wet and new monsters sprouted."

When Rose woke up today, Tom had been down in the kitchenette in his underwear, brewing coffee and slicing fruit. Her pounding hangover was buffering her from any tender, uncomfortably wistful feelings this display of half-naked domesticity might otherwise have engendered: *This is for me?*

"Did Boyd say who they were?" Rose asked.

"I don't think Boyd really knows. He said he came back

from his first morning jog and they were all here helping the first two tape the baseboards."

Boyd was in the center of the group, head and shoulders taller than most of them, looking like clickbait: *Great Dane adopts lost ducklings! He's a great dad!*

"They must be Snowy's or Puff's friends," Rose theorized. It was hard to remember the precise events of the previous day after the first or second bar, but both girls had made loud promises of assistance with the inn renovations once it became clear to them that Boyd planned on sticking around. "They must be here to help."

It was like someone else's package had been delivered to her door, but instead it was someone else's life. A week ago she'd thought this place would be full of her family instead of Boyd Kellagher's fangirls. A decade ago she'd thought she was going to have her family love her instead of Tom. It was a good thing she'd decided to embrace the unexpected, because she might otherwise have been reeling.

"They're shippers," Tom said dourly. "People with funny ideas about me and Boyd."

Rose surveyed the crowd inside. Several of them were casting inquisitive glances out at Tom, who was looking particularly handsome this morning in a faded *Rent* cast T-shirt that clung to a lot of places he hadn't had as a college junior. He had several days' worth of stubble, as he seemed to have forgotten shaving equipment while packing for this trip, but it only highlighted the strength of his jaw and the fullness of his mouth.

Rose was probably of less interest in her cable-knit sweater and comfortable corduroys. She wondered what Puff and Snowy had said about her. She'd responded to every personal question the previous day with a lengthy and entirely fictional account of her relationships with both men. She'd rescued Boyd from sex slavery in Peoria; she and Tom had been go-go dancers in Sugar Land and war buddies in Korea.

Served them right for doubting the very boring backstory that she'd met Tom in line at the registrar when he'd needed to borrow a pen.

Tom saw her expression tighten.

"What?" he asked.

"Oh, just remembering that Puff and Snowy seemed to doubt that a classy lady like me would ever have been seen with schlub like you," she said lightly. "Even if you're making an effort these days."

It was fine that nobody else's erotic fantasies revolved around thirty-four-year-old investment managers.

Tom cut his eyes to the fangirls, frowning. "Did they say something? I'll throw them out."

"It's fine. I'm sure you'll do something unexpectedly sexy, and they'll realize what I ever saw in you," Rose said.

"Hmm," Tom said, appearing to ponder the proposition deeply, though it had been a throwaway tease. He poured the rest of his coffee into the grass and set his mug aside on the vacant concrete planter at the end of the walk.

Before Rose could recognize his intentions, he'd seized her around the waist and swiftly tugged her against the full length of his body. He wrapped his second arm around her shoulders and hooked one of her ankles with his heel so that she toppled back into a theater clinch.

He held her like they were onstage, but he kissed her like they weren't. He held the curtain-drop position effortlessly, but he smirked right against her mouth and gave her a little aren't-I-clever pause he'd never have allowed a paying audience to see before he pressed his lips to hers.

Tom always did kiss with his whole chest, his kisses marking rare moments when he wasn't thinking of something else or doing three other things at the same time. He couldn't sing while his tongue was in her mouth, she supposed. Couldn't fidget or wander away with his hands supporting her. He was only kissing her, kissing her like there were no other things to do in the world. Rose dug her hands into the fabric of his shirt, off balance from the sudden shock of Tom's full attention.

He pulled back long enough to check whether he was going to be slapped for his presumption, then kissed her again, rubbing his stubbly face against hers hard enough to chafe her chin and bruise her lips. It didn't occur to her to be angry at him; it wasn't as though she'd ever wished he *wouldn't* kiss her like she was about to step onto the last plane out of Casablanca.

When he pulled back and set her safely on her feet, Rose held on to him, feeling absurdly as though she ought to have done something cleverer herself. Something interesting with her hands or tongue—she couldn't think of what. Something other than clinging to him like an understudy ingenue who hadn't learned her lines.

Still, she couldn't help but grin back at him, because his

expression invited her to be in on the performance with him. She was costarring today. *Thank you, everyone, we'll be back for the two o'clock matinee.*

"Sorry if today wasn't a kissing day," Tom told her, sounding anything but apologetic. He waved at the fangirls, who were all gaping in varying degrees of shock and consternation to see Tom rub faces with a random office lady, all except for Boyd, who was beaming like a gymnastics spectator who'd just watched a Ukrainian teenager spin three backflips and stick the landing.

Boyd extricated himself from the crowd of admirers and came outside, his phone in his hand.

"I just heard from my publicist. I told him about the inn, the basement bar, the whole idea, and he's going to pitch the feature to some magazines. He asked if we could send him a few pictures today."

"Oh my God," Rose said. "Are you serious? What magazines?"

"*People, Entertainment Weekly, House Beautiful* . . ."

Rose gasped in happy surprise. The inn had mostly served as a family retreat for the past several decades. There were much nicer places to stay on the island. She'd never imagined it attracting a wider audience, but if it *did*, Max could really use the extra income.

She needed to text the family group chat to tell them Boyd was here. She'd been posting nothing but bad news for months now. Finally she had something good to share. Wasn't her youngest brother a Meteor Man fan? Maybe he'd want to come out and meet Boyd?

"What would the article be about?" Tom asked, sounding cautious.

"The basement project could be a great angle," Boyd said.

Tom was not on board. "You mean the project you came up with while drunk yesterday and which only exists as a few notes on a teenager's iPhone?"

Boyd and Rose both frowned at Tom in disappointment.

"It looks better inside," Rose said. "You got the kitchen cleaned out, right?"

If she made a big breakfast spread, they could probably find an angle to shoot the kitchen where it looked appealing. She probably also needed to feed the kids if she wanted them to stick around.

"I only got the bees out yesterday," Tom complained. "It's not *House Beautiful* in there right now."

Rose opened her mouth to offer help, but Tom seemed to gather himself.

"But I've got it," he insisted, still looking a little wild-eyed. "No worries."

"Are you sure?" Rose asked. "Tell me what you need help with. I'll organize the fangirls."

"I can handle the remediation," he said, firming up the line of his lips. "Go have fun with the kids."

Aunt Max's "office" was more of a closet at one end of the third-floor bunk room, the air warm and wet even in winter, the only natural light coming through a screened-over ventilation hole high on one unfinished wall.

Tom had mostly happy associations with the bunk room: it was hot and stuffy there too, especially in the summer, and several of Rosie's cousins had snored, but he'd also gotten laid in secretive but spectacular fashion on several occasions. He'd never previously had a reason to go into the office, but it was a much less fun place. There were generations of spiders living in the corners of the room, a PC somehow still running Windows NT, and a couple of long-deceased orchids. Also the inn's records. After several days of fruitlessly calling contractors, Tom had gone up to see if there was any record of previous repairs.

Max had at some point exhibited Rosie's genius for planning and organization, but the files for the most recent decade provided evidence of Max's decline and the Kelly family's neglect. Papers were shoved haphazardly into folders and wedged in drawers with unopened mail and invoices that might or might not have been paid. He'd been going through it the entire morning with no success. Perhaps Rosie might have made sense of it, but the aromas of dust and mildew and the debris of storm damage made Tom fear she'd cough out a whole lung if she came in here.

Nonetheless, he brightened when there was a careful knock on the door behind him, because he thought it was her. It wasn't—it was that Puffin character, who was still lurking around the inn, bearing a covered paper bowl full of hot shepherd's pie. She silently put it on the desk and took a step away with her hands clasped behind her back. Tom checked his phone; it was already lunchtime, and he hadn't even found the papers he was looking for yet. He had a missed text from Rosie asking if he was coming down to eat with everyone else. From forty-five minutes ago.

Shit. Not only had he made no progress, it looked like he'd blown Rosie off. Fuck his life.

"Thank you," he told the girl belatedly.

"Rose told me to ask you if you needed anything," she said, looking hopeful.

"No, just tell her thanks for lunch," Tom said, shoulders slumping. He couldn't go back down and report exactly no progress. "Are things going okay downstairs?" he asked.

"Yeah," the Great Puffin said, fidgeting. "We got the hall-way walls and baseboards all painted, and now we're starting the crown molding."

"Um. Does she look like she's having an okay time?"

The Great Puffin blinked at him. "For sure. I mean, she made *Boyd Kellagher* go to Alley's and get her stickers for a chore chart. And he did it. That would be, like, a big day for me?"

Tom wondered when Boyd might be going home. Or at least away. While he was glad for Rosie to have fun creating years' worth of blind items for Boyd's publicist to rebut, or to enjoy the questionable thrills of commanding a dozen under-employed members of Gen Z, it was hard to imagine the two of them having time to work on their relationship while super-vising Boyd and the growing number of fangirls. He'd barely seen her alone for a single minute over the past week. She cooked and planned and organized from sunup to evening, then collapsed in a happy heap—alone—in the big bed in the loft.

Tom sent the Great Puffin back downstairs with instructions to get him if it looked like Rosie was not having fun at any point in the afternoon, then resumed his fruitless search for any documents evidencing the previous roof replacement. The insurance company was fighting him on how many years the roof was supposed to have lasted before being swept off in the hurricane. Finding no records, he made a last-ditch call for help. He'd called everyone he knew at this point. Cashed in every favor.

"Do you remember when it was that you last had the roof at the inn replaced?" he asked Aunt Max once he'd answered fifteen questions about his parents' health.

"Sweet boy, I don't even remember what I had for breakfast this morning," she told him cheerfully. "But I'm glad you called anyway. When's your next premiere? It's been a while, hasn't it? You're not getting too ambitious with your auditions, are you?"

"Mm, literally nobody has ever called me too ambitious, Max, but I'm waiting for the negotiations on a Broadway transfer right now," he said, identifying a folder of tax returns from the early 1990s. It appeared that the inn hadn't *ever* done much better than break even, gauging by the losses described. He tossed the tax returns in the trash.

"Broadway! I'll have to buy a new dress," Max said dreamily. She coughed, then cleared her throat. "I haven't been to New York in a couple years. Since before you were acting."

During the decade Tom had spent in exile in Boston, he'd made sure to send Max a couple of tickets for every show he appeared in. He'd started doing so in hopes of getting some intelligence on Rosie, or at least a little goodwill, but he'd continued as his parents grew older and more reluctant to travel up from Florida to see him perform. Max had come without fail, though she was hit or miss on whether she acknowledged that Tom and Rosie had ever married or divorced.

It would be more complicated to get her down to New York in her increasingly poor health, but keeping the approval of a single member of Rosie's family was probably a good idea.

"Sounds like a plan," he deflected. "Any idea on where you might have kept the repair records for the inn though? I'm in your office."

"Why are you up at the inn? It's awful there in January. Damp and gray. You should take Rosie down to your parents' place. Somewhere warm. I'd like a little great-niece next. One that looks just like her. She was the most adorable baby. Born with a full head of hair. Think you can manage?"

"We don't have *any* kids," Tom told her, confused. "Um. Yet."

"Well, what are you waiting for, then?" Max demanded, tone sharpening. "Rosie's not getting any younger."

"Yeah, sure," Tom said, shoving the drawer shut. "I'll get right on that." He slumped into the ancient, creaky office chair and bent over the desk to rest his chin on his forearm. *No, Max, you're thinking of how my life was* supposed *to go.*

"I hope I didn't scare her off the idea," Max mused. "I used to put her in charge of her brothers and cousins when we were at the inn. Had her feeding and dressing them, all that. She was the only responsible one in the whole bunch. My parents did the same thing to me, and I'd decided I was never having any of my own by the time I was married."

"Oh, I don't think that's it," Tom said lightly, though his

chest hurt. "She used to tell me we were having six or seven, all their names on a theme."

Not knowing whether she was joking had been part of the fun. Rosie could really commit to a bit, and he'd imagined telling some horrified nurse that yes, they really meant to name their second set of triplets Egbert, Fiona, and Gus.

"That's good," Max said approvingly. "Let me know when the baby shower is. I want to get the crib."

Tom promised as genuinely as he could, knowing both that Max would not remember this conversation in ten minutes and that Rosie probably had ten more trials for him to pass before she might reasonably consider him father material.

Maybe he should just put the roof aside for now. There were plenty of other problems in the insurance report that had not yet been tackled while he fruitlessly pursued roofing contractors and Rosie turned the basement pub into a karaoke bar.

He opened the binder to a random page. The gutters needed to be cleaned out and patched. He hadn't the faintest idea how that was done, and the insurance company had only allowed him the princely sum of $83 to accomplish it. As his heart rate miserably picked up, he heard cars on the front gravel.

It was probably just more teenage fangirls, but he was expecting Ximena today. *Please let it be Ximena.* He needed reinforcements, someone to keep Boyd and the girls out of Rosie's hair and Tom's jock.

Tom climbed up on the desk to peer out the single window. There was a traffic jam down below: the front drive was totally full. Ximena's roundly pregnant figure stood next to a rental car, in heated conversation with Rosie's cousin Seth and a middle-aged woman in a code enforcement uniform. A dozen or so teenage girls had stopped what they were doing—spray-painting furniture, beating throw rugs, taking selfies—to watch.

"What fresh hell . . . ?" Tom muttered.

He pounded down two flights of stairs and out the front door. They were being written up. Tom had never owned a car, so he'd never been pulled over, but he recognized the smugness of a civil servant engaged in a satisfying bout of ticket writing. The code enforcement officer was scribbling a novel onto her pad while Ximena argued with her and Seth stood by with a mildly anxious expression on his face.

Everyone stopped what they were doing when Tom made it to the front yard. They looked at him as though they'd been waiting for him to make an appearance, even though this wasn't his inn, it wasn't his circus, and these were not his monkeys. He swallowed hard.

Time to perform a Tom who was a respectable father of three, a Tom who paid his mortgage and voted. A person to whom anyone in the world might defer.

"Is there a problem?" he asked in his most authoritative voice, praying it didn't break.

The code enforcement officer flipped back a couple of pages in her notepad. "You've got no permits for construction work, you've got three vehicles parked in the roadway, and you've got no certificate of occupancy for all those guests you're lodging here, to start," she said.

"I told you that you needed a certificate of occupancy," Seth said mournfully, to nobody in particular.

"What—we're not renting," Tom said.

"Then you need to fill out the paperwork stating an intent to use it as a habitation again," the code enforcement officer said, unimpressed.

Paperwork. Tom was *terrible* with paperwork.

"Okay, I'll . . . do that right now. But do we really need permits? We're just painting. Nobody's paying to be here. Nobody's getting paid to be here," Tom said.

The code enforcement officer looked at Seth. "We got a report that someone was doing unlicensed renovations."

Tom cut his eyes over to Rosie's cousin, who was fidgeting with his tucked-in polo shirt. Had he narced on them to code enforcement?

"There aren't any contractors here yet," Tom insisted.

Seth scratched his head. "But you're still doing renovations. Rosie's been spamming the group chat with photos of Boyd Kellagher taking out drywall. That's renovations, right? Why didn't you get a permit?"

Everyone gazed at him judgmentally for a moment. In response, Seth blushed but didn't back down. "And I saw a TikTok of Boyd replacing some rotten studs too," he muttered, tucking his chin into his chest.

Tom briefly shut his eyes, praying to Old Testament God for some lightning bolts.

Ximena folded her arms over her bump before elbowing Tom to bring him back into the conversation. "Do you really need a permit if you're not doing anything structural?"

The code enforcement officer had perked up at Boyd's name.

"Wait, Boyd Kellagher? From the Meteor Man movies? Seriously? That's who's doing the renovations?"

Ximena and Tom exchanged lifted eyebrows.

"Meteor Man himself," Tom said. "Just hanging out. Not doing any renovations."

"Would you like to come inside and meet him?" Ximena smoothly suggested to the county official. "And I'm sure Tom's . . . young friends . . . will move their cars to a better spot if we just let them know they're in the road."

The other woman hesitated in the face of this blatant play for leniency in exchange for celebrity selfies. But as celebrity encounters had to be one of the chief perks for drawing a Dukes County salary in an expensive town, she agreed.

"I'll just verify that there are no renovations going on inside," she said, justifying it to herself as she slowly lowered her ticket pad.

"It's just some good friends spending some time together out at the vacation property," Ximena said, leading the code enforcement officer into the inn. "Having a relaxing vacation." She looked back over her shoulder at Tom while making an exasperated face at him, one that eloquently stated that she was too famous for this shit too.

Seth nearly went in after them, but Tom seized him by the back of the polo shirt and dragged him around to the side of the porch. Rosie had been texting her family all week, trying to convince them to join in the fun. Nobody had agreed to come. Now this douchenozzle showed up with the cops?

"Did you call code enforcement on us?" Tom demanded,

leaning in to the other man's shocked, pink face. "On your own cousin?"

"No," Seth yelped. "I didn't call her."

Liar. Tom glared at him. He wouldn't come eat Rosie's dinner, but he showed up now?

"No. I mean, Lettie's in my golf group. I just happened to tell her today that the property's value is going to take a hit if you guys wreck the place. If Rosie does sell, I mean."

Tom fisted his hand in the front of Seth's shirt, knuckles going white. Rosie would literally tape herself to the front door before she agreed to sell.

"If anyone else wants a vote on how I fix up this shithole, they can fucking show up and help," he growled. "And you. How do you not have time to help at all, but you have time to watch the stupidest content on the whole Internet and tell your *golf* buddies about it?"

"Hey!" Seth objected. "I'm not in control of what the algorithm shows me." His bland face turned threatening. "And anyway, maybe you shouldn't be getting all in my face while you're cheating on my cousin?"

"I'm . . . what? Cheating?" As aggravating as it was to be dogged by Boyd Kellagher allegations, it was news to Tom that Rosie now considered the two of them to be in a relationship. "When? I'm literally sleeping in the same cottage as her, and I think fifteen teenagers can report I haven't even been *alone* with Boyd."

Seth sneered at him. "Bro, there are like a *million* videos online of you two making out." He pretended to pick lint off his shirt where Tom had grabbed him. "I can't believe you invited the dude you're hooking up with to stay in the same house as Rosie, but you know she's gonna find out eventually. Maybe you should, um, go do some counseling about how you're into men?"

Tom goggled at this person who was somehow related to the love of his life despite sharing no personal qualities past their eyebrows.

"Seth . . . do you remember that I'm bi? I was always bi? Not to mention, Rosie and I were *divorced*? For ten years?"

From the vacant look of nonrecognition Seth gave him, Tom's absence had not been noted at the past decade's worth of holiday celebrations nor had Seth ever managed to absorb a single pertinent biographical detail about him.

Tom curled his fists and uncurled them. Rosie would not thank him for beating the shit out of her cousin.

"Why don't you go back to your property management office and look up whether there's any other paperwork you can fill out for us before I call *your* wife and tell her you've got plenty of time to golf and watch videos from my stupid queer-baiting Broadway play instead of taking care of your baby, huh?" he growled at Seth. "Next time you show up uninvited, you better have a paintbrush in hand or I'm turning the hose on you."

He shoved the hapless cousin off the porch, then gathered himself. He was a dependable version of Tom, a man who didn't lose his temper when asked to do home improvement tasks, a Tom who cheerfully managed houseguests.

After a deep breath, he went back inside. Boyd was slowly touching up a section of crown molding while the code enforcement officer and half a dozen young women watched with rapt attention, phones at the ready to document every second of this process.

Rosie came up from the basement, a flowered silk scarf tied on top of her head to hold her hair out of her face. She had a smudge of dust on her nose and paint on the overalls she'd rolled up three times at the ankles so they wouldn't drag. The smile on her face when her gaze landed on him washed all the week's frustrations away like rain. Whatever it was about this place, it was working for her. She looked happier by the day. Like his Rosie.

"I think I narrowed it down to three," she announced, unaware of any of the day's events and fanning three nearly identical paint samples in her hands. "For the accent wall behind the stage. What do you think?"

She waited for his answer, utterly serious.

"Hmm," Tom said, stepping closer to pretend to consider the paint chips. He put his thumb in his mouth and wiped it across the smudge of dust on her nose before answering.

"This one," he said, choosing a shade at random.

Rosie squirmed away from his wet finger on her face, then held the paint chip at arm's length.

"Are you sure?" she said doubtfully. "You don't think my dad will say it's too pink?"

Tom thought if Mr. Kelly cared, he would have shown up by now, but he wasn't going to break Rosie's heart by telling her that.

"I think it'll set off my summer tan wonderfully," Tom said.

Rose pulled the corner of her mouth out to the side, because she recognized both the evasion and the implied promise in that statement. Her expression was hesitant, but she took a deep breath, checked to make sure that nobody else was watching, then went up on her tiptoes to brush her mouth across his lower lip. Her palms splayed across his stomach for balance. Tom savored this tiny bit of sweetness, even though he wanted a lot more of it.

At least he was the romantic lead in this play. Now he just had to hope the show was a comedy.

17

"**B**ig day for the Tomboys," Snowy announced, scrolling through her phone. She gave Rose a significant look.

Puff and Snowy were helping Rose hem the new curtains she'd bought on remainder. Rose had thought she could teach them how to use a sewing machine, since she'd been the only one in her group of college friends who'd ever learned. But this particular group of kids not only knew how to sew well enough to make their own elaborate convention costumes, they could hand-bind books, scrub and decipher metadata on ten different social media platforms, and paint the human form like they'd trained at the knee of the old masters. Rose got the feeling that if she expressed interest in setting up a small nuclear reactor in the backyard to provide auxiliary power, Snowy would flip through her mental Rolodex of die-hard Boyd stans and muse, "I guess we could get MeteorManWhore at the Department of Energy. Or would it be better to see if AngelKisses96 can get a visa once she's done at ITER?"

So the sewing machine wasn't new and exciting to them,

but they'd still been keeping Rose company all morning. Which was . . . really nice, actually.

"Are people excited for dinner?" Rose asked, taking the next fabric panel from Puff. She was making king ranch chicken casserole tonight. It was really a shame none of her family had been able to make it out so far—that one always went over well when Max made it.

Snowy paused as though struggling for diplomacy. "Yes. Absolutely. Dinner. But I'm actually talking about the big post this morning about whether we should let multishippers use the Tomboy hashtag."

None of those words were in the Bible.

"Hmm," Rose said, trying to be supportive, though she found it much easier to relate to the girls when they were talking about window treatments than their fandom drama.

Puff made a troubled expression. "Are you doing okay?"

"Why would I not be okay?" Rose asked. It had turned out to be a wonderful month. They'd made so much progress on the inn, and everyone had been very considerate of her, personally, even though she'd just met everyone but Tom.

Snowy and Puff exchanged guarded looks.

"Well, you're sort of the main character of the day," Puff said.

"Me?" Rose said, startled. "What did I do?"

"Okay, so, you know about all the *Vogue* pictures with the pool, right? And someone else dug up your divorce decree," Snowy confessed. "Not me! And *then* someone posted a clip of Tom grabbing your ass last week. Also not me. Sooo . . . can you see where this is going?"

Rose did not see. She understood the interest in the thirst trap photos of Boyd and Tom carrying heavy things around the inn that Snowy had been posting, but Rose tried to stay out of the frame. Why would anyone care what she was doing?

"You and Tom. Tom and Boyd. Boyd and You. All here. So, a lot of people are having *all* the feelings about you," Snowy said. Puff nodded.

"*All* the feelings? Are some of them angry at me?"

Snowy bit her lip, then passed her the phone. The Tomboy Updates account—that was Snowy—had posted a poll on whether OT3 content, whatever that was, ought to be allowed in the Tomboy hashtag. There were 158 comments.

"Wow," Rose said faintly.

Some people on the Internet *hated* her.

"You know, it takes a lot of slut shaming and biphobia to shock a Groton School alum," Puff said, tapping her chest, "but I think some of these are real bad takes."

"I don't think you're a home-wrecker," Snowy said earnestly. "Like, you were with Tom first. Saying otherwise denies Boyd's agency."

Rose looked again through the comments.

"People are making *death threats*?" she squeaked.

Snowy snatched the phone away from her. "Okay, don't worry about those. I get, like, three a week, just from antis. That's just fandom."

"No, adding you is just, like, a big adjustment for everyone," Puff hastened to reassure her. "But I get it! I was a Boyd/Reader person for two years—"

"You are so brave to admit that." Snowy interjected.

"Shut up, Snowy. But anyway, Tomboy was my OTP for the last year. Still. I think I could come around on you."

Puff and Snowy gazed anxiously at Rose. "If you wanted us to," Puff added. "You guys are cute together. It *does* make sense. Order and chaos. Balance."

Rose finished with a curtain panel and took another from the pile. The inn was really reclaiming its feminine energy these days, even if everyone here was revolving in Tom and Boyd's orbit. The curtains were lace. The wallpaper was birds. This would be a wonderful place for weddings when she was done with it.

"Guys, you know I wasn't serious when I said I'm the dom in a tragically under-negotiated kink relationship with Tom and Boyd," Rose said, trying to keep it breezy. "I did not actually crate train Boyd Kellagher. Tom does not actually tongue-wash my kitchen at home."

"I mean, yes," said Puff.

"But also no," said Snowy. "I know you weren't serious. But we could be serious. You should see some of the videos we have. Puff could make some new art. We want to support you."

"I don't think anyone needs to stop having fun with the idea of Tom and Boyd together just because Tom and I—well, things are still up in the air," Rose said slowly, not sure what she ought to be sharing with these two and, by extension, the Internet.

The girls paused.

"Oh," Snowy said with faint disappointment. "You and Tom?"

"I mean, maybe me and Tom," Rose said. "We've got a lot to work out."

Or, really, Rose had a lot to work out. She'd spent her whole life imagining one kind of future for herself, and she could admit that that future wasn't going to happen. She was instead trying to take stock of what she *did* have: the inn, which her family would hopefully love when it was done; this unexpectedly fun experience realizing her pink, bird-accented renovation dreams with Boyd Kellagher and Ximena Tejeda-Souza and all these teenage weirdos; and also, maybe—maybe—something unconventional with Tom.

Puff bit her lip. "So, people aren't really imagining you with *Tom*."

Snowy passed her the phone again, filling the screen with a piece of fan art.

It wasn't Puff's work—it was gestural and monochrome rather than color block—but the unknown artist had clear drafting ability. Which they had used to depict three very happy, very naked people having an Eiffel Tower–shaped sexual encounter. The artist had a fantastic grasp of the human form and anatomical detail, and backs were arched, stomachs were taut, lips were slack—

"Oh God," said Rose. That was her. And Tom. And *Boyd*.

Somewhere in the back of Rose's mind, two soundtracks began playing. A reproachful "Ave Maria" warred with a low, suggestive seventies funk beat.

"That's . . . that's . . . uh," Rose said, struggling to identify the socially appropriate response to reviewing art of herself sexually pleasing two men at the same time. Puff and Snowy seemed to be waiting for a reaction akin to receiving an early birthday gift. *Oh, for me? Pornography? You shouldn't have!*

"I know!" Snowy said, fanning herself. "Isn't it amazing? The artist cross-posted a safe-for-work version too, and it's doing huge numbers. This really feels like a tipping point."

Puff leaned in, raptly interested. "So?" she asked Rose.

"So?" Rose replied, confused.

"So what are you going to do?"

Rose thought she was going to have a large glass of wine with dinner and avoid eye contact with Boyd for a while. Was there anything else she could possibly do about this?

"You know this isn't real either, right?" Rose said, tapping the screen. "Like the story Snowy wrote about Tom and Boyd playing hockey."

"Of course it's not real. It's a picture," Snowy said. "But it's also a vibe?"

"This is not even the vibe. You've been here three weeks. You know there's nothing going on involving me, Tom, and Boyd," Rose protested.

The girls gave her twin unimpressed stares.

"Once again," said Snowy. "It *could* be. Do you want it to be?"

Set aside that if Rose had ever wanted to have a threesome, she should have had one when she, her cute bisexual boyfriend, and everyone else in the world had been in their sexual exploration era—college. Set aside that she was a now a respectable thirty-four-year-old endowment manager. Set aside that she wasn't even sure Boyd was into women. How was she supposed to raise the topic?

Thank you for coming to this meeting! First on the agenda is reviewing bids for the gutter repair. Excellent work, Tom. Second on the agenda is this picture of the three of us doing it. Can everyone be ready to operationalize that before dinner?

"First off, you must have noticed that Tom barely tolerates Boyd now," Rose said.

"Which is an absolute tragedy, because we all know they're perfect for each other," Puff said. "But, you know, it's not like he really likes calling contractors on the phone, and he's doing that all day for you. I'm sure he'd have a threesome if you asked him to."

"I cannot have a threesome with my ex-husband and Boyd Kellagher," Rose said.

"What, just because you're short? I think it's totally doable if you and Tom get on the bed and Boyd—"

"*Please* stop telling me about it. No, I mean, that's not me. Under no circumstances is that me." She tapped the phone for emphasis.

"In the picture?" Puff asked, confused.

"I mean, sure, I'm guessing it's supposed to be me, but it doesn't even *look* like me."

Puff paused, considering. "They got your hair and your boobs right."

"Yes, but where's the rest of me?" Rose asked skeptically. The woman in the picture had the proportions of the porn actress who'd surely served as a reference image for the picture, wasp-waisted and underfed. Which only supported the larger point that nobody, including Rose, could ever imagine her doing anything like that.

Puff took another look at the artwork. "Okay, yes, I can see

that BakugoLuvs has some important lessons on body diversity
to learn. I'll talk to them. But also, like, why are you up here
sewing curtains when you've got Tom Wilczewski and Boyd
Kellagher wandering around and basically willing to do *anything* you ask? This is, like, totally wasted on you."

Snowy snorted. "Put me in, Coach," she said, mocking Puff,
who elbowed her in the ribs.

Puff had a point, Rose supposed. Stated objectively, who
wouldn't want to sleep with Tom, Boyd, or both of them at the
same time? Rose was just unable to imagine herself in that scenario, not least because sex with Boyd would be like a liaison
between a Great Dane and a Lhasa apso: theoretically possible
on account of them being members of the same species but uncomfortable and undignified for everyone involved.

"It's just not me," Rose repeated. It was a core fact she knew
about herself. She didn't have any desire to be intimate with
someone she wasn't in a relationship with. If there was any part
of her that was able to imagine herself down on her knees,
hands braced over Tom's bare thighs, it was the same part of
herself that had once believed they'd live happily ever after.

Snowy made another grunt of dismay.

"Rose. Can I call you Rosie? We're calling you Rosie online.
So don't get offended," she began. This was a thing people said
before they said something offensive. "But have you thought
about being someone else for a little while? Who cares who you
are most days? Today you're making curtains. Tomorrow you
could be Tomboy's third."

The isolation out here in Tisbury in winter was getting to

Rose if the fangirls were starting to make sense. Somehow these were presented as equally valid choices for how she should spend the afternoon. Curtains. Spit-roasting with Meteor Man.

"I'm not sure this is what I bring to the table," she mumbled. If this was what Tom was interested in, he was probably going to be disappointed. While he'd been out having interesting sex with famous people, Rose had been practicing serial monogamy and building a 401(k). If Tom missed clean sheets and food in the fridge, Rose understood what she had to offer. If he expected her to be the sex goddess in the picture, she wasn't sure she could keep up. "What if I look ridiculous?"

"Tom and Boyd get to take ridiculous roles," Snowy said. "I'm his biggest stan, but I think we can all agree Boyd shouldn't have been cast as young Henry Kissinger if J. J. Abrams really wanted that Oscar. But he still tried!"

This struck Rose as an unexpectedly convincing argument. Tom did get to be other people on a regular basis. He got to be a different person now, while Rose still felt like she was the same person she'd been since she was eight years old, searching anxiously for the thing she could do that would make people love her.

Rose took another look at the picture. *Maybe it's a metaphor for the female gaze*, she thought, almost deliriously. Some anonymous artist who was taken with the idea that a famous movie star had fallen in love with the unknown stage actor who saved his life had decided to bestow their fantasy on Rose. Some fantasy version of her was getting exactly what she wanted: a big hand curving over her hip, or one cupping her cheek—okay, good—but there was also the rapt expression on Tom's face.

Someone had imagined him looking at her instead of Boyd, his face suffused with desire. Rose could almost imagine it too.

"You don't have to stop anyone from posting about it," Rose told Snowy. Sure, why not let people imagine that Rose, Tom, and Boyd were living in polyamorous bliss. Flattering, really. "It's just as likely as Tom and the hockey stick."

18

The dinner dishes were cleared away, and Rosie had delivered final orders to prepare for the next day's work. Tom, Boyd, and Ximena were sitting around the great oaken table, which had been reserved for grown-ups during Tom's previous visits to the inn.

"But why does she cook like a 1970s housewife from Minnesota with eight children," the Great Puffin whined to Tom as she reviewed Rose's detailed instructions for preparing the next day's menu: bread pudding, glazed carrots, and baked ziti.

"You're lucky to eat like one of Rosie's eight hardy prairie children," Tom said, because Rosie had several times planned the dinner menu around the palate of Seth's toddler, only for her cousin to beg off at the last minute. If he didn't come tomorrow, Tom was going to *get* him.

Tom was still not wild about the number of barely legal girls roaming around the inn, but as Boyd had been a model of restraint and they were certainly at no risk of exploitation by

Tom, he had to admit they'd been surprisingly handy so far, and not just at eating the food Rosie had planned to serve her delinquent family. The whole place had been patched, primed, and painted; Boyd was prepared to start cleaning the gutters tomorrow; and the fangirls apparently knew how to sew, so the window treatments were being replaced and the linens repaired. Big progress! But it also brought into focus that Tom himself had not been getting anything done.

"Can we at least have something with seasoning?" the Great Puffin begged. "I can take a turn cooking."

Tom looked at the kitchen. Rosie was in there baking sunbutter cookies. She'd been very quiet all through dinner, but in a way that was more thoughtful than hostile. Tom couldn't tell if she'd noticed that he had nothing to show for his whole day's effort.

"Okay, okay, fine," Tom said, tearing a sheet of scrap paper from one of the notebooks. "I'll write down some things Rosie isn't allergic to. Don't get anything else. First person who brings a tree nut or an avocado into this building gets fed to the turkeys."

Boyd nodded at Tom's warning, impressed, even though Rosie had prepared and served him a *special* dinner of two whole roast chickens and grilled zucchini, which was on the list of forbidden foods.

Tom would never have asked Rosie to cook him something she couldn't eat, but Boyd had beamed at her and praised her cooking and made her smile and everyone else coo. The big dork.

After all the girls had cleared out, Tom looked back at his

laptop, where he'd opened the budget spreadsheet Rosie had prepared before her arrival.

The amount allotted to the roof sounded like a big number, but as Tom had spent many hours on the phone with the insurance company and various roofers over the past couple of weeks, he'd learned that this number was deceptive. The inn's roof was fifteen years old, and it needed to be replaced due to the storm damage. According to the claims adjuster, it had only ever been a "twenty-year roof." Tom wasn't sure what happened when roofs turned twenty: Did they pack their bags and move to the city, leaving the bunk room exposed to the heavens? Did they retire? Did they simply vanish? But per the insurance company's calculus, they only owed Rosie a check for 25 percent of a roof.

Tom was having difficulty procuring 25 percent of a roof. Roofers did not want to install 25 percent of a roof. They were in the business of installing entire roofs. Tom had asked whether they might install 25 percent of the roof and allocate those new shingles to the portions of the roof that leaked. He had asked whether they might buy shingles for the entire roof, install some small portion of them, and teach Tom to lay the remainder. No luck so far.

He was from Florida. Roofing was in his blood. He would just have to figure it out, he thought gloomily, deciding to copy and paste the painting budget and add it to the roof budget, the concept moving through his resistant brain like a marshmallow through Jell-O salad.

"What color do you want to have the outdoor trim painted?" Ximena asked, sliding some paint chips across the table.

"Rosie said she wanted it to be pink. Pink like flamingos," Boyd rumbled.

Oh, now she was *Rosie* to him, Tom thought with a glower.

"This is a classic Cape Cod–style building," Ximena objected. "Pink trim's for the Victorian gingerbread cottages up in Oak Bluffs. You can do white, eggshell, or ecru here. I'd go with ecru. It'll wear best."

"Did she really say flamingo pink?" Tom asked Boyd.

"Yeah. She said she wanted to do the same color as the interior of the little place you two are staying," Boyd said. "Her vision is feminine but playful."

"Then we'll do flamingo," Tom said.

Ximena made a noise of exasperation. "I thought you asked me to come out here to apply my good taste and sophistication," she objected. "It'll look weird with pink trim."

"Do it how she wants," Tom said, pulling back in his chair. "If her family doesn't like it, I'll just tell them I screwed that up too."

Tom's tone was perhaps sharper than he'd intended, and the other two fell silent.

Boyd was the first to move. He put one of his big paws on Tom's knee. "You're not screwing this up," he said sincerely. "Everyone sees you working really hard."

Which was all well and good, but Rosie probably planned to lodge her future dairy-fed children in an inn with a roof.

She came out of the kitchen just then carrying a tray of cookies and a wooden trivet. She set them down on the center of the table and waited for due expressions of admiration.

"I made them with honey instead of sugar, so they should

be lower on the glycemic index," she told Boyd, who gave her a doting expression and immediately shoved a cookie into his mouth, the first dessert Tom had ever seen him consume.

"Is the honey—?" Tom began to ask, putting his most appealing expression on.

"Yes, it's *local* honey," Rosie said.

Tom grinned at her and took a cookie for himself. She was coming around on his trash honey. The cookie was delicious, of course, because if Rosie decided to do a thing, she decided to do it perfectly.

Tom shut the laptop when he saw her leaning in to squint at his budget spreadsheet. Instead, he stuck out his arm, realizing only after he'd extended it that he couldn't assume Rosie would let him put his arm around her, especially in front of Boyd and the others.

Please do not leave me hanging, I will feel like such an asshole, he thought, and thank God, she moved to stand next to his chair. Tom gratefully turned his cheek against the round swell of her stomach and took advantage of a brief moment of peace with Rosie in his arms where she belonged.

"Mm. What do you want to do tonight?" he asked.

She hesitated, and he tilted his head up to see her catch her lower lip between her teeth. Her body was pressed against him, but surprisingly tense.

"We're done for the day, right?" he prompted her.

"Yes. It's looking fantastic. Thank you," she said, even though Tom couldn't claim any credit for the work that had been done today.

"Do you want to have game night?" Tom threw out, and

Rosie stilled, obviously interested. "I found the board game pile in the bunk room. Most of it survived the hurricane. Monopoly's a loss"—this was a lie; Tom just hated Monopoly—"but we could do Scattergories? Cards Against Humanity? Apples to Apples?" Tom thought he was being very generous to offer to play party games in which there was no possibility of him singing.

"Um," said Rosie. For some reason, her cheeks were bright pink. "I, um, I think I might just turn in early today?" She made this a question directed at him, even though she hadn't run her schedule by him up to this point. And it wasn't even eight o'clock yet.

"You don't want to do anything?" Tom asked, surprised. Rosie wasn't typically the first one to call it an evening.

"I . . . no."

"Are you feeling okay?" he asked, because if Rosie was skipping game night, she probably had tuberculosis or something. The seductive rattle of plastic tiles against cardboard had been one of the few sounds he could use to lure Rosie out of a finals-season despair spiral. He leaned up to put a hand on her forehead, but she dodged. She met his gaze, eyes wide and nervous.

"No, no, I'm good. Just going to bed early." Her throat moved as she swallowed. She gave tight smiles to Boyd and Ximena. "Good night." She ran her fingers through the loose ends of Tom's hair in a familiar way, then turned to go.

He sat back in such a funk of disappointment that for several minutes after Rosie left he didn't notice that everyone else was looking at him.

"Jeez, no wonder you're divorced," Ximena said.

Boyd giggled, then covered it with a hand.

"What?" Tom demanded.

Ximena rolled her eyes. "For a decent actor, you're sure missing a lot of cues."

"What cues?" he said.

"I think she wanted you to go with her," Boyd said from behind the hand he had clasped over his mouth.

Tom wheeled around as though the door through which Rosie had gone would tell him something.

"Are you sure?" he asked.

Ximena snorted in the way of smug married people, which was a lot less charming than when he'd been a smug married person himself. She made a shooing gesture with her hands.

"We'll see you tomorrow. Go make your wife yell happy yells."

She and Boyd were now widely grinning, marveling at Tom's confusion. Tom hesitated, trying to imagine what he'd possibly done today that would make him seem sexually appealing.

"Do you want me to ask her if that's what she meant?" Boyd offered, seeing Tom's hesitation.

Do you want to do it with Tom? Yes/No (Circle one)

"I'll just check on her," Tom announced. He stood up, head spinning like he'd tossed back a shot of something high proof. Why was he always the last one to know what Rosie wanted? He stalked off with his ears burning.

The windows of the cottage were dark when Tom reached the front door. He rapped quietly, just in case Rosie had actually gone to bed, but it was unlocked, and he heard her voice inside. She'd only turned on the single overhead bathroom light, so she was a silhouette by the suitcase rack.

Even though she'd told him to come in, she straightened up as though startled. She pulled her hands back from the suitcase she was going through, one he hadn't seen her unpack. When he drew closer, he recognized both the fabric at the top of the stack and the wide-eyed expression on Rosie's face. The fabric was lace on satin, shimmering even in the low light, the top of a pile that also held black mesh, silk, and velvet. The expression—he knew that one from other nights he'd spent with her.

"Oh," he said softly, putting two fingertips on something with tiny ruffles. "Were you going to put that on for me?"

Rosie's lips pressed together, eyes big and uncertain. "Maybe?" she said.

Tom walked his fingers along the edge of the garment. He wasn't sure what it was called. Rosie had always liked lingerie, in theory at least, but he understood that the stuff was expensive. She used to spend a few minutes looking at fantastic, lacy things online, add them to her shopping cart, and then quickly close her browser window.

"I'd like to see it on you," he said in his mildest voice, proud of the way he enunciated without choking on the rush of desire that was drying his mouth out.

". . . okay," Rosie said, with just a tiny flash of pink as she licked her lips. She looked at the pink toile chaise, which faced away from the bathroom, and made a little gesture toward it. "Go sit down."

Tom took direction well, and he went readily. He collapsed

into his seat, mind unmoored at this sudden change of fortune, and leaned back with his eyes closed to savor the rustling noises behind him. Fabric sliding across skin. Little snaps being fixed over Rosie's small, curvy form.

He spread his arms across the back of the seat when he heard Rosie's bare feet on the floorboards tiptoeing around to stand between his spread knees.

"Tell me when," he said, eyes still closed.

Her breath made a small shift in the air, in and out. "When."

He opened his eyes and paused on his own inhale. He hadn't been sure what he was looking at in the suitcase, but this was a whole outfit: a black net bustier that wrapped Rosie's curves and supported her round breasts with velvet-covered wires, then a short skirt that traced her hips and clipped to thigh-high stockings edged with the same black lace that formed her skimpy underwear. He was going to have a hell of a time figuring out how to get it off her, which he both wanted to do immediately and wanted to avoid doing at all if there was any creative way of working around it.

She was just an arm's length away, and he'd instinctively reached out for her, but he limited himself to resting fingertips on her hips and brushing his thumbs over the little satin ribbons that held everything together.

"Oh my God," he said. "Jesus Christ. You look so fucking pretty, Rosie."

Tom had been more eloquent in his life, but never as sincere, and his words moved a little of the uncertainty off her face. He put his knees together so that he could urge her onto his lap, the whole warm, soft weight of her.

"Mm," he hummed, burying his face against a bare spot over her collarbone, then kissing his way up her honey-scented neck. "I could have worn something better if I'd known I'd see this on you."

Rosie tilted her face to look at his ratty T-shirt and lifted the hem with one fingertip. "You look pretty good in nothing though," she suggested.

"I can pull off nothing," Tom agreed, leaning back to peel his shirt off and toss it away. Rosie sighed and put her palms against his chest when it was bare, and the expression of admiration on her face was worth at least half the hours he'd spent on the goddamn medieval torture device to get into this shape.

He leaned up to kiss her again, which had the side effect of pulling her flush against his lap, her warm, lace-wrapped body rolling directly over his hardening cock. His lips were already open when they pressed against hers, but she was sweet about kissing him back, giving him just the corners and edges of her mouth before she finally opened to him. His tongue slid along hers while his hands pulled her closer against him.

The feel of her under his hands left him giddy and intoxicated. He didn't know how this had happened to him, but he wasn't wasting this opportunity to kiss her as much as he wanted to.

"Should we take this upstairs?" he asked breathlessly, when his lips started to feel swollen and bruised. He had no objection to the chaise or any other piece of furniture that caught Rosie's fancy, but he'd have more room to maneuver around various strips of lace on the bed. Reacquaint his hands and mouth with every precious inch of her.

Rosie's eyes were glittering over flushed cheeks, and she hesitated before she answered.

"I thought maybe we *could* play a game," she said.

He thought she was teasing him.

"I don't think I can do enough math for Yahtzee right now," he said. "Even naked Twister would be pushing it." He kissed the tops of her breasts where they were pushed close to his face. Yeah, this thing should stay on.

Rosie shook her head, black curls brushing bare shoulders.

"I meant a game like—um. Bad secretary and the horny billionaire who never got HR training." Her cheeks flamed even brighter as she spoke in a rush.

"Oh," Tom said, surprised. "I . . . guess I've heard of that one?" He didn't know which role he was supposed to play; it wasn't like he'd never heard of gender norms, but if Rosie ever decided to be a secretary, she'd be a really good secretary, and who'd ever imagine Tom as the rich asshole?

He looked around the room, trying to imagine what she meant. "Am I supposed to make you coffee or spank you over the desk?"

He couldn't spank her, actually—Rosie bruised like a peach. If he spanked her, by tomorrow she'd look like she'd been in a car accident. Did she mean she wanted him to put on cologne and a nicer shirt?

"Maybe later," Rosie said, seeming to gather a little more courage. "I thought that—well, I thought I could start like this?" She rolled off his lap, then slid down to the floor, positioning herself on her knees and leaning up against his. Tom now had an idea of where things were going, but it was so close to a number of very unlikely fantasies he'd entertained over the past couple of weeks that he didn't do anything to assist beyond sucking in his stomach when Rosie unbuttoned the fly of his loose, tattered jeans.

He barely breathed, already dizzy with expectation and unable to think of a single thing he could say that wouldn't wrongly suggest he thought he deserved this. Where had this come from? What did he do?

Rosie pulled his cock out of his boxers with careful hands and propped her elbows on his thighs as though making herself comfortable. Tom caught himself about to close his eyes again and forced them open, because this was the very best sight in the world.

No matter how Rosie filled his arms, she was built on a base of delicate little bird bones, and she had small, delicate hands and a round, delicate mouth. The contrast of either one wrapped around the taut head of his cock was the hottest fucking view imaginable, one that always made him feel like a demigod.

The back of his head hit the back of the chaise at the first warm brush of her tongue. He was going to lose it in about thirty seconds. Time to think about baseball. The national debt. The missing insulation at the southwest corner of the roof.

When he lifted his head, Rosie was looking at him expectantly, and he remembered that he was supposed to be playing a role.

"Um, you're a bad secretary," he said, because he hadn't practiced his lines. "And you're going to have to work late collating things. Overtime."

The curve of Rosie's lips where they were wrapped around him convinced him he was going to have to dig deeper into his improv abilities.

"Keep going," she encouraged him, pulling off only long enough to press him against smiling lips before wrapping one fist around his base and leaning back in. This was the best thing that had ever happened to him.

"I'm an evil billionaire," Tom declared. "I spend all my time doing white-collar crimes and staring at your ass. But that's okay, because I work out."

Rosie's mouth felt like magic, like every good and sweet thing he'd ever wanted. This was going to be over *very* soon, and then he just had to hope Rosie understood that he wasn't eighteen anymore and he'd need a union-length break before he was ready to bend her over any imaginary copy machines.

"Dictation," he muttered. "Imagine I just made a really good dictation pun."

He couldn't concentrate enough to keep up the game. The tight, wet slide of Rosie's mouth wiped all conscious thought from the surface of his mind. He kept speaking anyway. He'd heard from more than one lover that he was a talker. Rosie had never minded, because the only things that he ever managed to say were compliments (*Your tits are so hot, the best in the entire world*), blasphemy (*Oh God, oh fuck, Rosie, please*), and forward-looking statements (*I'm going to come in your mouth*).

Rosie stopped abruptly and sat back. The shock of the cool air on his wet cock had Tom sitting straight up in discomfort, wondering what the hell he'd done wrong now.

"Are you still playing?" Rosie whispered, eyes worried.

What had he said? It had all been pure stream of consciousness. *Rosie, nobody does this like you, please, Rosie, I love you—*

That wasn't the line she'd been looking for?

Tom pressed a palm to his muddled head. He should have volunteered for Bad Secretary and gotten on *his* knees. His body throbbed with thwarted desire. "You can*not* expect me to stay in character while—Jesus, Rosie, Sir Kenneth Branagh himself couldn't stay in character with your mouth on his cock."

"I didn't mean—" she said, shoulders tensing. "I just meant you didn't have to say that."

Tom groaned and yanked his jeans and underwear back up over his hips. Served him right for sitting back on the couch to get his dick sucked like a king when he'd been begging her for weeks just to let him sleep upstairs with her. *And, scene. Let's take that from the top. Put in a little effort this time, Tomasz.*

"You're in a position that allows for too much heavy thinking," he told her. "Let's go upstairs. I have some better ideas."

He'd never thought the act where they got back together would start with Rosie on her knees in front of him, dressed like a wrapped present.

She sucked her lower lip into her mouth, obviously still wondering if she should shut things down. Tom stood up and hauled her up to her feet too, hoping to intercept any more thinky thoughts. He kissed her swollen mouth and swept her hair out of her face with his palms. "Okay?" he prompted her.

"Your ideas. Right," she said, seeming to calm down. "I thought that maybe this could be—an opportunity. To try some new stuff. So that's good."

"Uh?" Tom said. He thought he and Rosie had done it just about every way two people with their anatomy could do it, in the spirit of mutual discovery, and he'd also thought he'd gotten a pretty good handle on which ways she liked.

She put her hands back on his chest, smoothing the line of dark hair down his stomach in an appreciative way. "If there was ever anything you felt like you couldn't do—let's try it now. You know. Get it out of our systems."

Tom left his hands framing her face as he tried to pry instructions out of that. "Out of our systems?"

"I mean, we can see how it goes," she said, apparently under the impression she was being encouraging, even though he didn't like the sound of that at all. "Maybe it'll be fun. To stretch some boundaries. But if it's not, at least we'll know, right?"

Tom now had no idea what she was talking about. He hadn't ever thought there was a problem with the sex they'd had, only the sex they hadn't had. Her soft blue eyes searched his, and he wished he knew what she was looking for.

Tom put his most charming expression on his face. Jesus Christ, no pressure, right? Just go upstairs and rail her so good that she decides it's worth ever doing again. And make it new. And different. With zero specifics.

He swatted Rosie lightly on the rear and urged her toward the ladder. "Whatever you say, babe."

19

Tom had always been a giver. Patient. Open-minded. Devoted to the ideal of orgasm parity. Rose had never talked about their sex life with anyone else, but even in the politely repressed community of Boston College, she'd heard enough complaints about other men to know that this attitude wasn't something to take for granted. She'd known she was really lucky that the first person she'd ever slept with—the person she thought would be the only person she'd ever sleep with—put in a lot of effort.

Still, Rose couldn't imagine that with her encouragement to do whatever he wanted tonight, the absolute top items on Tom's priority list were kissing his way along the line of her high-top stockings, followed by twenty to twenty-five minutes of oral sex.

It wasn't like Tom had ever had a routine or anything that basic, but on occasions when he felt like extra effort was called for—her birthday, their anniversary, midterms—there was a certain way he'd begin, and she'd think to herself, *Oh, Tom's feeling romantic tonight.* That's how things were going. But Rose was caught in a muddle of familiar arousal and heart-piercing confusion.

"This isn't make-up sex," she told him as he covered her breast with one big careful hand.

"If you say so," he murmured, letting his lips just graze the lace edges of her bustier. He was propped up over her in the bed, supporting almost all of his weight on his forearms. All he'd done was run his hands over her body—big, sweeping caresses and gentle kisses—even though she could feel him still hard as a rock through the denim of his jeans.

"Because it feels like you're trying to have make-up sex," she said. "And you don't have to do that."

She should have given Tom the script in advance. Or at least the artwork. He was undoing the clasps of her garters one by one, fingers soothing the little red marks where the metal clasps had dug into her thighs, and Rose felt like she was going to jump out of her skin.

She took a deep breath. "I'm sure you can tell it's been a while for me," she said, trying to understand where he was coming from, "but it would actually help me get out of my head if you'd act a little less like my confusingly besotted ex, and a little more like a guy I just dragged home from a bar."

"What's confusing?" Tom asked, lifting his head from her skin. His fingers swept up her inner thigh but lingered just outside of the lace borders of her underwear. If he was thinking of edging her, they were *really* not on the same wavelength.

"I thought this would go a little different," she said, still trying to sound encouraging. "Like, faster."

Tom finally brushed a knuckle across her core, a mildly skeptical expression on his face.

"Babe, you're vibrating like a tuning fork. I assume the losers you drag home from bars don't care about that, but—"

"How do you know they're losers?" Rose grumbled, even though she'd never brought someone home from a bar in her life, and he was right about how tense she was.

"Well, because I'm here with you now, aren't I?" he said, sounding pretty smug for someone with his pants still on.

That's why I am confused. This? This was exactly what she'd had to offer before. Sure, she hadn't owned nice lingerie, and she'd never been part of some collective fantasy on the Internet. But any night of their marriage, he could have come home and had exactly this.

This couldn't be what he wanted.

Rose decided to take matters into her own hands, and she tried to put a hand on his matters, but he shifted his hips back and out of reach.

When she wrinkled her nose at him, Tom finally grunted and undid the fly on his jeans. He took out his wallet and produced a condom from the otherwise empty billfold. Noticing her disapproving look, he flipped it over it for her inspection.

"Not latex," he promised.

Rose's relationship with condoms was just as long but even more complicated than her relationship with Tom.

"Do you get tested? I finally found a pill that doesn't make me sick," she said, hoping to cut short what was usually a longer talk.

"I get tested all the time," he said. "But I don't mind wearing a condom."

"I believe you," Rose said, trying to flick it off the bed. He caught it.

"What, did someone else screw up and buy the wrong ones?" he said, managing a small smirk.

Yes, someone had, even though *I'm allergic to everything* was one of the first things anyone learned about her.

"Which is why I'm on the pill," Rose said. This conversation had not previously involved so much persuasive effort on her part. She used her foot to shimmy out of her stockings. She began unhooking the rest.

Tom screwed his mouth to the side. "Babe, I've done it raw like five times in my entire life, all of which *you should remember*, and I'm a little keyed up right now. Do you want to have thirty seconds of sex?"

Rose growled in aggravation. It seemed increasingly unlikely they'd be having any sex at all.

"I just—please, Tom. Let's do something different. I thought it would be different."

"Different how?" he asked, letting a little of his own worry into his voice. It was a reasonable question, but Rose's interior swirl of frustrated desire and fear couldn't articulate that she wished they were two different people entirely.

So instead, she said, "I don't know, maybe the mean billionaire thing. Pull my hair. Call me names. Jesus, I don't know. You haven't done that at least once?"

"Are you seriously into the rough stuff now?" Tom asked, and although his tone was light, there was an edge of skepticism that made Rose stiffen her shoulders because she *could have been*, maybe, for all he knew, she had fifty different floggers back at her apartment and a Saint Andrew's cross in her breakfast nook.

"Act like I am," she said, trying to sound like she was confident in that request. "I mean it. Rail me so hard I see sound and taste colors."

She rolled onto her stomach, even though the position left her feeling even more bare and exposed. It got the point across, she thought.

Tom put one hand on the back of her thigh and waited. Probably for her to say she was kidding.

"If you say so." His tone wasn't convinced, but he pulled her underwear over her hips and tossed them away. Her body felt like a taut wire, one filled with enough current to spark and ignite. Something was going to snap tonight, she was sure of it.

Tom put a palm against the hollow of her back and swept it down a few inches, but the movement was more soothing than authoritative. When he took a step closer and leaned over her, she thought he'd gotten on board with the idea, but then she felt his lips press tenderly against her shoulder as he curled his body around hers.

"Tom," she warned him, heart aching.

"Don't you want me to go down on you or something first?" he asked against her skin, letting her feel just the edge of his top teeth against the muscle in her neck. His hard cock pressed against the back of her thigh through his jeans, a lot more eager than the rest of him to do what she was asking.

"No," she said, thinking that a little burn, a little imperfection, a little pain might trick her brain into thinking this wasn't the same person she'd slept with hundreds of times. She risked a look back over her shoulder, saw that Tom's expression was growing even more uncertain.

Tom's lower lip pressed against his teeth as he slowly slid his hand up her back to tangle in the hair at her nape. He caught a handful of her curls in his fingers. Rose closed her eyes when he closed his fist, but her breath caught involuntarily at a firmer pull of his hand. He let go.

When she opened her eyes, Tom was half a step farther away. He shoved both hands into his pockets.

"I would pull your hair and spit in your mouth if you thought that was hot," he said with shadowed eyes. "If I thought you actually wanted that, I'd do it. But if you're asking me to pretend like I'm not in love with you, I don't think I'm that good of an actor."

Rose covered her face with her hands and curled her knees up to one side. This had been the worst idea she'd ever had. Why had she thought she could get away with this? This wasn't her.

The mattress bounced as Tom lay down next to her, fingers gently trying to pry her hands away from her face.

"It just feels a little unhealthy," he told her. He interwove his hands with hers, holding them tense between their bodies. "Different proposal. How about tonight we just do the things I *know* you enjoy? I call you nothing but nice words, I'm allowed to kiss you whenever I feel like it, we both come, we both cry . . . and if you still want me to bruise your ass afterward, we do that tomorrow?"

"It won't work," Rose mumbled.

"Why not?" Tom laughed, the sound forced. "Babe, I know how it *works*. I remember real well how it *works*."

"You can't think we are going to have frilly, floofy, emotional sex. Like, we look into each other's eyes and declare our undying love for each other from the missionary position? That sounds like a performance. Who are we trying to convince?"

"I mean, it doesn't have to be cheesy or anything," he said in a mildly incredulous tone. "But I think I could make you feel *very* loved, in the right position."

Rose made an unhappy noise in the back of her throat. Telling him felt much more exposing than bending over the mattress and asking for him to make it hurt a little, because it felt like asking for everything he hadn't given her and could never go back in time and give her.

"I want you not to have been in love with me," she said. "You weren't. You aren't. Stop saying you are."

"That sounds like a real bad game, Rosie," he said cautiously.

"I'm not trying to play a game. I don't get it. Why you want to act like it was all flowers and romance. Or why you're interested in that now. I'm not saying there was none of that ever, but we ended with you walking out of my life like it meant *nothing* to you."

His dark eyes widened in surprise. "I didn't walk. You *threw me out*—"

"We had *one* fight, and after that you never came home again. You couldn't treat someone you loved like that."

Her body felt tight and trembly, because all the adrenaline and desire and anger were mixed up together with no outlet.

She could have clawed the sheets or his shoulders, but he wouldn't do just this one thing she'd asked of him.

"We don't have to have been in love," she said. "It's fine that we weren't. That's why we got divorced. But that means we aren't now either."

She looked up at the ceiling, because the plan had been to get spectacularly laid, not to cry, and she didn't want to deviate from the plan any more than necessary.

She heard Tom's reluctant exhale as he propped himself up on an elbow. She flinched away from that and made a first move to roll over and start looking for her clothes. His hand on her shoulder pulled her back.

"No. You can't go. Because here's the thing, Rosie—I'm in love with you. I was always in love with you. We were in love. And I wish that meant we couldn't ever hurt each other, but I think you know it doesn't work like that. It doesn't work like that for anyone. So, yeah. I treated you badly. But I always loved you."

She tried to squirm away, but Tom kept his gentle grip on her wrists. Oh, *now* he was comfortable holding her down.

"That's not what love means," Rose insisted. "If you were in love with me, you would have tried to fix things *then*, not now."

Tom adjusted his hands on her skin, checking that he wasn't putting more pressure than necessary to keep her from getting away. Apparently satisfied, he leaned in. Rose tilted her chin away under the impression he was trying to kiss her, but he wasn't.

"I should've," he admitted from only a couple of inches

away. "And I didn't. I've got a dozen explanations and excuses—I was angry, I was embarrassed, and you'd always made all the decisions, so I thought you'd just call and tell me when I could come home—but I don't think the *why* of it really matters at this point." He pressed his forehead hard against hers and smooshed the tips of their noses together, ignoring Rose's pained grimace.

"We were only twenty-two. We were young and stupid, and we didn't know what we were doing." He held her gaze from so close that she couldn't even focus.

"We are just going to have to forgive each other," he said directly into her face.

After that announcement, Tom released her and sat all the way back on his heels, relaxing his shoulders and nodding as though he'd delivered a great and important truth. That was it?

Rose sputtered. "What?"

"Yep," he said, brushing his tangled hair back out of his face. "You're just going to have to forgive me. And yourself too, Rosie. For everything you said. You told me you hated me! I never really thought you meant it, but I did wonder for a decade if I had ruined your life. You can't feel good about having said that, so you're going to have to forgive yourself while you're forgiving me too."

She had to blink hard as she worked through that, not sure if she needed to be outraged.

"Why do I *have* to?" she said as her first response, instinctively objecting to any commands.

"Well, most urgently because, Jesus, look at us. We are so hot. We could be fucking right now," Tom said, forcing a smile to his mouth, even though it didn't reach his eyes. "But more importantly, because I think you want to."

He held the position, let her look at him. There was space for her to respond if she wanted to, but she could tell he didn't expect an immediate answer. She licked her lips, unsure whether she ought to test his commitment to either proposition.

She must have waited too long to speak, because Tom wrinkled his nose as he slid his legs off the bed. "Be right back."

"Wait, where are you going?" Rose demanded. Running away in the middle of the conversation was hardly persuasive if he wanted her to think he'd meant what he said.

"I'm going to take a cold shower," he said. He gestured at his lap, and when Rose did the math on how long he'd been hard, she did actually feel bad for him.

Tom ruined it when he put his feet on the ladder and dramatically frowned to himself. "Actually, you know what? I didn't do anything wrong tonight. I'm going to take a hot shower. I'm going to jerk off."

Rose's shocked intake of breath turned into an involuntary snort, making Tom laugh at her. She looked for something to toss at him, but he ducked out of view.

"I'm going to imagine we're doing it *respectfully*," he taunted her. *"Emotionally."*

"Go fuck yourself," Rose moaned, grabbing a pillow too late to catch him before he made it to the floor. She threw it after him anyway.

"That's the idea," he agreed. "Baby, you are going to be so sweet to me in my head. See you in a few."

I hate you. She opened her mouth to say it, but he was

right: she'd never meant it, she wished she'd never said it, and she couldn't say it now. So she didn't say anything. Instead, she grabbed another pillow and pulled it over her own head. She yelled into it, which did make her feel a little better, but not as much as the exotic, cathartic sex she'd spent all day thinking about would have.

After a minute, she heard the shower turn on, then the rattle of the glass stall door closing. No singing this time, even though she leaned out of bed to listen for it. Knowing Tom, at least half of what he'd said was bluster, and he had the shakes now.

And look, so did she. Her hands were trembling. It was that fight-or-flight system, she guessed. Telling her to do *something* when she was still just curled up naked in bed. Run away. Go down and yell at Tom for leaving her in a lurch. Go down and get in the shower with him.

Most of her clothes were on the living room floor, but her underwear was up here at least. Putting it back on didn't feel like she was making a choice, not the way going downstairs would be.

After this long, she ought to know what the right choice was. She wasn't twenty-two anymore. She ought to be able to decide what she wanted. But she remembered being twenty-two so clearly: miserable and alone in their bed, wishing Tom would come home—just not enough to call him and ask. It was ridiculous, she thought from the benefit of distance, how the thing she'd wanted most in the world was for Tom to come home without having to ask him. That wasn't the right thing to want *most*.

She wanted to forgive herself the way people forgave children: because they didn't know any better. She wanted to be sure that she did know better now, but she *wasn't* sure. So she just curled up again, stuck in the quicksand of her emotions, waiting for Tom.

Possibly he'd get out of the shower and sit down to watch some TV, she thought with dread. Then she'd have to either lurk alone in the loft like Mr. Rochester's attic wife or climb down the ladder in her underwear. She felt nearly nauseous at the thought of doing either. What if he just went to sleep afterward? What would she do then?

This time, though, Tom did come back. After his standard half-hour shower, he got out, toweled off in an unhurried way, and found a clean pair of boxers in his duffel bag. He checked the locks and turned off the bathroom light. Then he climbed back up the ladder as though he'd faced no similar crisis of decision.

"Oh, Rosie," he said when he spotted her in her defensive ball, attitude deflating. She put her pillow over her head and turned her back to him, defiant. "C'mere," he coaxed her.

He crawled across the bed to her and wormed his body under the covers, still damp from the shower. He kissed her shoulder again, then her jaw, just under her ear. She clenched into a tighter ball in response.

"I forgot to say the other part of it," he said, wrapping both arms around her so that she was half lying on his chest. He pulled at her knees and elbows until she unfurled like a nervous hedgehog, limbs still tense. "There's more."

"More? If you had a bunch of shit figured out, you should have shared it with me," she said unevenly.

"I always forget you don't know everything," he said into her skin. "But I think it's important you hear this. Just psyching myself up. Ready? Okay. Here it goes. I won't do it again."

Rose hadn't expected any specific words, but the short declaration still took her by surprise. "Do what?"

Tom exhaled against her neck, voice emerging rough and gravely. "I thought *I won't do it again* before I even knew what. I just knew that whatever I'd done, I'd *stop* if it meant you'd take me back. But I get it now. I know I wasn't there for you, and I should have been. If you let me, I will be. I promise."

Her sinuses burned, because that might have been enough if he'd said it eleven years ago. If she'd thought he meant it. It might have been as easy as that.

But now she knew not just that they were capable of hurting each other but that they were capable of not speaking to each other for ten years. Now she had to forgive not just twenty-two-year-old them but the two of them that existed before the first of the year: two people who could have fixed things but hadn't.

"Okay." She couldn't get any more words out.

But she meant, *Okay, I'll try to forgive us both.*

Okay, I believe you mean it.

Okay, everyone was right, and I am thinking about getting back together with you.

"Okay?" Tom confirmed, wrapping an arm over her stomach.

She tucked her chin into her chest and nodded, her body still electrified and unsteady.

"What's wrong?" Tom said when she didn't relax.

She didn't answer, but she squirmed. She was still in her underwear and bits of lingerie, and she needed to get changed and possibly take a hot shower of her own. She'd spent the entire day telling herself she was going to wipe all conflicted feelings about Tom from her mind by having elaborate sex with him, and now she wished she'd just taken him up on the straightforward orgasms and crying.

"Oh," Tom said, finally realizing her exact emotional state. His arms wrapped her tighter against him. He trailed his lips from her neck down to her shoulder, then left them there as the hand he'd clasped over his own forearm brushed down over her hip.

His palm, pressed against her thigh, fingers pointed in at the seam of her body, was a silent offer.

Rose shifted to lean back against his chest and part her legs in silent acceptance, and he sighed again, finding a more permanent spot to rest his mouth as his fingertips ran once down her thigh in a soothing gesture before moving to the elastic of her underwear.

He didn't take them off, just slipped his big, warm hand inside to cup her intimately. She didn't know if this was meant as a compromise or an olive branch, but she didn't plan to reject the gesture either way. Not after she was certain he'd done exactly as he threatened and jerked off in the shower—probably imagining her sobbing into his neck while she ground down on his lap. Or the kind of half-asleep morning sex you only ever had with someone you woke up with frequently. Tom had especially liked that, the mornings when Rose would tug his heavy, warm body on top of hers before she even had her eyes open then gasp good morning after he'd pressed inside her.

Tonight he barely moved the fingers that lay against her core until she rocked against them, desperate for friction. She wouldn't have blamed him if he'd been tentative, or even if he'd decided to play it a little cute, but as soon as she moved, he moved, sliding two fingertips in a delicate circle.

"I've got you," he murmured, lower lip hot against her neck. Rose relaxed at the implicit command, rolling her face into the warm muscle of his bicep where his arm supported her head. Nobody else would ever know her body as well as he did, because nobody else would have spent so many hours learning it alongside her. He knew how to touch her. He knew the exact tiny motions of his hand to have her arching her feet and whining within moments. He knew the precise moment to slip his fingers inside her body and stroke her tense and aching, the sound among all other sounds she made that meant he should still his wrist and hold her tight until the electric buzz of her orgasm had blurred into softness.

Rose closed her eyes hard against Tom's arm, willing the moment not to be over even as he slowly slid his hand over her inner thigh before replacing it on her chest. He let out a shaky breath—he must have been worried things worked differently now, especially with all the bullshit she'd been saying about pulling her hair.

"Can I stay?" he said into her ear, sooner than she'd have liked.

And that was the question, wasn't it? Could he stay? Would he?

"All these blankets are mine," she deflected.

"I remember," Tom said, making himself comfortable. "But since I just made you come, seems like I should get, like, a short-term sublease on them at least?"

He didn't wait for explicit permission, just grabbed a pillow and stuck it between his chest and her back. This was how sleeping next to Tom worked: he put his elbow on the pillow so that his arm didn't squish her boobs, and she put her feet against his shins so that her toes didn't get cold. If he was holding on to her tighter than he ever had before, she couldn't blame him for that.

"Okay," she said one more time. He relaxed.

"Good night, Rosie. I love you," he said softly.

She wrapped her hands over his and wished this had been every night.

20

The first thing Rose saw when she woke up was the pillow where Tom had slept the night before. She instinctively reached out to touch it, but he'd left long enough ago that it was cool now. Still, unlike all the other mornings she'd woken up to look at an empty pillow next to her, there was no denying he'd slept there. His jeans were still on the floor next to the bed, and the sheets were crumpled.

Rose went down the ladder and looked at the kitchen. He'd left her half a pot of coffee on the burner again and a couple of hard-boiled eggs in the fridge for breakfast.

She hadn't showered the night before, so she went into the bathroom to get ready, scooping up discarded towels off the floor as she went. She looked at the toothpaste and single toothbrush they were apparently sharing as she put on her makeup.

Across the street, the inn was bustling with activity. Boyd was enthusiastically leading the demolition of built-ins down in the basement to make room for the stage. Ximena was headed out to the hardware store with Snowy to get more paint. The Great Puffin was making a chickpea and red onion salad in the spotless kitchen to go with the lunch Rose had planned.

"Oh, I can eat that," Rose said, pleasantly surprised.

"I know," the girl said, pouting dramatically. "Who's allergic to *celery*?"

"Me," said Rose.

"I know," Puff said again, rolling her eyes toward a sheet of paper on the range hood titled *Kills Rosie*. The list was thorough and complete, apples to zucchini. At the bottom of the list was a handwritten addendum, *Safe for Rosie*, in Tom's messy handwriting.

The kitchen smelled like paint where the baseboards and crown molding had been touched up in gleaming white. When Rose imagined the bird-print wallpaper replacing the blue nautical theme, the place looked even brighter in her mind. Her younger brother's oldest kid was six; this summer she'd be old enough to start learning some of the family recipes. Rose's mind cautiously populated the inn. *There are birds now*, she'd tell her family, and they'd just have to deal with that.

"Is Tom here?" Rose asked Puff, who pointed upstairs.

Rose opened doors until she found him in the bathroom of the honeymoon suite. He was carefully applying silicone caulk to the cracks around the window frame, his back to her.

He turned his head to smile at her when she came in, but he didn't stop working. He'd found an ancient battery-powered radio somewhere, and it sat in the open window, turned to the Tisbury community station. It felt like spring today; the tips of the tangled brown branches forming the property line had not yet swollen to bud, but the breeze had a drier, warmer scent to it.

Tom wore a faded yellow T-shirt advertising a charity poker night Rose had organized their junior year. Rose was pretty sure he'd misappropriated this precise shirt from Adrian or Rose at some point, because it stretched across his shoulders, and Rose had ordered them roomy enough to sleep in.

She walked up behind him and pressed her cheek between his shoulder blades, arms not around him but tucked against his broad back. He felt warm and solid, and he smelled familiar. They'd been using the same shampoo and soap and detergent for several loads of laundry now.

"What are you thinking this morning?" she asked.

Tom finished applying a strip of gel before he answered. His tone was thoughtful and impassioned.

"So, I was just thinking that 'Take the Money and Run' doesn't deliver on its narrative promises," Tom told her. "It seems like it's going to be a three-act story, because the beginning is brilliant. Bobbie Sue and Billie Joe are small town kids, there's this call to adventure, and they start robbing houses. Okay, so then the narrator introduces this Billie Mack character. There's a buildup, and we're like, oh no, what will our heroes do? They're on a clear collision course. But then there's no denouement! How *does* Bobbie Sue slip away? The ending image, where they're still running today, it feels unearned. There should have been another verse with a shootout or something. The song's too short. Taylor did it better in 'Getaway Car.'"

"Oh," Rose said, lifting her eyebrows. "Was it on the radio?"

"Yeah, a little earlier," Tom said. He cleaned the nozzle of the caulk gun on a bit of paper towel and ran his fingers down the other edge of the window to check the seal.

The pleasant sounds of the morning filled the ensuing silence. There was the distant, muffled cracking of wood. The plaintive hoots of the turkeys off in the trees. The radio station playing Boomer standards.

"Or did you mean about last night specifically?" Tom asked, as though it had only just occurred to him to have more serious thoughts.

"Yeah."

Tom's big shoulders bunched and relaxed in a half shrug. "I've decided you're cut off from any kinky shit until you get better at getting words from here to here." He craned one arm behind him so he could tap her temple and her lower lip, but his look back was only mildly concerned. "Why, what were *you* thinking?"

Rose swallowed hard, because this wasn't easy. "I think I'm going to move into the suite. Now that the bees are gone, it's just as usable as the rest of the inn, and I'm still afraid we'll get arrested for trespassing."

"Okay," Tom said, looking through the doorway at the empty bedroom. "We can clean out the cottage after lunch."

Rose braced herself. "And I think you should stay in one of the other rooms."

Tom did *not* like that.

"What? What'd I do *now*?" he demanded, eyes going wide with surprised betrayal.

"Nothing," Rose said, putting her hands up on his chest. "You haven't done anything wrong."

"Why am I getting kicked out, then?"

"I'm not kicking you out," she said. She licked her lips. "I'm thinking about whether we should get back together. You know. After . . . after we're both home. What that would look like."

"Isn't that what we've been doing all along?" Tom asked, thick dark brows lowering in confusion.

Rose pressed her lips together. She'd thought they might do any of several different things, but none of them had involved any degree of *back*. She'd buried the dream of Tom as someone she'd spend the rest of her life with so deep that just to name it felt like breaking her own heart again.

She shook her head. Her fingertips snagged in his shirt.

"But is that . . . is that what you really want?" she asked.

Tom's mouth twisted, and he tried to run a hand through his hair, finding it tied back instead.

"I meant what I said at the beginning," he said slowly.

Although it was hard to breathe normally, she tried. She nodded. She'd try to think about it.

"Let's not just fall into things, okay?" she said, trying to sound like she knew what she was doing. "Let's be thoughtful about this. Aware of who we are and what we need to be happy."

Tom sighed. "Okay, Rosie. Okay." He slung an arm around the back of her neck and pulled her in to his chest. "Whatever you think is best." He kissed the part in her hair and left his chin digging into her scalp. She squirmed, but not to get away. It felt heavy and urgent.

"But I just need the same thing I always needed," he said, and she supposed he got to put all his cards on the table too. "You."

Rose closed her eyes and breathed against the V of his collarbones. If this was going to work, they needed to start being honest with each other. Even about the things that scared her.

"I love you too," she said.

21

March

Rose's phone screen displayed a close-up view of Aunt Max's jowls, chin, and pensive expression. The image occasionally shifted to show the ceiling of Max's Watertown condo. On her own side of the video call, Rose arranged her choices in furnishing for Max's approval.

She turned in a slow circle to transmit the video of the main reception area. All of the whaling paraphernalia had been banished, replaced by birdcages painted in bright colors and filled with wooden parrots, feathered hats, and mismatched porcelain bird tchotchkes. The new wallpaper was up. The floors had been refinished. It all smelled like new paint and hot coffee and the casseroles baking in the oven in the next room, which Max couldn't smell from Boston, but which marked the biggest difference from the day Rose and Tom had entered two months ago. It felt lived in.

"Do you like the curtains?" Rose asked when Max didn't immediately respond at the end of the tour. Rose liked the curtains, but this was her first time picking out window treatments. She held her breath until Max nodded once, very firmly.

"It's perfect," Max ruled.

The wave of relief that swept through Rose was so strong as to nearly leave her dizzy. She'd made so many decisions without any good image of what it was all supposed to look like at the end, she'd been afraid of what the rest of her family would think of the result. If they hated it, she knew she'd cry.

"Yeah?" Rose asked, as eager for Max's approval as she'd been at eight years old. "What about the suite? You don't think people will think it's too frilly?"

"What people?" Max asked grumpily. "It's my inn. I don't care what the boys think. Will it all be ready by Thanksgiving?"

"Thanksgiving?" Rose asked, confused. "Don't you want to come before that? Memorial Day? Or the Fourth of July, maybe?"

Seth and his manager had come by yesterday and begrudgingly allowed that the inn might be ready to reopen by the beginning of the season. If they were a little late in opening the place to tourists, that would be fine though. Rose could work out any issues with, say, housekeeping or landscaping while it was just family here.

Max scowled, reorienting herself to the day's date. "Of course I do. Just didn't have a calendar handy." She sat up straighter, and Rose saw that although it was midafternoon, Max was sitting in bed. "I'll come for Memorial Day," she said decisively.

"I'll drive you down," Rose said. She brightened as she imagined it—they could do something like a grand reopening party. Get the whole family here to see all the renovations. Soft-launch her relationship with Tom. That was the right tactic: build up a little goodwill with all the improvements, then casually slip into conversation that Tom had been responsible.

"Where is that handsome boy of yours?" Max demanded, punctuated by a dry cough. "I didn't see him on the tour."

Rose froze. She hadn't mentioned anything about Tom to Max yet. Maybe Seth had said something?

"Ah, you know that Tom and I are . . . working on things?"

"What does that have to do with anything? The little girl who does my hair has been showing me videos. Taken in *my* inn. I can't believe you tried to hide him from me. Go put him on so I can say hello," Max insisted. "Go on, put him on. I promised to show him off for the girls here. They're big fans."

Laughing to herself at how the Tomboys were *everywhere*, Rose went looking for Tom. She found him in the bathroom of the room he'd been sleeping in, supervising Boyd as the other man cut broken tiles out of the shower wall with a grout saw. Tom's face was concealed by clear plastic goggles and a dust mask, and his shaggy hair was pulled back by one of Rose's elastics and covered with a bit of scrap fabric from the new throw cushions.

Rose had noticed his laundry piling up in his bedroom and, as an experiment, decided not to do it for him. Today he'd run out of clean T-shirts and simply borrowed one from Ximena, although it was striped in orange and pink and way too small for him. This was a singular look, but one that was really working for him, highlighting his narrow waist below the impressive expanse of his shoulders.

Here's that handsome boy of mine, Rose thought, wondering if she might be developing a very specific sexual interest in construction workers who were very confident in their gender presentation. She'd ask Snowy if anyone had written that one yet.

"Can you say hi to Aunt Max?" she asked, passing the phone to Tom, who pulled off his dust mask to beam at her, then the phone screen.

"Hellooo," he trilled. "Max, you're looking radiant today."

Max coughed again and waved her hand in front of the screen. "Not you," she said irritably. The video screen zoomed out, revealing the two health aides who were crowded around Rose's aunt in her bedroom. "I've seen you. I want the other one. The big gorgeous hunk from the movies where things blow up. Boyd! That one."

Tom made a face when Rose snickered. She'd forgotten Tom wasn't considered the handsomest boy in the room.

"Do you mind?" Rose asked Boyd, who put down his grout saw and delightedly took the phone from a scowling Tom.

"My niece's husband got me tickets to your premiere," Max announced to Boyd, and that was news to Rose, both that she had a husband and that he'd promised Max theater tickets. "Is the show any good?"

"My agent said the reviews were mixed in the Off Broadway run," Boyd said modestly. "But it was very popular."

"Because it's racy?" Max said eagerly.

"Um," Boyd said, looking at Tom for help. "I suppose there are suggestive themes? And I have my shirt off for most of the second act."

"Wonderful," Max sighed as the nursing aides around her

burst into giggles. "It's a good thing I'm so open-minded. I've always supported the theater. It's just been a couple of years since I've been to New York."

More like five since Max had traveled anywhere except the Vineyard. Max needed a lot of help getting ready in the morning, and that meant Rose always had a health aide or a family member scheduled to assist.

"Where's she going to stay?" she whispered to Tom.

"With us?" Tom said innocently, unveiling a ton of assumptions about Rose's apartment and their future living situation. Oh boy.

Rose made big eyes at him. "Us?"

"In our apartment?" Tom said, recognizing the challenge and not backing down from it.

"*My* one-bedroom apartment in Yorkville?" she said, stressing the singular possessive adjective.

"Oh, is that where it is? You hadn't mentioned," Tom said, innocent tone not matching the devilish sparkle in his eyes. "That'll be convenient. We can take the same train to Midtown."

"It's pretty small," Rose said.

"I don't mind getting rid of my furniture," Tom said.

"Your aunt can stay with me," Boyd said, briefly lifting his face from his conversation with Max. "I'm renting a four-bedroom townhouse in the Village."

Max gave a happy gasp. "Oh, yes. That would be wonderful."

"Well, there you go," Tom said, waving one dusty hand, and Rose thought that meant he'd backed down on the question of their living arrangements, so she backed herself out of the room to go have a long think about the implications of Tom having proprietary thoughts about her own apartment.

When her eyes landed on Tom's dirty clothes, piled in the corner by the bed, she felt guilty about her experiment, since Tom was busy doing manual labor. Tomorrow he'd probably turn up in Ximena's maternity pants. She filled one laundry bag to the brim and headed for the door before Tom came out and intercepted her.

"Don't do that," he said heatedly. They had a brief tug-of-war over the full sack before he won and pulled it out of her arms.

"I don't mind," she said.

"You're not doing my fucking laundry, babe," he said.

Tom's face was alarmed far beyond what the situation called for, so Rose held up her hands in surrender.

"I was going to do it later," he muttered as he headed to the hallway and the back stairs, which led to the kitchen and utility room. Rose rounded up an armful of socks and underwear that had escaped the initial collection and followed him down.

"I'd like it noted that I know how to do laundry," Tom said when he'd loaded the big industrial washer. His movements as he added soap and collected the last odds and ends from her hands were rattled, but as Rose watched, he smoothed his face and turned on the charm like he was flicking a light switch.

"I'm noting it," Rose said cautiously.

"And did you notice that I have fixed many broken things around this place?"

"Yes, of course I've noticed," she said, backing up a step,

because she was wary of any conversation where Tom felt like he needed to pour it on thick.

"I'm downright handy," Tom said, following her. She was backed up against the line of washers, caught between his body and the counter. "I can also reach much higher shelves than you."

"That's true," Rose allowed. So that's where this was going. Tom was still pressing the point about her apartment. He leaned forward to prop his palms on either side of her and trap her between his arms, looming big and dusty over her.

"But not only am I useful around the house, I'm also decorative," he declared. He ducked his head to press a kiss to the point of her jaw, ticklish and open-mouthed, which was *cheating* because he knew she liked that.

"Uh-huh," she said, because Tom had slipped one hand up under her shirt to cup her rib cage with the spread of his fingers, and he was nuzzling down her neck. He made several very fair points, which deserved due consideration, but she had counterpoints.

"You have your own apartment," she said. "I've been there. It's not bad."

"My apartment doesn't have a Rosie in it," he said, lips brushing her collarbone.

Tom had nostalgia goggles on if he thought that would be an unqualified good thing. Rose had ruthlessly assessed the parts of herself that were difficult for other people to deal with and knew that she was unable to be the best version of herself on a sustained basis. For the length of a weeklong holiday vacation? She could ooze Christmas spirit from dawn to dusk.

For a date night in Chelsea? A cast party in the Village? She could sparkle. She hadn't lived with anyone since Tom though, because she knew there were nights when she'd come home from work drained of her ability to be a good Rosie. Sometimes *she* was nothing but work.

"It wouldn't be like this," Rose warned him. "Everyone likes me better in short doses. I'm not actually that fun to deal with every day. Remember? You didn't like living with me."

Tom froze with his face in her cleavage. "That's not true," he said. "We lived together for a whole year before we got married. Best time of my life."

Best of hers too. But it was important to pay attention to why.

"That wasn't just us. It was us, and Adrian, and Ganima and Meagan," Rose said firmly. Three other people who'd done not just housework but a lot of emotional care and feeding for Rose. She tried to scoot to the side, out from under Tom.

He exhaled in frustration, but he followed her to pin her again, with his hips this time. "Well, Adrian and Caroline are moving to New York in two months. Or what are Ganima and Meagan doing these days? Do any of them want to go in on a three-bedroom in Brooklyn? We could have them over, feel them out on it—"

Tom's expression was so deadly serious that Rose couldn't help but giggle.

"That's your plan? Get Adrian drunk and see if he wants to join the Wilczewski-Kelly polycule? If he had any interest in having sex with either of us, pretty sure he'd have let us know at some point in the last fifteen years."

Tom wrinkled his nose in mock outrage and leaned over to rub it against hers. She matched his face and snarled back at him until he laughed.

"I was just making a point about being creative," Tom said, stealing a brief kiss from the corner of her mouth. "I don't want some tiny space in your life just because you're afraid of my dirty clothes all over your apartment. I'll fucking become a nudist. I'll wear a single pair of vinyl fishing waders every day and you can hose me down in the hallway."

"I *am* being creative, and I don't care about your dirty clothes on the floor," Rose said, even if he didn't seem to believe her. Not living together, not falling right back into the same patterns they'd failed at before—that was her being creative. That was her thinking about which parts of her life he'd actually want to live in. "We'll just have to see what works."

"What more do you need to see me do?" Tom asked, and there wasn't any self-pity to it, but there was a whole lot of worry in those words.

Be happy with me, she thought, but that wasn't something she could actually ask someone else to do. In any event, she didn't have to answer, because she heard the doorbell ring.

"Must be the basement furniture I ordered," she told Tom, making an effort to seem bright and cheerful and not at all worried that Tom would spend one Tuesday night eating reheated pasta on the couch with her and remember all the better options he had for his time.

She hurried out the front door to greet the big moving truck that was laboriously backing up the gravel drive.

"We have the budget for new furniture?" Tom asked.

"It's not new. A department store closed, and I bought a bunch of the used furniture. Snowy found it, actually."

Tom looked glum, but Rose didn't think that expression was going to last past her reveal. She'd been incubating this surprise for several weeks. Tom might have thought the basement project was going overboard, but what was in the back of the truck was going to change his mind.

The delivery guys rolled up the back of the truck and set up the ramp to unload a big white leather couch and several groups of café tables and chairs. But the very best thing in the lot Rose had purchased was in the rear, covered in blankets and belted to a dolly. Tom's eyes landed on it, narrowed in concentration as he wondered what it was, and then flew wide open when he figured it out.

"An upright piano?" Tom breathed, his voice joyous. He jumped into the back of the truck and peeled back a corner of the blankets. The piano was slightly battered, lacquered in blinding white, and embellished with a rainbow of exotic butterflies.

"I got it real cheap," Rose bragged.

The piano straddled the line between beautiful and tacky in a way that precisely fit the vibe Rose was cultivating for the basement event space, even if it was butterflies rather than birds. It was going to be the centerpiece. Of her *vision*, as Boyd put it.

"You bought me a piano?" Tom said, wheeling around with an expression of delight spreading across his face. No, Tom was a stage actor; he smiled with his entire body. "*Rosie*. Baby. I always wanted a piano. This is amazing. You bought me a piano?"

"I . . . well. Technically I bought myself a piano for the downstairs bar," Rose said, feeling her pulse tingle in her fingers. She'd been sure he'd love it. Maybe part of her had also wanted to remind him that there were benefits to being in a relationship with her too.

Tom grabbed her wrist and held up her hand to splay his much-larger palm against hers. "But nobody in your family plays the piano. Because you all buy gloves in the children's section."

"Rude and true. But other people play the piano besides you. Adrian plays."

Tom snorted indelicately and put his hands on Rose's hips, pulling her closer. "You didn't buy this queer-ass butterfly piano for Adrian Landry so that he can play you a little anxious Shostakovich when he's out here once a year."

"Also rude and true," Rose admitted. She let her conspiratorial grin bloom on her face. "Okay, yes. I bought you a piano. I thought this summer, you know, if you do come, we could have musical trivia night with my family."

Maybe they wanted to try some new things too—not the same old bocce ball tournaments and fried turkeys from Rose's childhood. She couldn't imagine a better rainy-day activity than Broadway standards with Tom in the new airy pink space.

"This summer? But what about tonight? This is what we're doing tonight, right?" Tom asked, hands vibrating on her waist.

"Of course," she said.

"And you'll sit next to me and turn the pages on the music, right?" Tom asked, expression as sweetly intent as when he'd waited for her at the end of the Simboli Hall Chapel aisle.

"Of course I will," Rose said.

"And everyone will have to say nothing but nice things about my singing?" Tom concluded.

"Or they're turkey chow," Rose promised.

Tom whooped and ran off to gather enough people to move the furniture into the basement. Rose pressed a palm over her heart.

It was a bigger space than he thought, that she was making for him in her life. It was going to be the best part.

22

Rain had started at nightfall, and it was still rattling against the high windows that sealed in the humidity. The air was warm in the enclosed space of the basement, thickly scented with feminine perfume and styling products. Tom had pulled Rosie halfway into his lap and draped himself around her in the corner of the cracked white leather sectional couch that now faced the karaoke stage. His chin rested on her shoulder and his palm on one of her bare knees, round and pink below the hem of the cotton dress she'd changed into halfway through the evening. He was happy, and also a little drunk.

Tom couldn't keep up with both Rose and Ximena's conversation to his left and the parade of earnestly terrible karaoke singers up on the stage, so he was attempting neither, simply enjoying his rare feeling of accomplishment. The renovated basement was a nice space. He'd carried in most of the furnishings. He'd performed capably on the piano—"Watermelon Sugar," "Cruel Summer," and "Peaches" (*You are hilarious, but don't do three songs about oral sex while my parents are here*)—so

Rosie might now look forward to many similar evenings, tucked into his side as was right and proper. His life was all in order for once.

Rosie turned her head and shot him a slightly apprehensive look, and it took Tom a moment to realize that her conversation with Ximena had turned to Ximena's favorite subject: the baby. Tom immediately schooled his features into the appropriate attitude of benign interest. Acting squeamish about Ximena's deeply considered plans with respect to breast pumps and babywearing would likely dislodge Rosie from his lap, if not his life.

"—only take two weeks off, probably, which sucks, but at least Luísa gets three months at her firm," Ximena continued.

Having satisfied herself that Tom didn't object to the subject, Rosie turned back to Ximena. And why would he object? He and Rosie were supposed to be on their fifth kid by now under the original plan. He'd always wanted kids. And if, like Ximena had suggested, Rosie's biological clock was ticking, it was his ally in his campaign to win her back. It made him feel a little ruthless to think about it that way, but he'd take all the advantages he could get.

"They're making you come back two weeks after your first baby?" Rosie asked, scandalized.

Ximena shrugged. "I was lucky they didn't recast me. Probably would have if Lú's dad weren't putting up so much of the funding. So I'll perform right up till my water breaks. In the middle of the Sunday matinee, probably."

"I think portraying Berta as nine months pregnant and still dating two different men is a baller move, actually," Tom put in, because the play had few features to recommend it, and a heavily pregnant Ximena swaggering around the stage as a famed seducer of virgins was going to lead to some interesting reviews. "I think you should wear the baby onstage when you come back. Get them some Equity credits."

"And the casting director is throwing me a baby shower on the Eataly rooftop, so there's that, at least," Ximena said, disregarding Tom's half-serious suggestion. She looked at Rosie, then Tom, then back at Rosie. "You should come," she said to Rosie.

Tom held his breath, but Rosie easily pulled out her phone to add the details to her agenda.

Ximena did the same, holding her phone next to Rosie's to add her to the invitation.

"Oh, you've got your rehearsal schedule already?" Rosie asked, looking at the other woman's screen.

"Yeah, found out yesterday. All the way through opening night," Ximena said, pointing at the entries on her calendar.

"Do you mind if I add myself to those?" Rosie asked.

Ximena shook her head and passed Rosie her phone.

"Give me your phone too," Rosie said, absently tapping Tom's knee. He moved to comply before he'd really thought about it.

"Wait, why?" he asked when his brain caught up.

"Don't you want me to know your rehearsal and performance schedule?" Rosie asked patiently. "I'll add us both."

"I do, but—"

On the one hand, this was great news, if Rosie was thinking that they'd be seeing each other so much that she'd need to know his schedule. On the other, making her responsible for his entire life was one of the things he'd caught hell for last time around.

"I can do it," he muttered, taking all of the phones out of Rosie's hands. The looks both women gave him were unimpressed, but neither stopped him.

Feeling very conspicuous, Tom went through Ximena's calendar, adding himself and Rosie as invitees where appropriate.

Was this how she imagined their life? That she was still going to have to make sure he did laundry and went to work and made it to his friends' baby showers like when he was twenty-two? No wonder she was still skittish on the whole concept.

"Wait, how come Boyd's invited to the baby shower and I'm not?" Tom demanded when he made it far enough into May and opened the item to invite Rosie. "You told me it was girls only. I would have come." Tom did good baby shower gifts. He brought onesies with funny expressions on them if the pregnancy had been planned, or big boxes of diapers, if it had not.

Ximena hesitated, scanning the room as though checking who was in earshot, but all the girls were clustered up around the stage and the karaoke machine. Boyd was sitting alone at the other end of the bar, scrolling through a hookup app. As far as Tom knew, Boyd hadn't gotten laid since arriving on the island, and the other man might actually die if nobody paid attention to him soon.

"Boyd's mother is flying out for the shower," Ximena eventually said. "And he's bringing her."

"Why's Boyd's *mother* coming?" Tom asked, even more confused.

Ximena paused again. Then she gestured with both hands at her round stomach.

"What?" Tom said.

Ximena raised her eyebrows in exasperation. She pointed again at her bump, then shot her eyes at Boyd.

"Oh my God," Tom said, catching on. "Ew?"

"Shut up. You are in no position to 'ew' me," Ximena retorted, crossing her arms.

"*You* slept with Boyd?" Tom whispered heatedly, leaning behind Rosie to make an appalled face at Ximena. He couldn't immediately identify the source of his outrage; it wasn't that he was now one degree away from Ximena, sexually speaking, because if he got exercised about his friends sleeping with each other, he'd have a lot fewer friends, but more that . . . Boyd! Of all men in the whole world, Boyd?

"Jesus, no. This was a medical procedure," Ximena whispered back.

Somehow, that didn't even make him feel better.

"Pretty sure you don't get an opinion on this one, Tomasz," Rosie said. She swiveled to give him a cautioning tilt of her eyebrow, and Tom tensed, considering whether she was right.

No. He still had an opinion.

"Boyd!" he said again, covertly gesturing at the man, who was drinking his vodka neat to maximize his alcohol-to-carb ratio.

"You think we could explain to our kid why we chose some random broke pathology intern when we could have had Boyd? A movie superhero?" she asked.

"Why would you even think you could *have* Boyd?" Tom demanded.

"He saw me going through my clinic's donor catalog last year and asked if I'd rather have a known donor. Lú and I talked about it, and we decided we liked the idea."

"No, and I get that, but—" Tom struggled with it. "Okay, sure, your kids will probably be happy if they look like Boyd. But you're really going to raise kids with him? Boyd with the frog venom? Boyd with the car crashes?" Boyd, who somehow got endless forgiveness for *his* screwups?

Ximena shrugged. "It's not like he's moving in with us. He said he'll make sure to show up at Christmas and for birthday parties, and that'll be nice for the kiddo, but he's not going to co-parent. He doesn't want to be a *dad* dad, which is why he's donating instead of having his own kids—"

"I mean, it makes sense," Rosie said, frowning at an unconvinced Tom. "That's the kind of setup you want. Adrian said he'd be my donor if I hit thirty-five and I was still single, but can you even imagine him in the same room as a screaming baby?"

"*What?*" Tom said, head snapping back like he'd taken a hit to the face.

Rosie froze. "Wait, he didn't tell you about that?"

"*No.*" No, his best friend had not cleared with him a plan to knock up his wife.

She shifted uncomfortably, expression turning a little guilty. "Well, I turned him down."

"Of course you did," Tom said, trying to calm his heart rate by repeating that important fact. Though it was bad enough that there was some alternate universe in which Rosie had a passel of snobby redheaded cherubs. He hoped the Tom in that universe had been long ago hit by a bus and did not have to mail darkest-timeline Rosie baby shower gifts and pretend to be happy for her. God, the terrible turn his life had nearly taken.

"This was before he was dating Caroline, anyway, but I never wanted to have kids without a partner," Rosie clarified, as though this was the chief reason she wasn't having babies with Adrian.

Tom squeezed Rosie's knee as hard as he dared, willing Ximena to look away from this tense moment.

"Of course you're not having them without a partner," he said intently. *Why wouldn't you be having them with me?*

Rosie stilled, blinking.

"Um," she said, apparently realizing that this subject had gone from awkward to painful for everyone involved. "That's a . . . really serious conversation. For us to have later."

"We can have it whenever you want," Tom said.

The comfortable, celebratory mood of a few moments earlier had dissipated, leaving now-familiar expressions of exasperation on Ximena's face and vulnerability on Rosie's.

"Tom," she said, trying to pitch her voice in an undertone. "Let's figure out first whether you want to see *me* when your theater schedule picks back up before we think about adding a baby to the mix." She took the pile of phones back from him and reopened the calendar app.

As he had not realized that Rosie was at all concerned about that, or considered that to be an open question, Tom sat back heavily. Rehearsals had crept up on him, and he hadn't counted the days until he needed to go back to New York, but he'd assumed that if he managed not to mess anything else up before they got there, then on their return they'd just . . . be together. Their lives would recover from their decade-long divergence and fit together like the final pieces of a Lego model.

"It wouldn't matter if the ghost of Stephen Sondheim cast me as a lead in his new musical, Rosie, I'm not going to be too busy—" he began to say, but Snow Wolf clattered down the basement stairs and waved her arms at the room.

"We need more pots," she announced. "There are leaks all over the bunk room."

"New leaks?" Rosie asked, looking out the basement window at the pouring rain. "Oh crap."

She bounced up and out of Tom's lap and headed toward the stairs. Tom hadn't noticed, but most of the fangirls had vanished from the basement along with Boyd.

With a sinking feeling in his stomach, Tom followed Rosie up to the third floor.

Snow Wolf and the Great Puffin had tried to contain the water in a variety of pots and pans, but there was a puddle on the freshly refinished wood floor by one of the windows, and there was water dripping straight through a light fixture on the highest beam of the slanted room. The ceiling bore two spreading damp spots.

Rosie covered her cheeks with her hands and took in the scene with dismay.

"Oh crap," she said again. "The wind must have dislodged the tarps. Or there's just too much water . . ." She spun, trying to decide what they could possibly do in the middle of the rain-storm.

"I'll get some towels," Tom volunteered, even as a sludgy feeling of failure began to sink in.

Rosie nodded anxiously, gaze still flicking from disaster to disaster. "When is the roof going to be done?" she asked, al-ready moving to pick up a nearly full basin.

Tom swallowed. This had happened over and over again. This moment of cold sweat, when he realized he'd put things off too long. Wile E. Coyote looks down and realizes there's no runway left, plus he's tied an anvil to his ankle.

"So, I haven't actually found anyone who can repair the roof yet," Tom said.

Ximena winced, and even some of the girls—probably the ones who'd be sleeping in this wet room tonight—turned to look at him accusatorially. Rosie stiffened her shoulders.

"What, really?" she said, and Tom wasn't sure it was better that she looked surprised that he hadn't managed it.

"I did call a bunch of them," Tom said. "And two companies came out. But the insurance estimate doesn't pay enough to fully replace the roof, and—"

"Can't they just repair it?" Rosie asked, brow furrowing.

"I'm sure someone could, I just—nobody has said yes yet. When I've asked."

Rosie closed her eyes, disappointment playing across her features. They'd been out here two months now. They were leaving in two weeks. And Tom still hadn't handled the roof even though he'd said he would.

Rosie swept her hands back from her face, pressing curls flat as she thought, probably, about how Tom was still an unreliable flake after all these years. Tom wished devoutly that the earth would open and let him fall into a pit.

"Okay, okay," she finally muttered. "I'll deal with the roofers tomorrow. Can everyone else just help me clean up as best we can tonight?"

"No, seriously, I will do it before I leave," Tom said, suddenly concerned that this would be the screwup that led to him eating pudding cups alone in the nursing home on Christmas Eve fifty years from now while Rosie and her redheaded descendants feasted on roast goose somewhere else, probably in a building that had *a fucking roof*.

She shook her head, not meeting his eyes. "It's fine. You've done plenty. I should have stayed on top of the contractors too."

Tom's throat tightened, because he didn't want Rosie to let him off the hook, even if he was tripping over her low expectations.

"I *will* get to it," he reiterated, grabbing a pot at random.

Rosie tilted her chin back, partly in resignation, partly because of a new droplet that had just struck her in the face. The nor'easter was rattling the ancient windows and pulling entirely new leaks from the battered roof.

"Can you and Boyd grab one of the planters from the garden shed?" she finally asked. "I think we'll need at least one big basin if this keeps up."

"Where *is* Boyd?" Ximena asked, looking around the room.

As though in response, Tom heard a loud thud on the roof, louder than the surrounding clatter of rain and the snap of tarps coming loose in the wind. Like a very big, very reckless raccoon.

"Uh, he was going to see if he could hammer some of the shingles down and stop the leaks," Snow Wolf said, flapping her palms in distress.

"In the middle of a lightning storm?" Rosie demanded, wheeling on her.

"Oh my God, didn't you write a fic where he was hit by lightning?" the Great Puffin whispered to Snow Wolf, who gasped and covered her mouth.

Tom went to the window over the second-floor addition, looking down at the short section of composite-shingled roof. The main roof sloped sharply down on this side of the building, low enough that someone determined and not very bright could climb it. That was probably how Boyd had made his way up.

Tom opened the window, admitting a blast of wind and early-spring rain.

"Boyd!" he shouted with half his body hanging out the frame. "Boyd, you goddamn squirrel-infested sack of nuts! Get down! Get off the roof."

Tom thought he heard the other man call back, but he couldn't make out the words.

Ximena was dialing on her phone, even though it probably wasn't a good idea for Boyd to answer during the storm, and he was unlikely to hear it over the deluge.

Tom looked out the window again. Then he sighed and started taking off his jacket. Fuck his life.

"No, Tom," Rosie said when he put his hands on the lower

edge of the window. She grabbed him by the upper arm and held on, big blue eyes fixed anxiously on his face. "This is a Florida Man thing. I'm calling Florida Man on this. You promised no more Florida Man shit."

Tom apologetically shrugged her hands off, because that was true, but it wasn't like he could just let Boyd fall off the roof. There were a lot of loose shingles, and the tarps weren't very secure either.

And wasn't it all his fault too? That the roof wasn't done and that Boyd was even out there to begin with. She ought to be hoping he *did* slip and put them out of their misery.

He got his feet square on the addition roof and gripped the window frame to figure out his next step.

Rosie leaned out as though she intended to follow him.

"I'm the only one who's sober and not pregnant. I should go," she said.

Tom snorted, because there was no way in hell he was letting Rosie jump for the third-floor roof.

"Not a chance. I only get one Rosie," he told her, wincing as the words left his mouth. He only got one, and he couldn't blame a single other person but himself if he didn't have her anymore.

When he made his way to the crest of the roof, he found Boyd happily hammering down corners of a loose tarp while lightning crackled in the distance. Even though he was yelling for Boyd to stop as he crawled across the slope of the roof, the other man didn't look up until Tom was just a few feet away, and even then his expression only shifted to a genial, puzzled *Oh hey, you're here too?*

Tom opened his mouth to inform Boyd of the list of barnyard creatures that made up his probable ancestry, mind already moving on to what explanation he could give to Rosie about his roofing delinquencies, when a shingle that his left knee rested on abruptly broke loose. Tom made a grab for a nearby tarp to steady himself, but it ripped free as well.

Boyd lunged for his hand, but Tom was already sliding uncontrollably down the steep bank of the roof. It felt inevitable, not shocking. Of course this happened. What else had he expected? He heard the short, awful sound of Rosie's scream over the storm and had just enough time to think, *She's going to kill me if I survive*, and then he was falling.

23

How many fingers am I holding up?" Ximena asked, waving her whole hand in front of Tom's wincing face. Nearly a dozen people surrounded them in an anxious semicircle.

The rain had slightly slackened, but everyone was uncomfortable outside, Tom probably most of all, as he still lay on his back in the mud and dead leaves of the front lawn. Rose had put his head in her lap as she knelt behind him, but Ximena was the recent graduate of a pediatric first aid course and used that credential to insist that he not be moved until they figured out whether he'd broken his neck in the fall.

If he hadn't, Rose was ready to do it for him. Watching him fall, catch himself on the gutter, and then slide painfully down the rainspout had probably taken ten years off her life. He'd scraped the skin off both forearms and given himself a large abrasion on one cheek, and he still hadn't gotten to his feet. Her heart was still in her throat.

"Five fingers," Tom said, the first thing he'd said since *I'm sorry*. "Which is always too many."

"What day is today?" Ximena said.

"Oh come on, I never know that one," Tom said.

"Guess."

"I think it's Friday."

"It is Friday," she said, sounding relieved. "I think he's okay."

"I feel okay," Tom confirmed. "But I don't know who you are."

"What?" said Ximena, eyes rounding.

"Obama's the president, *Evita*'s on Broadway, and we just got married," Tom said, trying to look back at Rose. "Who are these other people?"

Rose wanted to strangle him, but her hands moved to gently smooth his wet hair out of his face instead. When he'd hit the addition roof, he'd *bounced*.

What was she supposed to do with this aching, painful tenderness she felt for him? She knew how to love him and not have him, because she'd done that for years, but how was she ever supposed to put away this fierce need to care for him? How did she put it back away if she lost him again?

"Tomasz Antoni Wilczewski, are you trying to make jokes right now?" she demanded.

Tom shut his eyes again. "It was worth a try," he said.

He took a deep breath and flexed his stomach to sit up. When he pulled up his knees, he yelped and fell back.

"I think I tweaked my knee on the roof," he muttered, clutching at his leg.

Rose groaned. He had rehearsal in *two weeks*. She was going to kill him. She was going to take care of him and then she was going to kill him.

"Boyd, put him in my car," she said. "I'll take him to the hospital."

Boyd, who had gotten off the roof as adeptly as might be expected of someone who'd done his own stunts in *Meteor Man 2* and *3*, nodded obediently and slung one dinner plate–sized hand under Tom's shoulders.

"Wait, wait, not the hospital," Tom said, holding on to Boyd with one hand and Rose with the other. "Just help me get inside."

He balanced wildly on his good leg.

"Someone needs to look at your knee," Rose said.

"I can see it. It's still attached."

"What if something's broken?" Rose said, putting her shoulder underneath his arm to steady him. "And someone needs to clean out these scrapes."

"I'll go if it still hurts tomorrow," Tom said stubbornly. "And I'll wash everything with soap."

"Go to the hospital, you lunatic," Ximena said. Rose tried to pull him toward her rental car, and he dug in his heels.

Tom scrunched up his face, lips tight and pale. "I can't remember if I have health insurance right now," he admitted.

"How can you not know if you have health insurance?" Rose asked before she could stop herself. Her internal filter wasn't working well under strain.

"How many weeks were you under contract last year?" Ximena asked. "You might still have insurance."

"I, ah, can't exactly math right now? I'll check tomorrow."

Rose could tell he was trying to play it off casually, but his mouth was tight with pain, and he wasn't putting any weight on his right leg.

"We're going anyway," Rose said. "You fell off my goddamn roof. I'll pay."

"I'm not going to *sue* you—"

Rose shushed him violently, holding her hand in the air.

"We're going!" she shouted, loud enough that several of the girls who'd surrounded them to make sympathetic noises and take photographs of Tom's prone form stumbled back.

She crushed all other objections and enlisted Boyd's aid in putting Tom into the passenger seat of the car.

The rain had slackened a bit, but the roads were still dark and wet and littered with tree branches when she backed slowly out of the inn's gravel drive. Both of them were breathing hard, Tom probably in pain, Rose because adrenaline and fear and anger were still running through her system. She turned off the radio, then pulled onto the main road, keeping their speed to a crawl. It took all her effort not to chew Tom out for his carelessness with himself, and she was able to avoid that only because she could tell from his face that he was having an absolutely terrible time. *Only one Rosie* indeed—how many of him did he think there were?

"I'm sorry I screwed everything up, Rosie," Tom said again when she didn't speak.

She didn't trust herself not to cry or otherwise deviate from the important goal of getting Tom's knee tended to as quickly as possible, so she just squeezed the steering wheel harder. He was always sorry about the exact wrong things.

Tom swallowed. The seconds crawled on as she drove down-island toward the hospital.

"You know," he said in a forcibly casual voice, "if you really want me to have health insurance, we could just get married again."

Rose laughed against her best efforts and swiped at her eyes with the side of her hand. Tom fractionally relaxed once he saw his joke had landed, and that instinctively relaxed her too.

"Would that solve the issue of you doing things that are going to get you killed?" she asked, satisfied with how calm she sounded.

"Maybe I'd feel less of a need to impress you," he offered.

"I am *impressed* when I see you onstage," she said. "I am *worried* right now. You need . . . a lot of things. You can't live like this."

"So that's a yes, then?"

Rose laughed again, even if the noise was strangled. "You asshole. It would serve you right if I said yes."

"Serve me right?"

"Sure. Let me ruin your life again. Let's get married again."

"Why's it ruined? I'd get your benefits package and move into your nice apartment, you'll probably file my taxes for me, plus, you know, I'd get *you*—and all you get is a fifty percent stake in my PlayStation 4 and some free theater tickets. I'd get the better end of the deal."

The windward side of the island was deserted this season, and the headlights of the car were the only source of illumination for the wet branches and brown fields flanking the narrow road. Rose stopped at a stop sign and paused long enough to sneak a look at Tom, whose face was still more drawn than his words would suggest.

"If you wanted to get married again, you'd have gotten married again," she said carefully, wishing the thought didn't hurt. "It's one of those things that, you know, I'm willing to compromise on—"

"I *do* want to get married again."

"Oh, come on. You were going out with people like Boyd Kellagher because you were in the market for a life partner?"

"I was barely looking for a brunch with Boyd. But no, I'm serious. We can get married again. I think it would be a little awkward to make a big thing of it, the second go-round, but we could do something nice at city hall—"

"Don't tease me about it," she warned him, chest throbbing. "This is *hard* for me. I'm not judging you for what you want, but you could at least be honest about it."

"You didn't get married again. And you wanted to. Still want to."

Rose looked back at the empty road. Going on dozens of dates with strangers from the Internet, putting on lipstick and going out after work when all she wanted to do was watch something brainless on TV, breaking up with nice men—Good people! Men she liked!—when she realized they didn't want kids or didn't believe in forever. She'd tried. She was sure Tom hadn't even tried. Adrian had once let it slip that Tom's relationships turned over like the dairy case at the supermarket.

"Did you think you would?" she asked.

Tom exhaled through his nose. "No," he admitted.

Lips pressed together, Rose nodded. That's what she'd thought.

"But, babe, we already *got* married," he said. "I didn't think I could get married to someone else."

"What?" Rose asked, shooting him a startled look out of the corner of her eye. "Wait. You don't mean in, like, a Catholic way?"

Tom paused. "I guess?" he said.

Rose snorted. "Is that what you tell people when you don't want to commit? Oh, sorry, I can't, I'm Catholic?"

"I *am* Catholic. So are you. Remember the priest at our wedding?"

"You're not *that* Catholic. You never went to mass." Rose retorted, because she had all the receipts on this. "I went to mass more than you, and I went, just, *when someone made me.*"

Tom sighed heavily and spread his fingers in concession. "Okay, okay, so I don't mean in a Catholic way. It's more that—"

She had to keep her eyes on the road as they approached the outskirts of Oak Bluffs, because now there was traffic, but she could feel him looking at her. She couldn't turn her head to look at him though, or she'd lose it.

"What," she said.

"I took vows. I said I'd love and honor you. And I knew what I was doing, and I knew what I meant. I said for all the days of my life, and I meant it. That's it."

"Tom," she said, like a warning. It was getting harder to drive.

"No, Rosie, listen. I meant it. I know I haven't always lived

up to my vows, not when we were living together, even, or in
the ten years since, but I always thought I should. I couldn't
make those promises to someone else, because I already made
them to you, and I meant it. I'm going to love you all the days
of my life."

He said it very fiercely, as though someone were going to
come into the car and dispute it. But what could she say? *Don't?*
Please don't love me? She would never have told him that, because what else had she been chasing all these years? No, *love
me*, please. Just do it in a way she might notice. Do it in a way
that mattered. *Say it and make me believe it.*

"You are—you're off the hook though," she said, aware that
her voice sounded watery. "You don't have to. I'm not going to
hold you to it. You're not stuck with me. You don't have to want
the things I want just because you made a promise when you
were twenty-two."

Tom leaned all the way across the center console so that his
arm just brushed hers. She felt the big shape of his body next
to hers without being able to see it, somehow sensing it through
the noise of their hearts beating too fast. He put a hand on her
arm for lack of any other part of her to hold onto.

"I don't want you to let me off the hook for once. I want to
stop screwing up. I don't want to be the person I was when I
was twenty-two. I want to be the guy you *thought* I was."

She pulled off the road into the nearest parking lot, a deserted Cronig's.

"I can't drive like this," she said, eyes welling up.

"I'm not in a hurry," Tom said, even though his knee had to
be killing him.

Once the car was in park, and the engine was shut off, she swung her head to check that there was nobody nearby, then lifted the hem of her skirt to wipe off her eyes, flashing Tom and Vineyard Haven both. She leaned over the steering wheel with her face covered by the loose fabric.

Actors had to cry onstage sometimes. Tom could cry onstage on command, like the excellent actor he was. Rose still didn't want anyone to see her cry. She didn't want to be a person who cried a lot, but arranging her life so that nothing made her cry had never worked, and it wasn't working now.

Tom grunted, got his good leg braced, then twisted around to grab her purse out of the back seat. He fished inside for the tissues he knew she'd have stashed there and passed her the packet without comment on her tears.

When she'd wiped mascara away, he reached for the crumpled tissue, but instead she grabbed his hand. She held on as hard as she could, fingers folded over his much larger ones.

I want that too. I want that so much. I want that for you, and for me, and, more than anything, for us.

They sat there in the dark for a long time, watching the red brake lights of the cars smear light on the wet roads as they spun past.

Tom's phone vibrated ten minutes later, and he fished it out of his pocket. He scanned his texts.

"Ximena checked with my manager. I have health insurance through next Thursday," he said with a note of triumph.

Rose took a deep breath. "Great. We'll go to the hospital. See if you can get some shots while we're at it."

She turned on the car and put it in reverse, but before she

could back out into the road, Tom put his hand on her arm again.

"I'm sorry about tonight," he said earnestly. "I swear it won't be this bad once we're back in New York. I take the subway, I listen to my manager, and I show up for rehearsal. This kind of thing doesn't happen—well, too often."

Another painful laugh forced its way from her chest. "You nearly got hit by a bus the night we met. I knew you were like this when I married you."

"Yeah," Tom said softly. "I know. But this had to wear on you."

She covered the brake long enough to look at him earnestly. "It didn't. It really didn't. I just wanted—I just missed you." She exhaled, long and tired. "I knew about everything else. Everything you don't like about yourself. And everything I didn't like about my life—I expected that too. I just thought I'd get you in exchange. It would have been worth it if I had you, but in the end I didn't feel like I did. I didn't think I should have to miss you all the time."

A complicated expression tilted the corners of Tom's full mouth and tight eyes. A little bit of surprise, a little more grief.

"Well," he said thickly, shifting in his seat so that he could stretch his injured leg out longer, "you could have had me at any time. But anyway, here I am."

The night was still and humid by the time Tom was discharged. They made their way slowly back to the car; his badly sprained knee had stiffened after the long wait in the emergency room, and now he had a brace and a cane. Not a handsome cane, a sexy cane, as he'd requested of the unamused rehabilitation specialist, but the aluminum kind with a big handle and a black rubber tip.

"This play is going to be such a train wreck," he said as Rose helped him into the passenger seat. "It was one thing when it was just Ximena on the prowl at nine months pregnant. Now I have to convince the audience that I'm a dewy-eyed twenty-year-old virgin in orthoses."

"I bet the *Times* will call it a remarkable comment on the intersection of disability and desire," Rose said, buckling him in.

"They're only going to review it if Ximena goes into labor onstage," Tom said sourly. "And then it will be in the Styles section and focus on maternity wear trends. Maybe Sara Holdren will throw us a bone if we're lucky." He pinched the bridge of his nose and leaned back against the headrest, face creased with discomfort.

Rose gently rubbed his thigh, worried for him. "Do you want to go back inside and see if you can get something stronger than Advil?"

"No. I want to go home," Tom said.

She paused with her hand on his leg, since she didn't think he was really talking about the inn. He was talking about her apartment, probably, a place he'd never been to. Or their studio in the East Village, which she'd vacated as soon as the lease was up.

"I think we missed the last ferry," she said, which was true but also cowardly. She winced and tried to do better. "You have been *so* brave. Do you want to go back to the inn to be fussed over by a dozen teenage girls and also me?"

"I guess that's as good as it gets for tonight," he said.

The roads were deserted as they made their way back up-island, but when they got to the inn's gravel drive, they found it blocked by a news van.

"What now?" Tom asked, squinting at the flood lights that had been aimed at the roof, where three men who were not Boyd were industriously nailing down tarps and patches.

Ximena, who had been waiting in a rocking chair on the porch, stood up when she saw Rose approach.

"What's happening?" Rose asked, gesturing at the news truck and the construction. Nothing went on in West Tisbury after seven p.m., especially not in March.

"So, Boyd and I put out a video about what happened. On all our official accounts. The local news picked it up, and an actual roofer came over and said they'd handle the project for the claim limits plus some promo," she said, pointing over her head. "But could you have Tom look like he's on the verge of death when he comes through here? Exaggerations about how close he was to dying may have been made."

Rose, who had been taking hard lessons in composure for several weeks now, managed to absorb these facts without demonstrating surprise or concern.

"Where is Boyd?" she asked. "You didn't let him get back on the roof, did you?"

Ximena shook her head. "He's filming videos about the

work that still needs to be done here. If it worked for roofers, seems like maybe we could get a real A/V specialist to wire the basement?"

"Would you be willing to go get him?" Rose asked. "I need his help to get Tom up the stairs."

"How is Tom?" Ximena asked.

"Grumpy," Rose informed her. "But he'll live."

When she went back to the car, Rose found that Tom had managed to get himself out, and he was gazing up at the late-night construction with a bemused expression on his face.

"Are those real roofers?" he asked.

"I think so," she replied.

Tom paused, expression shuttered. "And are they going to fix the whole roof?"

"Apparently it was your dying wish," Rose said.

They both looked up and regarded the roofers as they worked to render the inn waterproof for the first time in months.

"I really thought I could do something for you out here," Tom repeated glumly.

Rose rubbed his back through his shirt. She didn't care, but she didn't think he wanted to hear that right now. "You know, I only asked *you* for help. I didn't have anyone else to ask. And everyone else who came out is because of you. So, you know, in a way, everything they've done . . . that's because of you too."

"Huh," said Tom. After a moment, he slung a heavy arm over Rose's shoulders. When she peeked back up at him, his face was spreading into a weary grin. "I guess I did do it then."

"You did what?"

"The roof. I told you. I said I'd get the roof fixed, and I did." He beamed at her.

Rose giggled and elbowed him lightly in the ribs. "*You* did?"

"I did! Look, the roof's getting fixed, and you thought I'd flaked out again. But I got Boyd's weirdos to do it. Say you were wrong."

"Of course. This was part of the master plan. You lured Boyd out onto the roof, then fell off it just so that you could appeal to the sympathies of the hardworking roofers of West Tisbury," she said, helpless to resist mirroring Tom's smile.

"Don't question my methods, just my results," he said, tipping his head back and laughing. "But if I'm ever actually dying, I'm telling you now that I don't want a roof. I want hard drugs and sexual favors."

"I'll see what my cat tranquilizer guy can do," Rose said, going up on her tiptoes to kiss the smirk off Tom's face before Boyd and the inn crowd could approach. He rubbed the tip of his nose into her cheek, and she squeaked in a less than dignified way.

Boyd's expression was sheepish as he came over to support Tom's arm, and he seemed to anticipate being yelled at. He probably deserved to be yelled at. Tom had Rose, at least, but who kept Boyd from acts of Florida Man peril?

Tom looked up at the roof a last time, then reached out to pull the other man into a hug. Tom had recovered from enough of his Florida Man socialization that he didn't cut it off with any performative back slapping and arm punching. He gave Boyd a real hug, hard and earnest, and then he patted him on the chest.

"Thanks, bud," Tom said, to the dramatic sighs of nearby teenage girls. But he was sincere. "I mean it. Thank you for this."

Boyd didn't smile in any of his movies that Rose had ever seen, but he smiled then. "You're welcome," he said.

The whole crowd flowed into the inn and then up the main staircase.

They were completely booked. The fangirls were stacked up two and three to a room and filled the third-floor bunk room as well. Ximena, Boyd, and Tom had each been assigned a queen bedroom, and Rose had the suite. The inn was completely full for the first time since Rose was a small child, and the hallway rang with a dull background roar of female chatter, phone notifications, and hammering from the roof.

It was a wonderful din, Rose thought. She'd lived in New York for the past decade; she couldn't sleep if it was too quiet. All these noises were good noises.

Tom and Boyd made it to the landing, and Tom considered the long hallway of doors. The single room where he'd been sleeping. The suite.

"Drag my suitcase into the suite," he told Boyd, taking a first laborious step down the hall.

Rose made a small noise, not quite an objection, more a note of surprise.

Tom swung his head back toward her.

"Nope," he said, though Rose hadn't even finished thinking it through. "We're done with that. Not one more night."

The calm determination on his face wasn't an expression Rose was very familiar with. The features were familiar: the steady brown eyes, the straight bold line of his lips. But Tom never put his foot down on anything. He was never totally sure he was right. Except now he was.

Let's talk about it, she nearly said. But hadn't they already talked about it? She'd told him she got tired of missing him.

Rose had noted the occasional electric sensation in her brain of remembering something she had almost forgotten. Some memory about to be overwritten, some last item on the grocery list as she approached the checkout station. Wait, hold on a minute. I almost missed this.

"I can get him from here," she told Boyd, putting her hand on Tom's elbow.

As though she'd planned it all from the beginning, she guided Tom into the suite. She put his cane against the free nightstand and helped him strip down to his boxers. She collected the rest of his things from the other room. People were watching as she carried his suitcase down the hall, but not with a lot of surprise. They'd known this was where Tom belonged even before Rose had, and they'd been right then too.

D*omino* shot the basement with oversaturated Kodachrome filters to make the pink accents pop. *Country Living* took pictures of the handmade throw cushions in the honeymoon suite. *People* got them in the kitchen so they could take pictures of Boyd juicing oranges in his giant fists.

Boyd's slightly bewildered publicist had arranged it all, marking a sharp turn in Boyd's public persona from salmon-scarfing exercise maniac and possible sex fiend to cottage design enthusiast. But either way, Boyd sold magazines, especially with Tom dragged into the frame to slump over the furniture as though he'd just gotten sexed up so good he couldn't walk. By Boyd, the framing always suggested.

"Stop laughing at me," Tom begged Rosie and Ximena as the photographer's assistant poured water down the front of his white linen shirt. "And why do I have to be *wet*?"

"The concept is 'After the Storm,'" the photographer gamely explained. "The idea is that you and Mr. Kellagher found and renovated this little haven after the hurricane. There's a contrast—raw nature and domesticity. The storm, the inn. So you're wet. And all the textures are warm. Could you try to relax, please?"

"Be good baby. This is the last one," Rosie scolded him, barely able to speak for giggling so hard. "And they said they might leave some stuff behind that we can use."

Tom had been *very* good. He'd barely complained at all about two days of pretending to smolder at Boyd, even though Rosie was *right there* outside the camera frame. He wanted to point to her, say *Actually, that's my wife*, and have the story that the entire world heard be the real one: Tom had come out here for her, to do all of this for her, and he'd *done it*.

"You're whoring me out for table lamps?" Tom muttered, trying not to whine as he reluctantly leaned backward over the kitchen island. He and Boyd sucked in their stomachs and flexed for the test shot.

"Not just lamps," Rosie said brightly, her hands clasped possessively around a gilded birdcage. The expensive couches and antique rugs were going home along with the photographers, but the inn was dotted with a dozen vases of fresh flowers, several new potted plants, and an antique fair's worth of bird-themed miscellany.

Look at her! Tom nearly said to the photographer. He finally had the Rosie he'd longed for: she was pink-cheeked and smiling, wearing a pretty green dress, with her hair and makeup done just in case she popped up in the background of some picture. The Rosie he'd gotten the past two weeks was top Rosie—anxious about getting everything finished on time, baking five dozen bacon-wrapped dates about it, curling under his arm to press her face against his chest and then propelling herself forward to her next important task.

He didn't realize they were finished until she was standing in front of him, hands smoothing his damp shirt and resting against his stomach.

"That's it," she said, going up on her toes to press a warm kiss across his lower lip.

"That's what?" he said.

"Everyone's packing up," she said. And Tom was astonished to note that it was true—not just the photographers, but everyone else too. He'd been told that Rosie wanted everyone else out by the next day so that the property management service could clean and prep for guests, but the actual date had snuck up on him. People were carrying suitcases down the stairs, and the photographers were sweeping up after themselves. Tomorrow, that would be him and Rosie. He'd done it.

Tom had been involved in many theatrical productions that came together just before opening night, but he couldn't think of anything else that he'd started and *finished* the way the inn was finished. Rosie had her perfect place, and he had his perfect Rosie back.

"Back to the real world tomorrow," she said, and her smile dimmed a little.

Tom did not have any mixed emotions about that, but he slung an arm around her shoulders and kissed her temple. He didn't begrudge Rosie her holidays out here, and he'd be happy to come back when it wasn't fifty-five degrees and raining outside, but he was looking forward to going home. To Rosie's apartment, specifically, where he'd claim a side of the bed and a spot on the couch and a coffee mug in the kitchen.

"We should do something to celebrate," Tom said.

Rosie perked up a little. "Yeah? We should." She thought for a moment. "We haven't used the crêpe maker on this trip. We could do a dessert station. I could make crêpes suzette."

"Sure," said Tom, who had been thinking more along the lines of taking Rosie upstairs and bending her in half with her knees over his elbows. But these were not mutually exclusive ideas. Something of his own plans must have shown on his face, because Rosie colored prettily, looked around, then copped a covert feel on his ass. He was ready to pursue that impulse, and he turned to crowd her into the broom closet, but someone loudly cleared his throat behind them.

"Knock-knock," said Seth, sticking his head into the kitchen. Tom didn't appreciate the shit-eating grin the guy had on his face, nor the way he strutted into the kitchen like he'd done anything to contribute, but Rosie's smile was still fond when it landed on her cousin, so Tom controlled himself.

Seth warmly congratulated Rosie on the job she'd done and pulled up a chair to the kitchen island like he owned the place. He had a laptop and several binders bearing the name of his property management firm.

"I can't believe it," Seth said, shaking his head. "I can't hardly recognize it! You're the best, Rosie. This is, like, my biggest account now. I'm so glad you didn't decide to sell."

Tom recalled a relevant childhood fable in which a little red hen baked cornbread, but a bunch of other little asshole animals didn't help at all. Seth didn't deserve any cornbread unless Tom got to rub it directly into his face. Tom thought that he and his little hen should go eat cornbread in bed. But he needed to get the other man out of the house first.

"Have you had lunch?" Tom asked, deciding that conspicuous hospitality was the best tactic to take. He'd polished these floors. He'd caulked these windows. Seth was in *his* kitchen, but he'd barely acknowledged Tom's existence, which Tom did not intend to tolerate. Tom crossed his arms and went to stand next to Rosie. "We've got a lot of food left. Can I fix you a snack?"

"Oh, sure," said Seth, not at all picking up what Tom was laying down. He looked at Rosie. "Always love your cooking. It's too bad we've been too busy to get out here. The baby is just too much. But next time."

"Next time," Rosie said, shooting a cautious glance at Tom as he stomped to the fridge to get out the previous day's fajita meat. "Did you have a chance to look at all the bookings?"

Seth nodded in amazement. "Boyd Kellagher! Everyone wants to come stay with Boyd Kellagher. Any chance we can use him to promote the inn?"

"Like the white tigers at the Mirage hotel?" Tom called as he picked the meat apart for nachos. "Boyd needs a *lot* of enrichment in his enclosure. He's leaving for New York tomorrow."

Seth chuckled. "I get it," he said. "But won't he be back? Aren't the three of you all . . . you know?" He made a half-hearted gesture with his hands that could have been obscene or merely confused.

Rosie turned bright red, but she didn't flinch.

"Are we three what?" she asked innocently.

"You know," Seth said. "Or is it just, uh. Is it—you know?"

"I don't know," Rosie replied, digging in.

Tom stuck a plate of nachos in the microwave and came to stand behind Rosie again with his hand on her shoulder. *Sure, Seth, ask me in front of my wife which of us is fucking Boyd Kellagher.*

Seth folded and grabbed a binder. "Never mind," he muttered. "I brought all the bookings like you asked."

Rosie took the binder from him and eagerly flipped through the pages.

"We're totally booked through October," Seth boasted. "Even the bunk room. Some girls want to have a convention out here. About Boyd. See? In August? They're calling it Boy-Con. I had to get extra permits to have commercial booths on the front lawn."

"So it's going to make money?" Tom asked, headed to the microwave.

"Well, yeah," Seth said. "Should break even by the end of the season, even considering all the storm stuff. And if this keeps up through fall, Max might do very well."

"Maybe next summer we could put in that hot tub you were thinking about, babe," Tom called to Rosie, who was continuing to flip through the pages with a small frown on her face.

She murmured an agreement, but unenthusiastically. Tom looked over her shoulder to where she'd turned to listings for Memorial Day weekend. The suite was assigned to Max, and Rosie's name was listed for the next queen bedroom down the hall. Tom didn't recognize any of the other names on the list.

"Didn't you get an email with reservation links?" she asked.

Tom didn't understand the thrust of her question. He'd gotten the email. So had hundreds of other people, if the number of reservations was evidence. "Yeah, but I didn't make a separate reservation because I assumed I'd be with you?" he said, voice tightening. He'd thought this argument had been put to rest.

Rosie saw the flash of panic on his face and quickly put a hand on his arm. "No, of course you will." She turned back to Seth. "Did everyone else think they had to pay, do you think? We're still not charging family to stay here, right?"

Seth shook his head. "No, I sent out a separate email to all the people on the friends and family list. It's a different sign-up system." He flipped to the Fourth of July and pointed at one entry. "These are Max's friends. See the little code here?"

"I do see," Rosie said, her hands resting on the pages. She was very quiet and still. The microwave beeped, and Tom turned around to get Seth's snack out.

"You know," Seth mused. "It might even be better if you and Max did something else this year while everyone is so interested in the inn, yeah? We could charge a premium for the suite. Like a thousand a night. Hate to take those rooms off the market. I've got people on a waiting list. What do you think?"

The plate was hot, and Tom had to hunt for an oven mitt to pull it out. He was waiting for Rosie to tell Seth off, but when he turned back around with the nachos, Rosie was halfway up the stairs.

25

Even though she'd gone up to the suite to have a private cry, some part of Rose's soul was still bewildered to find herself alone there. After she'd matched the curtains to the throw pillows? After she'd gotten the wires for the basement sound system invisibly taped to the baseboards? After Tom had nearly broken his neck getting the roof fixed? After the windows, the pool, the *bees*? After Boyd Kellagher oozed his ambiguous sexuality over every piece of furniture in the foyer?

Was there a single thing she could have done to make this place more inviting? Was there a single way she could have made this easier for her family? Was there something wrong with the email? Had she not sent enough texts? Had they not seen the new pictures, or the magazine proofs, or the newsletter? Could they have somehow not realized it was time to sign up?

No. Even with every possible inducement, even with each tiny amount of friction eliminated, they didn't want to come.

Nobody in her family except Max had blocked a single day at the inn.

Maybe it was true, Rose allowed, that they'd never felt the same way about this place as her. They thought it was inconvenient to travel here. They were neutral at best on board games. They'd eaten the same meals too many times. But some part of her had thought that they'd do it for her, at least. They had to be somewhere on Memorial Day and Thanksgiving and Christmas, and she'd invited them to be with her. But it wasn't enough for them that she wanted them here. She wasn't enough.

Rose picked up one of the stupid floral throw pillows she'd spent hours embroidering and wrapped herself around it. Eleven years ago, when Max was still ruling this place with an iron fist, Rose had come out here for two weeks, fresh off filing for divorce, and tried to rearrange her ideas of how her life was going to go. She'd held her baby cousins and flipped pancakes for her uncles and driven her younger brothers to the movies, telling herself that she had a big family and she was never going to be alone. But there was no guarantee she wouldn't be, no matter how many cushions or casseroles she made.

Ten minutes was enough time in one day spent indulging her suspicion that there was something fundamentally unlovable about herself. She needed to start dinner and pack. But the same part of herself that had engaged in what she now knew to have been a great deal of magical thinking about her family still wished that someone would come find her.

And Tom did; she heard his voice calling her name, not worried, just confused. She immediately wiped her face, but his expression fell when he saw her sniffling. He looked around, then shut and locked the door behind him before coming to sit next to her on the bed.

He put his arm around her and pulled her against him. "What happened?" he asked in that overly gentle voice of concern people used with small children who'd taken a tumble on the sidewalk. Hearing himself, he cleared his throat, apparently deciding that a different character was called for. "Actually, first tell me *who*. I'll drag their ass in here, and that'll give you a moment."

Rose forced a laugh at his ominous tone. "That would fix the problem, actually. If you could drag them here."

"Drag who?"

"My family. Did you see? Nobody signed up. Nobody blocked out any time here." She laughed again and tilted her head up. "I thought it looked perfect. Max likes it. But she's got early signs of dementia. Maybe it doesn't look good. Maybe it's too frilly."

Tom rubbed her shoulders, face creasing in confusion. "Babe, this place looks great. It's never looked better. You can't even tell there was a storm."

"That's not good enough," she said. She leaned back on her palms, hoping her nose would clear if she stared at the ceiling. "Or is that just another lie I tell myself? That there was ever a single thing I could have done here that would make anyone want to spend their vacation time with me."

She was very glad that Tom was there with her now, just grateful for his presence, and had not really considered what he might think of her pity party. So she was surprised when he stood up and stalked away to the window. He set his hands on his hips, attitude agitated.

"Babe, tons of people wanted to spend their vacation with you. And did," he said, and Rose realized she'd stepped in it. He'd been here almost three months when he could have been at least earning money if not having a wonderful time as an up-and-coming actor living in New York. Not to mention all the time Boyd had been here, and Ximena, and all the girls.

"Oh no, I'm not saying I'm not incredibly grateful," Rose tripped over herself to explain. "You were incredible. Everyone was! This is not on you. No, oh my God—I could never have imagined everything you've done. You've been so good. I'm just sorry it ended like this."

What a waste of everyone's time. Jesus. She could have just sold it. Tom had told her, hadn't he? Everyone thought it was a shithole, and he hadn't wanted to stay. She should have just listened to him.

"That's not what I mean," Tom said sharply. "Rosie! What did *you* want? What were you doing out here for all this time?"

She blinked at him in confusion. She'd wanted to fix this place up so that her family would have somewhere to get together during the holidays again, and he knew that.

Tom tapped urgently on his palm, as though counting. "Because here's what I see. You have me, and at one point, at least, you knew that *I* was your family. You have your Aunt Max, who is thrilled to come out here as soon as possible. You have this place, which has never looked better. And I have fucking *filled it up* with people who think you're wonderful in every way." He cocked his head at her, expression pained. "Isn't that what you wanted?"

What she wanted? She'd never thought of it. Never in her wildest dreams would she have imagined that letting Tom come help with renovations would set off a daisy chain of events leading to more than a dozen vivid artistic depictions of Rose in a clinch with both Tom and Boyd Kellagher. She hadn't even thought that at the end of it she'd have *Tom*.

Tom shook his head. "I know this isn't how you pictured it, but isn't this what you actually wanted? Babe, it's going to be great. We're going to come back here this summer, as soon as the Broadway run wraps, and you're going to love it."

Tom sat back down next to her and tugged her into his chest, his hands curling into her hair to soothe her, even though she knew she was being a bit of a brat.

"Wouldn't that be enough?" Tom asked. "If I'm there, and Max, and a bunch of our friends? Adrian and Caroline are back from Singapore this week. My parents would come if I asked. Every other inmate in this asylum is dying to come back. Is that enough?"

Rose scrunched her eyes shut, willing away the sting of disappointment because she heard the note of uncertainty in Tom's voice. Of course it would be enough, if Tom really did show up. But hadn't she asked too much of him already?

"You're not tired of this place?" she asked tentatively.

"Never," Tom said stoutly. He rubbed his face into her hair, lips warm against the shell of her ear. "I'll be there, and I'll make sure everyone else comes too. I can't even get rid of Boyd. I'm sure he'll be here. Didn't I do that?"

"That was all you," Rose agreed. She knew she was being coddled, but this was filling up a little crack in the very base of her, the part that only ever felt loved for the things she did, not the things she was. And Tom was enough to fill her heart all the way up to the brim. He filled it to overflowing.

Tom pulled her tighter against him. "Because don't I take care of you?" he demanded. "Haven't I done everything you asked?"

"You did! You did. I'm just sorry I asked you to spend so much of your time on this." She could have taken Tom up on his offer of crashing at Boyd's vacation house, and she could have been sitting under an umbrella with sea turtles bringing her coconuts full of rum this whole time.

"I'm not sorry," Tom said fiercely. "I'm glad I got this chance. Because you know I can do it now. All the things I said I'd do the first time around."

"What—this wasn't a *test*," she said, finally realizing what Tom was getting at.

Tom scoffed. "Of course it was a test. But the important thing is, I *passed*." He stood up and held her face between his hands. "I said I'd do it for you. And I did. Because I'm going to keep taking care of you."

Rose closed her eyes and let the weight of that promise sink in. She wanted so badly to believe him. Tom's thumbs stroked her cheekbones, soothing her, and the way she wanted it to continue scared her with the intensity of the feeling.

"Was there anything else?" Tom prompted her, fingers tangled in her hair. "Was there anything else you wanted?"

His tone was such a volatile mix of pride and uncertainty

that Rose's heart ached for him. "No, I couldn't have asked for anything else," she said honestly. He'd given her so much more than she'd ever expected to have.

She put her hands on his waist, just steadying herself against the solidity of his body, and he looked down at the touch. His mouth pursed.

"Oh wait," he said. "I guess there was one more thing."

She didn't know what he meant by that, so she tilted her face up just as he leaned in to kiss her. His kiss wasn't delicate or gentle in the way he often approached her these days. He held her still with both hands so that he could kiss her at his pace—a hot sweep of tongue in her mouth and the sweet pressure of his lips claiming hers. He sat down again and wrapped her in muscular arms, holding her until she relaxed into his embrace.

She could have done that for a long time. Kissing Tom was an activity that didn't allow for a lot of extraneous thoughts, and she would have welcomed the opportunity to drown out any inner voices that told her she was doomed to be alone in the fully absorbing activity of making out with him. She couldn't do anything else while kissing him; she never *wanted* to be doing anything else while kissing him.

It stopped before she was ready. She didn't expect it when Tom gave her a light shove against her shoulders that had her landing flat on the mattress. She gave a single surprised huff of amusement, because Tom had been treating her with kid gloves, and she'd wondered when he'd decide to reopen the question of whether she was allowed *any kinky shit* if she used her words correctly. She expected him to climb up onto the bed next to her and continue things on a horizontal plane, but her laugh turned into more of a gasp when Tom none-too-gently rolled her to her stomach so that she was bent over the side of the mattress.

She pushed up on her elbows to look back at him.

"Um," she said in a skeptical tone of voice. She was fully dressed, and so was he. What was he even planning to accomplish with her in this position?

"You asked for it, Rosie," he said calmly, hands at his belt and eyes warm on her body bent over before him. With unhurried movements, he undid his belt and yanked it free of its loops with a heavy *snick* of leather against cloth. Even then, Rose didn't connect any dots until he loomed back over her and gathered her two wrists in his right hand.

"You're going to need to scoot a little," he said, giving her a light slap on the ass to urge her down toward the foot of the bed. "If you still want me to pin you to the mattress and rail you. In a loving way. In a respectful way. Do you want that?"

The noise she made through her nose was mostly one of disbelief, but she was seized with a sudden molten impulse of want that slid through her core like a drop of water down a hot pan. Yes. She did want that. She wanted to be the desired thing for once. She wanted the heated undercurrent of desire in Tom's voice. She didn't move, not sure whether she was actually supposed to.

Tom leaned back down and put his mouth next to her ear.

"Are you going to be a good girl and move, or are you going to be a bad girl and I move you?" he asked, and thank God he was an actor, because there was no way Rose could have ever delivered a line like that and not died of embarrassment, but he sounded like he'd never made a more serious offer in his life.

Rose considered whether she wanted to be good or bad. This was the choice, as Snowy would have put it, of the whole vibe. She could have Tom's big hands gripping her hips or maybe the back of her neck. The idea behind being bad was that she could make up for it, and then she'd be good. But she wanted to be good from the start. She wanted Tom to think she was good, to whisper *You look so fucking pretty* in her ear. She wanted to do it just right for him. So she moved down to the edge of the bed and put her arms straight out in front of her.

Tom looped his belt around her wrists and neatly tightened it so that it held her wrists together. He ran a thumb over the places where the leather rubbed against her skin, checking that it wasn't too tight.

"Jesus Christ," Rose said, blinking at the adept way he'd done that, the practice it implied.

"What, did you think I didn't know *how* to do the kinky stuff?" he asked, sounding warmly amused. "I know. I just didn't think our first night back together needed to be a softcore bondage scene."

He ran his hands all the way down the length of her body from her wrists, letting her know he could touch her anywhere. His fingers lingered on her hips, cupping her ass in a possessive way before hiking the skirt of her dress up to her waist.

"I, um," Rose said, trying to imagine how this was going to go and coming up blank. She'd never done this. She couldn't even recall talking about this other than in a joking way. She laughed politely, feeling the absurd need to distance herself from this act even with her wrists tied together. "I was bluffing, really. You don't have to do this."

"Babe, I'm tying you up so that *you* don't have to do anything," he said, hands petting her ass over the satin of her panties. "I mean, if you want to make some really good noises, I'd like that. But I'm going to take care of you. That's what it's about, right? Control. Having it. Losing it."

He slipped his hand around her hip, under the elastic, and curved it in toward her core, just parting her folds with the tip of his thumb. He traced his fingertip back and forth in a small soothing orbit, his other hand tightening on her body. He leaned back in. "You're really wet for someone who was bluffing," he confided softly, mouth dipping in long enough to catch the edge of her earlobe with his teeth. Rose shivered violently as Tom eased her underwear down to her ankles.

She was totally exposed to him, bare from the waist down, bent over like an offering. Tom nudged her legs apart with a foot as though considering his options.

"I don't think this is enough," he said thoughtfully, and she felt a cool breeze on her exposed legs as he stepped away, returning in a moment with the two curtain tie-backs from the window. When he tied a loop around one foot and secured it to the foot of the bed, Rose took a deep breath and held it. Yes. She really couldn't do anything from this position, her hands and legs tied. Tom would take care of her with his strong hands and big cock and better ideas of how to fulfill her very vague idea of doing something kinky.

"Do we need a safe word?" she asked, feeling hot and shaky

through her stomach even though he'd barely touched her. Was there anything else she was supposed to do?

"Just say stop if you want me to stop. I won't remember what you mean if you start yelling colors," Tom said, voice already rougher and deeper. He stayed on the floor behind her once both her legs were secured, but Rose was still shocked at the slide of both his hands up the backs of her thighs. She tensed when his palms gripped the globes of her ass.

"Up on your tippy toes, Rosie," he said, and then she felt his breath right against her entrance. She obeyed more out of instinct than because she understood what was about to happen, but Tom's hot, wet mouth landing over her core was a thing she both wanted with every fiber of her body and would never have been able to ask for.

She buried her flaming face against one arm, mind snagged on the delicious image of herself bent over the side of the bed with Tom kneeling behind her, his face buried in her pussy. Both of them still mostly dressed. It was *hot*.

Tom's thumbs spread her for his mouth, and tension coiled faster than she could have thought possible. She held her eyes firmly shut as he devoured her. She couldn't have thought of colors. Or numbers. She didn't count how many times his lips and tongue rolled over her, because her mind went blank and fuzzy with sensation. It never happened this quickly for her. Her orgasm wasn't its usual slow, twisting climb up an impossibly high summit but a hard, careening rush that rocked through her body like a sudden impact with the floor. She gasped, immediately sensitive and aware of the textures of Tom's mouth.

"Already?" Tom said, sitting back on his heels and rubbing his jaw with one palm. "God, I'm amazing."

Rose tried to turn over to look at him—to laugh with him, thank him—but Tom stopped her with a hand on her lower back as he stood up. She didn't have the time to feel self-conscious again, because Tom was moving decisively.

"No, no," he said. "I'm not done with you. Stay still."

He didn't bother to undress, just undid his jeans, shoved them to his ankles, and let her feel his hard cock pressed against the seam of her body. Oh. She was already adrift. She felt the need to grip the world to hold on to herself because she was lost in the moment. Her hands weren't secured to anything but each other, but she knit them together and went on her toes again when he notched the tip of himself against her core.

"Breathe, baby," he said, rubbing his hand over her lower back.

She'd once had the idea that the two of them were fundamentally built on different scales, like puzzle pieces from different sets, and this position had always made him feel impossibly big. He had to work at her, coaxing her body open every time. Even the wetness from her previous orgasm didn't make it much easier, and there was nothing she could do to control the angle or the speed at which he filled her. She just arched her feet and took it, inch by inch, until Tom's weight was spread over her back and her mind was wiped entirely clean by the hot press of Tom's body inside hers.

He hadn't even moved yet, and her heart was pounding as though she'd run a marathon. Tom lowered his face to the side of her neck and ran the flat of his tongue against her pulse there. The unexpected sensation jolted her, and he slid fractionally deeper inside her.

Sighing with satisfaction, Tom wrapped one arm around her chest and splayed his palm over her collarbones, just over her heart. "There," he said, rolling his hips experimentally. And, yes, there. Exactly there. Precisely *there*, which nobody else in the world would ever know but him.

It made her head swim like a third glass of wine, the sensations he was pulling out of her with every slide of his hips. It was slow, but not lazy. Controlled, but only by him. In and out. This was new, the intimacy of his focus on each tight movement.

"I want you to come again," he said, each word clipped with effort.

She wanted that too, but that usually didn't happen. Tom was the only one who'd ever consistently gotten her there the first time. He gave a sucking kiss to the side of her neck, hard enough to leave a mark, and let her feel the edge of his teeth on the muscle of her shoulder. Her body tightened with desire, but she could barely predict her next breath, let alone whether this deluge of sensation was going to wash into another orgasm. She couldn't think herself into or out of it. She could barely think at all.

"I know you weren't bluffing," Tom rasped out. "So you've got to do this one thing for me. If you're gonna make me top you, you're going to at least come on my fucking cock."

This was the hottest thing anyone had ever said to her, and she would have done anything for him at that moment. She wanted to do everything he asked. Faster than she'd thought possible, she was lost in such a vibrating rush of feeling that she was barely aware of Tom freezing in place, his palm clenching against her chest. She'd done it, hadn't she? She'd been good. Her body was floating like dandelion fluff, though Tom's weight anchored her to the bed. He pressed his forehead against the mattress next to her, weight falling over her back.

"Shit," Tom said.

26

The post-sex shuffle didn't have to be very awkward. Rose might not be built for strength, and she might not be built for speed, but by God was she ever built for cuddling. She could cuddle like a champion. Thirty minutes of spooning while they listened to Adele was her core competency. Her heartbeat had begun to slow, and she felt adored and cared for and very much in love with the man in bed with her. She just needed perhaps ninety seconds to scamper off to the bathroom to take care of some biological realities—and also for Tom to help untie her. Tom, however, was wrapped tightly around her, his chin digging into her scalp, and his attitude was brooding.

"Did you hurt your knee again?" she guessed, covertly trying to wiggle her wrists free. Things had been pretty intense for the last couple of minutes, and he wasn't wearing his brace.

He grunted a negative, wrapping his arms more tightly around her. When she squeaked, he seemed to realize that she was still anchored to the feet of the bed. He sat up and began untying her.

"Tom? Are you okay?"

Rose felt deliciously floaty. Tom looked shaken.

"I—" He sighed. "You're still on the pill, right?"

Rose snorted and relaxed at that being the thing he was worried about. God. Even tied down, she'd worried she'd somehow hurt him. She jerked her dress back down over her hips and smoothed her hair out of her face. "A little delayed on that question," she teased him.

Tom winced, finally getting the last knot around her ankles undone and standing up to put his own clothing to rights. "I was going to pull out," he defended himself.

"Oh yeah, I could totally tell," she said, grinning at him. "During that part where you were saying how perfect I felt, especially."

"I was! I was planning to," he said, face twisting with concern. "I thought I could—well. I couldn't."

Rose laughed and reached to pull him back to her, glad he wasn't hurt or worried about something serious. She wanted to pet him and soothe him, because she was feeling amazing, and he deserved all the kudos for turning her mood around. "Just as well. I would have thought you were trying to do it in a porny way, and I would *not* have appreciated that."

"You're welcome," Tom said, but his expression was still troubled.

Rose went to the bathroom to clean up, and when she got out, Tom was sitting on the bed, arms crossed and not looking thrilled to have just railed her brains out, like he should have.

"Are you actually worried about getting me pregnant?" she

asked, mildly shocked. "You *never* worried about that. And it was probably a lot more likely before I was almost thirty-five."

He gave her a begrudging nod to acknowledge the truth of that, then held his arm out for her to curl under. She rubbed her lips against his neck and hands over his chest, encouraging him to unwind and give in to the afterglow.

"I know, I know, I'm sorry," he said, though she wasn't sure why he was sorry. They'd been pretty careful. Not one hundred percent careful. But still careful enough that they'd made it through four and a half years of banging like rabbits accidentally stowed in the same Petco hutch without incident.

"I just—I didn't feel like I had to worry before." And he cringed, probably knowing how that sounded. Rose would have been terrified if they'd gotten pregnant in college, or even the year they were married. "It's different now, you know?"

"No?" Rose said. He couldn't think she'd be angry at him if he accidentally knocked her up. She would never have blamed him for something that was equally her fault, and it wasn't like she was in a situation where she couldn't take care of a kid. "How's it worse?"

She told herself these things very carefully to avoid imagining it happening. She'd done enough magical thinking today.

Tom sighed and rubbed the back of his neck. "Before, the worst thing that could have happened—well, I mean, aside from any of the worst things that can happen to anyone—was that we'd have to figure out how to be parents earlier than we planned. How to finish school. How to get a job that would actually cover baby food and stuff like that. But I thought we'd figure it out."

Rose dropped her head onto his shoulder and pulled his arm off her so that she could wrap both of her own around it. She'd thought that too. So she still didn't understand what he was worried about now, when she had health insurance and parental leave.

"But now—I guess the worst thing that could happen is you'd decide *you* wanted to be a parent, and you'd figure things out without me. Tell me I was welcome at birthday parties and Christmas, like Boyd."

"Oh my God," Rose gasped. "I would never do that to you."

Tom exhaled, somewhat reassured but not yet in the happy postcoital state of bliss Rose's hormones urged her to dissolve into. She clutched his arm tighter.

"You wouldn't do that to me because you'd think it was wrong, or you wouldn't do that to me because that's not what you'd want to do?" he asked, eyes still shadowed.

It hurt to think about it. It hurt to imagine how she'd feel, a preemptive sort of pain based upon the experience of wanting things, planning for them, and not having them. She wanted Tom even if they never had kids. She couldn't even let herself imagine she got more than this, because this was more than she'd thought she'd have.

"Why do you think I wouldn't want you there?" she asked. "Of course I'd want you."

Tom gave a pained laugh. "Babe, I don't even know your *address*. I'd have to ask Snow Wolf for it."

Rose's mouth formed a little O of surprise as she realized he was right. They'd talked very little about what would happen once they were back in New York, both because she knew his rehearsal schedule would be intense and because she didn't want to jinx it. But this worry, she could put to rest. She tapped on his pocket and got him to take out his phone.

"It's not going to happen because I *am* on the pill," she told him as she entered her address into his phone. And even though her lower lip trembled, she decided not to be a coward. "If it did, though, I'd be happy, I think? No, I know I'd be happy. And we'd figure it out, just like we always would have."

Some of the tension ran out of him at that.

"Yeah?" he said, encouraged.

She always forgot that Tom had probably thought his life was going to go a certain way too. They'd imagined a lot of things together that had never happened. He *wanted* her to imagine futures in which they were together.

She pushed him to his back and climbed on top of him to straddle his stomach.

"I *love* you," she pointed out. "It wouldn't be too tough. We'd stick the crib in my kitchen, I'd tell my boss I need my second extended leave in a year, and then you and Ximena would both babywear during performances."

Tom left his hands on her thighs and aimed a little smile up at her. "My love, the play's going to be terrible. It'll wrap as soon as all of Boyd's fans have seen it a couple times. I'm going to be unemployed again long before this imaginary baby is cooked."

"Okay, even better," she said, reaching down to gently sweep Tom's hair out of his face. "You'll stay home and save me a million dollars on Manhattan daycare. I'll be able to hold on to my retirement savings until we send the kid to preschool."

"You say that as though having no responsibilities except carrying a ten-pound person to anarchist vegan drag queen story hour at the Yorkville library branch every day isn't a literal dream for me," Tom said, putting his hand over hers and gazing up at her with such an expression of fragile tenderness on his face that her heart ached. It sounded awfully close to her dream too. Both the old one and the new one she was afraid to articulate.

Instead of responding, she swallowed hard and leaned down to kiss him. They ended up spending the rest of the day in bed, leaving all the other adults in the house to fend for themselves for once. Rose blew off packing, blew off cleaning, and thought about what she'd wear to Tom's premiere. She thought about Tom standing on the beach this summer with the wind ruffling his hair. A few times, before she could stop herself, she thought about whether a crib really might fit in her living room.

Every single vision she had of him felt like enough. She hoped he decided to be one of them.

It would have been the perfect evening, except for the call that came in at eight thirty that night. It was Rose's uncle Ken at last, and she would have been annoyed to discover that he did have the ability to get in touch with her when he wanted to, except that he was calling to confirm she had medical power of attorney over Max, who'd just been admitted to the hospital after a bad fall in her condo. Just one of those things that happened as you get older, he supposed. Did Rose want to go over and manage things? Oh good. She could keep everyone else updated, thank you.

27

Tom hadn't been able to coax Rosie into getting a little sleep until after midnight. And she was up again before six, making huge quantities of breakfast about her feelings. Nobody found out that anything was amiss until Boyd got up to feed the turkeys and do his morning exercise routine and Puff and Snowy, who were the only two of his fans still there, got up to watch him for the last time.

"Is she okay? She looks really upset," Puff muttered to Tom, both of them watching Rosie dice potatoes from a cautious distance.

He shook his head. Rosie's eyes were red-rimmed from fatigue and crying—though he thought the real problem was that she couldn't *do* much before taking the first ferry out.

"A broken hip's real dangerous for the elderly, isn't it?" Boyd whispered as the crowd gathered at the entryway to the kitchen.

"Yeah, it's not great," Tom muttered, and he must have looked like *he* was having some feelings about this, because the other man made his sorrowful Doberman face in response.

"Rosie couldn't get much information out of the hospital over the phone. But Max is having surgery this morning."

"If Rosie's aunt dies, what happens to this place?" Snowy asked, and Puff elbowed her in the ribs. "I'm just asking!"

"She's *not* going to die," Rosie said from over the stove, voice tight and frustrated. Snowy clapped a hand over her mouth.

Boyd sheepishly went into the kitchen and put a big paw on top of her shoulder. "I'm sorry, Rosie," he rumbled. "What can I do?"

Crap. Tom should have said that. He was suddenly afraid that he hadn't gotten any better at this. What would Tom, good supportive partner, say in this situation? Line, please.

Rosie paused as though choking back emotion, then patted Boyd's hand.

"I'll take a taxi to the ferry, so would you mind returning the rental car when you leave?" she asked him.

"Of course," said Boyd.

"What about us?" Snowy called, face reflecting some guilt that her first thought had been whether BoyCon would still be able to go forward this summer.

"My cousin will be over this afternoon with the property management company. Could you strip all the beds that have been slept in so they know which laundry to do? And just make sure everyone's stuff is out by then? I'm so sorry to ask you, I was planning to do it myself, but—"

"Of course we can do it," Puff said, running over to wrap both arms around Rosie. It might have been an excuse to lay hands on Boyd at the same time, but Snowy rushed in and the two girls enfolded both Boyd and Rosie in a slightly soggy group hug.

The sad little noise Rosie made was enough to jar Tom out of his frozen worry that he'd fuck this up.

He went upstairs and started carrying her suitcases out of the suite and down to the front drive as Rosie finished a breakfast he was sure she had no intention of eating. Salmon croquettes for Boyd. Spinach omelets for the girls. The corned beef hash that Tom loved but was not going to have time to eat before Rosie's taxi arrived.

"Is there anything else that needs to be done here, or should I go with you?" he asked Rosie when he was done and she was plating food for other people to eat.

The expression she shot him in response was confused. "I'm sure Boyd can get you on the plane with him," she said, confirming this with a glance at the other man.

"Are you sure?" he asked.

"Don't you have rehearsal tomorrow?"

He hadn't exactly forgotten that, but it had plummeted down his list of concerns. It didn't feel very important right now. The last time Rosie had been in a crisis—well, the last one before a hurricane hit this inn—he'd totally flubbed it.

"I can miss rehearsal if you want me to go with you," he said.

Rosie looked doubtful at this confident statement, and Boyd's face reflected the same thought when she checked with him.

"I could talk to the director for you?" Boyd offered.

Rosie hesitated, looking between the two of them. Her lips

thinned as she visibly struggled to think on little sleep. Then she shook her head, closing her eyes.

"Thank you," she said, fists curling. "But I'll be okay. You can still make it back to New York today."

Tom wished very much that nobody else was watching this conversation. He'd thought he was going to have a few more hours in which to find an opportunity to have this talk.

He cleared his throat. "To New York—do you want me to go to your apartment, or—"

Tom didn't know whether she had plants or pets or anything that needed attention there, but mostly he wanted to know if he was going to live there.

She blinked her red-rimmed eyes in response, and it was obvious to Tom that this question hadn't been answered in her head yet. She hadn't thought they were going home together. She hadn't decided.

Tensing up, she reached for her purse, fumbling for her key chain. "Is your lease up? Of course you can stay with me—"

"Remember I have three spare bedrooms in the townhouse I'm renting," Boyd chose that unfortunate moment to chime in, no doubt thinking he was being helpful. Rosie paused before handing her keys to Tom, hesitating as though checking whether Tom wanted to take Boyd up on his offer instead.

He didn't want to *stay* with Rosie any more than he wanted to stay with Boyd, if the word implied a temporary state.

Well, shit. He really hadn't pulled it off. Rosie was headed out, and he still wasn't even sure they were together again. It didn't appear that they lived together. He didn't even know when he'd see her again.

The anger that rose up in his throat was directed entirely at himself, but he still resolutely forced it down. Rosie was so tired she was nearly swaying on her feet, and her day had just begun. She looked overwhelmed and scared.

The last thing she needed was for Tom to make this about him.

"No, my lease isn't up for a while. Just text me if you need anything in the city," he said. "And call me when you know something at the hospital, okay?"

The crunch of gravel outside heralded the arrival of Rosie's taxi. Her eyes flashed with panic.

"I still have to finish breakfast for everyone," she said, turning to survey the stovetop and ovens. "And thank everyone for all their help. And I was going to talk to you—"

"Babe," he interrupted her. "I'll get breakfast out. And everyone knows. Don't worry. You can go. I've got it."

She grabbed his hand, hesitating. She looked out the door, then back at him. She squeezed his hand harder, jolting when the taxi outside honked but not letting go. Her little fingers curled in under the edge of his sleeve as though trying to hang on.

"I love you," Tom said, leaning in to kiss her temple, giving her his blessing to go. That was his cue, right?

"Love you too," Rosie said, releasing him at last.

28

Three weeks later
Boston

Tom thought it would have been more dramatic if it was raining when he arrived, but it was a rare and lovely clear spring day. The modest Dorchester neighborhood where Rosie had grown up was full of people outside in the sun to wash the last winter salt off rusting cars.

He paced the sidewalk opposite the white two-story home he'd last visited more than a decade before, wishing he could smoke. It had been almost six months since his last cigarette, and it hadn't been a regular habit even then, but Rosie's uncles and cousins were cycling in and out to smoke on the porch, and either the secondhand waft of tobacco across the street or Tom's nervousness about the situation was making him crave a big carcinogenic punch of nicotine straight to his lungs.

After twenty minutes, someone called him on his lurking. A redhead emerged from Rosie's house and crossed the street to fix him with a judgmental stare that took in his poorly fitting oxford and ratty old backpack.

"You're late," his best friend grumped at him.

"I was on time. I just . . . didn't know everyone was going to be here," Tom told Adrian, eyeing the full house across the street. It looked like Rosie's parents were throwing a party to welcome Max home from the hospital, and Tom had not exactly been invited.

"I assume from Rose's reaction when *I* turned up here that you didn't tell her *you* were coming either?"

Tom nervously rubbed the back of his neck at this accurate statement. He hadn't seen Rosie since she'd left Martha's Vineyard, though it wasn't like she hadn't been in touch. There was a long chain of perfectly domestic texts from her on his phone, ones that began early in the morning and ended late at night.

> Rosie: Max has Playbills for all your shows in a file in her desk. Thank you 🖤

and

> Rosie: I put both our names on the play gym for Ximena's baby shower. The registry had all this beige linen stuff but I think they'll hear about it in family therapy if they assign the kid Victorian explorer at birth?

and

> Rosie: I got my period in the hospital billing department. Somehow life-affirming?

If Tom had been hit by an MTA bus on his way to rehearsal, any stranger who found his phone might have looked at these messages and assumed, *That's his partner.* And while he was glad to know exactly where Rosie was and what she was doing if he couldn't actually be with her, he would really rather have been with her. For one, he *missed* her. And for another thing, her dickbag family had predictably dropped everything into Rose's small hands, even though Max had three perfectly capable younger brothers and half a dozen other nephews and nieces in the Boston area alone who could have helped out. Instead, Rosie and Max were both staying at her parents' house while Rosie figured out what level of care Max was going to need and how she was going to afford it.

So Tom spent his days looking at his phone, wishing for a life with Rosie outside of it, and his nights awake and fixated on the terrible unfairness of Rosie dealing with hospital bills, outpatient rehab, and health aides all on her own. After three weeks of this, he sat bolt upright with a realization: *Oh fuck me, I did it again.*

Why was he waiting for Rosie to ask him for help? She never asked.

He got out of bed and started to pack, then took the train to Boston the next day.

"I've been making awkward small talk with Rose's dad for half an hour. I had to pretend to care about *basketball*," Adrian said with a grimace.

"Maybe we should do this tomorrow instead," Tom said, sweating at the idea of facing down Rosie's entire family to inform them that they could not be trusted with their two most valuable players. He hadn't thought anyone but Max and Rosie's immediate family would be home. Rosie certainly hadn't mentioned anyone else helping her move Max out of inpatient rehab.

"Caroline needs her car back on Tuesday," Adrian said, making a shooing gesture with his hands. "If we're doing this, we're doing this today."

Suppressing stage fright he hadn't felt in years, Tom headed across the street and let himself inside the house. It was much cleaner than he remembered; the stacks of magazines and old mail that Tom had seen during his early visits had vanished, and the place smelled like Windex and Pine-Sol over the lingering odor of cigarettes. Rosie had probably cleaned it. There was a dull roar of male conversation from the back of the house.

Tom still had a poster, somewhere, with the names and faces of Rosie's relatives pasted onto the full family tree. He'd crammed it before each holiday, trying to recall which name went with which set of Kelly eyebrows. It was all beyond him now, but he recognized Rosie's dad in the dining room as he entered, standing over a large spread of sandwiches and cold appetizers laid out on the battered oak table. Tom didn't see Rosie herself, but if he was due to be dragged into the backyard for an ass-kicking, it was better to get it over with where she might not observe it.

"Derek," Tom said, drawing himself up to his full height—five inches taller than Derek Kelly—and extending his hand. Last time it had been *Mr. Kelly*, but Tom was going to pretend to all the trappings of adulthood today. "Good to see everyone rally together."

Derek stopped with a stuffed mushroom cap halfway to his mouth, replaced it on the platter, looked at his fingers, wiped them on his trousers, and took Tom's hand.

"You bet," he said vaguely. "Celtics should pull this thing off, I think."

Tom looked at him with flat consternation. Basketball? What? That was not the greeting he'd been expecting. Wasn't everyone there to see Max?

"Is this party just . . . is everyone just here for the playoffs?" Tom asked.

Derek shrugged, still confused. "Rosie kept complaining that nobody had come over yet, so I said we'd get the boys here on game day. And, you know, that girl loves a party."

Tom couldn't stop a faint derisive noise in the back of his throat. He was sure that what Rosie had actually wanted was a little help making the house clean and safe for Max. The only sport Tom had ever known Rosie to watch on TV was figure skating.

Derek gave Tom another looking over, eyes lingering on his expensive but poorly fitting shirt, because Tom was not quite back into Boyd's shape yet.

"Are you another one of Rosie's friends, then?" Derek asked Tom, and Tom abruptly realized Derek didn't even know who Tom was. "I thought she said we were just inviting family. I could've asked the guys from the office. We're gonna have a lot of leftovers." Derek gestured at the plates and plates of food.

Tom drew upon all his performance abilities to keep his expression neutral.

"It's Tom?" Still nothing. "Tom Wilczewski?" *The only son-in-law you've ever had? We've met dozens of times? You gave Rosie away at our wedding?*

"Oh!" Derek said belatedly, surprise creasing his pink features. "I didn't recognize you with the—" He sketched a hand over his whiskered upper lip.

Tom reflexively rubbed his own itchy mustache.

"It's for a role," he said unhappily.

"A role? Oh! So you're still planning to give the theater thing a go?" Derek said, mildly curious.

"For fifteen years now, yeah," Tom said.

"Huh. Well, nice of you to stop by. Did you . . . did you come to see Max, then?"

"Rosie and Max," Tom said.

Derek laughed politely. "Rosie's fine, of course. And Max's doing all right under the circumstances, I guess. It's not ideal." He made a face.

"Yeah, of course," Tom echoed.

It seemed that Derek was not holding any grudges. He just didn't care at all. And as infuriating as that was, it only made it simpler for Tom to get the girls and go. Derek wouldn't try to stop him.

"I didn't realize you still saw either of them," Derek said.

"I've been helping out at the inn over the last few months," Tom said.

Derek grunted and shoved more food in his mouth before answering. "Don't suppose I have you to thank for the new pink trim?"

"That was all Rosie. But it looks nice, don't you think?"

"Nice?" the older man snorted. "It'll sure add to the time it takes to get the place sold. Christ, what a mess."

"Sold?" Tom said warily. "Did Rosie change her mind?"

"Well, she had to. Max obviously can't stay here forever, and assisted living's damn expensive. Rosie finally said she'd put it on the market after I walked her through the finances. It's the smart choice."

It didn't seem to occur to Derek that Rosie might be both smart and devastated. God, the futility of it all. Three months pouring her heart into the place, only to lose it after all. Tom barely kept his fists from clenching.

You don't deserve her. The thought was incendiary at the top of Tom's mind. Not just him, because he'd always thought that, but her family. People like Rosie kept the entire world turning, managed baby showers and home health aides, remembered birthdays and anniversaries. Didn't they know how lucky they were to have her?

"Do you know where she is?" Tom managed to ask without shouting.

Derek pointed upstairs. "She said she wasn't feeling well. Hope it isn't the food. I've had about five of these salami roses, and so has everyone else."

This was so offensive to Rosie. Derek should have dragged Tom outside to yell at him for breaking Rosie's heart ten years ago. He should have demanded that Tom state his intentions. He should have given Tom a hard time, *at least*.

"Well, good to catch up," Tom lied, shaking Derek's sticky hand again and excusing himself. He didn't greet any of Rosie's other relatives, just wove through the crowd of short, round people until he was in the living room, which was dominated by a big entertainment console and a sofa bed with Max's suitcases tucked behind it. Nobody gave him more than a half-curious look.

Max was seated in a new armchair, one of those zero-gravity seats, but the pained expression on her face didn't seem to have to do with her broken hip. Everyone else was standing, eyes glued to the preshow. Tom knelt down next to Max's chair and kissed her cheek.

"Hello Tomasz," she said, clearing her throat. Rosie had said she was on a lot of pain meds, but she seemed with it enough to be bored watching basketball with her younger brothers and their sons. She rallied her face into a smirk. "Did you come to watch the game too?"

"Definitely," he deadpanned. "I love how those shorts fit them. Go green."

He was rewarded with a faint snort and the dramatic roll of Max's eyes.

"Can I get you anything?" he asked.

"I was supposed to go shopping with one of my girlfriends this past week. To get a new dress for your premiere. But Rosie keeps scheduling these terrible doctor's appointments instead," Max complained. "I haven't been able to go out yet. The play's not tonight, is it?"

Max looked put together, her hair and makeup done, tasteful clothes, but someone had put a tacky fleece Celtics throw over her lap and pointed her chair at the TV.

"No, in two weeks. I'll take you," Tom promised her, hoping

he'd be in a position to do that. He could do this. He could be a Tom who was Rosie's actual partner.

"You're a good boy," Max said, patting in the general direction of his shoulder.

"I'm glad someone thinks so," Tom said. "Let me just get Rosie. I'll be right back."

Gathering all his courage, he went up to the second floor. He still knew the way to Rosie's former bedroom, the door adorned with holographic stickers of kittens and unicorns and pictures of Rosie in her prom dress, some teenage asshole's arm around her. Tom knocked, heard no answer, and decided to let himself in anyway.

"Rosie?" he called. "It's me."

It was dark and full of storage boxes inside her old room, the only light coming from under the bathroom door. As Tom approached, now even more cautious, Rosie flung the door open. She was wiping her face with a wet hand towel as though she'd just finished crying, throwing up, or possibly doing both at once.

His stomach was a lead ball of worry and dismay, but the wave of surprise and relief that passed over Rosie's face when she saw him did a lot to dissolve it.

She dropped her towel, ran to him, and immediately locked her arms around his waist. Tom let out a breath he felt like he'd been holding since he'd left the island as she buried her face against his shoulder. He'd been right to come. He was late, but he'd been right.

"You're here," she mumbled into the fabric of his shirt, her breath smelling of spearmint toothpaste.

"Of course I'm here," he said gruffly, pressing his cheek to the top of her head, feeling dizzy with his own relief. He held her tighter, fingertips gripping her like that would really make her his. He bent to kiss her temples, her puffy eyelids, everywhere he could reach without letting go of her. "*You're* here."

He wasn't really referring to the bathroom in particular, but Rosie's face flushed when she glanced back toward the toilet.

"I'm not puking because I'm pregnant," she said quickly. "My mom forgot I'm allergic to fish, I guess, and she didn't mention the Worcestershire sauce in the three-bean salad. And I forgot to ask. Oops."

Tom tensed even though Rosie was trying to play it off like it wasn't a big deal. Nobody was allowed to be that careless with his Rosie, but it was his own damn fault for letting her leave without him.

"Do you need me to take you to the hospital?" he gritted out.

"No, I think the Benadryl's going to stay down," she said, pressing her palms against her eyes. "I'm fine. Really."

"We'll discuss this later," he promised, eyes narrowed.

Future family meals would not be potluck. They would not be *here*, where Rosie's asthma had to be acting up. He didn't care if they ate scrambled eggs and toast in his building common room or if they all flew to Boca to eat his mother's cabbage rolls. The days of Max and Rosie carrying the entire Kelly clan on their backs ended now.

Back to the original plan. He took a few short breaths to hype himself up. He wasn't sure exactly what he'd say. It had felt wrong to practice for this—this wasn't a performance; this was his life and Rosie's.

"Tom, I'm—I'm really glad to see you. But what are you doing here?" she asked before he could find the words.

"I came to get you," he blurted out.

"Get me?"

"Back to New York, I mean," he clarified.

"Baby, I'm sorry, I know, I want to. But—look, I'm sure you saw. Max can't even get to the bathroom by herself right now. Medicare's fighting with me on aides . . . I can't leave her."

"Both of you," Tom said. "Let's go home. I've got Caroline's SUV—it can fit all Max's stuff. Adrian's going to help us get everything packed. We can go right now, be back in New York tonight. You know that anything your dad could do for Max, *I* can."

He'd been more eloquent in his life, but for a moment Rosie's eyes went soft and wondering, and her breath caught.

"I thought about it," he reassured her. "As soon as performances start, I'll have every day to get Max to physical therapy, or the senior center, or wherever. You can get back to your job. We'll take it in shifts. Max can't stay here in your dad's living room—"

Rosie had recovered, and she started shaking her head.

"*You* can't stay. Tech week starts tomorrow. This is your first Broadway opening in a decade! Did you even tell your stage manager you were coming up here?"

"I did," he said, wounded, because he wasn't *that* unprofessional. He just knew where his priorities were. He locked eyes with her. "I can miss a day of rehearsal when my girlfriend has a family emergency." He took another deep breath. "I can for sure miss a day of rehearsal when *my wife* has a family emergency."

There was the gauntlet, thrown down.

"Tom . . ." Rosie's voice trailed off, expression going fragile and worried. "We can talk about that when I get back."

"Are you sure you're not staying up here because you're scared of what happens next?" he asked, and she flinched, because he had her all figured out now.

He put his hands on her upper arms and chafed them, aching again to just lift her up and carry her to safety.

"Just give me a real chance, okay?" he begged. "Don't sell the inn just because your dad's bullying you into it. Give it a chance to work out. Give it a chance to be a huge success. We've got time. And give *me* a chance to be everything I promised you I'd be. Okay? I'll bring both of you back to New York with me, and I'll take care of you there. Come home with me."

He swallowed hard, because Rosie's tiny body had gone very still. She was listening.

"If you don't think Max can live alone anymore, she can live with us. We can go to city hall if you want to get married again. We can just tell everyone it's back on if you don't. And as soon as the show wraps, we'll all go back out to the inn. Do you still want kids? We can go ahead and have the kids! Though if you want six of them, we probably need to get started, like, *tonight.*"

This finally got a reaction out of her, a startled laugh.

"Six? We live in New York. We can afford one, maybe," she

said, wiping at her eyes with her hands until Tom ducked into the bathroom to get her a fresh towel.

"Here," he said, brushing wisps of her hair away from her eyes until he cupped her face in his hands, fingertips careful. "Did I get it right? Is that what you want?"

"Of course I want that," she whispered, big blue eyes swimming between hope and hurt as she looked up at him.

"Then please just have it. Have me. That's all I'm asking. Please accept it from me. I wish I didn't have to rush you, and I know I don't have the right to show up after ten years and tell you right now is the right moment, but if you're ever going to settle for me, please do it now, because you shouldn't have to be alone in all this either."

Rosie pulled back against his hands, back going rigid. "Nobody would be settling for you," she said fiercely. "Stop thinking that about yourself. That's not what I'm doing. I *love* you. I have *always* loved you. And I wanted you to have what *you* wanted even when I didn't think that was me. I'm just being careful with us. There's nothing more important than getting this right." She fiddled with the hem of his shirt as though trying to fix the lines of it, face conflicted. "I just want you to be sure this is what you want."

But that was the one thing he hadn't needed to figure out. He'd always known he loved Rosie like he loved breathing. Knowing he wanted her was the easy part—the hard part was knowing how to have her.

"The only thing I ever knew for sure about my life was that I wanted you in it," Tom said. "You're the planner, Rosie. But you're my only plan."

He pulled off his backpack and set it down, coming out with a big manila envelope and a ring of keys and fobs. He hadn't been sure how this gesture would be received, any more than showing up uninvited. But she couldn't say she didn't know what he wanted after this.

"I brought you something." He took Rosie's hands and turned them palms up to fold them over the key ring. "I talked to my roommate, and he's willing to extend my sublease for two more weeks. He won't be in town, so that's two bedrooms. Here's a copy of my key. The day before that lease is up, Ximena's getting induced, and then she's staying with Luísa's parents for the six weeks after the baby comes. I'm housesitting. They've got two bedrooms. Here's a copy of their key. After *that*, Boyd has reshoots in Dubrovnik, and we can have his whole townhouse to ourselves. Here's the key and security code. And then he's back through the end of the run. And . . . happy to have us all stay with him. So. That's three months, but I'll start looking for the next place tonight. Somewhere big enough for us and Max." Tom took a deep breath, aware of how scraped together his proposal sounded. "I can take care of both of you." That was the part he was dead solid on. He could promise they'd be safe, and he could promise they'd be loved.

Rosie wavered on her feet, looking tired and scared and so, so beautiful to him, the way she had since the day he'd first laid eyes on her in the registrar's line and scrambled for an excuse to speak to her. He put his whole heart into his voice because his entire world was there in his arms, and he didn't know if he could keep her there. All he could do was offer this to her and know, finally, that he could make good on every word.

"I spent a decade waiting for you to call me and tell me I could come home. Well, I could have called too, any day before I did. That's what this is. *Come home.* I miss you. I love you. I want you in every single one of the days of my life, the good ones and the bad ones. Come home whenever you're sure. I already am."

29

Adrian found Rose sitting in the dark fifteen minutes later. Her parents had converted her bedroom to storage while she was in college, but it still felt a little like her own private space.

Rose's very bones ached for Tom to come back and hold her through the rest of this uncomfortable, lonely day, but he'd have missed his train if he didn't leave right then. It was bad enough that he'd spend eight hours riding the train in a single day—missing the start of tech week would have been worse.

"Did you really make him leave?" Adrian stuck his head in and asked, voice wary.

"He has rehearsal," Rose said.

It hadn't been easy to talk him into going. It had taken the threat of getting Boyd and Ximena on the phone to mediate the situation before he agreed to leave. And Rose wasn't even positive he wouldn't be back tomorrow. Her heart felt overfull enough to shatter again.

Adrian's pretty face was unimpressed, but it was probably

stuck that way. He came and sat down on the same stack of plastic tubs as Rose while he waited for her to say more. That was one of Adrian's better qualities. He wasn't a hugger, which Rose could have really used right now, but he was good at companionable silence.

"I didn't expect him to come," Rose eventually said.

"I think he knew that," Adrian replied, sounding judgmental.

Rose chewed on what Adrian might mean by that. Adrian openly disapproving of her was a new thing. Their entire friendship was predicated on giving each other sober, adult advice that they knew the other person would not follow.

"It's not that I didn't want him here," Rose added.

"Hmm," said Adrian. "That part, I'm not sure he knew."

Her hands clenched on the little pile of papers and keys Tom had left her. It was beyond thoughtful. But he had the chance to celebrate a career-topping triumph right now, and she was an exhausted mess who had a new dependent, a finance job to get back to, and an inn to sell. She didn't know how they started again, exactly, but if she hadn't worn out his enthusiasm for the idea with three months of renovations, asking him to turn into a part-time caregiver for her aunt was probably not the best follow-up.

She knew Tom wanted her to expect more from him. That just ran directly against her instinctual suspicion that nobody would love her if she made it at all hard to do.

"You know, he asked me to give him his wedding ring back," Adrian said.

"Why do you have his wedding ring?" Rose asked, startled.

Adrian shrugged. "He tossed it across my living room after you served him with some particularly nasty piece of divorce paperwork. I thought he might still want it someday, so I picked it up and stashed it in my garlic keeper."

She gnawed her lower lip. "Do you know why he wants it now?"

"I assume because he wants to start wearing it again?" Adrian said, casual expression not quite hiding his interest in her reaction. He reached into his jacket pocket to retrieve a garlic-scented plastic baggie containing a slightly tarnished white-gold band.

Rose took the ring and clutched it with her pile of keys and door codes. One more thing she didn't know how to handle. It felt almost like it was burning in her hands.

"I don't still have mine," she muttered, cheeks heating. It had just been a cheap little fourteen karat gold claddagh ring, because that had been all Tom could afford, but she'd never taken it off until the day she dropped it into the East River.

How did this happen? How did they pick back up? What would she even *say* to people?

After ten years apart, Tom and I have decided that divorce is no longer working for us. We ask for your support as we consciously couple, determined to remain friends as we transition to a life together.

"I didn't—I really didn't think this would ever happen," she admitted to Adrian.

Adrian wrinkled his aristocratic nose at her. "Really?" he asked, great skepticism in his voice.

"What," she said. "No? We literally didn't speak."

"I guess you didn't see him mope for the last decade. See the *both* of you moping. God, it's been difficult. For me, especially."

She elbowed Adrian in the ribs. "You could have told me," she said.

"I said I thought you two should get coffee when he moved back to New York. I said that twice! What, was I supposed to say, 'Rose, you realize you're the love of his life, please take him back and put him out of my misery'?"

"Yes, that. That second thing, that would have been helpful to hear," she said dryly.

She groaned and rubbed her face with her palms. Everyone seemed to think this would be easy, and she knew it wouldn't be.

Feeling that under the circumstances she could take liberties, she put her head on Adrian's shoulder.

"What if," she said in a small voice, finally giving words to her real worry, "it's just too much for him to handle? We just started seeing each other again after ten years. I made him do three months of renovations in a different state. Now I'm going to ask him to help me take care of my aunt? Maybe forever? That would be too much for a *lot* of people. And I'm not even asking him to do it."

Adrian sighed and crossed his arms without dislodging her. He didn't do easy platitudes, which was one of his better qualities. He looked out the window in the direction of the train station.

"You know, Tom's always told this story that he's a big screwup," he said thoughtfully. "He told Caroline that when they met, and he still believes that, somehow. Because he messed up with you. None of the rest of it—this movie star he's friends with, the Broadway show—it doesn't really count for him. He just wanted to be married to you."

Adrian gingerly reached across his body to pat the top of her head, a thing that only he could have gotten away with.

"I think you should let him tell a different story about himself. Because he always knew that getting married meant this was what he was signing up for. It's not too much. It's what he always expected he'd do if someone he loved needed help." He ducked his head, trying to make her look at him. "And he loves you."

Rose's eyes watered. How was she supposed to believe in a love she didn't have to work for? What did that even look like? She wanted Tom with her. Even more than that, she wanted him happy.

She exhaled through her nose, added Tom's keys to her key chain, then opened up the giant envelope Tom had left her, expecting it to be full of lease paperwork.

To her surprise, it was instead filled with greeting cards, some pastel envelopes printed with Max's name, others with hers. Thank-you cards for Rose and get well soon cards for Max from Ximena, Boyd, and the girls. It was sweet of Tom to bring them up.

She used the corner of her key chain to open them up, flipping through Hallmark inanities until a folded piece of paper fell out of the card signed by Snow Wolf and the Great Puffin. Rose shot a cautious glance at Adrian before she unfolded it, but for once Puff's work was G-rated.

It was a beautiful colored pencil drawing of Tom, Rose, and Boyd in the style of a 1970s family Christmas portrait. Tom and Rose, wearing matching Fair Isle sweaters, were posed with their hands on Boyd's shoulders. Boyd, seated in this composition, clutched a wild turkey in his giant muscular arms as though holding the family cocker spaniel. Everyone was smiling.

"The draftsmanship is pretty good," Adrian said, casting a professional eye over the work.

"Puff's very talented," Rose said, feeling delirious tears spring to the corners of her eyes.

"It's a little weird though," he added.

Snowy had written an inscription at the bottom: **My parents who raised me.**

"So fucking weird," Rose agreed, a laugh coming out of her throat like a sob.

Thanks, girls. I don't think Boyd needs parenting, but somehow I do think Max and I will be cooking him keto-friendly side dishes this Thanksgiving while Tom falls off the inn's roof hanging Christmas lights.

None of Rose's plans had ever worked out the way she thought they would, but, then again, their little adventure in West Tisbury had happened wonderfully and unexpectedly. She'd asked Tom to come with her, thinking it would be a punishment for him and a chore for her, and instead he'd brought so many weird and beautiful things back into her life. All the music and laughter and love and sex that had been painfully missing for the last decade. She'd never seen it coming. And she wouldn't trade it for anything.

She didn't know what it would look like if she and Max just picked up and told Tom to build them a new life in New York, but she believed he'd do it for her. It would be just as wonderful and unexpected as every day since Tom had careened back into her life. And finally Tom might feel both forgiven and loved.

Rose stood up and opened her mouth to shout for someone to find Max's shoes because she wasn't spending one more night without Tom. But when she looked down at her watch, she realized he would already be on the last train out of Boston, and, once again, she'd told him to go when she didn't mean it at all.

30

Tech week was always the process of turning chaos into order, but a general sense of impending doom clung to the cast and crew of *All's Well That Bends Well*. The quick changes were running ten seconds too slow. The props table had been mislabeled, and two other actors were about to strangle each other over custody of an antique champagne flute. Tom had tripped over the wiring for a practical lamp while the assistant stage manager was hunting down more gaff, and now his knee hurt again. They'd been held over for bonus rehearsals of the final scene, and even Boyd was beginning to look a little sulky because Ximena kept fumbling the cue to sweep him into a dramatic clinch at the climax of their love declarations.

It wasn't really Ximena's fault. The director and playwright were still arguing about whether the ending should hint that all three principals would form some kind of happy throuple after the curtain dropped—a patent sop to Boyd's fans—or whether they'd hew closer to the original Shakespeare, in which Ximena's character spent the entire play running as fast as she could from Boyd's affections, only to change her mind in the last scene. The kiss kept getting added, dropped, applied to Tom instead, then put back on Ximena's reluctant lips.

Tom was pretty sure he wasn't supposed to be there. Why *was* he there instead of with Rosie?

"You've got to sell this, or the whole arc falls apart," the director urged Ximena. "Put your back into it."

"My back *hurts*," Ximena snarled. "And I need to pee. This isn't working. I can't bend him over my hip—he's like a foot taller than me."

"Then at least give us a little tongue," the director said. "Nobody is going to believe you chose him over Tom if you don't nail this kiss."

Ximena made a long-suffering face. "Can I slap him on the ass or something instead?"

The director's lower eyelid twitched, and he wandered off-stage to do two minutes of breathing exercises rather than scream at his principal cast.

"Is there ass slapping in Shakespeare?" Boyd wondered aloud, looking at Tom for confirmation.

Tom shrugged. Shakespeare had been kind of a perv and a lot more lowbrow than most people thought, but this play was to *All's Well That Ends Well* what the live-action *Lion King* was to *Hamlet*.

"If you're trying to avoid Boyd's cooties," Tom drawled to Ximena, "I think that ship has sailed."

"His cooties are kicking my bladder," she muttered under her breath, but she walked back to her mark. When the director had recovered, they took it from the last cue: Ximena announced that she'd changed her mind and wanted to marry Boyd, seized him by the shirt collar, and did her best to lay one on him. Even in the original folio, this moment occurred about two pages from the point where Ximena's character informed the king that Boyd's character was an irredeemable, lying hooker, so five hundred years of audiences had suspended disbelief about this happy ending.

Ximena finally got Boyd bent backward and their lips glued together, but this time his knees wobbled, Ximena let go of him, and he collapsed to the stage floor, nearly taking out an expensive rented bicycle.

"Sorry, sorry," Boyd yelped when everyone jumped away from the impact. "I got a little lightheaded."

"What *now?*" the director begged.

"I'm on a mustard fast," Boyd explained, staggering to his knees. "It's where you only eat foods that are covered in mustard. I'm doing it with just mustard though, so it works faster."

"So *that's* what you smell like," Ximena moaned. "I can feel my morning sickness coming back."

Tom covered his face with both palms, wishing for the fifth time in five minutes that Rosie had come home with him. He really needed her to envision how this embarrassing spectacle of a play was going to lead to future fame, artistic satisfaction, and exciting cast parties.

"Boyd, why the hell are you doing a mustard fast?" Tom asked, speaking through his hands.

"I have my shirt off for the entire second act," Boyd repeated defensively.

"You need to eat a carb before you pass out onstage," Tom growled, and Boyd gave him a kicked-puppy blink.

"I'm not angry at you," Tom immediately retracted. "But seriously. This is not okay. I'm making you an appointment with a nutritionist. One with a science degree."

"Are *you* okay?" Boyd rumbled in an undertone.

"Sure," said Tom.

He wasn't sure he was. He was still trying to figure out what he could have said to Rosie to convince her.

I promise you don't have to do it all alone anymore. I promise a million times. He should have said that.

He should have convinced Max first; that would have been the best maneuver. She would have been an easy sell.

Well, Rosie, you can do what you *want, but Max and I are going back to New York together. We're picking up jerk chicken and watching* Love Island: Australia *until we pass out on the couch. Are you in?*

He'd try that next. He'd try that tomorrow.

The director despairingly announced that they'd wrap for the day, and the house lights came back up. Tom didn't immediately look out at the audience, because he'd pulled his phone out to look up the train schedule. It was Boyd's happy noise of recognition that alerted him to scan past the crew and theater staff who'd stretched out in the front row to watch them stumble through cue to cue.

Enter Rose Kelly, stage left, once again. She was seated in the second row with her embroidery hoop and big purse, ankles delicately crossed as she waited for Tom to finish rehearsal.

Dressed in the Manhattan commuter's uniform of waterproof jacket and comfortable sneakers, like she'd stopped by to pick him up on her way home from work. Max was on the aisle to her right, walker folded behind her seat, a journal in her lap like she was going to give him some notes on today's rehearsal.

Tom dizzily walked toward the edge of the stage as Rosie put her things away and approached from the audience. She folded her arms on the edge of the stage and made big eyes up at him, the same face she made when she pulled a perfect birthday gift out of hiding. Waiting for his reaction.

"Hey, don't we have security? How'd you get in?" Ximena called before Tom could say anything.

Rosie shot her a quick smirk. "Showed them my boobs. Same way I got Tom into bars freshman year."

"That'll do it," Tom breathed, a giddy wave of relief floating up from his toes.

"So we only have to worry about stalkers with good boobs?" Ximena groused.

"I can live with that," Boyd said confidently.

Tom waved at them to shut up. This was important.

"Did Adrian drive you down? Are you guys moving in?" he asked.

Rosie nodded. "He and Caroline are unloading her SUV at your apartment right now. Though Caroline was disappointed to miss rehearsal. She made me promise to get some good pictures of you making out with Boyd for the Christmas card this year."

"Did you get any?" he asked, throat feeling tight. "For our Christmas card?"

Rosie nodded slowly, a shy smile spreading across her face. "Though I'm not sure they'll make the highlights after we host BoyCon this summer. I was thinking the theme could be Vikings. You know: Bonfires. Feats of strength. Roast meats. I started putting together a Pinterest board on the drive down. Snowy's been in touch."

She nervously tucked her hair back behind her ear. A glint of metal during the movement caught Tom's eye and froze him again.

"I want to hear more about your vision," Boyd said. "I love roast meats."

Tom loved *her*. His heart filled his entire chest, choking him speechless for once in his life.

"Guys, I know you're having a moment here, but let's not just brush past the security concerns," Ximena said. "Are we really going to live with groupies wandering in and out like they did on the island?"

"Actually," Rosie said, clearing her throat and looking up at Tom with a shy tilt to her head, "I didn't flash my boobs. Security checked my ID. They may have thought I was your wife?"

She made it into a question. As though he actually had the opportunity to say it now and make it true: Rose Kelly Wilczewski was his wife; she was his, and they were going to be together for the rest of their lives, the way they should have been from the moment they first met. Tom's pulse started to pound, so fast he wondered whether he might be the next one to pass out onstage. "I think you are too," he said.

The corners of Rosie's pink lips trembled upward. "I guess that means we're married?" she said tentatively.

Tom finally vaulted down off the stage and grabbed Rosie's left wrist so that he could examine her hand. He recognized the ring on it, even though it was so large on her dainty little ring finger that it was in danger of sliding off.

He retrieved it and slid the ring back onto his own hand. Still fit perfectly. But that left her without one.

"I'll get you a new one," he promised Rosie. "Boyd's probably got a corporate sponsor who'll give me a discount. I could even get you something made of real gold this time if you don't mind a logo for a testosterone supplements company on it."

"I don't think anyone's ever given me a ring, but I got a watch made of space-grade titanium last week," Boyd immediately offered. "And it's waterproof to two hundred meters. Do you want that?"

Rose looked at her bare hand. "No, I think I have something that'll work," she said.

She bent to rustle through her purse, coming out with a ring of door keys. "Just in case you gave me your only copies, I made you a bunch of spares," she said. She carefully peeled the keys off a little steel spiral, then slid it onto her ring finger.

And just like that, it was done. The entire arc of Tom's life snapped back into place like a broken bone that had finally been set. Rosie held up her hand, displaying the band of cheap metal.

"Ready to go home?" she asked, body tense but tone casual.

Rosie loved a big moment, and she loved a party, and she'd loved his first proposal, with a sunset and a real ring and Adrian taking pictures. But she'd done this for him so that he'd know there were no tests to pass, no apologies to deliver, no more promises to make.

After a decade, he was finally going home.

Rosie's small, hopeful smile spread into a real one as he wrapped his arms around her and tugged her against his body. They had a bit of an audience right now, which made it even better when he rolled her over his hip and bent her backward in a move he'd been working on since they were eighteen. One perfect kiss, projecting love from every angle, dramatic and over the top and totally, totally sincere.

Rosie's tiny fists curled in his shirt as he savored the endless moment with her lips against his.

"That! That is what you're supposed to be doing," the director yelled to Ximena. "Do what he's doing there."

Couldn't be done, Tom thought smugly. Nobody did this like him and Rosie.

ACKNOWLEDGMENTS

After I nearly failed out of fifth grade, I was diagnosed with ADHD. It's underdiagnosed in girls, but I had very classic symptoms: even though I did well on tests, I was always in detention for falling out of my chair, failing to raise my hand, and never doing my homework.

As an adult, I am a flawless chair sitter, hand raiser, and homework doer thanks to lots of practice and modern medicine, but I still imagine myself as the lion tamer with a whip and a flaming hoop and my brain as the dangerous beast I must force to perform tricks. Making it write books is a group effort.

I'm a Tom, forever amazed by the people like Rosie who keep the world spinning. The people who cook holiday dinners and send greeting cards and plan parties. I'm so happy to be invited and remembered. I wish I were more like you.

The list of people I am grateful for with each book only grows, because this book wouldn't have existed if the earlier ones hadn't. Thank you to everyone who supported, preordered, cheerleaded, and read my first two books. It is such a privilege to be able to do this, and I couldn't do it without you.

Thank you to my Berkley team: my editor, Cindy Hwang, first and foremost, for being fangirl prime, the alpha fangirl, and the reason why so many perfectly weird and hilarious books exist in the world; editors Angela Kim and Elizabeth Vinson; publicists Yazmine Hassan and Dache' Rogers; marketer Elisha Katz; production editor Caitlyn Kenny; production manager Jennifer Wong; and cover artist Vi-An Nguyen, who created my three gorgeous covers. Thank you also to copyeditor Abby Graves, proofreader Emily Pearson, and cold reader Daisy Flynn.

Thank you to my wonderful agent, Jessica Watterson.

Thank you to Jenna Levine, Celia Winter, Ashley Mackie, and Anastacia Bersch for reading my drafts and wiping my tears. Someday, God willing, we will all write books where nobody cries while we're writing them.

Thank you to Sarah Hawley, Ali Hazelwood, Julie Soto, Thea Guanzon, Kirsten Bohling, and Kate Goldbeck for charging the hills with me and all the other 🐗 🐗 🐗. Every time I see one of your books in the store, I turn to the other shoppers and say, "I know her! From, uh, work."

Special thanks to Linnea Adler for behind-the-scenes advice on Tom's career. She gave me the Broadway details that are both interesting and true, and I then added mistakes and filler.

Thank you again to pocket friends in Getting Off on Wacker, Hyun Bin's Burner Phone, All That [G]litters, Berkletes, Fen'Harem, and *Animal Crossing: Pocket Camp*. I'm glad you're always with me.

Thank you and I miss you to Mr. Kitten, who hung on until I was almost done with dev edits. And thank you to Inky, who is lying on half my keyboard as I write these acknowledgments.

And, finally, thank you to my family, especially my Chris, my Mini-Shep, and my Baby Boy Shep. I know you didn't actually want to go swimming for three hours every Sunday afternoon. This book is the result of your patience, love, and support.

♥ Shep

Katie Shepard is, in no particular order, a fangirl, a gamer, a bankruptcy lawyer, and a romance author. Born and raised in Texas, she frequently escapes to Montana to commune with the trees and woodland creatures, resembling a Disney princess in all ways except age, appearance, and musical ability. When not writing or making white-collar criminals cry at their depositions, she enjoys playing video games in her soft pants and watching sci-fi shows with her husband, two children, and very devoted cats.

VISIT KATIE SHEPARD ONLINE

KatieShepard.com
🐦 YTCShepard
📷 KatieShepardBooks

Ready to find
your next great read?

Let us help.

Visit prh.com/nextread